THE DEVIL'S RANSOM

ALSO BY DOUGLAS MEADOR

Technical:
THE NEW VITICULTURE

Novel:
FACE THE TIGER

THE DEVIL'S RANSOM

a novel

Douglas Meador

ELLEM PUBLISHING, INC.
www.ellempublishing.com
+1-831-238-2998

THE DEVIL'S RANSOM
Copyright © 2012 by Douglas Meador
First Edition

ISBN 978-0-9843079-1-3
LCCN 2011940193

AUTHOR'S NOTE

International Health Emissaries is a loose-knit organization of dentists, dental assistants and oral hygienists who volunteer their time and talents to aid children in less-fortunate areas of the world.

Started in 1990 by a pediatric dentist in Monterey, California as a "pay back" project in Guatemala, IHE draws participating dental professionals from throughout the United States – all volunteers and all paying their own expenses. They have quietly alleviated children's' pain and suffering worldwide for twenty years.

The IHE projects have expanded from permanent dental clinics regularly visited every year or two in Guatemala, Peru, Ecuador and northern Argentina to building of schools, clean water projects and hygiene educational programs.

Working with non-governmental organizations (churches, hospitals, etc.), areas of most need are identified and, as funds are available, expeditions organized and scheduled. Missions have been done in the remote areas of Nicaragua, Belize, Honduras, Cambodia, Nepal and others. Wherever they go donated clothing accompanies and is distributed directly to the child patients.

Some contributing businesspeople are allowed to accompany the professionals on the excursions but they are expected to work in supportive roles. The daily workload is Herculean – often treating over one hundred children a day utilizing portable power generators and make-shift facilities. Flying doctors do a great service but diagnosis is one thing, cure is another. Dentists can "fix" on the spot. I observed a fourteen year old flowering girl whose front teeth were rotted away from the ubiquitous soda pop and 'dopa' – stall-made sugar, water, and flavoring. A dentist from Pennsylvania and his team took four hours to re-construct her mouth. Upon completion her smile lit up the countryside while tears of gratitude flowed from her, her mother and her grandmother. There were also tears from the staff – and me.

Funding of the associated costs of transport of equipment, supplies, materials, clothing and all the mobile paraphernalia needed for their mission is from donations. For many years I have sent my donations to:

IHE
8 Somerset Rise
Monterey, California 93940

Those who have suffered tooth pain understand what these children are experiencing with no relief – unless an IHE team arrives.

THE DEVIL'S RANSOM

PROLOGUE

In *FACE THE TIGER*, three old warriors (Vietnam vintage) were pulled by fate, thirty-some years after the war, back into events that happened there. The path led from murder of a navy legal officer to a drug 'railroad' running from Cambodia to the United States. Two of the corrupt military police officers running the show had meanwhile become high ranking political figures. Their fortunes were based upon the Heroin business both during the Vietnam War and after. An ex-navy security officer – by force part of the 'railroad' – was dying of pancreatic cancer. He thought a final atonement was possible by luring Douglas Mitchell, a highly decorated ex-naval aviator and close friend of the murdered legal officer, into being the point of the sword in his parting thrust.

Douglas Mitchell, attack fighter pilot veteran of 329 combat missions off aircraft carriers in two tours in Vietnam, had left the Navy and become a winegrower in Monterey, California. Along the way – after his service – he became acquainted with two career Army pilots who became his closest friends in his mature life. They, of course, joined with him to bring down the evil group and avenge his wartime murdered friend.

Bo Hanson, Lt.Colonel, USA (ret), left the Army after twenty years. He flew Huey gun ships, then Cobras, in Vietnam earning two Silver Stars and three Distinguished Flying Crosses among other trinkets. He had some workings with the CIA. He transitioned to Apaches, commanding a company, and then retired. In civilian life he became a successful businessman, founding a corporation he later sold then founding another in Monterey.

Ken Grazing, Col, USA (ret), spent twenty six years with the Army before retiring. A heavily decorated Cobra pilot in Vietnam – sporting a Purple Heart in the medal mix – he had been given Last Rites at a MASH (Military Advanced Surgical Hospital) and was expected to die. He didn't.

Using their network of now older officers who were their young juniors back in the day and their old compadres, retired but still active as civilians, they were able to generate sufficient information to penetrate and understand the evil empire. Unfortunately, none was usable for courtroom action on the two powerful main actors. Fortunately, the terminally ill ex-navy security officer engineered a recording, and transmission thereof to Mitchell, of his own execution. That was sufficient for the court of public opinion but still not for a court of law. However, the two miscreants served justice by apparently taking their own lives.

EXCERPT

FROM THE EPILOGUE
OF
FACE THE TIGER

"As for the 'no bruises' aspect, there is a type of garrote that is designed primarily to disable, not to kill. Instead of a wire, it is composed of an inch wide soft braid. The center two and one half inches is padded with sheep fleece. On each side of the fleece, there is a flexible but firm silicon ball which is incised and slid up the braid to the fleece. Properly used, the device quickly renders the subject unconscious leaving no marks or bruises on the carotid arteries or the surrounding areas. Of course, it can be used to kill but its use would then be detectable at autopsy, or, at least, its effects would be. Once the subject is unconscious, the rest can be done such that even the GSR (gun shot residue) pattern is consistent. The signs are apparent only if the searcher knows exactly what they are looking for. Or cares. Most MEs do not. The fishing line leaves a very fine line in the GSR."

"Mitch, how the hell do you know this shit, for God's sake?"

"Must have read it somewhere, I guess. Gents, once again we faced the Tiger and won. No more of this stuff. We're getting too damn old." Then Mitchell's cell phone rang.

His face blanched. His jaw dropped, then clenched. His eyes became steel hard. He quietly said "Christina, Christina, try to calm yourself. I'm on it. They'll be okay. We'll get them out. Bo and Ken are here with me. We'll be there in six or seven hours. Joanne is coming? Good. Talk with you very soon."

"Guys, we've got a problem. That was Christina Blaylock. Mark and her two boys, Jack Troia and five others have been taken captive in Guatemala for ransom. Twenty million. We know what that means. We've got to go in and fast."

Broderick said "Who are these people?"

"Dentists who do charity work there. Friends of ours. Boys are in high school. Five businessmen and dental assistants who went along to help. This is eastern Guatemala – jungle country around the Rio Dulce. It's going to be a bitch finding them and getting them out. I know, I've been there with them before." Mitchell answered.

"Mind if I join up? Sounds like my kind of work. Got some friends who'd probably like to tag along. We've got Guatemala and Nicaragua time. No offense, but you guys are a little long in the tooth for this sort of thing. Got a Lt. Colonel, SF, recently retired, who'd help with the assets." Scott Broderick (ex-Army Special Forces) said.

Hanson said "Who's the Colonel?"

"Deke Stratton."

Hanson exploded "The Deke? I know this guy. You're on, kid. Let's roll. I got some calls to make."

"Damn – another Tiger." thought Mitchell.

THE DEVIL'S RANSOM

PART ONE

THE SAVIORS*

*a person who saves someone or something from danger
—The New Oxford American Dictionary

2

CHAPTER 1

Troia home
Monterey, California
0630 hours local; Day 2

Kelly Troia awoke to the ringing phone. As soon as she heard Frank Lombard's voice she knew there was a problem. The time, Frank and his tone when he said her name all brought her to her full senses.

"Kelly, we've had an incident here. Nine of the group have been kidnapped, Jack and Mark among them. I've e-mailed the list of who's been taken. It's on your computer."

"Oh my God" Kelly shrieked. Then she immediately shifted to the stoic demeanor she carried as an influential businesswoman and said "Tell me what happened, Frank. Is everyone else okay? Who did they take?"

"Yes, they're okay although a couple were a bit hysterical. They're quiet now. Asleep." He then related the general events of the night and recovery of the rest of the group. He finished with "If this is true to form, we should be getting a ransom demand before too long. These were Maya. This isn't normal around here but in the western highlands and around GC (Guatemala City) it's becoming a cottage industry. Not as bad as Mexico but growing. A couple of years ago a local group took four Belgian tourists to trade for their jefe who was held by the Army. They hurt no one and released them a day or two later. This is probably something like that. I'm positive about that."

"God, I hope so. I'm not sure exactly what to do. I guess we have to wait and see what they want. I guess I should contact the spouses. Damn, I hate it when my brain stutters."

"Kelly, I'll keep you informed as things develop here. Remember, for awhile no word is good word. Keep cool. This'll work out. The Maya around here are not, repeat not, violent people. They cherish these dentists. We're on it. The word is out among the locals. We'll find them."

"Keep me in the loop. Going to have a bunch of panicky folks on my hands. Bye, Frank."

"Wait a minute, Kelly. You haven't read the e-mail. They've got the boys. You'll have a major problem with Cristina."

"Oh, no. Please God, no."

"Kelly, they'll be okay. The Maya love children. They won't hurt them. Be talkin' to you. Bye for now."

"God, what to do now?" she thought. "I can't make these calls. I can't. I can't. I have to. I can't. I need to make coffee. I need to think. What will I say? I need coffee."

She was losing her self-imposed stoicism. Panic was creeping up on her – she could feel the anxiety contractions in her belly. She needed to move, couldn't sit. Her right leg spasmed. She almost ran to the kitchen. The ritual of coffee making occupied a few minutes. She rinsed the last three days of dishes and placed them in the dishwasher. She carefully measured in the Cascade powder, closed and started the machine. It wasn't enough. She still felt the compulsion to move. Her left eyelid twitched.

She exited to the deck overlooking Monterey Bay and lit a cigarette. She paced the deck wishing her stomach to calm, begging her stomach to calm. "Goddamn coffee. Why isn't it ready? Goddamn slow thing! Jesus, why is this happening?" She paced. Her breathing wasn't right. She stopped and looked at the Bay. She paced. She heard the gaggling hissing sound of the coffee maker finishing. "About goddamn time." she thought. She fetched a cup of coffee, spilling about half as her shaking hand lifted it. She re-filled it and returned to the deck to pace.

By the time nine o'clock rolled around she was well into her second pot and had lit and put out nearly a pack of cigarettes. She punched numbers into her phone.

"Williams Law Offices. May I help you?"

"This is Kelly Troia, Jacquie. I need Jonathan right now. It's an emergency."

"Kelly, he's on the phone. I'll have him call you."

"No. I need him right now. Get him off that goddamn phone and on this one. Right goddamn now."

"I'll speak to him, Kelly. Just a sec."

"Kelly what's the problem?"

"Jack, Mark and his boys and five others have been kidnapped in Guatemala!"

"What? Oh my god! Okay, Kelly, I'll be right over. I don't want you driving. Just try to be calm. I'm on my way."

"Jacquie, cancel everything on my calendar and stand by here in case I need something. Jack Troia and eight others have been kidnapped in Guatemala. I'm going to Kelly's house." he said as he raced for the door, leaving her with mouth agape.

He arrived at the Troia house nine minutes later. She was standing in the open doorway, shaking. Williams wrapped his arms around her, hugged her a long while then said "Okay, Kelly. Let's go inside. You need to tell me all about this then we need to see what we have to do. Let's go."

They went into the kitchen. She poured two cups of coffee, lit a cigarette and related to Williams everything Frank Lombard had told her two and one half hours earlier. She told him of her anxiety attacks and near panic. She told him of her inability to make the calls to the others, of her inability to function.

Williams said "You did the right thing to call me. You could have called me earlier at home. Anyway, I'll take care of the calls, that's what attorneys are for. You just be calm. This is the list?"

"Yes. Frank e-mailed it to me. This is the roster information on everyone on the trip. Contact information is there."

"Kelly, I'll be awhile working on this. Just sit tight."

She picked up her coffee and went out onto the deck.

Williams spent the next two hours notifying, consoling, assuring, explaining, calming, arranging for lawyers, priests and doctors to visit, and cautioning not to drive. His steady hand was on the tiller, his professional demeanor smoothed the waters as much as was possible.

Christina Blaylock was not at home. Williams left a message at her home to call him immediately, her cell went unanswered. He left a message there as well.

Then he was done. The hell of waiting began, the purgatory of impotence, a level of Hades below Dante's eighth where your entire existence is at the whim of another – an unknown 'other', an evil 'other'.

At twenty-seven minutes after one o'clock Kelly's phone rang. She answered. What she later described as a Spanish accented voice said "Check your e-mail." and hung up. She did. There was the ransom demand. She hit the print icon. Ten times.

Williams had been looking over her shoulder. He took the copies and returned to his phone. He called each spouse to see if they had received the same call. They had not. He advised them to check their e-mail. Christina Blaylock was the exception. She still didn't answer her phone.

CHAPTER 2

Blaylock home
Carmel, California
1530 hours: Day 2

Christina Blaylock had been visiting her mother in Southern California. The thought of home was an elixir she desperately needed. The accelerating decline of her mother into dementia had left her an emotional wreck. She needed sleep, blessed sleep. And perhaps one valium for good measure. She arrived home and took her suitcases to her bedroom. She unpacked, took a quick shower and jumped into sweats and tennies.It was four o'clock by the time the beeping of the answering machine attracted her attention. She listened then punched in Kelly's number. Jonathan Williams answered the phone.

"Oh, hi, Jonathan. Christina. Just got home. Your message said to call immediately. What's up?"

Williams, drawing upon his vast experience, informed her as gently as he could that her husband and two sons were held captive by natives asking twenty million dollars ransom. Unfortunately, there exists no experience or skill that enables gently breaking such news to a wife and mother. Particularly a mother.

The devastation was instantaneous and almost complete. She found herself on the floor clutching the phone, knowing not how she got there – nor caring. She found enough awareness to call Joanne, Mitchell's wife, who lived just down the hill. All she screamed was "Come fast. Is Mitch there?"

"No, he's not. What's the matter, Christina?"

Christina screamed again "Is Mitch there?"

Joanne said "Try his cell. I'm on my way." She had no idea what it was all about but she knew it was serious. Christina sounded completely freaked out, terrorized even. She knew she had to get to Christina immediately. This was bad, bad, bad. She had never heard that tone in a voice before. It scared her profoundly, a soul-deep fear, a primal gut-wrenching foreboding.

Christina punched the automatic button for Mitchell's cell phone. When he answered all he heard was hysterical yelling about kidnapping in Guatemala, twenty million in ransom and others taken. Mostly it was about her boys.

CHAPTER 3

Peppermill Casino
Reno, Nevada
1620 hours: Day 2

Mitchell looked at Broderick and said "Scott – you have a rental car?"

"No, took a cab. Have my bag checked up front."

"Good. Get your bag. You're with Bo and me. Ken – go home. Free yourself up. We'll call. I'll brief you when I can on Guatemala. We've a ton of calls to make. Maybe we'll need you in Monterey. Think on it – drive over if it fits. Bo, let's hit the road."

Hanson said "Mitch, brief me enroute. I know you were there last year with these guys. I've never been there. You thinking about going in?"

Mitchell nodded and said "Something like that but we'll need this Stratton guy's assets and contacts. Broderick's right – we're too old for the heavy lifting. We're going to need CIA and DEA help. You and Kenner are going to be pulling in a lot of favors. Start thinking on it. This 'boots on the ground' stuff is so far out of my zone but I know what this shit means and we have to move fast. Back channels. Up front won't work – too slow, if ever. The heavies never authorize what's really necessary – not in time and not ever. No balls. Just excuses and false sympathies. They'll waste anyone to cover their asses. We've got to get them out. Ransom or no ransom, if we don't they'll never be seen again. You know that and I know that. Damn."

Broderick returned, bag in hand. Mitchell said "Let's go. Kenner, we'll be talking."

As the three moved towards the parking area, Mitchell was deep in thought. Broderick started to speak but stopped as Hanson held up a finger and nodded towards Mitchell. When they got to the car, Mitchell stopped at the driver's door and, speaking over the top, said "Scott, you say Stratton lives in Monterey? Bo, you know him. Get on the line after Scott. Set up a meet at his house in about five and a half hours. You know where he lives? Good. Brief him with what we know now. We'll update him as we have more. Tell him to pull up maps of Northeast Guatemala – the area from Lago de Izabal to Livingston and north to Belize. Study them to brief us. We need to put together a mission fast but we don't yet know to where – just somewhere in that area. I've got a couple of calls to make." Mitchell unconsciously assumed that Stratton would be aboard. Opposite some unfounded and ignorant beliefs, these sorts of men subscribed to high standards of integrity and honor, will respond to needs without question or hesitation, and despise bone-deep those who prey on the weak or defenseless.

They swung out of the lot onto the back streets, jumped onto Lakeside to pick up McCarran – the fastest route to I-80 west over the Sierra Nevada Mountains. Mitchell immediately dialed in Christina's number. Joanne answered. She described what a mess Christina was in emotionally, a complete disassociation with her surroundings.

Mitchell said "Glad you got there. She needs you there. You know she's been out of sorts lately. Call Charlie Daniels to meet you there. She'll need sedatives to calm her but tell Charlie not to put her out. I'll need to talk with her before too long but I've got a meeting first. Say, about seven hours from now. If I can I may talk with someone who knows more – maybe Kelly. We'll see. Remember everything she says in her hysteria before she's sedated. I want to hear it. Better yet, record it if you can. There's a recorder in your glove box. Call me if you need anything. Love you. Bye." He hung up.

Meanwhile, in the back seat, Broderick had reached Stratton on the first ring.

"Colonel, this is Scott Broderick."

"Scotty, how the hell are you? Great to hear your voice. To what do I owe this honor?"

"Doing great, Sir, but we've got a serious problem and need your help. I've got Colonel Bo Hanson here with me – you know him. If it's all right with you I'd like to put him on the horn and let you colonels sort this out."

"Sounds serious. Sure, put him on."

"Deke, Bo here. Got some local dentists, kids and businessmen taken hostage in Guatemala and held for ransom. I'm enroute from Reno. Be there in five hours. Need a meet as soon as we get there. We're probably going to have to go in. You know how these things come down. Don't know much now but pull up charts for northeast Guatemala from Lago de Izabal to Livingston and north to Belize. I'm with Scotty and an old navy fast mover named Doug Mitchell. He's been there and has contacts. He's checking in with them now. We'll have more intel before long. I'll keep you posted. Be thinking covert op."

"Jesus Christ, Bo. You know how to make a man's day! This is something else! Actually, it sounds like fun if it weren't so damn serious. And, yah, I know of that navy puke. Haven't met him yet. Looking forward to that honor. See you when you get here. I'm already on it. Adios."

"Mitch, Deke's on board. He's on it."

"Okay. Bo, I've got to call a guy in Guatemala – Frank Lombard. He owns the hotel where the group stays when doing the dentistry missions. Good man – American. Flew my kind of airplanes back in the day – before me, actually. Married there and stayed. Started the hotel in '69 or so. Sits on an island in the Rio Dulce River. Depending on what he says, we'll need assets in Punta Gorda in Belize – CIA and DEA, if we can get a connection. Your area and Deke's. Think on it. I'm calling Frank. Hope I get through in these damn mountains. Scotty, how about you driving? I'll be busy." Mitchell said as he pulled over.

After swapping places, Mitchell leafed through his red phone/address book until he found Frank's cell number at the Outrigger Hotel. "Hell of a world." thought Mitchell as he punched in the numbers. "From my car in the mountains of California calling a hotel in Guatemala in the middle of nowhere. Incredible!"

"Frank, Doug Mitchell. Just heard. How're things going? Can you brief me?"

"Thought you might be calling. I called Kelly Troia early this morning. Jack was the lead on this group so I figured Kelly had all the contacts. She call you?"

"No. I just got a call from Mark's wife."

"Well, I gave Kelly the short version. Skipped the details and softened as much as I could. It's a zoo around here. Let me bring you up to speed. The group was returning from the clinic late yesterday – not quite dusk. Jose had them all in his launch – you've been on it. There were four indigena fishing boats in their route but Jose steered to miss them, of course, going slower between them. One cut in front and Jose cut power to avoid collision. At that point, weapons appeared and the boats closed. Another power launch like Jose's made a fast approach and joined up. Three guys boarded Jose's launch. One had a folder that he kept looking at then pointing at specific individuals. Each was put on the bandit launch. It seemed that the bandit was looking at pictures but nobody actually saw what was in the folder. All the bandits wore balaclava-like face covering which is a good sign. Didn't want to be identifiable later. Shortly the fishing boats left under power – they had the common small outboards. The bandit with the folder returned to his launch. One of the bandits pushed Jose into a seat and took over the motor. The other was in front pointing his rifle at the remaining passengers. Both launches proceeded high speed down river and into the middle of El Golfete. They stopped. The two bandits took Jose's gas tank, disabled his Suzuki 250 and returned to their launch. They had searched everyone and thrown their cell phones overboard. They left them stranded in the dark, floating in the middle of nothing."

"When the jefe spoke to the captives it was in very poor Spanish but they spoke Q'eqchi (kekChee) among themselves, not Poqomom which would place them south and west of here. Jose said they were unsure about what they were doing, like they weren't sure they should be doing this at all. Seemed afraid. Jose speaks Q'eqchi – his cradle language. Jose says they are native to this area – probably a bit north of here. You know that there are 23 languages in Guatemala so it helps to locate to an area."

"When they didn't show up here, I got concerned and we searched the route. Found nothing. Became really concerned. The people at the clinic area confirmed they had left late. We know they hadn't come upriver past us so we started working downriver, shining spotlights everywhere. One Maya fisherman who was gill-netting told us he had seen two power launches going downriver high speed earlier. We proceeded downriver to the Golfete. You know how big that damn Golfete is! Fortunately, sound travels well here at night. Finally, after midnight, we heard a faint sound. We had run around near the shore with the spotlight and were moving across towards the other side. They had slowly drifted in that direction and had seen our lights. They had been yelling for quite a while when we finally heard them."

"They were okay, unharmed but a couple were nearly hysterical. The Maya people here are pissed – to say the least. For twenty years these folks have been caring for the children. Some of the mothers now were patients when young. The word is out to find where they are. The jungle drums and all that. We know they didn't make it to Livingston – at least they weren't seen there. Several fishermen at the Golfete outlet heard nothing."

"I'm starting to suspect that they went up the Chacon-Machaca River, which makes sense. That is dangerous country up there. Remember, I wouldn't let you go up there when you asked? Couple of years ago, when the military imprisoned a tribal jefe, they captured four Belgian tourists to trade for their jefe. Didn't hurt them and released them after two days. A little further up is all narco country, cocaine transit country and heavily defended. Historical bandit area – some mean sons-of-bitches there. Lots of crazies who sample the wares in transit."

"Frank, you say they were looking at pictures in a folder and selected the hostages accordingly? So it wasn't just a random snatch and grab. That means preplanning and serious intent. Where the hell do tribe people get pictures? And why?"

"Don't know. But we don't have absolute proof of that. It just looked like that. But – they were selective, that's for sure. Here's who they took. You ready to copy?"

"Go."

"Jack Troia, Mark Blaylock and his sons, John and Travis, Karen Smith, Charles Wilson, James Villareal, Peter Rust and Imelda Watson."

"Got it. An e-mail already went demanding twenty million ransom in English. Can they do that out there?"

"Mitch, that's not Maya. Twenty mill? E-mail? Maya wouldn't think like that. In English? No way! Somebody's behind this, somebody connected. Maybe narcos trying a new racket. They think big money and that is narco country up there."

"This mess is appearing stranger and stranger. Frank, I need intel as you get it. Right now were blind, the chessboard is fogged in. As it clears, if it clears, got a few things in mind."

"You going in, Mitch?"

"Don't know yet. Do know the spineless government heavies can't and won't handle it. We can't rely on safe release once the ransom is paid. Got to figure out something. Like I said, we desperately need intel. Location, numbers, etc."

"As I get it, you've got it."

"Roger that. Talk soon. Adios Amigo."

Mitchell gave a summary to Hanson and Broderick and said "Bo, give Deke a heads up on Chacon-Machaca. It's a river running north off the Golfete. I've got to call Kenner." He clicked in the number.

"Kenner, Mitch. Some changes. Think you need to come to Monterey. Got some intel from Guatemala. Seems the bad guys had photos to select specific hostages – not a random group grab. Something is going on. We need you to gather together all the spouses and their lawyers or accountants. The ransom payment has to be coordinated and delayed when the instructions come. You also need to generate as much info from the group as possible. There is a connect somehow. All I know so far is that they want twenty million – or so Christina said. You need to ramrod that whole side of the show. Calm them, focus them, pick their brains. Without a leader it will be chaos. FBI may step in. Let 'em but fly tight wing and feed us info. You concur?"

"Good plan. I'm on my way. Nice to be needed. What's going on down south?"

Mitchell quickly briefed him on all that Lombard had passed.

"Wow." Grazing said. "Sounds like he's really on it. Something should break. Shouldn't piss off that many mothers. Bet they've got their men beating the bushes. I'll be at your house in about six hours."

"Call me when you get here. I'll have more for you then. You know where your quarters are. Joanne's with Christina. Chase is around. See ya." He clicked off then punched in Joanne's cell.

"Hi, Honey. How's Christina doing?"

"She's sedated and calm. Charlie will have to leave to check on two others who are also his patients. She keeps asking when you'll be here and what are you doing."

"Honey, I've got Kenner coming to head up a gathering of the spouses – tomorrow, I think. Guess our house is a good neutral location. I've got a list of all the captives" He read the list to her. "Call each. Suggest they bring their lawyer or advisor. Accountants would be good. This thing has got to be coordinated. Ken should be at our place in six hours or so. I'll be along about then as well. Maybe a bit later. On second thought, call Jonathan Williams. I'll bet he's got a meeting in mind. Let's let him take the lead on that. I'll introduce Ken there. Okay?"

"Will do. See you soon. Drive careful."

"Bye."

When he was finished, Hanson said "Okay, Mitch, bring me up to speed on Guatemala. Never been to Central America. Wasn't operational for the Contra stuff in Nicaragua. Was privy to a lot of it from our side but no need to immerse myself in their history, no need for the 'feel' of the place. I know we were running ops in support from Honduras and a supply route from Guatemala. Know we still maintain a presence in each of those countries – both overt and covert. Mostly FBI and DEA but also CIA. There is Army presence, again both overt and covert. So – give me some 'feel'. You went there last year. I know you always develop a two inch thick study before we travel anywhere. You must have done one for Guatemala – give. You have two or three hours but please don't use it all. I get sleepy on information overload."

Mitchell said "Broderick, you ever draw Guatemala time, CIA time?"

"Ahhh – traveled through it but operated a bit out of Honduras. No disrespect, Sir, but I'd rather wait until I can speak with Colonel Stratton. I don't really know you guys and what I can say. I mean, I know of y'all and you're cool and he's a friend of the Colonel but still a lot of that stuff is still classified and I don't know where the line is until the Colonel tells me. You know what I mean?" With that he took in a deep breath and held it for a moment while he looked questioningly at his two companions.

"I'll be damned. Good for you Sergeant." Hanson said. "You're absolutely right about waiting for clearance. We respect that."

"Bo, Scotty, I'll give you the short version while were traveling. Correct me, Scotty, if you spot mistakes. Geography first. Guatemala lies south of Mexico, on the western portion, and of Belize on the Caribbean side. On that side, Honduras is to the south and El Salvador is to the south on the Pacific side. It stretches across Central America from the

Caribbean to the Pacific, sitting astride the Cocaine Highway from South America to the U.S."

"The Spanish established their center of administration for Central America here, locating in Antigua Guatemala which is a tourist center now. Along the way a huge earthquake destroyed much of the town – some of the ruins are viewable today – and the government center was moved to what is today Guatemala City or Ciudad Guatemala, often shortened to CG. In the northeast of the country are the Maya ruins which also run up the Yucatan peninsula of Mexico. Those ruins and culture were all from low-land Maya which seem to be different from high-land Maya. Probably food supply led to differences. The low-landers probably had more food capability which allowed greater and more dense population which allowed the development of a parasitic priest class thus the monuments to ego and, ergo, the ruined temples. They supported some pretty advanced astronomy, mathematics and writing. The highland Maya culture is the one you see today scattered all over the country. Even today's low-landers are more in the nature of the high-landers – scattered pueblas, not high densities with centralized organization."

"Even before the Spaniards there were internecine wars, primarily between language groups. Languages were a function of area and some conquest. Today, there are 21 indigenous languages spoken in Guatemala plus Spanish. Throw in some English and you have 23 languages prevalent. Even after all this time, many Maya do not speak any Spanish at all!"

"The Maya sense of loyalty and commitment is first to family then to puebla – a small village or enclave. There seems to be little or no idea of State or interest in commitment to central government. They are the majority of population but have not seen fit to exercise their numbers except in sporadic local rebellions against severe abuses."

"There are apparently three divisional classes among the, shall we say, 'elites'. For a long time the dominant was the *peninsulares*, the Spain born. They gobbled up huge land tracts as spoils of conquest. Then, over time, there were the *creoles*, Spanish blood but born in Guatemala or Central America. These are the children of the peninsulares. Of course, along the way, there was a little fraternization and the *mestizo* group arrived – Spanish and indigenous blood mixed – and formed a middle class functionary role. Landowner families and business families became the power and governing structure. It is so today - as one would expect "

"You had, and have, the foreigners coming in, non-Spanish, who worked their ways with the local elites. These were heavily towards Germans and North Americans with some English. Way down the power list – so far down as not to even be considered – came the indigenous people, the Maya. And it is still so today."

"In general, slang talk speaks of Guatemala citizens as in two groups, *ladinos* or *indigenas*.Ladinos are all those city, elite non-tribal folks. It includes Maya who have forsaken the way of the puebla, of their forebears, and are trying to participate in the ladino culture. The indigenas are the ones true to the old way, growers of maize, of Maya blood and honor the gods or God as demanded by the Church but modified or localized by the people."

"The Maya were, and are, largely uneducated – not stupid. They receive little government supplied education. They are not required to attend school until some minimal age. To a very large degree, the highland lifestyle is as it has been for more than two thousand years as far as I can tell. They have survived incredible abuse at the hands of the Spaniards – both from forced labor and decimation from European diseases. The landowners, through the Caudillos – military dictators bought and paid for by the landowners and business owners – had various methods of forcing labor. Though not calling it 'slavery' it was in essence just that. One method was a requirement to provide labor for so many days a year to the government. Of course, the people were turned over to the fincas – ranches. Others were the so-called 'vagrancy laws' – snatch and grab type stuff. Brutal, by our modern standards."

"Ag exports were the only real source of money. They needed to maintain an inexpensive and docile labor component. Fear was the tool and they were severely exploited. Coffee was king. Guatemalan coffee has consistently received high prices because of its high quality. The ruling oligarchy was coffee based. Bananas then came along with the advent of rapid steam shipping ability. The United Fruit Company (UFCO or 'the octopus'), formed in 1899, became a major player on the scene. Through its workings with, and funding of, the caudillos, it wrested huge amounts of land concessions and other 'deals' from the state. There was a railroad from Ciudad Guatemala to the Pacific – since 1880 – but none to the Caribbean. UFCO formed a subsidiary called International Railways of Central America and acquired, from the state, the exclusive right to rail traffic to the Caribbean, exclusive mail carrying, exclusive rate setting, exclusive right to develop Puerto Barrios as the Caribbean port and, of course, free land. It finished the railroad in 1908. It formed another entity called the Tropical Radio and Telegraph Company which was the only communication with the U.S. – which was the banana market. Bananas became a giant, foreign-controlled, plantation crop. Bananas are a low-land crop. Few workers from the highlands could be induced to come to the hot, disease-ridden Caribbean coastal plains. UFCO imported some Jamaican and West Indian Blacks to work there. Thus, today, along the Caribbean coast is a population of blacks – called Garifuna or Black Carib – which produces significant social tension. They're a mix of Black and Carib. The Carib were indigenous to some of the West Indian islands and aggressive sons-of-bitches. As a group they're essentially extinct now."

"The economic conditions in Ciudad Guatemala improved as they tried to emulate the U.S. forms. But all was not cool. The influx to the city created slums – the same old story. Caudillo Cabrera handled all dissent with armed force. However, university students were active and some labor unions developed."

"Then, 1929 happened. The collapse of the western economies was devastating to a country completely dependent upon selling coffee and bananas. Same old solution – a hard-core dictator guy named Ubico. Corrupt as hell and a pure power hungry ego. He did all the right things for the land-owners and foreigners becoming rich in the process and storing his money in the U.S. What's new? However, the greater the force the greater the resistance seems to grow. I think it's one of Ohm's or Faraday's Laws on electricity and social affairs. Students, labor and some junior military officers formed a strange group of companions. By 1944, Ubico was in deep tapioca and a series of labor strikes hit. Railroad workers shut down the transportation system in late June. Ubico quit, claimed bad health, scooted to New Orleans and turned the government over to a triumvirate of senior Army officers. Seems you Army guys always want to run the show. Never hear of government by Admirals. Strange. Anyway, the head General wanted to be the Cau-dillo but the force of public opinion, and as a condition of restarting the economy, he had to re-instate constitutional protections, hold elections in November and permit unions and political parties."

"Dr. Arevalo, an exiled professor, was elected. There was some other unimportant rebellion action along the way but one young rebellious Captain Arbenz becomes important later. Arevalo followed a program of structural change – not at all radical, even restrained, but change non-the-less. A new constitution. A new war on illiteracy. Voting rights. Workmen's compensation. Health services. Trivial stuff like that."

"Here's some numbers, if I can remember them right, of what he was facing: One-third of Guatemala is deemed arable. Only one-half of that was in use – the rest left fallow by large landowners. 2.2 percent held over 70 percent of the land. Less than one sixteenth of 1 percent owned 14 percent of the land. 22 percent owned 20 percent of the land including portions already mentioned. Bottom line – less than 10 percent of the land was for 90 percent of the population!"

"And it goes on. Jesus, the place was one big plantation with 'Massa' running the show with an army! The Church turned against him because the new constitution had anti-clerical clauses imposed by the 1879 constitution. They started criticizing Arevalo. His government eventually shut down the Church's print and voice media, accusing them of spreading lies among the uneducated population. Imagine that! He scaled back the military. The Army revolted but was put down by armed workers – can you believe it?"

"The defense minister Arbenz – the young captain I mentioned earlier – was the front runner in the 1950 election. He won. Under Arbenz, Guatemala moved towards the left but really that was closer to the center. Agrarian reform became the centerpiece of his regime. That planted real fear among the landlords. Young Che Guevara, employed in the Agrarian Reform Department, urged that labor unions be armed. Arbenz refused to do that. Later, the Army's fear of Arbenz doing just that led to their refusal to stand up for Arbenz against an invasion."

"In those days, the U.S. was berserk about communism – or so it seemed. The U.S. said that Guatemala was becoming a communist outpost of the Soviet Union. The reality? Arbenz, in total, over three years confiscated about 400,000 acres of unused land from UFCO and set out to redistribute it. Arbenz offered to pay for it at the price that UFCO had listed as its value for tax purposes. UFCO screamed 'foul'. Isn't that funny? They value the land to cheat on taxes and the government says 'Great. We'll buy it for your stated value'. I love it! The planning for the overthrow of Arbenz began in 1953 by the CIA. It was activated in June of 1954 and the CIA placed Castillo Armas in the presidency. End of confiscation."

"Communism? Let's look a little bit closer. Remember the honesty of our leaders in Vietnam times? Well, get this. Remember I told you about UFCO getting all those land grants and concessions from Ubico in the thirties? There's a Wall Street law firm that represented many American interests in Central America. An attorney partner in the firm – later the executive partner – negotiated those deals for UFCO. His brother was also a partner in the firm. Both held significant quantities of UFCO stock and stock in the bank UFCO used. In 1953, the U.S. Secretary of State was John Foster Dulles and his brother, Allen Dulles, was head of the CIA! Want to guess the name of that attorney that negotiated with Ubico? Want to guess who engineered the overthrow of the Guatemalan government? Want to guess why some Central Americans aren't too fond of Norte Americanos? Ain't that something?"

"Castillo Armas was placed in power and it was business as usual for the next thirty years. The military establishment came out on top in the shuffle, over the other players. No more talk about 'cutbacks'."

"In response to the horrid military suppression, covert resistance developed even though death squads and tribunals continually weeded their numbers. More joined. Tourism plummeted. That, and a drop in coffee prices, caused more poverty and more resistance. For example on poverty, in 1981 nearly 80 percent of the population had less than

300 dollars per month income. In 1985, the military conceded to a new constitution and later that year a civilian was elected president."

"Cerezo was unable to quickly end the essentially civil war of thirty years. He also could not handle the rising narcotics trade that was responding to the U.S. hunger for the powder. But he made great efforts even though he served at the pleasure of the high ranking military officers. It was a step."

"Rigoberta Menchu (she was Maya highland young lady) was the subject of a book, supposedly of true experiences recounted by her, that brought world-wide attention to the plight of the indigenous people even though the book was full of falsities. She received the 1992 Nobel Peace Prize. Nobody realized then that the book had been written by the wife of a French communist organizer in Paris. Didn't matter though – it brought attention. As late as 1990 all leftist political parties were banned."

"In 1996, under President Arzu, a peace accord with the guerilla rebels was signed. The thirty-six year civil war ended. Their last area of control was in the north east and north central – the Peten, low land jungle just north of where we are thinking the hostages might be located. Arzu purged military officers accused of human rights violations. Still, violence remained and even increased in the countryside. Murders and kidnappings increased. As late as 1999 a survey found 88 percent of Guatemalans feeling that the administration of justice was inadequate. A United Nations sponsored report listed Guatemala City as the most dangerous city in the Americas!"

"Today, violence and human rights abuses still plague the country. The Maya are beginning to organize a little bit and focus on the central government. They hold six of the 80 seats. They are 60 percent of the population – it is a start. In 2000, an agreement with the U.S. was reached allowing

U.S. agents to operate within Guatemala to fight the drug interests. This is very important for us now. American assets are on site."

"That's sort of my take on a quick history lesson of the country. The two recent presidents – Berger and Colon – seem to be making great strides but to where, I don't know. Population pressures, not much in the way of natural assets, a history of violence and the god damn drug trade look like big hurdles. For us, though, the presence of agents from DEA, FBI and CIA means we won't be alone – we should be able to generate back-channel help and support. That, Gentlemen, is about it. Take out paper and pen. There is a small written exam to see if you were paying attention. Bo, you awake?"

"Jesus Christ, Mitch, how do you keep all that crap in your head?" Hanson exploded.

"It's only been a year since I was there. Still kind of fresh, Bo. Actually, the place fascinated me – particularly the Maya of the east and north. Really wonderful people. I enjoyed them immensely. I have to say, though, that I did receive a few tentative guarded looks that I took to reveal an underlying distrust of the Anglo. From what I could learn it was a well placed distrust and fear. And remember, where we think we're going is right into that guerilla holdout, historical bandito, now narco country! Ain't life sweet?"

Broderick said" Wow. That's quite an off the top of the head summary. Never heard one unprepared like that. It sure gives me a feeling for the place and people I didn't have. And I've been there."

Hanson said "Don't be impressed, Scotty. He does that stuff before every country he visits. Says it broadens the experience once you get there and meet the people. Some places he even learns the languages. Me? I just tip well. They remember me more than him. One other important point; don't encourage him. We'll just get more detail."

Mitchell said "Scotty, that's true. Places we've re-visited, they say 'Hi, Bo' as we walk in the door. Bo has to re-introduce me."

They drove silently for some time, each lost in thought contemplating the upcoming probable mission. Hanson and Mitchell, in their minds, planning out scenarios and probable asset needs associated with each. People's names were popping up in their heads as possible routes to follow for needed solutions.

"Gents, let's slack off a bit, wait until we meet with Stratton. No point in getting headaches over wild schemes. Let's get a plan and then work it out. I'm going to close my eyes. Scotty, you okay?"

"Yes, Sir" Scotty replied.

CHAPTER 4

Stratton home
Monterey, California
2000 hours: Day 2

Hanson had called Stratton for a refresher on directions to his home. As they pulled into the lower entrance to the garage they saw Stratton on the upper deck waving them up. "Trust coffee is needed." Stratton said in welcome. "How ya doin, Scotty?"

"Great, Colonel. You know Colonel Hanson. This is Doug Mitchell. Mitch, Deke Stratton."

"Pleasure to meet you, Deke. Scotty and Bo have said some nice things about you. It's an honor."

"Lies, I'm sure. Welcome. Bo says you were Navy. Fast mover. What'd you drive?"

"A-4Fs in combat. Instructor in A-7s. Tested some others."

"Combat?"

Hanson broke in. "He had 329 missions in 'Nam – mostly in the north. Marines tried to give him the MH (Medal of

Honor) or a Navy Cross. Another time some in the Navy tried to give him another Navy Cross. Problem was, he was disobeying orders both times. Naughty boy."

"Think I kind of like you." Stratton said. "No shit, the Medal, huh?"

"Aw, it was bullshit. Just trying to save my own ass. Snagged a few Marines out along the way. They're mad dogs but they're *our* mad dogs so we have to look out for them from time to time. Navy noblesse oblige and all that."

"How'd you do that in the air?"

"Wasn't. Was on the ground. Time for that another day. We've got a huge problem facing us here and now."

"Someday I'd like to hear the story. Someday."

"Right."

Stratton looked around. "Everyone got coffee? Good. We'll work in here. I've got some stuff put together. Got a lot more to assemble. Started work on lists of needed stuff. Need way more intel but I'm coming along on a skeleton program that can flex as needed. I need to call a few folks, get some folks standing by, eat up some lead time. Probably stuff we won't use. I'm planning the Chacon-Machaca until we know differently. This will take me some time."

Mitchell said "I think you guys can do the preliminary stuff. We definitely need more information. Frank will call us when he has more – Deke, Frank is the guy on site, lives there, Bo will explain. I've got to go see about Christina and the others. Deke, can Broderick bunk here?"

"Absolutely."

"Bo, you going to stay or should I drop you?"

"Drop me."

"Okay, how about we meet here tomorrow, ten hundred hours. Should have something by then. Grazing should be arriving any time now. I'm off."

On the way out, Stratton said to Hanson "Seems to take command."

"The Lieutenant thinks he's an Admiral – but he probably should be. He's our resident genius. Sometimes frighteningly so. Does have a little problem with rules and regs, though. Despises gutless wonders – meaning bureaucrats, politicians, and rank with no merit."

"I knew who you meant."

Hanson laughed and joined up with Mitchell.

As Mitchell pulled out of the driveway he rang up Grazing. "How ya doing?" Mitchell inquired.

"I'm on Highway one. Should be at your house in about twenty."

"Great. I'm on my way and should be about the same. See ya there. Gotta drop Bo off first."

CHAPTER 5

Mitchell home
Carmel, California
2330 hours; Day 2

Enroute home, Mitchell called Joanne." How's she doing?"

"So, so. She is completely demolished. I've got to stay here tonight. There's no need for you to come up. Probably start her off crying again. The sedatives have her pretty knocked down. She's said nothing of any help to you."

"Okay. Kenner should be arriving about the time I do. Have you talked with anyone else?"

"Yes. Jonathan Williams is at Kelly's. He's handling everything, notified everyone. You need to be talking with him. Think he's setting up a meeting for tomorrow at eleven for everyone at Kelly's house. I'm not sure Christina will be able to go."

"Find out, if you can, who their main lawyer is and their accountant. Get me their names and I'll get them there for her."

"Okay. Hon. Do you have something in the works?"

"Tell her that I will do my very best to get her men back. I'm on it full power. Oh, by the way, Ken will be here but Bo and I will probably be out of the country for awhile."

"Ohhh, God, Mitch! You're too damn old to go chasing bad guys in a jungle! You'll have a heart attack. Are you crazy? We'll lose you and them! NO, NO, NO!"

"Wait a minute, sweetheart. We've got younger guys to do that. All ex-snake eaters. Bo and I will be in safe areas. We open doors and write checks. Okay? We are not going into the bush ourselves."

"Oh. Okay then. But you'll call? Often?"

"When I can. I'll be talking with Kenner as we develop information. He'll know where we are at all times. Some of this you can't know. Okay?"

"Just be careful."

He thought to himself "Why do women always say that? Like, ah, yeah, I need to be reminded to do that – be careful. Jeez!"

Mitchell arrived home before Grazing. He had some time to verify that his son, Chase, was winning his video game and that Nazis or aliens were dieing by the hundreds. He thought that maybe Chase was speaking to him when he said "Hi, Dad." Chase's eyes were locked on the screen as more bad guys bit the dust.

As Grazing entered, Mitchell was on the phone to Williams. They were friends. Williams brought Mitchell up to date and informed him of the meeting the next day at eleven at the Troia home. Mitchell confirmed that he'd be there. He had some things to say to the group. He discussed his thoughts on having Grazing involved. Williams concurred. Mitchell then said "Have you notified the FBI?"

Williams said "No. Why? They are not being held in the U.S. The FBI has no jurisdiction there."

Mitchell quietly said "Jonathan, I'm thinking there's some U.S. connection but I can't tell you why. Also, the FBI has agents that specialize in kidnapping. They have a lot of experience and knowledge that we don't and they have abilities that we don't. And they have assets – read agents and connections – in Guatemala itself. See what I mean? I'll call and see if we can get an agent there tomorrow – even if just to listen and advise. Okay?"

"You put it that way, I'm kicking myself in the ass for not calling them earlier."

"See you tomorrow."

Mitchell turned and said "Hi. Guess you heard that. Now what do we do – look up FBI in the phone book?"

"Good a place as any."

CHAPTER 6

Stratton home
Monterey, California
1000 hours; Day 3

"Mitch, Frank here. I've got what you need. The dentists are being held in a small puebla up the Chacon-Machaca like we guessed. It's quite a ways up river. Like I told you, the Maya are pissed off about this. These people are cherished by the mothers – which means the whole family."

"You know that there are antagonisms between pueblas, just like people everywhere else. Lower down the river the boats were seen heading up river by two young members of a nearby puebla. At the time they thought it strange – so many people – so they told their jefe. Of course, nobody knew then about the kidnapping. When the jefe later heard about it, it connected and he knew where they were headed. The kids knew the boats even though they couldn't clearly see the guys. Nothing's a secret in the bush."

"This puebla only speaks Q'eqchi but they have one young man of ambition and curiosity who was having a continual problem with the old ways. His name is Enrique. To cut to the chase, he left for the outside world. He, so far, has only made it to Nana Juana's – there by the bridge. If you guys look it up it's called 'Fronteras' because the road used to end there. He works on the docks – you know, where I picked you all up. He's a good kid, hard worker and smart. He's already learned a lot of Spanish and a touch of English. Anyway, the old jefe sends off Enrique's little brother, Emilio, in the puebla's one motorized panga to tell Enrique. As you know, that's a long way in a little fishing panga and its nothing of an outboard. Kid's lucky he had enough gas to get there. But, he did."

"Enrique promptly came to me. He showed me on a map exactly where that puebla is located. Took some time. He'd never seen a map before. Once I explained certain locations he knew he was able to pinpoint the spot. I've already e-mailed the GPS coordinates."

"Frank, wait. Here is a different address – where I am now. Just a sec. Deke, what's your e-mail address?" Mitchell quickly passed it to Frank then said "Go ahead."

Frank continued "According to Enrique, it's pretty complicated to find but it is waterway accessible. It is up a small channel off the river. The entrance to the channel is through the trees that line the river. If you aren't exactly perpendicular to it at the right spot you won't see the entrance. Even then, some hanging vines have to be pushed aside. If you are going in you will need guides. I mean it – you won't find it by yourselves. Enrique and his brother are more than willing to be your guides. Doctor Mark and Doctor Jack have cared for his family for years. They're mad. Their jefe is mad. *Their mother* is mad!"

"Enrique has been to this puebla several times. Seems there is a girl there. Sort of upset both tribes. He says there are sixteen houses in that puebla. There are twenty-eight males over twelve years old and twenty eighteen and older.

The village is called Las Arenas because it is on a sand hill running up from the channel."

"He says the jefe's name is Felipe. He has a wife and three small children – boy of twelve, girl ten and a little one. Felipe's house is quite a ways back from the channel. It is the fourth one up the avenue on the right, right beside the avenue."

"If you guys are going in, I can fly Enrique and his brother to wherever you wish. I'll need a little time to arrange. You guys figure out what you're going to do and then give me a call. Run it by me – maybe I can spot problems or add to it. At least now we know where and who."

"Frank, you're fantastic. I'll get back to you. We've got a lot to do now. And thanks."

"No need to thank me. You've got the football. Keep me posted. Adios for now."

Mitchell explained everything to the others then said "We've got a target, Gentlemen! Deke, you pull up that e-mail?"

"Got it right here. Already plotted while you were talking. Must have some Y chromosomes the way I can multi-task! I'll deny I ever said that. The map we have doesn't show that little channel. I think there is merit to that guide business. Used local guides before. Also, none of us speaks Q'eqchi. That kid does. We don't know if 'Felipe' speaks any Spanish. Most of the remote ones don't."

"Okay, let's spread out these maps I've already taped together. The internet is great but it is a shitty way to put maps together. Happily, I do have some old Central America maps. Did a little project or two there some time back. Was Nicaragua if I remember correctly. Yeah, that was it. Wonder if Ollie ever knew what really was going on? Well, that's another story. Here we go. There – that's where we have to go. Let me study this a bit. Hope you all don't mind me taking the lead here but it is kind of my thing."

"Go for it. I'll get some more coffee while you're cranking up that Army brain. Know it takes some time from being around Bo here." Mitchell said.

"Up yours, fast mover." Hanson replied.

After about ten minutes filled with Stratton swinging finger arcs over the maps, wrinkled brow, measuring with index finger and scratching of head, he leaned back and announced "We can do it. Bo, you still plugged in deep with the Company?"

"Somewhat. Don't know how far but, yeah, I think I can get us some help. What do you need?"

"Well, here's what I'm toying with. Six of us would go in. Don't like working with eight – never did. Six is enough."

Mitchell interjected "Six? Six for twenty-eight – maybe more? You sure?"

Stratton looked at Mitchell and said "Navy, put a sock in it. Even if it were forty or so we'd only need six!"

"Jesus." Muttered Mitchell.

"Anyway, as I was saying before I was so naively interrupted, six of us would go in. We'd need to go to Punta Gorda in Belize. There's a domestic airport there. More important, there's a CIA and DEA presence. On the far side of the airport the CIA maintains a fairly large hanger under some phony name and several aircraft. They share, somewhat, with DEA. If we can get cooperation, back channel, they can get us south to an insertion point. See this little airfield on the Guatemala side of the border with Belize. There, just at the southwest corner of Belize – at a place called Modesto Mendez. From there it is a few miles to connect with the upper reaches of the Chacon-Machaca. Once there, we go down-river in hard bottom inflatable boats – three of them. We have small outboards and carry a small gas tank for each. Down river we pre-position another boat with more fuel aboard for use on our way out. It is a simple run to the hotel."

Mitchell said "Downriver? Why not go upriver to get them? This seems overly complicated."

Stratton gave him a condescending look and said "Going up river the outboards are running. Everyone knows you're there. We go downriver – no noise. In the dark. After we have the hostages we crank up the engines and go like hell. Then we don't care about noise."

"As my son would say, 'sweet'." Mitchell responded. "But, that long overland trek carrying Zodiacs, motors, fuel and gear looks to me a bit forbidding. Further, you go into that field in the heart of narco and bandito country, everyone will know you've arrived for some reason. That area is notorious bandit country and has been for centuries –it's a way of life up there. Looks to me more men would be needed to carry then return to the waiting plane. A plane waiting might not be such a good thing. I'll bet there is an Army detachment at Modesto Mendez – it's a border town.. That would not be good."

"Yep, those are problems. So, let's solve them. Getting a team is no problem. I've made a few phone calls. Guys are standing by. I just have to decide which are best for this op. Spanish speakers are priority, of course, but that really isn't a problem. The next problem is money. This could be very expensive."

In unison, Mitchell and Hanson said "No problem."

"Ok." Stratton said with a raised eyebrow. "Third – transportation and to where. Mitchell, why don't you get on the horn to this Frank guy. Ask him if there are any decent dirt or grass runways anywhere near the upper Chacon-Machaca. Four thousand feet would be nice but shorter okay. Just ask what there is. If there is, e-mail us coordinates and a map would help. Maybe we go to a remote strip from Punta Gorda. I've got another call to make."

Mitchell wandered off to the kitchen to make his call. Stratton picked up his phone and punched in some numbers from memory. Hanson raised an eyebrow quizzically. Stratton said "Pope."

His call was answered "Joint Special Operations Command. Command Sergeant Major Robert Williams speaking."

"Hey, Bobby. Deke here. How you doing?"

"Hey, Boss. Good to hear your voice. What's up?"

"Got a big favor to ask. We okay to talk? You got a few minutes?"

"Always for you, Deke. Shoot."

Stratton explained about the dentists and the kids. He left out the businessmen thinking that wouldn't carry any weight. At one point, Williams interrupted saying "Think I'll shut my office door about now. Have a feeling where you're headed." He did so and returned to his desk chair. He said "Go."

Stratton continued "A few of us guys are going in after them. You know they won't be released even if the ransom is paid. We need legs and clearances from CONUS to Punta Gorda in Belize. One of those C-130s you've got would work nice. We have to carry three inflatable boats with 25HP motors. We need six full kits, six suppressed Ruger 22s, subsonic loads, 2 MA4s with extra clips, goggles – both ambient and IR (Infra-Red – heat signature), Tac com and Sat phones, six Tasers – the new three shot if you can - and a full box of preloaded syringes for 120 to 140 pounders. Want them out for an hour at least. Give me a few with antidotes. Oh, yeah, I need to be in the air within forty-eight hours. All back-channel. That's about it. Oh, and yeah, some Fer de Lance anti-venom."

"Jesus Christ! Deke, you don't ask for much do you? Anyone else I'd tell to go to hell – or at least a mental hospital. I guess that's the same thing. God Damn – kids! Damn it. Know why you're going. Who's with you?"

"Broderick, Munoz, Gray, James, and Garcia. Called them last night. All in."

"Damn you, Deke! Hoped you'd forgotten this phone number. Well, I've got some bad news – The 130s are CONUS use only right now. Got some stuff brewing and they can't leave. What I *can* do is provide the stuff – returned, of course. I mean that! Problem getting boats back to me? It's over my signature. Forget the syringes and ammo, use as you must. I can put this stuff anywhere in CONUS you say. Won't be a 130 hauling, though – that stuff will fit in a lot of planes. You give me cords and time and it'll be there. Don't suppose there's room for me, is there?"

"Bobby, as a Command Sergeant I'm sure you've gone to fat with a gut over your belt. Besides, you're active duty – no way. You'll have enough work if your General gets wind."

"Yah, he probably will anyway. That Marine is one detail – oriented guy. But, he's one of us. I'll be okay. You know, the active duty part would have been enough – didn't have to insult. Probably can still outrun you. Always could – except when the shooting started. Never saw a guy could outrun you at the sound of gunfire."

"Bobby, I'm trying to figure out how you mean that! Thanks for all this. Hopefully we're there in time. I'll work on legs to Belize. When I know a drop location I'll call. Be prepared quickly. Talk soon. Bye."

Stratton turned to the others and briefed them on the situation. Hanson leaned back in his chair thinking. Mitchell had already returned. He said "Why sub-sonic bullets if your 22s are silenced?"

"Navy, the word is suppressed, not silenced. Regular

rounds still make a noise. Sub-sonic just a puff but you've got to be close for them to be effective. We'd be close."

"Okaaay. Yes, there is a strip. Map and cords on the way. Besides bandito country, it's also been cattle grazing country forever. Strips were cleared both for that and it used to be great sport hunting turf – particularly for cats. The one he's thinking of is only two hundred yards from the river – over open sand slope. It's all lowland there and swampy. The higher ground is open to light jungly growth. Not a lot of nourishment in the sandy stuff. Lots of rain. Everywhere else heavy vegetation. He wasn't sure about the length but it's taken some heavier twin engine planes. Doesn't know if the narcos use it. Nobody goes there anymore."

Hanson leaned forward and dialed his cell phone. He said "Hi, Alli. Go into my computer. Pull up my files. Go to one marked PRSA. When you pull it up you need a password to enter. The password is DEEB. Got that? Good. Inside is a phone number. That's all. Call me back when you have it. Okay?"

Stratton said "What's that all about?"

"Might have our legs. And our CONUS strip. We'll see. Haven't used this number in more than twenty years. Hope it's still good."

"To who?" Mitchell asked.

"Can't say."

"Oh."

Shortly, Alli called Hanson and gave him the number. Hanson punched it in then held up a finger across his lips. Everyone nodded. After the fourth ring a voice spoke, saying only "Yes.". Hanson said "May I speak to Ross?"

After a long pause the voice said "Who is speaking, please?"

"Bo Hanson."

The voice quietly said "Stay by your number. We will return your call."

Hanson hung up, looked around and said "Now I wait."

Stratton said "Well, while we're waiting let's see if those maps have come through. Bo, when you finish with whoever you're calling, I think we've got to exercise some of your old CIA connections. We need cooperation from the CIA guys in Punta Gorda, the use of their hangar and equipment. I'm sure they've got good detail maps of the area also. Find out what they've got that can haul us to this remote strip. I know they've got wings. From time to time they insert or pick up DEA guys, SF and SEALS. Anyway, they used to back in the day. Probably only DEA stuff now."

"Man, this is going to have to be Command down. I don't know any of these young field tigers. My guys are heavies now. Maybe I can get a message passed to cooperate with us. Don't know. Some folks get real territorial. I'll work it but why don't you get that Command Sergeant 'Bobby' to make a call to them at P.G.? I'll bet JSOC has worked with them before. Two prongs on their asses might be more effective or twice the chance of one getting through. We're going to need their clearance into that airport. Also, bet these guys will know of this strip, maybe others in the area, or at least can find it. They might even check it out to see if it's usable by their equipment. I also think those guys should be told exactly what is going on and why we're coming. When I finish with the call I'll get on it."

Mitchell said "What's with a password like DEEB?"

"Means Deeeep Black, brother."

"What about PRSA?"

"Play with it, cowboy."

"Jesus Christ! You gotta be kiddin me!"

"Nope. Got the T-shirt too!"

Hanson's phone rang. Once again he put his finger to his lips. Then he answered. "Hanson."

A Texan voice said "My goodness. A voice from the past. Bo, to what do I owe the honor of your call? Using this number I know it must be of great importance. Tell me what I can do for you."

Hanson said "Ross, I have a very serious problem similar in some respects to our last little adventure. I've got a bunch of American dentists, children and businessmen taken hostage for ransom in Guatemala. You and I both know what that means. I've put together a team of ex-special ops guys. JSOC has confined their 130s to CONUS. I can't get us a ride but they will supply our asset needs back-channel. I need a runway with no eyes – maybe in Texas – where the Air Force can deliver our gear. I also need an airplane with long legs to take us to Punta Gorda in Belize. Later, it may have to come get us – don't know about that yet. Upon our return we need that strip again to return all our gear to the SF. I guess that's all, Sir."

"These dentists, what were they doing there – looking at ruins?"

"No, Sir. They go several times a year, and have for years, to work on Maya children in eastern Guatemala. Everyone in the group, including the children, work. The businessmen, and others like them, work and do the funding."

"Sounds to me a *lot* like our little 'adventure', as you call it. Same principles involved. Last time we spoke I told you how thankful I was for what you and the Colonel did for me and mine. Major, did any of it ever see daylight?"

"Don't think so, Ross. They eventually made me a Lt.Colonel so I'd guess that would be a 'no'."

With a weak laugh, 'Ross' said "Well, I also told you if you ever needed anything to call me. Bo, I'm declining quite rapidly. Time is running out for me. You no doubt notice that you are on a speaker. Standing here beside me are two men you should know. They know who you are. My son, Ross junior, runs the show now. Dave Armstrong is corporate counsel. He is Junior's right hand man. They have had their instructions for quite awhile in case this phone ever rang and with which they agree entirely. As far as this mission, they both nodded that they will cover it. Bo, I'm growing weak. I'm going to turn you over to them. Before I go though, I want to thank you again for helping us then and for helping these fine people now. Goodbye, my friend."

Ross, junior, spoke, saying "Colonel Hanson, our chief pilot is Gerald Ford – no relation. He will be in contact with you within one half hour. He will provide you the field information and, after discussing your requirements, will be prepared to transport you and your team wherever it must go. He is totally at your service until the completion of your mission. Is there anything else you require of us?"

"By the way, my name is Bo, not Colonel. No, that is more than generous. I try not to bother your father more than once every twenty-five years, or so, but this *is* such an emergency. I knew his heart would go out to these people just like it did before. Please thank him profoundly for me – and you and Mr. Armstrong as well. I look forward to hearing from Mr. Ford. Goodbye."

"Goodbye ---Bo."

Hanson clicked his phone closed and said "Gentlemen, we have our legs. We may proceed." He explained the gist of the call though he did not divulge the first 'adventure' behind it. Each figured it out for themselves.

Everyone was somewhat stunned that Hanson could get those assets – private assets –just like that. One phone call. To 'Ross'. They sat there looking at Hanson. Finally Hanson threw up his hands saying "What? We needed transportation. There it is. No big thing. That's what old guys are for. Let's get to work."

Stratton's phone rang." Stratton."

"Deke, Bobby. Got some good words for you. You get to Punta Gorda you've got help. Command two – that's me – made a call. The head guy there is CIA. Name's Jackson Kenworth Thompson – yah, that family. Goes by 'Jake', better known as Jake the Snake. Little loose with rules, likes to do what's right, compassionate, fearless, pushes hard – an all around good guy. He's got aircraft. Here's his number. He's been briefed. He's a go."

"Bobby, I love ya. Thanks. This'll work. We've got legs to Belize. I'll call soon with GPS of the field for the gear transfer. We're going to move fast."

"You're covered, Boss. Good hunting."

Stratton clicked off, turned and said "Guys, we've got our hookup in Punta Gorda. Now the planning gets serious. Bo, would you mind going down to West Marine. They rep Zodiac – probably others. We need three hard-bottom inflatable boats, stripped, three twenty-five HP outboards, five gallon tanks, wood paddles, three batteries and one electric air pump, with cable, for inflation. Get about three hundred flex ties – the black ones, not the whites. Get three fifty foot packages of nylon rope – 3/8ths. We need four hundred foot packages of ¼ inch cotton rope. We'll want two electric spotlights with cables to batteries and some handheld spots with batteries. There'll be black duct tape in the kits but get some more -black if you can, gray if you must. You might have to go to OSH for some of this stuff. Can't return the SF boats as far as I can see. Everything else we can pack up and transport to Guatemala City."

"They won't have all three boats here – maybe at the factory – but find them. Used is okay. We'll have to fly them to where we need them in Texas. Your project, Bo. After you talk with that pilot – Gerald Ford. He should be calling soon. I'm going to talk with Jake the Snake. See what they've got."

"On it, Deke."

Mitchell said "In your plans, Deke, keep in mind that I'm going in with you."

"That would be a NO, flyboy. This isn't your world. You would endanger us. Also, simply put, you're too old for this type of work."

"You're in California. We've got an Elder Abuse Law here and I think you've just crossed the line. Besides, have you ever heard of the Golden Rule? You know, the one that goes 'Them with the gold makes the rules'?"

"Yeah, I've heard of that one but it changes nothing. You would seriously endanger us and the mission. I understand your feelings but it cannot be."

"Ah hell, you're probably right. I do seem to have lost half a step. Then, Bo and I will go with you to Belize and continue to La Aurora Airport in Guatemala City. We'll get to the Outrigger Hotel and await your arrival there. We will be the com center."

"That'll work, Mitch."

Mitchell said "I've got to go to another meeting. Talk soon." He left.

Stratton said "I've got to get some guys moving." He quickly rang up each of his four compadres informing them that the mission was a go – two by message. "Get to Monterey now!" he said. "Drive or rental plane, whatever – just get here quick." He had purposely called earlier only men who lived in California. The furthest away lived in Los Angeles. They could assemble within a few hours.

Hanson's phone jumped alive. With a pad and pen in hand he took the call, wandering into the kitchen to hear clearly.

"Colonel Hanson?"

"Gerald Ford, I presume, and yes, but I go by Bo. No longer in the Army."

"Bo it is. Call me Gerry. I am completely at your service, Sir. My directions are to do everything you request. But first, I have a field for our use. It is one of Mr.....I mean, one of Ross' fields. Are you ready to copy cords?"

"Yes. Go."

Hanson copied the GPS coordinates and said "Where is this?"

"South and a little west of San Antonio. Kind of in the middle of nowhere. It'll serve your purposes, if I understand them correctly. Where are we going?"

"You – and only you – are to know this, okay? We'll rendezvous here in Monterey. From here we go to Texas then we are going to Punta Gorda in Belize. We will drop off six men, three Zodiacs and various other materials. Then we will continue to La Aurora Airport in Guatemala City where you will drop off two more people. Then you will return to Punta Gorda where we will need to be picked up later. When, I don't know. This is all subject to change. Your crew must be blind, deaf and dumb."

"How soon?"

"I'm thinking tomorrow but I'll have to let you know. Just be ready. Okay? Can you put a couple of guys at your field to receive materials when they arrive? I'll get you an ETA. Hey. Wait a minute. Just had a thought. You know any source for hard bottom rubberized inflatable boats? Like Zodiacs? Need three about twenty or twenty-five feet long with twenty-five HP outboards and five gallon cans. Need batteries, electric spots and cables. Need an electric air pump and fittings. A patch kit would be nice."

"See what I can do. Probably come through. When Mr. ---- 'Ross' wants something it usually happens. Be talking to you."

"Thanks."

As Hanson returned to the room, Broderick said to Stratton "Boss, they're all enroute. Be a few hours."

"Great" said Stratton as he looked up from the phone and held up a finger. "Right, Jake. That's the situation. There'll be six of us, three boats, outboards, tanks, bunch of other stuff and full kits. There's a strip that a local gave us a heads up on. Here's the rough coordinates – very rough. It sits about two hundred yards off the headwaters of the Chacon-Machaca river."

"Hey, we know that strip. We were in there about a year ago. Took down a small plane load of coke. Yah, we can work that strip. It's rough but workable."

"What kind of equipment you using?"

"You'll probably laugh but we love our old crates. We've got two C119s or what everyone calls 'Flying Boxcars'. They're older than dirt. But, we've maintained them perfectly. These are the upgrade version with twin Wright R-3350-89 Cyclone engines. Each develops 3500 HP. We've got a 1700 mile range so we can cover a lot of area. We don't really use them for intercept – they max out at 215 MPH – but for hauling guys in, stuff out or loiter time, they're great. Low, slow and off radar! Love 'em. One will handle all your needs. We've got a flyover airborne as we speak. I'll radio the cords and we'll just take a quick peek at conditions but we won't draw attention. Let you know if a problem."

"Thanks. That's good." Stratton said.

`"Since Command two briefed me, we've re-adjusted our schedule. We've got a bunch of DEA guys here also. Your clearance into this airport is NCI765. The tower will recognize this and vector you to Savannah Air Services – which be us. When are you coming?"

"If we can put it all together I'm hoping to head out before dawn tomorrow. Getting the boats and stuff together could be a hang-up. Put a Colonel in charge so it'll probably be fucked up."

"Deke, I understand that you're a Colonel also."

"Sorry. Old habit. Fucked up. See what I mean when you make Colonel? Hoping to go in as late as your pilots are willing – say dusk. I'd like to hit the water dark as hell."

"Keep me informed. We'll be ready."

"You got it." Stratton snapped off his phone with a wrist flick and turned to Broderick. "Scotty, take care of getting all the guys here. Pick up the ones coming by air. Do you know the Millionaire Terminal?"

Hanson stuck his head in saying "I'm off to West Marine and OSH. I've got the Texans working on the boats. Bet their purchasing department can move faster than lightning – about the same speed as me. Maybe a little slower. They'll find them anywhere in the country and get them to the field on time. I'll get the rest of the materials."

"Bo, I'd like to head out of here about 0300 tomorrow. Think your guy can pick up the six of us here, go to Texas, load up and head to Belize?"

"That would be the *eight* of us by my count."

"Right, right. Can you put it together?"

"No problem. I'll call Gerry." After he arranged the flight, Hanson called Frank. "Can you have Enrique and his brother at the strip just before dusk tomorrow?"

"Sure. No sweat. Good timing. Weather's been clear but tomorrow night will be overcast and possible rain the middle of the night."

"Frank, we'll have both UHF and VHF in the planes. We'll be in an old Flying Boxcar – twin tail. Don't land unless we're in contact. We'll clear the area first. When you land get the boys out fast and you get the hell out of there. Don't fly down the river. Don't let Enrique and brother know anything. Just take them to the plane and leave. Don't tell anyone."

"Understand. Probably should lay in some extra beer. Have a feeling there might be extra call for it. Maybe some champagne."

"Frank, I and Mitchell will be arriving at La Aurora tomorrow late afternoon – private flight. Could you arrange a van and driver to pick us up? We're coming to the Outrigger. You gather us at Nana Juana's?"

"Jose will be there. See ya then."

The pieces rapidly assembled themselves. Stratton was X-ing his checklist, point after point. Munoz, Gray and James had driven in to Stratton's home. Broderick had picked up Garcia at the Millionaire Terminal. Each had his personal gear and weapons. No airport security would be encountered.

Once together, Stratton and his team became single-focused over the map table. In a monotone, Stratton's voice discussed all facets of the mission, step by step, from beginning to end. No aspect was left untouched. He even discussed the Fer de Lance (the killingest snake in Central America), its night hunting habit and its liking of riverine inhabited areas. They could be territorial. He cautioned about the baby ones who couldn't control their dosage and thus were even more deadly. Tonight, all snakes are bad snakes!

Gray said "Let me see if I've got this straight, Boss. Your plan is that the six of us are going to invade Guatemala, paddle down an unknown jungle river in the dark, guided by two children, enter a jungle village, take on twenty-eight armed men on their turf and rescue nine civilians?"

"Yeah, that's about it. You still in?" Stratton responded.

Gray looked around at his companions then said "Colonels must stay up all night coming up with this stuff. Sounds like a great plan to me – genius actually. Wouldn't miss it for the world."

Hanson said "I'll call Frank and have him pre-position some gas where the Chacon-Machaca enters El Golfete. Probably won't need it but your exit weight will be heavy. I'll tell him lights on a boat – say, two lights. It'll be there if you need it. Say, by 0200, morning following drop off of the guides."

Stratton nodded.

The Texas magnate's staff had found the boats and all associated attachments. They would be at the field waiting with the other equipment. The Air Force had already delivered the promised kits and arms. The SF boats went back to JSOC. All was under guard awaiting their arrival.

The 'plan' was absorbed, refined and smoothed. But – as every combat person knows – even the best of plans goes out the window as soon as the first bullet is fired. The answer? Fire no bullets. Be silent and swift, and deadly if one must.

CHAPTER 7

The Troia home
Monterey, California
1100 hours; Day 3

Grazing had arrived early. An FBI Assistant Special Agent in Charge Mark Harrison of the San Jose office was awaiting him in the driveway. They introduced themselves and went to the door. It was ajar so they entered. The living area and the kitchen were full of people, some in suits and others dressed casually. Some were clear- eyed (the suits) and some red-eyed (the others). Grazing thought to himself "Wonder which are the lawyers and accountants?"

Grazing went to Kelly, whom he knew well, hugged her saying not a word then stepped back and said "Mitch will be along any minute. He'd like to speak to this group and then he has to leave."

"Where's he going?"

"Kelly, you know Mitch and how much he loves those boys and Mark and Jack. He and Bo have some other things going. Enough said?"

Kelly looked at him with a questioning tilt to her head then nodded with a half smile.

As Jonathan was calling the meeting to order Mitchell arrived. He hugged Kelly and whispered "Ride with me." He hugged Christina and then his wife. He strode to the front area where Williams was standing.

He said "Excuse me, I need to speak to you. For those that don't know me, I am Doug Mitchell. To those that do – hi. At the request of Kelly and Christina, I have been asked to provide some assistance. I would like to introduce Special Agent Mark Harrison of the FBI. We called him in late last night. He may call in other FBI specialists in kidnapping. We should pay attention closely to any suggestions he or his associates may make. They have experience in these matters. I should also tell you that the FBI has agents in Guatemala doing a variety of things who may be able to help as things unfold."

"I also asked my good friend, Colonel Ken Grazing, to assist here in coordinating activities. I am told that the ransom demand is twenty million dollars. To raise that, many assets from the various parties will have to be pledged. With many lawyers, accountants, bankers and principals involved, a neutral referee may be needed. He should be the center of information. We are exploring other support activities primarily handling the people upon release. That is all I have. It is up to you folks to satisfy the captors and achieve the release. Ken, why don't you take the floor?"

Williams spoke up "I sort of arranged this meeting and have a flow line laid out."

Mitchell said "That's great, Jonathan. Share it as it goes along, help the Colonel. Don't you think you would be better advocating for your clients not as the leader? Kind of hard to do both, if you catch my drift."

Williams said "I catch it and you're right. Colonel Grazing, here's the outline I wrote up."

Mitchell slipped away. Best not to be there as a distraction, let Ken establish his authority. He last heard Grazing say "Shall we get to it?"

Grazing began "I'm sure everyone here knows each other but Special Agent Harrison and I do not so perhaps we should have introductions. Jonathan, could you do the honors? Please take each family and advisors separately so I can get it straight in my mind."

Williams pointed at each as he said "Myron Smith, husband of Karen Smith, with his attorney Peter Biegel and accountant Maxwell Jones. CEO, Berchel Construction. Martha Wilson, wife of Charles, attorney Mark May and accountant Jerry Andrews, CEO Peninsula Motor Group. Marianne Rust, wife of Peter, accountant Bill Woods, Private Investor. Jane Villareal, wife of James, attorney Alan Winslow, Archibald Abernathy, CFO of Central Bank Holding. James is chairman and CEO of the bank. Winfred Watson, husband of Imelda. Winfred is the CEO of PineTree Financial.

"Thank you. I think at this point I should step aside and just listen. First, as I understand it, the demand has been made for the twenty million but no instructions about delivery or timing have been received. Correct?"

"That's true." Williams declared. "The demand came by e-mail. I made copies. Here."

Special Agent Harrison spoke up, "The instructions will probably come the same way – and fairly soon. They are giving you time to accumulate the money. When they come they won't allow much time for conformance."

"Why?" Abernathy asked.

"This will be an electronic transfer. Twenty million is not going to be put in a paper bag and left in the park or somewhere. It will be electronic and it will race from place to place hoping to avoid our trailing it.

Abernathy said "Our bank can be the accumulating site.

Yesterday, Mr. Williams asked each party to have their people break down their assets that are collateralizable for security on advanced cash for their portion."

"What do you mean by 'their portion'?" Grazing asked.

"Haven't you looked at the demand? It's broken down by individual."

"What?" exclaimed both Grazing and Harrison in unison. They quickly looked at their copies which Williams had handed to each earlier but had gone unread.

There it was:

Jack Troia	$2,000,000
Mark Blaylock	$1,000,000
John	$ 500,000
Travis	$ 500,000
Karen Smith	$4,000,000
Charles Wilson	$3,000,000
James Villareal	$5,000,000
Peter Rust	$3,000,000
Imelda Watson	$1,000,000
	$20,000,000

Grazing studied it. Special Agent Harrison said "I've never heard of something like this. I thought the twenty mil was for the group. Why would anyone do such a thing, I wonder."

Attorney Williams said "Whatever their reason, we have to come up with the money. Max, why don't you start?"

"Maxwell Jones for the Smiths. We've assembled all the readily merchantable assets, real estate, stocks and bonds, valued them at sixty-five percent of appraisal or fair market value. The Smiths can collaterize their share."

"Andrews for the Wilsons. The same process. We can cover."

"Woods for the Rusts. The same."

"Williams for the Troias. Our accountants have confirmed to me the same conclusion."

"Anderson for the Blaylocks. I concur. We can cover."

"Watson for the Watsons. We can cover, barely."

Archibald Abernathy, the Chief Financial Officer for Central Bank Holding, rose and said "Gentlemen, that won't work. The furthest we can go is fifty percent. We can go to seventy on PineTree Financial holdings. That is local, many of our clients hold it and want more. It is an immediate sale, if necessary. The bank's exposure is minimal. Anything else we won't go above fifty."

There was a moan of disbelief from among the accountants and looks of the betrayed on the faces of families.

Jones said "My lowest calculation was fifty-seven percent."

Andrews said "We're around fifty-three."

Woods said "We're around sixty."

Williams said "We need sixty-one."

Anderson said "We're at fifty-eight."

`Watson said "I'm at sixty-four."

Williams said "Mr. Abernathy, this is not right. This is a community emergency. These are high income families, families of wealth and the very fabric of our city. Any day of the week lower income families can borrow at sixty-five percent of value. Why are you saying this?"

Abernathy responded "Mr. Williams, loans are based not only upon value of the collateral but also on the ability to repay. Banks are not pawn shops as you very well know. In Mr. Villarreal's case we are fully prepared to cover through our executive insurance. However, we cannot cover the other portions without being fully protected. We have a fiduciary responsibility to our shareholders mandated by Law. You are absolutely correct – these are high income families. I emphasize income. If these people are not returned there is no income. Thus, we must have a higher margin."

The entire room was dumbstruck at these cold-blooded comments. Christina began to sob uncontrollably. So did Martha and Marianne. Tears appeared in Myron Smith's eyes. Tears flowed on Winfred Watson's cheeks.

Jane Villareal stood, speaking on the way up "Archibald, my grandfather started this bank. My father expanded this bank into what it is today. My husband is Chairman of the Board. Together, we hold the majority of the voting stock along with our children and my sister – a fact you damn well know. Listen carefully to me. As of right now you will say not another word along this line. There are people's lives at stake. There are children at risk. You are a brilliant man. You will use every ounce of that brilliance to accumulate the money within twenty-four hours. Anymore insensitive and heartless comments like you just made and you will find yourself living on food stamps. You still may when my husband hears of this. Am I making myself unmistakably clear, Dear?"

"Yes, M'am, you are. You are authorizing me to take any necessary steps to raise the money. Even if we have a problem with the examiners. You are very clear. And I apologize for my comments."

The room again was dead quiet except for muted sobs. Everyone knew Jane. No one knew she had a backbone of steel like that. She was truly her father's daughter.

To soften the tone in the air, Grazing said "You said that this PineTree Financial thing was local and marketable. I don't know what it is but if anyone here has holdings in it, perhaps they could buy it back at full value. That would certainly change percentages and please the bank examiners that Mr. Abernathy is worried about."

Williams said "I guess you missed it but Winfred, there, is the Chairman and CEO. His wife is one of the hostages."

"Oh. Yes, I didn't connect it. Sorry. But, still, it is a possibility."

Winfred Watson stood, tears still on his cheeks that he was trying to wipe away. He said "I wish it could be so. Each of you families is aboard with us at PineTree. You know we make money by being fully invested and the returns are excellent. They are long-term mortgage backed positions. As such they are not easily convertible to cash. I, myself, need to borrow to fulfill Imelda's ransom. Sorry, Mr. Grazing. Sorry, everyone."

Mr. Abernathy stood and said "If you accountants will get your thoroughly detailed lists of assets to me, my staff will begin all the associated paper work for collateralizing the cash advances. Tomorrow I will need signatures. You can pick up the papers at tomorrow's noon meeting. They can be signed there. If for any reason your client can't be there, you can take the papers to them or bring along a proper Power of Attorney and you can sign. We'll handle the notary part somehow. My orders are to proceed."

Grazing stepped forward saying "That seems to be it for today. Mrs. Villareal, everyone thanks you for your decisive action. Tomorrow at noon, everyone. This was a very productive meeting. We should be prepared when delivery instructions arrive."

Small groups gathered around the room mutually needing human interaction in their misery. Grazing fetched a cup of coffee and returned to the room. He found himself next to Martha Wilson, the wife of Charles Wilson of the motor group, who was standing alone appearing deeply introspective. Not far away, Winfred Watson was commiserating with Kelly and two others. There were fresh tears on his cheeks. He was saying "I don't know why she had to go. I begged her not to. She just had to contribute, she said. She was a dental assistant in her youth. I can't believe this. It's just terrible. I pray that they'll be fine. I can't wait until she's home."

Grazing heard Martha Wilson quietly say under her breath "Bullshit! That's a god damn lie. Asshole."

For a moment Grazing wasn't sure that he had heard correctly. He looked directly at Martha and saw that she was getting red in the face and breathing a little fast. Something had sure fired her off. Grazing took her elbow gently in his hand and said "Should we get some fresh air out on the deck? I could use it about now. I think it might cool me off. Don't you find it stuffy in here with all these people? Please join me."

"Good idea, Colonel."

On the deck, Martha took a deep breath and gazed out at the magnificent view of Monterey Bay. After a short while Grazing commented quietly "Something really upset you in there. Care to talk about it? As an outsider I'm a good listening wall."

Martha shook her head no. Then almost at the same time she said "I just cannot stand that man. My husband thinks he's such a financial Midas, everything he touches turns to gold. Charles plays golf with him fairly often then drags me to dinners with him. He knows I don't like to be around him. His poor wife, Imelda, puts up with him. How, I don't know."

Grazing said "You said something about a lie in there when you got so upset."

"Oh, when he said he begged her not to go. That is such a lie. Imelda didn't want to go. He demanded she go. He ordered her to go for the 'business', he said. We were at dinner with them a few months ago. When Charles talked about going along, Winfred said to her that she should go too. She was adamant about not going. She's afraid of flying, deathly so. He was even more adamant about her going – to the point of a fight about it. It was so embarrassing. To stop the fight from escalating she finally said yes. To stand there with tears on his face and saying he begged her not to go was too much. I lost it. I'm truly sorry, Colonel."

"Not a problem. Everyone's under a lot of pressure and pain. Do you feel a little better now? Talking often relieves the pressure."

"Yes. It was a help. Thank you. Tell me, Colonel, exactly *why* are you here? I know what Mitchell said and it makes some sense but I also feel that there is more to your presence than meets the eye. I'm a big girl. One doesn't spend their life in the auto business without seeing some of the dark side. You are listening so carefully to everything and studying everyone as if you're trying to read their soul. The hostages aren't going to be released, are they? We'll pay and then they'll disappear. Something else is going on. I feel it. Isn't that so, Colonel?"

"Mrs. Wilson, I really can't address that, your feelings, I mean. I am here to help in this time of sorrow and pain. I will do anything in my power to ensure a good outcome to this mess. Does that answer your question adequately? I hope so because it's all I can give you."

"Actually it does. It is so opaque that I take it as confirmation of my feelings. Worry not. I will keep my thoughts to myself and pray for your success. Thank you for whatever it is you folks are doing."

Grazing smiled at her and nodded his head in gratitude.

CHAPTER 8

Mitchell's home
Carmel, California
1400 hours; Day 3

Mitchell and Grazing sat in cushioned chairs on the patio. Mitchell had prepared avocado, bacon and cucumber sandwiches and opened a bottle of Ventana Vineyards Gewurztraminer wine. There was also a pitcher of water. The sun was shining warm and the surrounding roses scented the air. Out here he could have a cigarette if he wished. Not allowed in the house. Even if it were raining Joanne didn't allow it and had absolutely no sympathy for his filthy habit – as she called it. Addicted as a child, he believed he needed it in order to think. An addict's delusion.

Grazing had briefed Mitchell on what had transpired at the meeting. The itemized demand note surprised him. From his recorder Grazing had made summary notes of the things the financial guys had said. Mitchell and Grazing were both taken by the relatively tight ranges of the percentage numbers at the sixty-five percent leverage figure. Probably a coincidence.

Mitchell didn't like coincidences. He gazed off into the distance and sat silent. Grazing was used to Mitchell's semi-trances when he contemplated issues. He said nothing, ate his sandwich and enjoyed his Gewurztztraminer. He was able to think while he ate.

Mitchell finally spoke saying "Not liking this. Don't know how it fits but those indegenas in Guatemala appeared to have pictures of the captives they wanted. Where the hell would Maya tribespeople get pictures of Anglos? All wealthy. Then an itemized ransom demand. In English. Then similar collateral percentages on assets relative to demands. Don't like this at all."

Mitchell briefed Grazing on what was coming down on the rescue effort. Hanson had filled Mitchell in on what had transpired after he had left for the eleven o'clock meeting. Mitchell said "I'm out of here at 0200 tomorrow. We launch at 0300. Kenner, we'll have satellite phones. I'll keep you posted. Anything new of interest here alert me. Here's a phone number. The guy's name is Frank Lombard. He owns the resort where we'll end up. Use my name with him. He's our man on the scene and he's damn good. Flew A-4s before me. Also, my cell works there."

"Yeah. You already told me twice. You're starting to do that old man thing of saying things over and over."

"That's because I am an old man. Got to fit the role. Actually, it's an act so you youngsters won't feel bad. Also to let you know what's ahead of you."

"Sure."

"Kenner, you say they were all invested in this PineTree Financial or whatever it's called?"

"Yes."

"And it's a local thing?"

"Yes. The head of it is named Winfred Watson. His wife, Imelda, is one of the hostages. According to the banker guy the thing is doing very well. Real Estate mortgages and such. Unusual in this day and age."

"Yeah. And it's the only nexus among them all that we see so far. And it's financial. But, it's local and we're a small community. Figures. Another subject. To calm Christina I told Joanne to tell her we'd get her guys back. Probably shouldn't have done that. Keep an eye on her. Don't let her talk about that at these meetings – at least for the next two days. Caution her again about not a word."

"You're right, you shouldn't have. If there is something local, that's a risk."

"Kenner, you know where the computer is. My password is A7NAVY. Use as you will. I've got things to do. Got to pack, some stuff to buy. See ya later."

CHAPTER 9

Del Monte Aviation
Monterey Airport
Monterey, California
0230: Day 4

The Gulfstream 550 had arrived at 0100. Refueling was completed. Gerry Ford had arranged the after-hours fueling service before he left Love Field in Dallas. It cost but what the hell. There was no fuel until Belize or La Aurora in Guatemala City. It had been a little 'iffy' getting in. The notorious bay fog was starting to move in but slowly. They were still above the minimums of 200 feet ceiling and one-half mile visibility and would be for another hour – probably.

At 0245 Ford cranked up his engines. Once stabilized, he ran through his checklist and continued through his take-off list. He wasn't going to mess around before taking the runway – just roll and go.

Hanson and Stratton came up the stairs. A smiling, lovely young lady said "Mr. Bo? I'm Clara. Come this way." as she guided them to the cockpit.

Ford looked up saying "You must be Bo. I'm Gerry. Thought I'd drive you myself. This is Pete." gesturing to his co-pilot.

"Good to meet you." Bo responded. "This is Deke – the head snake eater. He's in charge. I'm here just for quality control and assuring compliance with all rules and regulations."

Ford and Pete laughed. Ford said "Deke, get everyone on board quickly. I'm worried about dropping below minimums. Then I've got a problem with tower. Enough questions already. Let's go."

"We'll be aboard within five minutes."

Deke and Hanson returned to the cabin, Deke continuing to the door. He raised one arm and swirled his hand, index finger up. His men responded immediately. Within four minutes they were aboard, gear stowed and strapped to their seats. As the last one came aboard the young lady raised the stairs, closed and locked the door. The aircraft began to move.

Ford was wasting no time. The taxi out was quick and he didn't pause at the end, accelerating as he turned onto the runway. He went to full power.

Once airborne, Mitchell wandered up to the cockpit. "That takeoff seemed a little familiar. You Navy?"

"Some time back. You, too?"

"Yeah. Further back than you, though. Drove A-4Fs in Vietnam, instructed in A-7s. Name's Doug Mitchell."

"I was sevens then eighteens. I'm Gerry Ford. The youngster is Pete."

Mitchell nodded at Pete who, looking up from the instruments, nodded back.

Ford said "You know, I heard about a guy – think the name was Mitchell – putting an A-4 aboard a carrier with no flight control stick. Only one ever done. Ring any bells?"

"Seems familiar. I forget things anymore but, yah, it might have been me. 1968 it was, I think. Yah, It was me come to think about it. Young and stupid."

"No shit? Wow. That is something else. Pete – you know what were talking about?"

"No."

"He's the guy that flew a jet aboard an aircraft carrier with no flight control stick – only trim motors, rudders and power. Can you believe it? You can't believe how nearly impossible that is."

"Hell, its just naval air. What's the old saying? The difficult we do immediately. The impossible takes a little longer. Pete, if you look at it carefully, actually all naval air is insane. Airplanes mating with ships is not a natural act. Yet, Naval Aviators think it's just another day at the office. No big thing. This is really quite a machine. Never been in one before. Nice to fly, Gerry?"

"Yeah. Real gentleman flyin'."

"What's our ETA?"

"I'm looking at about 0730 local. Everything is positioned for fast loading. We'll be on the ground about thirty minutes or so, max. You guys don't have to lift a hand. We've got it handled. Could be there sooner but I'm dawdling along. Use less fuel even though we've got long range tanks and there's no lights on this field."

"Great. Think I'll get some shut eye. Going to be a long day – and night."

The aircraft droned on towards Texas.

* * * * *

Kelly Air Force Base
San Antonio, Texas
0715 hours: Day 4

"Lieutenant, this is kind of interesting. Yesterday we had that Special Ops flight touch down at that private field about eighty miles, 210 degrees?"

"Yes, but why do you think a Special Ops flight?" she asked.

"Came and returned to Pope. Besides, what's an Air Force plane doing going to a private field?"

"Okay. So – what's interesting now?"

"Got a civilian Gulfstream 550 canceling its flight plan, Center says. Gone VFR (Visual Flight Rules) and its going into that same field."

"Okay – and?"

"Nobody's used that field in the two years I've been here. Now, two planes less than eighteen hours apart – one of them JSOC. Something is going down somewhere."

"Well, they're not our worry as long as they stay clear of us are they?"

"Just curious, M'am."

"Keep an eye on them."

"Yes, M'am."

* * * * *

Remote Field
Southeast of San Antonio, Texas
0740 hours: Day 4

Stratton strode up to the cockpit of the Gulfstream. "Gerry, everything is aboard and secured. The boats, even deflated, were a little tight but we got them in. You don't mind we knocked down that wall by the kitchen, do you?"

"It's called a galley, Colonel. And you're kidding, right?"

"Yeah. Everything's aboard okay. Not even a scratch. Time to go." Stratton said as he left the flight deck.

His team had already extricated the weapons supplied by the Special Operations command and were breaking them down. Each piece of equipment was carefully inspected and placed in its appropriate place. Each weapon was broken down, inspected and re-assembled. Upon arrival in Belize everything would be ready to go.

* * * * *

Kelly Air Force Base
San Antonio, Texas
0745 hours: Day 4

"Lieutenant, that Gulfstream just lifted off that private field. Center shows a flight plan filed to Punta Gorda, Belize. Something is definitely going down down there!"

"Then they're out of here. Not our problem, Sergeant."

"Yes, M'am. Thought I'd let you know. They're headed southeast."

* * * * *

Airborne over Texas
0800 hours: Day 4

From long experience and knowing the need, the entire insertion team was soon fast asleep, Stratton included.

Mitchell and Hanson sat opposite each other, an oak table between them, hot coffee in front of them. They had been watching the speed and efficiency of the inspection and positioning of the equipment. Upon completion the maelstrom of activity simply ceased and the men were asleep – in the blink of an eye.

Mitchell said "Brings back the old days, doesn't it? Remember laying down in any ready room corner, helmet as a pillow and instantly asleep. Fifteen minutes, two hours, whatever. Grabbed what you could. Took the opportunities 'cause you didn't know when there'd be another. These guys still have it."

"Used to sleep in the cockpit sometimes. Gunner'd wake me when it was time to crank up." Hanson recalled. "God, we were young."

"Bo, from here on, what comes down, comes down. We've done all that we could do. It's in their hands and the will of fate. Now I know how the Captain and the Admiral felt when they sent out young men to do the job. Much rather be going myself. Know you feel the same. Damn old age. A willing spirit trapped inside obsolete equipment!"

"I'm with ya. Can't hardly stand it sitting here. The old itch is eating away at me. Haven't felt like this in a very long while. You know, bringing down the Senator and that Congressman a year ago wasn't anything like this. God, I wish I was going in with them."

Mitchell said "Damn me! I did love heading out on a mission."

Hanson responded "Found coming home from one better."

"You got a point. Well, we'll be close by at the hotel. Hope Stratton is able to get information as well as the hostages. If not he's going to have to bring the jefe out with him. I'd sure like to talk with that guy. So much seems bizarre. I know in my gut that this isn't a Maya thing. This sort of thing is beyond these indigenous folks. Waiting is the shits! Think I'll copy them and get some sleep."

"Me, too. We've also got a long day and night ahead."

Sleep they did.

The aircraft droned on toward Belize.

CHAPTER 10

Office of PineTree Financial
Ryan Ranch Business Park
Monterey, California
0915 hours: Day 4

Grazing casually entered the office. He had risen at dawn, old Army habits not dying out, random thoughts congealing somewhat with sleep. Long ago he had learned not to chase the phantom thoughts that tried to rise to consciousness then evaporate when his mind tried to grasp them. Let them be. They would appear in full form when his unconscious mind had worked with them – usually after sleep though sometimes days or weeks were required.

At Mitchell's he had been the only soul stirring. He knew that Mitchell's son, Chase, was doing what teenage boys did best – sleeping. Joanne was at Christine's and Mitch was long gone. After putting on coffee he performed his ablutions. Those finished, the coffee was ready. He did love the coffee at Mitch's house – a special Guatemala blend Mitchell had discovered the year before and was sent regularly by a merchant there. With his mug in hand he wandered out onto the patio enjoying the bite of the chill Monterey morning air. The cold air vaporized any residual sleep fog. The mind responded with alacrity. "How different from waking up to warm humid air" he thought. On the other hand, loosening up old muscles took longer!

Mitchell's advisory that he felt that there was some local connection to the hostage taking had him sensitive to every nuance. Actually, Mitch more than 'felt' the existence of the connection – he was fairly positive about it. For unknown reasons, Grazing had the same 'feeling'. The only nexus that had arisen was the PineTree Financial thread. That 'thread', however, had perfectly reasonable reasons for its existence which could render it a non-thread for their purposes.

He was bothered by Martha's outburst but people are often acting or exaggerating during moments of group trauma, some trying to appear to be more moved by the event than others, to cover a lack of feeling or to hide a sense of relief that it is not them. One often saw those performances at funerals.

A little more bothersome was the comfort zone Watson was in when discussing financials with Abernathy. Any sadness or pain was completely absent from his eyes. But, again, escape to known comfort zones was often a defense mechanism to suppress that very pain. If one doesn't let the mind recognize the pain it doesn't exist. It is a form of denial even if for a short stretch.

He found the soaring financials of more interest. There were collapses all over in the Real Estate sector yet here was an operation flying high. Might be worth exploring. If nothing else it might be worth investing in. That twelve percent return PineTree had been paying for a long time looked awfully good compared to his four percent money market returns – and those looked like they were going to dive. A visit seemed in order. He had time early this morning.

PineTree occupied spaces on the second floor of one of the newer buildings. It had a superb view overlooking the Live Oaks in the small canyon below and the green expanse climbing the hills beyond. The office was empty. He picked up one of the brochures on offer and was reading when a rather plain young lady – though obviously proud of her abundant cleavage that Grazing immediately noticed – charged into the room stopping with a startled look when she saw Grazing.

"Oh, hi, Sir. May I help you?"

"My name is Grazing. Ken Grazing. By any chance is Mr. Watson in?"

"No, but he should be here any minute. Is he expecting you, Mr. Grazing? I don't have you on my calendar. My name is MaryLou. I'm his assistant."

"No, he is not expecting me. Thought I'd just take my chances. I know this is a very trying time for him. I thought I might look into PineTree as an investment after hearing him yesterday. Perhaps someone else could explain the opportunities to me."

"His partner, Richard, will also be in shortly. Would you like coffee? It'll be ready any minute." Looking past him her eyes began to sparkle.

At that moment Watson had come flying through the door. He pulled up short as he spied Grazing. "Colonel, hello. Is there some new development? Please, tell me they are released."

"No. Nothing like that I'm sorry to report. There is no transmission message yet. Abernathy should have the paperwork finished by noon and the money ready soon thereafter baring any unforeseen glitches. Now – we wait."

"Waiting is so god damn hard. I want her – them – back. Yesterday. God, I'm sick over this. It is such hell."

"Yes, it is, Mr. Watson. Actually, I'll excuse myself. I shouldn't bother you at a time like this. How unthoughtful of me. We'll keep you posted. Goodbye."

"Mr. Grazing, I'm okay. Just why did you come by?"

"It was nothing. I became interested in PineTree listening to you and Mr. Abernathy. Thought I'd explore it for investment possibilities but that can wait for happier times. Sorry to have bothered."

"No, no. That's quite alright. Come in. Work is good for me. This way, Colonel. MaryLou, we'll have coffee when ready."

They entered Watson's office, MaryLou following with a coffee tray which she placed on the table. Off to the side of the spacious room were comfortable chairs arranged around the glass-topped table. Watson's desk was near a large window on the opposite side. Watson waved at the chair area saying "Make yourself comfortable. I'll be back in a few minutes. Need to take care of some earlier coffee."

Grazing nodded. He remained standing, gestured towards Watson's 'wall of fame' and said "May I?"

"Of course."

The large wall was covered with diplomas from both Harvard and Wharton, certificates, licenses and pictures. Pictures of Watson with the local Congressman, the Governor, local movers and shakers, actors, musicians, local literati, people beyond count. It seemed to Grazing that if anyone stood still anywhere near Watson their picture was taken. He was sure that the wall was impressive to locals – sort of like the caricature walls of The Rio Grill, a local institution. Probably a status thing to be on Watson's wall.

Watson returned, all smiles. "Well, Mr. Grazing, how can I be of service? Let's sit over here."

"First, call me Ken. That's an impressive wall you have."

"It's fun to put up pictures of friends and partners in our ventures. All participate with us in some fashion. Of course, there's not room for everyone up there. We'd need several more walls!" Watson said with a chuckle.

Grazing said "I might be interested in joining the wall, in any opportunities available but I would need guidance. I'm not a sophisticated investor – just taking the easy way of keeping money in money market accounts. Listening to Mr. Abernathy valuing PineTree as he did certainly raised thoughts in my mind. Perhaps you could tell me what PineTree is all about, how it works, give me any brochures, reports or prospectuses for study that you can or, if there are no openings, send me away."

Watson hit an intercom button saying "MaryLou, be a sweetheart and gather some reports from Richard's office for Mr. Grazing." She shortly appeared with a thick stack of papers, set them on the table and left. "Richard Ortiz is my junior partner, a fine young man. You will meet him, I'm sure. He's an MBA in finance, USC. Spent some time with Bear Stearns."

For the next hour Watson laid out financial summary spread sheets, brochures prospectuses, outlined up-coming projects and essentially threw Grazing into input overload. Grazing thought the performance one of the best sales jobs he had ever seen. Eventually he begged off pleading the overload. With a stack of information in hand he took his leave from a beaming Watson. MaryLou was waiting and escorted him to the door.

For some time Grazing simply sat in his car contemplating all to which he had been exposed. In its totality it was fascinating. The body language and its implications were particularly tantalizing. The constant reference to ten to twelve percent returns – though not absolutely guaranteed – certainly implied a promise. The actual returns of the past supported that promise. The example projections used that range on into the future. In today's world that return seemed dubious. He needed to understand exactly how it was done. Serious study time was in order – for many reasons, MaryLou not the least.

CHAPTER 11

Porta Gorda Airport
Belize, South America
1240 hours local: Day 4

Ross's lead pilot, Gerald Ford, earned his pay. Receiving his clearance to land after giving his CIA assigned call number, he fought the elements through the entire approach. There was no Ground Controlled Approach radar assistance. Given clearance, he was on his own. The driving rain squalls - actually walls of water - complete with raging uplifts and downdrafts turned the approach into a wild, blind roller-coaster ride beyond the imagination of Six Flags Amusement Park. Point of fact, it was more like riding a bull blindfolded! Ford caught glimpses of the runway here and there through the squalls – just enough to keep it coming in. Breaking through the last squall, he had time for one quick lineup adjustment before he touched down. Amazingly, it was a one light- bounce landing. He went to full thrust reversers. The main tires were hydroplaning on the thick layer of water on the runway. The rollout was uneventful. The taxi instructions in English took him directly to the SAS facility. The hangar door was open with several men standing inside beyond rain depth.

Ford stopped the Gulfstream in front of the hangar but kept the engines running. He keyed the cabin intercom announcing "Disembark." He turned to his co-pilot saying "Pete, hold her here. Think I'll go change my underwear. Also hit the head, get a cup of coffee and say goodbye. Be right back."

"That was something else, Gerry. I think I'm glad you were a *Navy* pilot. Bring me a fresh pair of underwear on your way back too. Coffee, too."

By the time he unstrapped and made his way aft, Stratton's crew was well along in their disembarkation. The boats and a few miscellaneous bundles remained.

Stratton said "That was quite a ride. You always try to shake us Army boys up like that?"

"Nah, just old habits. So used to a ship moving around and correcting for it that I forgot runways don't move but I still correct. I'll do better next time." Ford answered.

"That was some kind of weather. Wild ride. Gerry, thanks for the lift – and thank your boss. These hostages needed this. We'll be finished in ten more minutes. Vaya con Dios." Then he was gone.

Ford approached Hanson and Mitchell who were watching the activities. They had long said everything with Stratton that needed saying. Ford stood there for awhile watching also. Then he said "Hope it's a bit better at La Aurora. Anybody need coffee? Clara, I need some if you don't mind. Guys?"

"Sounds good." Mitchell replied.

"Me, too, with a little medicinal brandy." Hanson added.

"Good job, Gerry." Mitchell commented. "Bet you were busy as hell up there. Nice control of the hydroplaning."

"Thanks. That was one of the hairier ones. Wonder when the shakes will start. Hope it's not on takeoff."

They all laughed.

Ford went to the head then was off to the cockpit with his coffee. He returned, got a cup for Pete and disappeared forward again. The stairs came up, Clara secured the door and they taxied out. They took off through the maelstrom, rough but climbing out is a lot easier.

The aircraft droned on toward La Aurora Airport, Guatemala City, Guatemala.

* * * * *

The waiting men rushed to help move the equipment into the hangar. Nothing was said. Several returned to help with the deflated boats and motors. Stratton advanced toward a tall, slender man to whom the other men had looked before moving. "Hi. I'm Deke." he said.

"Kinda figured that. I'm Jake." The CIA agent said. "Scary landing, that. That's one hell of a pilot ---- or a damn lucky one."

"Same thing." Stratton said.

Laughing, Jake said "That could be true. Anyway, welcome to sunny Belize. This stuff will blow out in about an hour. Be high overcast until around ten tonight. We're expecting more rain about then – all over the region, even where you're going."

Stratton replied "That's good for us, the rain. Got everything?"

"Let's close this hangar." Jake yelled. To Stratton he said "Get your guys and let's go to our conference room – sometimes called our locker room. It's this way."

Stratton raised his arm, swirled it and pointed the index finger down at himself. His men joined in trail. Stratton glanced back. His men were fully armed. Foreign country, take no chances.

Jake had chairs arranged, two large high resolution aerial photo assemblies taped to a wall, a black board with a large area map affixed and a plain blackboard centered in front. He waved towards the chairs, moving to the center black-board himself. He turned, saying "Gentlemen, I'd normally introduce but names are unimportant. In fact, to the best of my knowledge, you aren't even here."

"Now, we did a recon of the subject area. These pictures over here are where you'll unload. The X marks where your 119 will offload you. See that water at the edge of the picture? That's the Chacon-Machaca River. All in all, you've got less than one hundred yards to travel. Ground's too soft, sandy, for us to get you any closer. We've looked at this carefully since we were briefed and you told us your plan. This map over here shows where we'll be going. The route bends around a bit. It avoids any possible radar contact and doesn't indicate our destination. We're going to use both 119s. Our guys, all volunteers, are going in in one to clear the area, a narco raid if you will. If our guys come under fire, you guys will land and come at them from a different direction. The narcos will run – simply disappear. If no re-sistance is encountered, we help you to the river, cover your launch and then we depart. You concur?"

Stratton said "Impressive. Yes I concur and I thank you all. One added factor, though. We have to coordinate with a small plane coming from near Lago de Izabel. It will carry two Maya guides for us. The airplane will land, they'll exit and the plane will immediately take off. He has VHF (Very High Frequency) – here's the frequency. I think he should land right behind us. Your call, though."

"Concur – and good plan. Don't know how you accom-plished that, though. Probably shouldn't know. Okay – we together on this?"

Everyone nodded.

Jake looked at his watch and said "We'll mount up in four hours. Your gear has been placed in your plane. The boats have been inflated. Gas cans are full and gas squeezed to the motors. They are stacked upright – one on top of another. Batteries and cables are in place. Lights are lying on the bottoms. There's lots of room in these 119s – you'll see why we like them. There's food and drink over there. Heads are to your left.

Munoz looked at Gray saying "I like these guys!"

Deke took Jake aside asking about distances and flight times. "I've got to give this guy a heads up about what time he's to arrive at the strip. It's been a long while since he's been there and he may need a count for direction finding. He has the ability. He has about a half hour holding time. He'll be coming out of a small field near him – across the Rio Dulce. There – I think. While you take a look at it, I'm calling him to get in position."

Stratton punched in the number. Frank answered immediately. "Frank, this is Mitchell's friend. You need to be at your airplane so you can launch ......" he looked at Jake questionly.

Jake said "He's a little further than us so, say, at 1700 hours. He should be there at 1800 hours."

"Frank, you need to be there at 1800 hours sharp. You using that little field across the river?"

"Yeah. Think I'll lift off at 1700 and putz around a bit. I'll be there at 1800. See ya – well, no I won't. Enrique is the taller one – by half an inch. Take care of these boys."

* * * * *

Frank Lombard had previously, to their complete excitement, housed Enrique and Emilio at the hotel to have them close at hand when needed. Frank had given them run of the place with no particular limits. However, their cultural reticence and the insecurity of youth led them to spend most of their time with the women staffing the kitchen. Two were mother-figures for the boys, clucking over them and encouraging them to eat. The boys gladly obliged, of course only to keep the ladies happy. Of course.

During the waiting time Frank dispatched Jose with the hotel's launch to bring the boy's parents to the hotel. Frank knew that the boys needed mental preparation and used that time to explain to the boys how they were going to fly to the rendezvous location. The idea of flying, of actually going up into the air in an airplane, of being like a bird, both scared and excited at the same time. It was impossible for each to determine which feeling was dominant. They could not believe that this impossible gift was to be theirs. The idea that someone from their puebla could ever do such a thing was beyond fantasy, beyond dream. Perhaps there was a reason it was beyond fantasy and dream. Perhaps man was not supposed to go where birds and spirits lived. Perhaps. What if?

Frank, using soothing words and tone, calmed their fears. He understood their fear of the unknown and the possibly forbidden. He spoke of all his time in the air and how he, too, had been fearful at the beginning, how it was normal for everyone to feel that way.

Emilio asked "What happens if the motor stops? Sometimes the motor on our panga stops and we have to paddle. How do we paddle in the air?"

Frank explained that if the motor stopped the airplane doesn't just drop right out of the sky, that it could glide without the motor a long way. If that happened they would land on a road, a meadow or even on a river. He knew how to do it. It was not a problem about which to concern themselves. They believed him. Sort of.

When it was time to depart the hotel they both had calmed considerably and retreated into their demeanor of quiet restraint. As they crossed the river, however, their eyes regularly connected and huge grins would appear, the underlying excitement breaking through the tension barriers to spread across their faces. Brother talking to brother yet not a word was spoken. They understood where each was. Part of them loved it immensely. Part of them feared it – no matter what Frank said.

Unknown to them, they were embarking on one of those life-turning points, one many men never face. The fear of flying would have to be overcome if they were to continue on the frightening work ahead. Unknown dangerous men would be their companions. Unknown, though somehow familiar, terrain would be faced – at night – in unfamiliar equipment. They would knowingly be invading a stronghold occupied by armed men who had shown themselves to care not for moral conduct. As youths they were about to enter an arena built for men – and face the tiger, be the point of the spear, go deliberately in harm's way. Many men, perhaps most, cannot bring themselves to climb that mountain, turning away before the trek begins. Others silently thank their God they were never offered the opportunity to make that choice.

But those who are offered the choice are never quite the same again. Those who accept are profoundly changed. They have crossed a threshold, a dividing line, which separates them from most of their fellow men. It doesn't matter if they succeed or fail in the outcome of the issue, only survive. The change came when they accepted the challenge, overcame their rational fear and proceeded. That is the turning point, their Rubicon.

Enrique and Emilio were at that point as teenagers. They would be changed forever. There would be no puebla life for them – at least not until they were old. They would become men of the world in some fashion. In the next twenty-four hours what they would experience would render them unable to be satisfied with the bucolic life. Enrique was already partially upon that path. Emilio was fated to follow.

They reached the grass airstrip. Frank positioned the boys in the aircraft then removed the chocks, checked the oil, did his walk-around and mounted. The boys' eyes followed his every move. He cranked up the Continental engine and released the brakes. The aircraft eased forward at the idle RPM. He let the engine warm up as the aircraft crept towards the end of the strip. Upon arriving he stopped the aircraft and conducted his takeoff checks. Satisfied, he said to the boys "Here we go, guys. The fun begins" as he pushed the throttle to full power. The boys' eyes grew large at the noise.

When sufficient speed was reached the aircraft smoothly slid into the air leaving the earth behind. The boys were mesmerized by the sensation of flying and the never-before experienced speed. Once the flaps were up and desired altitude reached, Frank pulled the throttle back and leaned the mixture for cruising.

Both boys were looking down at their home territory happily pointing out to each other known locations. Every aspect was being deposited in long-term memory cells never to be forgotten.

Once again Frank explained exactly what would happen upon landing at the rendezvous strip and what was expected of them. He counseled the two to trust these men completely and to obey any directives given immediately. Then he received the call from Jake. It was time to begin.

CHAPTER 12

Troia Home
Monterey, California
1200 hours local: Day 4

Attorney Williams tapped the water glass in his hand several times with a spoon. The talk died down. He said "Mr. Abernathy and his staff will be twenty minutes delayed. They are finishing up. Not to worry. Everything is in order. We will have a signing session when they arrive in order to release the money. The ransom money itself has been raised." There was some slight clapping. Many heads turned towards Jane Villareal in gratitude, eyes leaking. Mrs. Villareal gave a slight, embarrassed, shrug of her shoulders and her beatific smile.

ASAC Harrison nodded his head sideways at Grazing and moved towards the front door. Grazing drifted toward the door through the various gatherings, nodding and smiling at each. Two stopped him for excited talk from which he extricated himself shortly. Exiting the front door he looked for Harrison and found him off to the side by the hedge. Approaching, he asked "What?"

Harrison said "I've taken some liberties on actions. First, up in Seattle there is an Interpol agent finishing up some business. I know him. This kidnapping is international and I believe the ransom instructions will definitely involve international money movement. This fellow is very plugged in in this area. I've called him and he should be here later this afternoon. He's enroute as we speak. Second, I've been assigned for the duration on this matter. We are bringing our abilities to bear."

Grazing interrupted with "You're out of the San Jose office. I thought the FBI had specialized agents for this sort of thing."

"Colonel, specialized agents don't sit around awaiting an event. There is a lot of other work to do. I was on Temporary Assigned Duty to San Jose to help out. I am, in fact, one of those kidnapping specialists and normally based in D.C. That's why I was sent in response to the notice. I assure you that we're on it."

"When the instructions for transfer come it will be electronic. That amount dictates it. We are prepared for that transfer – both us and our friends at NSA. Upon activation of the transfer it will be monitored by several different entities each with its own approach – not necessarily overlapping. I'll go no further into the methods. We expect there will be repeated rapid transfers through different offshore banks and probably fractioned but ultimately reassembled somewhere. In most cases we can monitor the fractionalization and subsequent movements in real time when we have the starting point – which we do here. However, we're not perfect. Cutout servers in Uzbekistan, Tajikistan and the Ukraine have not been fully penetrated yet. If they use those routes we have to fall back on traffic analysis on outputs and probabilities to let us pick up the trail again. We have algorithms for that work but we lose real time monitoring – they take time. Each receiver has to be entered and the data analyzed for relevance."

"Interpol will be in the loop. But, I will control the information provided to them. Some information may not be shared if it compromises any of our, perhaps, extra-legal methods, shall we say."

"Your clearances are at the highest level. I've told you more than I would a civilian but you know most of this and can guess the rest. Yes, we've already run you. Colonel, bring us in. It's your turn. We're here to help. But I sense that you and this Mitchell guy have some other action in the works. Give. We need to know so we don't stumble over each other. And ----- we may be able to help. You know, we do have out of country assets – and we do work outside channels sometimes."

Grazing listened and contemplated Harrison's comments. The quiet was becoming strained as Harrison awaited a response. Eventually Grazing overcame his DNA-level military distrust of civilian bureaucrat operators. He needed their capabilities. It was that simple – he needed them. Almost. Maybe.

"You say that this Interpol fellow will be here in a few hours. Here and now is not the right place. When he gets here let's meet at Mitchell's home – it's secure and I'll cover it once for both. Sound good? I'll give you the address and your GPS will take you."

"Got the address already. We've also run Mitchell. Seems your friend Hanson is also missing at present. A coincidence, no doubt?"

"Jesus, you're a nosy bunch. Don't mess around do you? Thought you were just listening but you did have to piss a lot. Guess those were phone calls as you heard something."

"Umm, yah. Don't like flying blind. Time is critical in

these matters. Like to know the players and see the whole chess board as soon as I can. We're looking at each of the principles now. Gave you cowboys, you and Hanson, priority. Mitchell popped up. Your names rang a bell. Loud bells, actually. You know, we did clean up that little mess of yours in Carmel six months or so ago. Someday maybe you'll tell me the whole story – off the record, of course. Not for a minute did we believe the D.C. events. Politics. Would sure like to know how it came down."

Grazing said "Why don't we go back in? We've been talking out here long enough. And – ah – the whole story might be above your pay grade. It sure as hell should be above mine. Not my call. I'll be leaving soon. Come to Mitchell's. I'll be there. And bring what you have on the principals, if anything, why don't you?"

"It's a plan."

Grazing returned inside and worked his way through the mini-groups exuding calm, hope and empathy as best he could. He was thankful when Abernathy arrived with his team of seven.

Each staff member was assigned to one family. Mr. Abernathy, the personification of efficiency, said "When your name is called go, with your advisors, with the designated person. That person will have all your documents. Mrs. Lorraine, here, is a notary. She will move from group to group taking care of her business. Stay in your group until she releases you. It will go faster for all that way. This shouldn't take long. When we finish the funds will be released for transfer. Thank you. We got it done."

Everyone clapped softly.

CHAPTER 13

Troia Home
Monterey, California
1400 hours local: Day 4

At two o'clock it came. The bank to which the funds were to be transferred was in Grand Cayman. The transfer was to be accomplished within fourteen hours. There were to be no extensions or excuses. If not done within that time, at exactly fourteen hours hence cutting into pieces would commence. The boys would be first. Pictures and sound would be transmitted by internet in real time. There would be no further communication. Nothing was negotiable.

Archibald Abernathy fluffed the lapels of his suit and said "As I said, the funds are ready when we get all the paperwork finished and reviewed. We should finish here within the hour or so. Once I verify everything is complete we can transfer."

Jane Villareal said "Archibald, everything is complete when we finish the signing. No need to verify. Isn't that right, Dear?"

"Yes, M'am. Of course."

Grazing thought of the time difference. It was now after four o'clock in the afternoon in Guatemala. The guys should be pushing off into the river soon. The drama had begun. He needed to delay the payment. He stood and quietly said "Mr. Abernathy, Mr. Williams, Mrs. Villareal, could I speak with you – out here?" as he pointed at the deck area. No one else paid any attention. They were busy on their papers. Once they were outside, Grazing closed the heavy sliding glass door.

Abernathy said "What's this about, Colonel? We have work to do."

Grazing said "I'm aware of that, Sir. In due time all will be clear. Mrs. Villareal, please sit down here, in this chair. I have something to tell you."

"Colonel, please call me Jane."

"And I am Ken." Grazing continued "Jane, you have given Mr. Abernathy orders to transfer the money as soon as the papers are signed. I ask you to rescind that order. The money must not, absolutely not, transfer until thirteen of the fourteen hours have passed. Will you so direct him? Please. Trust me on this."

"Ken, I will do no such thing. I want my husband back as soon as possible! I want those children back as soon as possible! I want everyone back now! No. I will not rescind. You ask me to trust you. Ken, with all respect, I do not know you, Sir. I have no reason to trust you in this life or death matter."

"In that case, I have some unpleasant things to say and some hopeful things. Jane, you need to be very strong, very strong and very detached from your emotions for awhile. Also, what I'm about to say absolutely cannot leave this deck for the time being. Can you all do that – say nothing?"

They all nodded, dreading what he had to say. His tone and demeanor had them at a high alert level. He was no longer the 'nice guy'. He had re-clothed himself in the aura of an Army bull Colonel in combat mode. The drama of it was severely intimidating. Intentionally so.

"Here are some things you must know and understand. Jane. You folks have plenty of competent advisors here and Mr. Williams is certainly more than competent to organize and run the show – as he has amply demonstrated." Williams nodded his head in acknowledgement.

Grazing continued "Why am I here? I'm certainly not needed for that yet that was what you were told. I am here because there is a whole different part of this of which you are unaware. Well, now, here's some unpleasantness. When Mitch was informed by Christina of the capture it was immediately clear to us – we military types – what it meant. There were nine captives. Taken in a particularly remote area. Held deep in the jungle. With further information we acquired from Guatemala, the conclusion was clear. In order to release the captives they would have to be transported out. There are eyes in the jungle. That would be very risky and complicated for the captors. They could be just released into the jungle but this isn't that type of jungle. It is somewhat open and is tribal. There are groups that would aid all around. Bottom line – there would be no release. There is past history in Guatemala and Mexico of no release after payment – even here in the U.S."

"No, if that ransom is paid, it is a death sentence for the captives. They would have the money and no further use for the hostages. They would no longer be assets – only risky burdens." Jane began to weep.

Grazing said "Jane, bear with me a while longer. There is no good reason to believe they will be released when the ransom is paid – only faith and hope in the veracity of folks who have shown themselves to be reprehensible. Some of us believed that they were kept alive so real time images of abuse could be sent to encourage payment. The transfer instructions confirmed that position. The payment would be a death sentence for them all. We must delay as long as possible."

Attorney Williams cleared his throat and said "In that scenario, then what difference would it make when we sent the payment?"

Grazing looked off into the distance at the bay, hummed, hawed then looked back at them and said "You notice that Mitchell is not here. Along with another friend, he is in Guatemala with a team of ex-Special Forces guys. As we speak, they are in the process of effecting a rescue of the captives. It will go down tonight. They are in transit. It is critical that not one word of this gets out. No discussion away from this deck. We know exactly where they are. And I know that now only you three know this."

The three looked at Grazing dumbfounded. Finally Williams found his voice "When did this start?"

"Within one minute of Christina's call informing Mitchell."

Williams said "What difference would a leak make? They're in Guatemala."

Grazing answered "Funny how fast and far a story can travel in this day and age. When this is over successfully – and it will be successful, I believe – nothing of the details will be released. People are risking their lives, their careers, and their general well-being to assist in this rescue. Nobody will know the full story. Government cannot and will not do the necessary things in any crisis. They will talk but take no action until it is too late. That is reality. Individuals operating without rules can make things happen. Individuals who accept responsibility. That, too, is reality. Force is the only thing evil fears. There are many good men within the government who understand and are assisting – outside the rules. They feel for the children and the spouses."

"Jane, knowing this, can you rescind your directive to Mr. Abernathy – and trust me?"

Abernathy interjected "I don't think that's such a good idea, Jane."

"Archibald, you do as the Colonel orders. Thank you, Ken. I don't know if that's adequate but, *Thank You!*"

"Mr. Abernathy, that transfer will be in the middle of the night if it occurs. Have several people there with you. Even though they said no more communications they could change that at any time. Don't want someone falling asleep and miss the transfer or a message. Probably the FBI will have someone there. If a transfer is going to be made I want you to give me a ten minute warning before hand if I'm not there. That's me, personally, on my cell phone. God willing, we'll have them out before the transfer. When I get the word I'll call your cell – make sure it's charged and don't use it. Okay?"

"If anyone asks if the transfer has been made – and they will – say 'soon'. Perhaps you should absent yourself. That would avoid questions but perhaps worry people more. From now on not a word of this. Okay?"

They all nodded.

"Good. Let's go back in. Jane, I believe you have some small signings to do. Now, all we have to do is wait. Jane, these guys are really good – the very best. They'll do whatever it takes."

On the way back in, Grazing leaned close to her ear and asked "How long has Abernathy been with your bank?"

"I believe slightly over four years. Why?"

"No reason. He seems to be somewhat of a contrarian."

She laughed and said "That's the basic nature of a good banker."

Waiting and not knowing is absolute hell. But, wait they must. And wait they did.

Grazing, with his twenty six years of military service was well conversant with the waiting game. The only way to beat the game was to occupy the mind, a diversion. He decided to study PineTree Financial. Boring, but what the hell. It was something to do.

CHAPTER 14

Savannah Air Services
Punta Gorda, Belize
1645 hours local: Day 4

The two C119s started cranking their engines at the same time. While the pilots were conducting their checklist exercises, a group of ten helmeted men trotted to one of the Boxcars. They were clad in flak vests and camo gear. Each carried some version of the AR-16 – some regular barreled and a couple short barreled. Various other devices hung from their vests. They were the volunteer mix of resident CIA and DEA agents providing insertion firepower if bad guys were present.

Stratton's group, standing aft of their 119, watched them board. Gray said "You know, I really do like these guys!"

"Okay, men, let's mount up. Party's about to begin. Everyone cool?" Stratton yelled.

The first Boxcar was taxiing out. Stratton checked his men aboard entering last. While his men positioned themselves Stratton went to the cockpit. "How's she lookin', Jake?" he asked. As he did so, the left engine began to sputter and cough. Stratton looked that way in alarm. "What's that?" he asked.

"Oh, she's just got a little colic." Jake responded. "They'll do that sometimes. Not a problem. Probably blowing through a little condensation. It'll go away when she warms up and I add a little power."

"Oh – ohhhkay. Well, we're aboard." Stratton said.

"Roger. Let's rock and roll." Jake said as he released the brakes.

Each man was lost in his own thoughts. There was no conversation. There was no need. Even if conversation had been desired the outrageous noise in the belly of the Boxcar would have made it nearly impossible. It was a time to mentally prepare for the challenging task ahead

CHAPTER 15

Troia Home
Monterey, California
1525 hours local: Day 4

The last of the banking staff was packing up to leave. Their work was complete. The Notary had completed her last entry and returned the driver's licenses. Archibald Abernathy was hurrying them along. Most of his staff had already departed for the bank. Winfred Watson approached saying "Archibald, thank goodness that's finished. I'm so anxious over Imelda. Now we can transfer and get her home. You'll transfer as soon as you get back to the bank. Probably in the next hour?"

"Winfred, it won't happen that fast. Now that we're collateralized I have to get the electronic funds transferred from the Federal Reserve to us. You, of all people, should know that banks don't sit around with millions stacked in their vaults. We've got hoops to jump through for them. I can't say exactly when we'll have it for transfer. We've got time. We were given fourteen hours, that's four o'clock tomorrow morning, to accomplish the transfer. It'll happen."

"Archibald, we've done a lot of business together. There's more to come. I'm good for the bank – you make a lot of money from my ventures. Now I want something. I want my wife back. I want her back now. Every minute delay on her return is a minute too long. I'm sure the others feel the same way. We don't want to hear about Federal Reserve or any other bullshit. We want the transfer made and our people released. Now. You said the funds would be available when we finished signing. We've signed. Transfer the funds."

There was a murmur of concurring voices among the principals remaining. Jane Villareal smiled benignly at Abernathy allowing him to dance alone among the swinging blades being unsheathed. His earlier hard banker comments had not endeared him to the group and they were not inclined to timidly accept his statements as fact.

Abernathy defensively said "I'll get it cleared as fast as possible. Then the FBI has to authorize the transfer. They've put a hold on it for now." Jane Villareal's eyebrows shot up thinking "Where did he come up with that one? That'll throw gasoline on the fire. Thank goodness that agent isn't here now."

The room groaned. Watson was irate. "Where the hell is that FBI agent? They've got no damn business interfering, they've no jurisdiction. This is a private matter, no government funds are involved. Who the hell do they think they are? I'm calling the San Jose office. I want that SOB on the phone as fast as they can reach him."

CHAPTER 16

The Mitchell Home
Carmel, California
1615 hours local: Day 4

It wasn't long after his arrival at Mitchell's home that he opened the door for ASAC Harrison and his companion. Grazing rapidly took in the tall Interpol agent noting his wrinkle-free Savile Row fine chalk-lined, dark blue suit, the immaculately tucked pocket silk, the faintly pink silk shirt and rather flamboyant cravat. "Oh, Christ, a dandy." thought Grazing.

Harrison made the introduction "Colonel Ken Grazing, Inspector Michael Loddington." The courtesies were exchanged.

Upon hearing Loddington's accent, Grazing asked "Brit?"

Loddington said "Yes. American?"

Grazing laughed and said "Yes – a point for you. Never had that done before. Dover?"

The shock on Loddington's face was striking. His jaw

dropped down while his eyelids rose up. After a pause to recover his composure, the Inspector said "As a matter of fact, I am from there though I've been gone a long while. What in this bloody world would elicit such a question? I simply don't believe this! No one knows that – outside the service of course. What is going on here?"

"Easy, Inspector. There is no breach of your security. You have an uncommon name. I happened to have spent a night in Dover some time ago. I stayed at the Premier Inn on the waterfront. I went for an evening walk along the beach walkway and I noticed a small hotel opposite, along the base of the cliff, called Loddington House Hotel. It had been there a long time. Only place I'd ever seen the name Loddington, admired it. Thought it must be the name of a long-standing local family. That's all."

"I'll be damned. Yes, that's my roots. I'll be double damned! This world is entirely too small." With that he laughed heartily. "Hate to tell you what I was thinking – or wondering."

"Me, too." said Harrison.

Grazing offered drinks which were accepted. Once prepared and handed out they exited to the patio. Grazing proceeded to narrate the schematic as it then existed to the extent of his knowledge and what they had in mind. Not yet having spoken with Mitchell about the day's progress much was not disclosed. Grazing deliberately left out his recent phone call to Tom Hellman. He also failed to mention any names of the participants in the rescue attempt nor did he bring up any participation by active duty military or use of military assets. He gave the impression that all support was private except he did ask for any on-scene FBI assistance if it became necessary.

Of course, the two agents registered the vagueness in the story. As officers of the law and the courts they also recognized the need for the vagueness. They were very interested in the timing. Grazing put the desired departure date two days out but emphasized *desired*. Inside he was hoping that he'd provided enough time for a fate accompli. He emphasized that loose lips sink ships and that there was no need for any information on such a possible action to reach their respective agencies. Their function should be limited to the ransom and its trail.

He pointed out that the actual transfer of the funds should be delayed as long as possible without further endangering the hostages. Time needed to be provided to the rescuers if indeed there was any rescue attempt. The reality of the attempt was itself in question at the moment. It simply might not be possible. At the present it was only being explored. He did inform them of his conversation earlier with Mrs. Villareal, Abernathy and Williams to delay.

"Yeah, I know about that. After you left, it came up. Abernathy laid the hold on the FBI. Luckily, I'd had most of this figured out and realized what happened. I did a nice song and dance about setting up tracking equipment. Calmed that Watson guy down. Told him we'd lift the hold when the equipment was ready and the funds were actually in the bank's account. Told him a few hours at the most. Also told him we'd be there at the bank with Abernathy to release when able."

Grazing thanked him and threw out as many caveats as he could as he finished up.

Loddington and Harrison nodded their heads in understanding. Really understanding. They knew it was on. They knew it was probably coming down tonight. They knew military assets were in play covertly – after all these were plugged in officers. People's asses were on the line. These agents were not short-ball hitters. They knew Grazing had given them everything he could, enough so that they would not be surprised or blindsided by any future events. Yes – they nodded in understanding. They also knew that there was no overlap, nothing on the one side that would subvert or compromise their efforts. These were two separate campaigns – the money trail and the hostage trail. In fact, they perceived that it was in their best interests to not know about the hostage rescue. Armed invasion of a foreign sovereignty, advance knowledge of, was not where they wanted to go. Ignorance was, in this area, bliss – and job security. They were thankful that Grazing was recognizing their limits and not exposing them to possible sanctions while at the same time keeping them in the loop. It was skillfully done.

When Grazing finished silence descended while the information was digested, the permutations calculated, the self-interest evaluated and the appropriate roles concluded.

Harrison said "Thank you, Ken, for your candor. I clearly see our position in this drama. Our end is covered. Between Interpol and us, we should be able to track. It is interesting that you and Mitchell are so sure that there is a Monterey basis in this. If subsequent information so indicates, it is a domestic situation and we – the FBI – take full operational control. At that point you civilians would have to cease and not interfere."

"Oh, if that were the case, far be it for us to interfere with the FBI. Goodness me, no." Grazing responded.

"And any and all information in your possession would be turned over to us – no matter how acquired." Harrison growled.

"Oh, that would go without saying. Of course we would do that. Absolutely for sure."

Loddington looked at Harrison saying "Why do I feel that he's jerking you around?"

"Because he is!" said Harrison. "Ken, any domestic stuff, I'm serious. You guys went around us on that Senator and Congressman. We don't want that here."

"Actually, we didn't. When we had it nailed down, every law enforcement in sight, Congress and the media were given everything we had. Nothing was hidden."

"That's true, I guess. But your methods were a bit off the chessboard. We couldn't prosecute."

"Ultimately it didn't matter." Grazing answered.

"You guys do that too?" Harrison said.

Grazing said "No! We did not terminate them. Period."

Loddington said "What's this all about?"

Harrison said "Tell you about these cowboys over dinner. So, Ken, we've got a working agreement?"

"D'accord. We're in agreement."

After Harrison and Loddington departed, Grazing opened a bottle of Scheid Vineyards Chardonnay liberated from Mitchell's cellar, leaned back and replayed in his head the day's words, facial expressions, body languages and everything else he could pull up from his memory banks.

He played through his call to Tom Hellman, his longstanding friend from his years at Pamplona drinking and running the bulls. Tom had had a career at Treasury, first as a bank examiner then as a tracker of funds for Treasury in the war against drugs and terrorism. Upon his retirement from Treasury as the finest tracker they had, he was immediately contracted by Treasury to continue that work as an independent contractor at four times the pay. There wasn't a bank account on the planet that, given enough time, he couldn't find and penetrate. He was the best there was at what he did. And he was on it – with all the technology of the U.S. government at his fingertips *and his personal string of hackers* – each of whom owed him in some way or another.

"Yes, it had been a good day." Grazing thought. "A very good day indeed, considering."

CHAPTER 17

Headwaters; Rio Chacon-Machaca
Guatemala
1745 hours local: Day 4

At treetop level the ride had been bouncy. Every different color, no matter how slight, had created a different thermal – an updraft. The high lift wing of the Boxcar had found every one – it didn't miss a single burble.

The first Boxcar had the strip in sight. It circled the area one time then rolled down and in. The wings rolled level just before the wheels touched down. The side door was open, eyes scanning the adjacent scrub. The aircraft turned and high speed taxied to its assigned location. Upon stopping, the aft ramp swung down, men pouring out before it touched the ground. The men immediately scattered to a tactical skirmish formation. The pilot remained as he was – at the controls with engines running.

The scrub and jungle were silent.

The skirmish line proceeded outward. There were no encounters. There were no signs of footprints. Nothing. Nothing human, that is.

About ten minutes in, the pilot radioed Jake "The signal's clear. The guys are finding no human signs."

"Roger. We're coming in." Jake said. Then he changed radios saying "Frank, I have you in sight. You a tally on me?"

"That's affirm."

"We're cleared in. Join up and come in right behind me."

"Go for it. I'll cut the corner. Be right behind." Frank responded.

Jake said "Two of our guys will meet you. Warn the boys to not be afraid of the armed men – we're the good guys."

"They're already briefed. I've instructed them to talk with Deke."

"Okay, here we go."

With that, Jake did the same roll-in maneuver as the other Boxcar. No smooth, gliding approach that any gunner would love. Bend it around, level wings and plant it – that was the way to go. Frank followed suit but from the opposite side, touching down about one hundred yards behind Jake to avoid any vortex turbulence from Jake's wings. Taxiing a little faster, Frank pulled up to the Boxcar as it stopped. Two men appeared as if squirrels popping up from the ground. Enrique and Emilio were snatched up as quickly as each foot touched the step. The door was slammed shut and Frank taxied off gaining speed as he turned.

Stratton's team hit the ground the instant the ramp touched down. Kits were deposited on the ground. The inflatable boats were lifted then trotted towards the riverbank where they were deposited adjacent to the water. The men returned for their kits and miscellaneous gear. Everything was placed aboard the boats in its proper place. Fifty foot lengths of rope were laid out to tie the boats together, nose to tail, with about twenty feet of slack between each. The slack could be taken up or lengthened as desired on the river. Jungle black is nearly absolute black. The boats must not become separated.

The outboards had been locked in their upright position and so remained. Once in the water they would be lowered, fuel squeezed, motor started then shut off and returned to their up position. Their wood paddles had been wrapped with black tape to deaden any knocks and to kill any possible reflection of moonlight. For the exit run light would be needed. Cable was strung but not hooked up to the batteries. All was prepared. The CIA/DEA men maintained their perimeter guard.

Meanwhile Stratton, Jimmy Munoz and Javier Garcia were speaking with Enrique and Emilio. They were making acquaintance and working at getting their language straight. The general hand signals were easy. There was no attempt to teach the guides the hand signals used among Stratton's men.

Munoz explained to Enrique that he, Munoz, and Stratton would be in the lead boat, Gray and James in the second and Emilio, Broderick and Garcia in the last.

Deeper dusk was rapidly approaching. Jake gunned his engines twice. Ten men slithered from the scrub. They had been pulling back for some ten minutes. Five went to each aircraft, ramps were pulled up and the aircraft departed. With their departure the jungle came alive with night sounds. The men sat, leaning against the boats, looking out, weapons at the ready. They quietly waited, the deet fending off the mosquitoes and in their stillness they were slowly absorbed by the deepening dark.

CHAPTER 18

Rio Chacon-Machaca
Guatemala
1900 hours local: Day 4

Stratton stood. With his movement the others rose. Without a word the six men moved one boat into the black water, then the next, then the next. Munoz' hand guided Enrique to his boat, Garcia the same with Emilio. The men boarded, one to a side, paddles in hand. Munoz placed Enrique in the prow, putting himself to the left. There he could see Enrique's movements as well as paddle as necessary. Night goggles were dropped into position and a green world appeared. The old ones presented a hazy, blurry, ghostly green image. The new ones were far superior, presenting crisp, more natural images.

Frank James, in the middle boat, and Scott Broderick, in the third, were in IR mode. They were the lookout for any heat emitting entities. Of course, their primary interest was in anything vertical and slender resembling mankind.

The Chacon-Machaca moves at a sluggish pace through

lowland swamp country. Here and there it picks up the pace but overall it wanders at a leisurely one mile per hour rate. They needed to cover three miles per hour – a little slower than an average human's walk. Therefore, two miles per hour had to come from muscle work. Fortunately, they were paddling with the current and the lightly loaded boats seemed to glide as if on ice. Stratton had wanted to hit at one in the morning but two or three would be fine.

The river was shallow – perhaps eighteen inches to thirty inches deep. The bottom was sand and mud as they saw before dark. Enrique confirmed – that was its nature throughout its run. The new goggles were giving them excellent vision. Enrique, however, seemed to be able to see without goggles as well as they could with them.

Fifteen miles to go. Twelve miles to go.

"Contact. Eleven o'clock. Three hundred yards." Broderick whispered into his tactical com mike. "Looks like a bonfire, maybe twenty, thirty yards back from the river."

James whispered back "Got it."

Stratton said "Jimmy, have Enrique keep us right. Hunker down, safeties off, paddles feathered; we'll go with the flow."

"Two hundred yards."

"One hundred yards."

"Four armed movers, near the river."

Eight prayers wafted their way to the god of weather asking for the solid overcast to continue. Mouths open breathing shallow only enough to sustain life, each was willing invisibility. The night obliged, creating the non-contrast of black on black not detectable by the human eye.

The river slowed. They knew it slowed. It must have slowed. It took half a lifetime to drift ten feet. Or so it seemed.

The four men were clearly visible to Stratton's team,

whether on ambient goggles or IR. Two approached the edge of the water looking and scanning the expanse. *"What the hell had caught their attention?"* thought Stratton.

After a few minutes of observing he then laughed to himself with relief as he saw hands lowering zippers. They were peeing into the river! They weren't scanning or searching! They weren't on alert. The other two had split and squatted down. That was a latrine area for whatever group they were!

The river continued carrying them lethargically past the encampment. The two men standing fiddled at their trouser fronts, turned and sauntered back up the trail toward the fire. Of the other two, first one then the other rose, tugged trousers into place and retreated along the same path.

Eventually Broderick whispered "Clear" when no more heat signature registered on his IR goggles.

Stratton said "Center of flow. Paddles."

Ten miles to go.

The welcomed rest from paddling had rejuvenated those muscles. Now oxygenated and fresh they were ready again for the long remaining distance. As the blades bit strenuously into the black water to accelerate, the overcast cover split allowing a shaft of moonlight to shine through. It lit them and the river up like a spotlight. The jungle didn't seem to care.

"Thank you for the delay, God." James whispered into his mike. God answered. As quickly as it had opened, the split closed plunging them once again into absolute black.

Stratton said "Gents, I think God just winked at us."

The night ebbed on. Light drizzle changed to rain. Dark and rain – friends to attackers, enemies of defenders. The men paddled then rested, then paddled some more. There was a rhythmic pattern that each fitted into with the ease of long experience and conditioning. Every so often Enrique would point a direction. The boats adjusted immediately. There were branches into other channels, probably false. The slow movement of the river didn't allow distinguishing between the channel and false pockets by watching the flow. Somehow Enrique could tell. The hours passed.

The boats slid gracefully silent across the black water, its surface appearing oily in the slivers of moonlight seeping through gaps in the overcast. The paddles dipped in and out in a rhythm born of training and practice though not as natural as that of a native born to a lifetime of paddling a panga. Enrique could feel the slight difference even as he appreciated the learned skill of his companions, learned as adults, not learned while in their mothers' wombs.

He marveled at these men he was guiding, at their courage, at their skills, at their modern equipment. Yet, as good as they were, they were strangers to *this* jungle, *his* jungle. Though still a teenager, Enrique was already a full adult in this world. The men *looked* at the river. Enrique *sensed* the river. He could *feel* the minute differences in the slow-moving flow rate, stronger towards the main channel, weaker towards misdirections. He could feel the incoming flow from feeder waters and the faint whorls of the flows blending into one. His hand signals were following those faint signals sensed by his bones and ligaments. He had never been in these upper reaches of the Chacon-Machaca but it made no difference. It was unimportant. Recognition of past familiarity had nothing to do with his guidance. That would come later. He was sensing the heart and soul of the living river, its very essence, its fundamental nature, its search for the sea in its obedience to a basic law – gravity. And at the centerline of that main route the current would be infinitesimally greater even in this flat land river. During the times when no wisps of moonlight broke through he made no effort to see at all. His eyes were often closed; he focused only upon feeling the flow.

He had been shown the night goggles during the wait for dark. He had been first frightened then amazed when he looked through them bringing chuckles from the men. The goggles were incredible for seeing at night. But, he himself did not need goggles to give him warning of threats – except maybe from scorpions and the Fer-de-Lance. Human threats, even Jaguar threats, were evident to him through his ears. The jungle noises were different, or absent, in the presence of any such threat. Even their passage on the river affected the sounds of the jungle. Silent as they were they were not silent enough. The jungle heard their presence. The jungle sensed their presence. The jungle reacted – marginally, perhaps, but react it did. Enrique, child of the jungle, could hear it. He knew all was well as they progressed. His concern was the arrival. He knew it was possible that a sentry, with patience and time, could embed himself in the fabric of the jungle so no noise change gave warning. He hoped that the IR goggles would solve that problem should it occur.

Emilio, younger still, was also in complete harmony with his environs, as many teens are. While not participating in the guidance, from his third boat position he was monitoring his brother's performance. If anything, he was more sensitive to the character of the waters even though they were slightly disturbed by the preceding two boats. Several times he had almost tapped Broderick on the shoulder to correct his brother's direction only to observe his brother properly adjusting. Each time he smiled to himself, both proud of his brother and pleased that he himself had picked up the error first. Even in such serious circumstances the younger sibling striving to rise above the older reigned. Some things are eternal and succumb to no circumstance. The deference and respect the men paid his brother swelled Emilio's chest with pride. The respect of such men was no small thing!

Javier Garcia mused upon the upcoming action. It felt

good to be back in the game. The addictive taste of adrenalin was welcome as he felt it course throughout his blood stream, reaching every fiber of his being. Rosa would never understand what he had given up for her. Damn, he missed the life! Work at Blackstone Security was okay but it wasn't the real thing. At least it wasn't a nine-to-five completely boring civilian job but at times it was damn near. Civilian life would have killed him – withering away from the nothingness. Probably would lose Rosa along the way down. Employing many men like Javier, this time off was understood by Blackstone. It definitely wasn't by Rosa. She was *mad* – until he told her about the children. Okay, he shaved some years off the ages but – what is it they say? 'All's fair in love and war?' This was both, wasn't it?

Damn, he felt for the hostages. Could anyone believe it? Not only men but women and boys. How god damn perverted can they be? He hoped to hell that someone got cute, had a major attack of the stupids. Not totally in agreement with the Colonel's approach. These kinds of folks should be eliminated. Left alive, they'd do it again. Anyway, it sure felt good to be back in action.

Frank James was totally focused on the mission playing 'what ifs' in his mind. Ever the preparation man, he ran through all possible scenarios that he could think of and mentally rehearsed his responsive actions. In his experience, when a scenario became a reality instantaneous previously-thought-through response was a life-saver, the difference between success and failure. He believed that the fact that he was here today was proof positive of that premise. He could recount several instances where it was true. Tonight could possibly be one of those.

James was there neither for the adrenalin nor for the adventure. He had no compulsive need for the action though there were those who may think otherwise. His wife had her suspicions. In truth, he did have a compulsion – it was a need to protect. His combination of that need with exquisite combat skills had made him a highly desired team member among his peers. Highly. Those features had led to Stratton's call. There was no way he could deny aiding those hostages; no way could he refuse to bring his skills to the effort. His renowned practice of contingency planning and his cold efficiency when engagement occurred was needed. He took ten days vacation leave from his accounting firm and, with his wife's blessings, here he was. He prayed for success.

Bob Gray was a blank. Deliberately so. Going into action he cleared his mind of all thought, mission or otherwise. He was all senses, infinitely aware of his surroundings. He was a firm believer that plans were plans and action was action. Plans were good for general objective before the fact but when action started plans were history and a fairy tale at that. To him, all action was re-action. Once the fray began the event was never as that planned. The dance steps were created on the spot, procedures invented on the go. Believing that, he did not wish to clutter his mind with thought that might interfere with his sensing – the precursor to re-action. Of course, his training had been so completely absorbed that his re-action to any stimulus was exactly what his teammates would expect. He was a complete team player – exactly as he taught his high school students they should be.

Jimmy Munoz had Enrique on his mind. He was the first responder to Enrique's gestures, Stratton taking his cues from him. Munoz, often called 'The Wizard' by his teammates past and present, was gifted with empathy, language affinity and a near-mystical rapport with the computer world. Many times he was responding to Enrique's directions nano-seconds before Enrique actually made the gesture, feeling the body change preparing to give the directive. Others found it uncanny – almost like the Radar character in the old MASH series on television. In fact, he thought it was quite simple – his brain did not put up protective or self-centered barriers. It took in what was available and worked at connecting the dots uninhibited. Language assimilation and computer comprehension followed as naturally as night follows day.

Munoz hoped that tonight went safely. He was concerned for Enrique and Emilio, what brave young men they were! He would make sure that Enrique was not exposed to danger as much as possible. Unfortunately, he did need Enrique with him when confronting the jefe but he'd keep him behind the jefe and out of the way in case the situation deteriorated. Garcia would have Emilio positioned down during the take-down of the banditos. No problem there. At one point, before re-focusing, he chuckled to himself thinking what a world, two days ago solving a computer system problem for a client and tonight paddling down a jungle river to engage some bad guys! Amazing!

Stratton checked his watch. If he had figured anywhere near correctly, and the twisting river was anything near the measured distance, and the progress rate was somewhat accurate, they should be getting close to the place. *"Lots of variables"* thought Stratton. *"Hope not too many."*

Enrique, kneeling in the bow, was looking hard into the black, his head canted somewhat. Stratton tapped Enrique's leg. Without looking back Enrique held up his hand, palm toward Stratton, all five fingers splayed. Stratton whispered in his mike "Coming up."

Enrique started pushing his hand, palm down, up and down – the taught signal to slow. The paddling ceased. The oars held flat in the water then streamlined awaiting the next directive. Enrique then tipped his palm forward and gave a little 'come along' movement. Paddles bit the water gently. Suddenly, Enrique's left arm came up and pointed directly across the river. He made jabbing motions with his index finger. The boats turned hard left, outboard paddles taking full bites of the water. Stratton strained his eyes looking for what Enrique had seen. Nothing. Just a dense wall of jungle – trees with branches bowed to the water, vines hanging down as if to drink, dense brown Mangrove roots forming a nearly solid barrier. "What the hell?" he thought.

As they neared the vegetation wall, Enrique continued giving small corrective hand signals. The bow of the lead boat pushed into two vines reaching down for the water. They were no different than a million other vines along the river. Enrique, with both hands splitting the two vines, pushed one to each side of the boat. Stratton couldn't believe it. They were in a vegetation tunnel! Enrique put one finger to his lips and sat down. He pointed directly ahead and nodded. There was a satisfied smile on his lips.

CHAPTER 19

Las Arenas Puebla
Rio Chacon-Machaca, Guatemala
0100 hours local: Day 5

Stratton was momentarily stunned by what Enrique had done. *"Put it aside."* He thought to himself. *"Time to work."* The boats moved stealthily up the channel. Broderick and James focused ahead with their IR mode seeking the warm body of any sentry. Munoz and Garcia pushed their young charges low down in their boats, arms at the ready. Enrique, however, was head up looking over the prow. There was a branching and Enrique pointed right. At the next he pointed left. Then came a slow down signal followed by a sweeping swing of the arm ending with a finger pointing to the left.

Ahead, Stratton saw a large sand bank devoid of vegetation. There were several pangas and one launch beached on the sandbank. Enrique was pointing at it, jabbing his index finger hard towards it. *"This is Las Arenas (The Sands)"* thought Stratton. Boat two beached first. James and Gray were instantly ashore and deployed forward. All was quiet.

After the short hesitation for clearing the area, the other two boats touched the beach. All exited. The boats were lifted, not slid, a very short distance – only the front third of a boat was out of the water. The group moved forward. Emilio was placed in the rear, Enrique forward with Munoz and Stratton. They caught up with James and Gray who were looking at a rickety wooden elevated walkway over a swampy area. That walkway would make a lot of squeaking noise – for sure! Enrique grabbed James' arm and shook his head no. He pointed to his left, went that way and gave the 'come along' gesture.

About forty yards away the swamp dwindled to nearly nothing. Enrique led them through it. Beyond the sand continued its rise. It was shorter and simpler for the villagers to have the walkway near the sand-beach channel access. Enrique led them on a well-used path to the beginning of the puebla.

It looked exactly as briefed, losing little as the description had passed from Enrique to Frank Lombard to Mitchell to Stratton. Amazing. A large 'avenue' perhaps thirty feet wide covered in grass and low shrub ran the length of the puebla. There was a well-worn dirt path wandering through the middle. The people obviously walked single file through it. Off to the side of the 'avenue' were well spaced-out houses and living areas.

A quick foray confirmed a cross avenue up ahead. Some of the houses were in little 'compound' arrangements, separated for privacy by walls, or 'fences', of some tropical vegetation placed for that purpose. The houses were dirt floored, open-doored, single layer wood walls with a thatched roof. The wall planks appeared to have deliberate small gaps between them – perhaps for air movement. Most of the main houses had smaller out buildings associated with them – one here and there two. The IR goggles showed every living thing as well as the cooking pits indoors and even residual warmth in utensils used the evening before. In one of the 'compounds' the main house had two out-buildings more in the nature of large sheds. IR showed those sheds containing nine heat-emitting units, four in one, five in the other. There was one guard in front, off to the side of the door, of each shed – and each was fast asleep!

Nothing moved. There was no chirping or other night jungle noise. The jungle had sensed their presence. The resident humans had not. There were no dogs – as Enrique had said. One pig grunted then was quiet. The chickens made no sound. Each invader moved according to plan. James, Gray and Garcia moved to the outer houses, duct tape, Tasers and needles in hand. Tasers first for the males. Then the females, tape over the mouth, flex-tied, hand on the head, needle in the neck and count four. Next, flex-tie the males while still disabled from the Taser shot. Older children were flex- tied and left in place. Small children were untouched. They slept on unaware of the phantoms among them.

Broderick began in the near houses. Stratton, Garcia and Enrique counted out to the fourth house on the main avenue. Enrique pointed. Garcia, with his hand on Enrique's shoulder, pushed him gently to the ground and signaled 'stay'. Garcia then joined Stratton and together they entered the house. They first went to the jefe. No Taser for him. Couldn't chance a terminal reaction before interrogation. Mouth and ankles received pre-cut duct tape and flex-ties. He was flipped and wrists were secured with flex-ties. He was completely immobilized before he was half awake. The wife was next. The twelve year old son awoke. He was promptly duct taped on the mouth. He struggled but the flex-ties quickly went on. He was no match for these apparitions. The two girls were loosely flex-tied and duct taped. It all happened so fast in those skilled hands that no outcry had time to happen.

Stratton signaled Garcia to help Broderick. The jefe's house was secure.

Shortly Munoz, Garcia, Broderick and Enrique appeared. "Got the count. All down. James and Gray are working with the hostages. They are well but somewhat debilitated. They're also very happy." Garcia reported.

"Good. Now for the end play. Scotty, take the two girls. Javier, the wife. Separate area as we discussed. Jimmy, time to go to work. Keep Enrique behind the jefe out of sight. Put a scarf or something over his face. He needs to hear and see the jefe. The recorders are on. You've got it." Stratton left, going to the hostages.

The men re-entered the jefe's house. They switched on a flashlight and set it upright. They lifted him and sat him on a bench. They forcefully ripped off the duct tape. The jefe yelled in pain. Then he yelled again, louder. And again, even louder.

They just looked at him. Then they took the wife and girls away. Roughly. Not a word had been spoken. More fear spread across the jefe's face. A wet spot appeared on his pants.

Stratton made his way to the hostage sheds. Stratton said "Good job, guys. Jimmy's interrogating the jefe. Bob, relieve Scotty. Send him to me. When Jimmy's done, cover him on the way out. Stay close on the kid. We'll work on getting these folks to the boats."

Stratton turned and went to the captives taking off his balaclava along the way. He wished to increase their comfort level by seeing an American face. "Good morning, folks.

Hope you don't mind being wakened so early. We thought it would be a nice surprise. Your transportation awaits. Any complaints about our service? My name is Deke Stratton and we've come all the way from Monterey to make your day – as one of our residents would say. Seriously, how ya'll doin'? Anything physically that we need to look at right now?"

Jack Troia stepped forward saying "We're okay. Nothing serious, minor stuff. We're okay to travel. Thank you, who-ever you are." There rang out a chorus of 'Thank you's'.

"Sir, my name is Charles Wilson. I think I've met you at the Pasadera Golf Course. What the hell are you doing here?"

"Actually, Charles, we have met. As to what I am doing here – I really sliced one off the third tee. Looking for it led me here. What a coincidence to run into you again." Deke replied, laughing.

"I meant it. What's a golfer at Pasadera doing coming here for us?" Wilson asked.

"Charles, in real life it was Lieutenant Colonel, United States Army, Special Forces. They wanted to give me a desk and make me a Colonel. I said no. Ended up in Monterey. When you folks went missing on your little adventure, as I understand it, Mark's Christina called an old military guy and friend – Doug Mitchell – who pulled in Bo Hanson, another old military guy. They, along with one of my ser-geants, pulled me in. I pulled in some of my guys. And here we are – ruining your vacation, forcing you to come home. Your families want you home. And, Charles, we have an eight o'clock Tee-time in two days so we've got to get on with it."

"Jesus Christ." Wilson whispered.

"Well, maybe He did have something to do with it. Right now we've got to move. Lot's of miles to go before we sleep.

So, folks, pack up and let's proceed quickly down this way. And I mean quickly. Shall we?" Stratton said as he gestured at the way out. "Speak of the Devil! Folks, this is Scotty, the sergeant I mentioned. There are more of us outside. Let's get them in the boats, Scotty."

"Good God, are Mitch and Bo here too?" Blaylock asked in amazement.

Stratton said "They wanted to be but they're a little too old – and maybe too chubby – to run around in the bush anymore. They're at the hotel anxiously awaiting your arrival. They're worse than a couple of old hens clucking and pacing. It's really tough on them not being out here with us. They're good men."

As they hustled them along the path, Travis looked at Broderick and said "Are you really a Special Forces guy?"

Broderick said "Yes, we are. All of us. This is what we do. Help people."

"Wow." Travis said. "This is so sweet. I can't wait to tell my friends."

"In that case, let me be clear here. We *were* Special Forces. We're all civilians now. Remember – were – not are. Clear? Also, you might not be able to tell anyone. It may have to remain a secret. That will be covered by the Colonel later, I'm sure."

"Ya, but this is so cool."

"It's not over yet. You ready for a scary boat ride?"

"I'm not scared."

"I know. But I am."

"For real?"

"Not bad. But some. It's dark and we'll be moving fast."

Stratton said "Watch yourselves on this walkway. The boats are at the end of it. Board as we direct when we get there. Move to the back. Guys, help slide them back. Leave room by the motor for one of us."

As they slid the boats back everyone else arrived. Munoz said "Got everything, Boss. No need to bring him along. Think you'll like the tape. Here's one for you. Broderick, one for your boat – just in case."

"Good. Everyone set? Wait a minute. Young man – you get in that boat there with Scotty. Balance the loads. Enrique, get us out of here. Everyone – no sounds, be quiet until we crank up the motors. Then you can talk – if you can. Let's go."

They paddled down the channel, pushing on the bottom with their paddles through some of it. It was definitely harder work with this load. The shallowness was a risk to their propellers – a risk they didn't want to take.

Soon, they were in the river. Enrique said "It is deeper out here but there is a part in the Parque – the refuge – that is shallow again. We are heavy but I think the motors will be alright – maybe."

"Give me warning when we get there. I think we won't risk it even though the bottom is sandy or muddy. We've plenty of time. We'll paddle or go very slow. Guys, hook up the lights. We need to see."

The ex-captives huddled together on the floors of the boats. Their faces were displaying or shielding, as the case may be, their thoughts as they bounced gently along. One showed exhilarating joy at the rescue. Another dwelled upon the depth of fear he had felt at his situation, now shaking worse at the memory. The boys, not understanding the true depth of the past danger from their privileged viewpoint, were fascinated by everything they were seeing and experiencing. Still, a primordial sense of relief lurked down deep within them. Karen Smith was silently crying from thankfulness, thankful to see her children again, to see her mother again, to see her husband again but mostly for the two boys.

Mark Blaylock, too, had wet spots in his eyes. His sons

were safe. He had spent his captive moments trying to figure out how to save the boys. His ever analytical mind had been in afterburner working on scenarios wherein he could trade himself for them. The problem was, they already had him. He had never felt so helpless, so impotent, so weak in his entire life. His massive intellect was of absolutely no use whatsoever in the face of pure force. At times might is all there is. There is no right – it is totally irrelevant. The Lady of Justice does carry scales but a sword is in her right hand. It is there for a reason. Sometimes it needs to be used. For the first time in his existence he had experienced an overwhelming desire to kill a human being. He had even begged God for the opportunity. The revelation that he was capable of such a desire was having profound affect upon his psyche. He was not sure how he was going to deal with it. Nothing in his life experiences had prepared him for this. Perhaps time would blur the contradictions into irrelevancies and life would go on. He thought not.

Jack Troia, Jack the Lionheart, Jack the Leader, had been so occupied leading his 'children', his cohorts, that he'd had little time for himself. Except at night. Then he dwelled upon what a great life he'd had. He relished it all. He knew what was ahead for them. There would be no release. If released they could lead authorities to their captors. Nope, this is where it would end he had thought. He was at peace with that. Actually, it was a good place to die he had thought. And now this incredible rescue! God must have more important work for me to salvage me in such a fashion he thought. The Clinic will continue but I'll bet not so many businessmen will come along in the future. Probably will be only us dentists and assistants but maybe not. Spice attracts. We'll see. Thank you, God.

The boats churned down river, their lights playing off the still black waters. Eventually, Enrique waved a hand, palm down. Throttles were reduced. Enrique pointed towards the right side. "Deeper there." he said. A little later he pointed at the middle and raised his hand palm up. A short while later he lifted his right arm pointing hard right. The river had disappeared, debouching into El Golfete. The boats laid over and went to full power. They flashed their lights at the waiting re-fueling boat to follow. It turned into their wake and tagged along. Now it was a straight run up El Golfete and continue up the Rio Dulce to the Outrigger Hotel. Deke had notified, by satellite phone, Mitchell and Hanson that they were in route with all. Mitchell and Hanson thought they'd let the ex-captives announce their rescue to their families themselves when they arrived.

CHAPTER 20

Rio Chacon-Machaca, Guatemala
0130 hours local: Day 5

Peter Rust leaned his sore back against the side of the rub-ber boat, his long legs reaching nearly across to the other side. His analytical and reticent nature had served him well as a private investor. He had always followed his own coun-sel neither soliciting nor considering the opinions or con-clusions of others. His method by inclination – now habit – was to obtain such 'facts' as were ascertainable by any means available. He then contemplated their possible inter-relations. Each newly acquired 'fact' would start the process anew. Each of those interrelations would require a separate analysis. Each analysis could generate branch points along the process creating sub-paths, each essentially a new line of analysis and contemplation.

The years of practicing the method had rendered it auto-matic, essentially beyond his control, simply the essence of his existence. It was done without any conscious effort or intent. Observation and registering of detail were inherent factors native to him. Outward reactions were not.

During his captivity he had said hardly a word, using head nods to respond to Troia's questions about his condition. His eyes and ears absorbed the responses of each of the captives as Troia made his periodic leadership inquiries. Sprawled on the bottom of the boat, he continued speechless, observational and contemplative.

He was not surprised that he had felt no particular level of fear throughout the ordeal. Okay, maybe a little but at a nearly subliminal level. His mind's analysis operation had kept it occupied, occupied sufficiently to enchant it and allow it to suppress signals sent from the 'lizard' brain – the amygdala. For him that was normal. In general, emotions were foreign to him. Their suppression was an instinctive part of his being. They were irrational. They were unreliable. They interfered with rational thought if their presence was allowed. They could lead one to stupid actions. Emotions were the enemy of everything he valued, of everything he was.

He was surprised at the equanimity with which he had accepted his fate. By the time the hostages had reached the captors' puebla his analysis had concluded that it was here he would die. They had been selected not at random but for some specific reason or reasons. There would be no release even if a ransom were paid – which he assumed would be demanded. Once clear of the non-captives the captors had removed their face coverings. No attempt had been made to blindfold the captives. No attempt had been made to secret the route to the puebla from them. No attempt to hide the villagers' faces had been made. Yes, here he would die.

That, too, he contemplated. So be it if that is Fate's wish. He'd been granted an excellent and rewarding life. His wife and children would be well-off. They would miss him for awhile but then life would go on. That would be the same whether he died here or at home from whatever. Yes, why not here? This jungle is actually a beautiful place to end.

Que sera, sera. That concluded, his mind shifted back to its normal mode. Actually, that had been its normal mode.

He had experienced a sense of shock at the appearance of black-clad men speaking English. They had simply materialized, like apparitions, among them. The emotion of shock rapidly changed to curiosity as he observed the coordinated and professional actions of the rescuers. He found the economy of movement, every action containing a purpose, fascinating. Outside of novels and movies, those rarely engaged, he had never really been exposed to the physical action world. It engrossed him to be participating even in his passive role. Exiting their hutch, additional black-clad men joined. And two Maya boys. Were they captives? No, their body language was as if they were one with the black-clad men, now known to him to be Americans, at least one of whom was known to Charles Wilson. Most curious! Special Forces? Amazing!

Once underway in the boat he realized that one of the boys was a guide. His hand directions were being obeyed without hesitation. Each of the rescuers radiated some distance a force field of dangerous competency that he found strangely reassuring. He was in good hands even if he did not know from where they had come and who they really were. *American* was as good as it gets.

Now that pardon from imminent demise was at hand his mind recovered from the distraction of the escape activities and returned to its haven – contemplation. The roar of the outboard had a peaceful white noise effect, the vibration of the boat a soothing massage. He appeared to be asleep but it was not so. He knew that the matrix had huge gaps, missing facts and that key points were not connecting. But enough were present to generate intriguing possibilities, probabilities, conjectures – all indicators of pathes in the pursuit of facts, more points in the matrix. And pursue he would. This vicious insult would not be forgiven. They may have been rescued but the murderous bastard behind it was still out there. And 'there', he suspected, was Monterey, not Guatemala.

He had observed and registered the demeanor and body language of his fellow captives. Truth be known, he had been fascinated by the broad spectrum of reactions among the group – and the speed of changes when they occurred.

James Villareal – the personification of the corpulent banker – had at first been indignant that anyone would presume to interfere with his person. When understanding of his predicament pushed aside the indignation, fear emerged full blown - skipping awe, amazement, shock or any other intermediate emotion. His eyes grew large, the face flushed deep red, and his breathing became labored. Watching, Peter had been concerned that a heart attack or stroke was imminent. He shortly noticed that the breathing stabilized but still at an alarming rate. However, there was no hand moving towards the chest or throat. Eventually the flush subsided, the breathing slowed but the fear-stunned eyes remained. They were locked upon the weapon of one of the captors. His eyes never wavered from the weapon until arrival at the puebla. He appeared mesmerized by the potential evil of the thing. As a banker his almost every waking moment had been spent avoiding crisis of any kind. Now he found himself embroiled in one of no escape. It was anathema to his very essence. It was inconceivable that this was happening to him. It must be a dream from which he would soon awake. Unfortunately it was not. The thoughts played across his face. His descent into despair was swift.

During the captivity Villareal was disoriented and distant, a blank look in his eyes, perfunctory in his movements. Though food was offered he ate little. Stripped of the importance accoutrements of his world he had ceased to exist, had become a non-person, a cipher. Cognition of the reality of the rescue effected a profound change. Peter observed from behind that James' shoulders were raised during the walk to the boats. Before, they had sloped down. His stride was smooth, his demeanor forceful. The rescue was his due. Once again he would rule his barony. As he approached the boats Peter saw the broad confident smile before he faded into the dark of another boat.

Mark Blaylock rapidly alternated between anxiety attacks and remorse attacks. The recurring anxiety followed each recognition of impotency – he could do nothing to protect his boys. The remorse came from his self-castigation for exposing the boys to such danger. Peter could see that he had not one thought for himself. Mark's eyes were back and forth between his sons. He held them close to his sides, his arms around them like a mother hen gathering her chicks to safety. Only there was no safety. While his body was fixed, his eyes told Peter where his psyche dwelled. He was desperate to protect but knew not how. A conundrum, supercharged with emotion that could, in a weak mind, lead to a shutdown.

Early in the captivity Blaylock shifted to a nurturing role, solicitous of his sons' needs, both physical and mental. He, too, had reached the conclusion that this was the end, that they would not survive. His conundrum was solved – there was no solution. The answer to no solution was to accept the will of the gods – and hope that Zeus was feeling magnanimous. His work in this situation was to ease the passage. At moments he experienced profound sadness creeping up on him and it showed itself to Peter. Blaylock mentally forced it back into oblivion. Peter saw that Herculean effort as well.

Blaylock ensured that the boys ate the offered food. He kept their minds occupied. They discussed the adventures throughout the world they had had together. They discussed what each had learned, liked and disliked about each adventure. They even discussed the foods the Mayans served them. Blaylock had always prized communication with his sons, sharing their thoughts and feelings. If die they must then they would die living their lives as they always had.

When black-clad rescuers had appeared among them, startling them all, Blaylock had immediately recognized the significance and calmed the instinctive fear of his sons. He had said "They're Americans." How he knew he did not know. The boys' fear subsided instantly. Then their excitement grew. Boys being boys, each thought that this was really 'sweet'.

During the march to the boats the boys were well along in relegating the danger-laden event to the adventure category. Rescuers, guns, black clothes, boats and escape. What could possibly be better? They were living a video game! Blaylock himself was almost in ecstasy, his boys were safe or, at least, almost so. Peter heard him say "Thank you, God. Sorry about the Zeus appeal." Peter chuckled imagining what Blaylock had asked of Zeus.

Imelda Watson had been another sort of problem. He could read very little about her because she was not there. She simply had gone somewhere else – mentally. She disclosed nothing in body language. Her eyes transmitted no information. She wasn't catatonic with its associated jerky sporadic movements. It was more of a stupor but there was clarity to her eyes, a horizon gaze of introspection. Jack Troia worked on her to eat and drink. She did so under his ministrations but showed him no reaction while doing so.

Peter had found her lack of response or recovery from the rescue even more curious. She displayed nothing – no happiness, no joy, no relief, no gratitude to the rescuers. She perfunctorily walked to her boat and sat exactly as she had during captivity. Peter wondered where she was.

Jack Troia, after his initial surprise, shock and fear, appeared to have buried himself in his leadership role. The escape from the reality of the situation could be achieved by work and his true innate concern for the well-being of other human beings was apparent. His entire life had been one of nurturing and relieving suffering and pain. The role obviously was a natural for him and he excelled at it. He was always busy – negotiating food and drink with Felipe or his wife, walk around space, toilet facilities, water for washing and the miscellaneous living needs.

At rescue he was efficient at aiding the rescuers herd the group toward the boats, moving up and down the line offering aid if needed. None was. He was ebullient in a controlled way. There was a hyper spring to his step. His joy radiated.

Karen Smith he had found intriguing. At first she had registered shock then fear which suddenly diminished, replaced by anger. Her anger had been one of a moral outrage at perpetrators of such an evil. It showed in the disgust radiating from her face. Her slow-burning anger seemed not to have diminished during the captivity. In spite of, or because of, that anger, she assisted Troia in his efforts and made good with the others. She seemed to relish her time with Blaylock and the boys. She made periodic efforts to reach Imelda – wherever she was. She failed each time. She still returned for another attempt.

Peter concluded that she had a backbone of steel, that when adversity struck one wanted to be on her team. Watching that anger burn, Peter knew that in her there was no forgiving a major moral transgression.

When the lights of the Outrigger Hotel came into view, Peter knew that they were not at the end. This was only a way-stop. The true end was miles down the road – a road he intended to travel.

Karen Smith at first felt shock when taken, then fear and dismay. The covered faces and the weapons struck a primal chord deep within – not unlike a rabbit cornered by a fox, nowhere to run, no escape. Freeze. She observed subliminally the selection process from the file folder, its import not recognized at the moment. She knew of tourist kidnappings in Guatemala and was sure a modest ransom payment would be coming soon. Not a problem. Then she realized the boys had been taken.

The selection process sank in. Her anger rose mildly as she realized the boys were deliberately being subjected to this traumatizing act. That was unconscionable! Her outrage at such a heartless, despicable depravity reached soul deep and her anger rose accordingly. Someone would pay for this when it was over. She fumed internally as the launch progressed across El Golfete. Face coverings came off, first one then another until all were uncovered. Understanding hit her like a club! No blindfolds. Now, no face coverings. There was no intent that they would survive the taking! This was a one-way trip. They could not be allowed to lead authorities to wherever they were going or to identify their captors.

They entered a river off El Golfete. The realization that she would soon die was met with a wave of resolve. If that was what was in store then she would meet it with honor, with fortitude. She would assist the others, focusing on their needs – physical and mental. And if she could find a way out she would take it. She could not. And if she could find a way to take one of these scum with her, she would. She, again, could not.

She had sensed Peter Rust studying her but took no offense. She had observed him studying intently each of her fellow hostages like bugs under a microscope. She was only another bug. Sitting in a rubber boat with rescuers, she allowed tears to flow. Peter may think they were tears for her own salvation. That was alright but he would be wrong. The tears were for the boys, for *their* salvation, their futures now assured. Knowing that their short lives were coming to an end had been excruciatingly painful to her, so painful she could not allow her mind to dwell there. Let Peter think what he will. It was not important.

CHAPTER 21

Troia Home
Monterey, California
0000 hours local: Day 5

The e-mail went to each residence. It was time dated as of 11:59 PM. The new instruction was that the fund transference was to be done within the next fifteen minutes. At the expiration of that time one hostage would be killed. Each five minutes after that with no transfer another would be killed. The children would go first. No reason for the change was given.

After looking at Grazing and getting a nod, ASAC Harrison instructed Abernathy to initiate the transfer in five minutes. Harrison notified his tracers. Grazing thought *"Damn. It had been a good day – until now. It is what it is in Guatemala."* Then he also made a call. To Tom Heller. He went back to waiting.

CHAPTER 22

Outrigger Hotel
Rio Dulce
Guatemala
0330 hours local: Day 5

All the lights were on with floods covering the docking area. The bar was lit. Beer and champagne were on ice. Rosalee, Nora, and Ingrid had prepared mountains of food. The cheering started when the approaching lights were first seen.

"It may be four in the morning but I believe a fine brandy is in order. Fortunately I happened to find a bottle of Duca d'Alba. God damn it, Bo. We did it! Jesus – WE. DID. IT. Can you believe it?"

"It is pretty incredible when you think of it. Thank God for Stratton and his men, actually! God does work in mysterious ways, doesn't She?" Bo murmured.

"I'm really interested in what they found. Deke said the jefe talked. Can't wait to hear that. Somehow it's going to lead us to the drug trade. But, I don't know, there's something else here. It's too organized. Another thing, the hostages are in the possession of a tribe that doesn't speak English in the middle of nowhere yet within one day e-mail ransom demands go out to each family. How the hell do they get the addresses? And where did those pictures come from? Had to be pictures, he was looking then pointing. Damn – I'm missing something. Boy, I really want to hear what that jefe has to say."

"Me too. None of it makes any sense." Hanson responded. "This is damn good brandy. Perfect for the occasion. Suppose we should reserve some for Stratton and the guys? Nah. Stuff's too good for snake eaters. I'm just going to be happy for the dentists and kids."

The boats gently nudged the dock, lined up nose to tail sideways against it. Multiple hands held ropes and others pulled people onto the dock. Mitchell grabbed the two Blaylock boys in his arms holding them for the longest time. There were tears of relief in his eyes while his heart danced with joy. Finally he released them, looked into their eyes, smiled and said "Quite an adventure you've had." They nodded. There were hugs and kisses and tears and laughter, questions and answers, dancing and jumping all around. It was bedlam. As quickly as it began it subsided with Frank's whistle. He brought forward Stratton, Enrique and Emilio after separating the boys from their mother. When he had everyone's attention he said "Everyone, there is lots of time to hear all the war stories and how things happened. But, first, here's Deke Stratton who'd like to say something. Deke."

Stratton gathered the Maya boys, one arm around each, and said "You all will eventually get the full story – or as much as can be told to you – but I want to introduce the true heroes of the evening. The rescue could not have been done without our two guides here, Enrique and Emilio. With all of our expertise and equipment we were totally lost out there. We probably would not have found you. These are the two people you owe your thanks." With that, he raised his hands and slowly began to clap. The others joined in until it became a thundering roar. The boys grinned from ear to ear. Then they changed to embarrassed as they were hugged and kissed by all. Their father looked on beaming with pride in his sons. Their mother shed tears of relief. Frank watched and grinned.

Stratton then turned somber saying "Folks, listen up, please. I can't emphasize enough how important it is that you all forget who rescued you! We'll leave it that some locals rescued you. You must not speak of who it was. I also emphasize that you were NOT rescued by United States Army personnel! There were no Special Forces personnel operating in Guatemala. None of us here are members. Maybe we used to be but no longer. You absolutely must not talk to the press, any media. Any comments, if made, will be strongly denied. Am I clear on this? Any questions as to why this must be?"

Almost everyone nodded affirmatively.

Karen Smith said "I'm sorry but I need a bathroom and a shower."

Frank's wife Sylvia said "Everyone, your rooms are as you left them. All your clothes are there. If you'd like to freshen up, the food and champagne will be waiting."

Amidst the euphoria only Agnes – one of the dental assistants – noticed that Imelda Watson was not participating. She had gone to a couch and was sitting looking at the floor in a form of disconnected stare. Mitchell noticed Agnes approaching her and followed. Peter Rust had done the same. Agnes put her arms around Imelda and held her. Imelda had tears running down her cheeks. Agnes was making soothing sounds and saying "You're safe now, you're safe."

As Mitchell came close he heard Imelda sob "I was supposed to die."

Agnes again reassured Imelda that she was safe and continued to hold her, helping her through her trauma. Her pain and sadness was manifest and deep. She would probably need professional help upon return. Now, she was in Agnes' capable hands. Mitchell and Rust turned back to the others. As they did so, Agnes was helping Imelda towards her room.

Except for Troia all the ex-captives left for their rooms. Troia approached Mitchell and Hanson. Troia, watching Agnes aiding Imelda along, commented "Poor lady. She was traumatized the worst. Said not a word while we were captive. She was so scared she was nearly catatonic most of the time – like you see her now. She seems so sad even now being rescued." Mitchell handed him a vodka and tonic, squeeze of lemon. "Your usual, old friend."

Troia took the drink, looked at it, looked up at Mitchell and Hanson and said "What took you so long?"

Hanson said "Had a barbecue to attend."

Troia looked at them for awhile then said "How the hell do I thank you guys?"

Hanson said "Easy – you pick up the wine tab at dinner for the next year."

Mitchell said "What? I think two years for sure."

Mitchell raised his glass. The others followed. Mitchell said "Welcome home, old friend. Jack, no offense, but you really do need a shower. Go. We'll be here."

Troia nodded and wandered off as Stratton and Munoz approached. Stratton said "Okay. Boats are empty. Gear's secured. We need to listen to that tape. I was going to give Jake a call to pick us up at that strip across the river over there when Jimmy said he didn't think so. 'Hold off a bit' he said. Said 'We might have another little job to do!' We need to listen."

Mitchell said loudly "Frank, why don't you join us. We've

some time before people return. Let's go up to the dining area. Little more room there."

Frank directed Jose to return Emilio and parents to their puebla and Enrique to the marina when he returned. He joined the others.

They gathered around a dining table.

Munoz started the player.

* * * * *

Munoz' voice played softly. "Felipe, escuchame. Me llamo Sargento. Entienda Sargento?"

"Si, Sargento. Pero no pienso de Guatemala."

"You are correct – I am not from Guatemala. I am much worse than the Guatemalan Army. You will tell me what I wish to know. You are a peaceful Maya cacique over your puebla, a grower of maize, a man of honor. You are not a bandito, not a narco. Why did you take these people?"

"We need money. I think we get money for these people."

"Felipe, you took the people. How were you going to get the money?"

"I don't know."

"Felipe, don't lie to me."

"I no lie."

"Then tell me how. Someone else was going to get the money and give you some?"

"I don't know."

"Felipe, how can you not know?"

"I don't know. A man, he say I take people. He will give me money. We not hurt the people."

"Who is that man?"

"I don't know."

"Felipe, I don't have much time but I need to know the truth. Do you love your children? Your wife?"

"Yes."

"One more lie and I will hurt them – not you. I need you to talk like an honorable man, a grower of maize, so I won't hurt you. I will hurt them – very badly. Do you understand me?"

"Yes."

"Good. Who is this man and how can I find him?"

"I don't know. He comes when he wants to."

"Verdad? I don't think so. I think he had some reason to come to you and you know who he is. I think you just lied to me."

'Sargento' nodded at Enrique who was by the front door saying "Wave one arm." Immediately there was a shriek of pain from a child and a terror-filled scream from Felipe's wife. Felipe blanched.

"Felipe, next I will cut off a foot or hand, not just a finger, and hand it to you. Now, you must tell me what I need to know or all your children will be in pieces. Who is this man?"

Felipe began to weep. His shoulders sagged. His chin dropped to his chest. Wracking deep sounds of pain struggled from his mouth. "He is mi primo, my cousin. Please, don't hurt my family. We didn't hurt those people. Don't hurt us. He said there would be no problems."

"What is your cousin's name and where can I find him? Remember, he got you here."

"He calls himself Manny Bonano – not his real name. It is a name he took on when he became a ladino. His real name is Pablo. That's all, just Pablo. He lives in Ciudad Guatemala. I don't know where. He has a restaurant there."

"Where is the picture book?"

Felipe nodded towards the corner. Munoz picked it up and glanced through it, saying "Did the man give you this?"

"Yes."

"How old is he? Describe him."

"He has about thirty five years, I think. He is about one and two thirds meters. He is a little fat."

"How much money did he promise you for this taking?"

"200,000 dollars. That is a big amount of money for my puebla."

"Yes, that is a lot of money for one puebla. No wonder you didn't refuse – but it was wrong, Felipe. In what part of La Ciudad does he have his restaurant?"

"I don't know – it's true, I don't know. I've never been beyond the bridge or Livingston."

"What is his wife's name?"

"I don't know. We not talk about wives."

"How did he come to find you? Tell me all you know about him."

"By boat. His mother left the puebla with a man. They went to La Ciudad. The man got killed. Las Armas killed her husband – a student. The mother worked as a maid. At a big place. She talked about it. Lots of people worked there but some lived there. She cleaned for his Excellency. She called him 'ambassador', American, I think. Yes, American. Then she come home when Pablo was ten. She died. Pablo left at about sixteen. He could speak some English and Spanish so he went to the City. I hadn't seen in – oh – it makes twenty years. He came with his plan. Later he brought guns and the other stuff. We don't like the guns. He talks to me by the radio."

"That radio?"

"Yes."

Munoz smashed it.

Munoz looked over Felipe's head to Enrique. "El habla Verdad?" –Is he speaking true?

"Pienso que si." –I think yes.

"Me too. I don't think he has more to tell us. You?"

"No."

"Okay. We're done."

"Felipe, we are going to leave. Thank you for your help. We did not hurt your child bad, only a little pinch to make her scream. She is okay. Do not attempt to contact your cousin in any way. If you do we will come back. You don't want that do you?"

Felipe vigorously shook his head.

"Just relax. We are going to put you to sleep for awhile – like the others. You will be alright. Adios, Felipe."

"Adios, Senor Sargento. I am sorry."

CHAPTER 23

Outrigger Hotel
Rio Dulce, Guatemala
0530 hours local: Day 5

"Play it again, Jimmy." Stratton instructed. They listened carefully.

When it finished, Mitchell said "Ahhh – what we have is a name, owns a restaurant in the City, has access to weapons and com, is short and somewhat fat, thirty-five years old, is Maya ladino, mother worked at the American embassy twenty-five years ago and he speaks Q'eqchi, Spanish and English. Anything else?"

"Where'd you get Spanish and English?" Munoz asked.

"CG and narco business – needs it. Embassy until ten. Felipe said it."

"Right."

Hanson spoke up. "We need to get help from DEA and CIA in the City. Run Bonano's name through the data base. Let's have Jake do the input as well. Frank, you know anyone plugged into the restaurant game in the City?"

"My wife's cousin owns two in Zona 10, another one in Zona Viva and another up in Zona 1. I'll call him. See if he's heard of this guy."

Stratton said "Think I'll call Jake. See what he can come up with. I'll also call Ford, let him know we might be a day or two longer. Also let him know the mission was successful – so far."

At that point, Jack Troia and Mark Blaylock came rushing in, both speaking excitedly at once. Mitchell said "Whoa, one at a time. What's up?"

Blaylock said "The ransom was paid a little over two hours ago. The money was transferred."

"How the hell?" Mitchell erupted. "I told them to delay. No call. Damnit. What happened?"

Troia said "At midnight their time, two o'clock our time here, an e-mail came giving them fifteen minutes to transfer or one of the kids would be killed. Then another of us every five minutes. The money was ready. The FBI authorized the transfer. It was a complete change from the earlier instructions. They still had four hours to go until that change. They had to act."

Mitchell said "Bo, I blew that one. We had them in hand a half hour before the transfer. Damn. I should have called. We really need to speak with this Bonano guy. Now!"

"Don't think you're going to be able to do that." Frank said.

"Why?"

"Just spoke with my wife's cousin. He about choked when I mentioned the name. This guy is bad news, a real nasty. Roberto almost couldn't say his name. This is a cocaine heavy. He does have a restaurant – of sorts. It's in Barrio El Gallito – the absolutely worst area of the City. The worst! There is no entry. You wouldn't get within six blocks of the so-called restaurant much less to him. The restaurant is more a club for ranking narcos. The entire Barrio is heavily armed. Nobody goes there. Not the police. Not the Army. Certainly not you guys."

This information was quietly digested by all.

After some thought, Stratton said "Looks like we need some intel. Lots of it. We need to hook up with the on-site DEA boys. Bet they've got a handle on someone like this."

Frank said "A handle, maybe. But they sure as hell don't have him. And they sure as hell don't have assets inside *that* Barrio!"

"Never know until you ask." Hanson said. "Think I'll make a few phone calls. Deke, you need to make any calls about now?"

"That would be a yes but I've got to think about it a bit. Not quite sure who to call first. I'm on it."

The two of them slid off to separate private zones, Hanson's cell phone at work, Stratton's in hand. Then Stratton's came into play.

Mitchell sat down and gazed off into the distance. Troia and Blaylock also sat. Blaylock said "What are you thinking about, Mitch?"

"How bad I fucked this up. How bad *we* fucked up. Not the rescue. I mean the communication among us on the ransom and my decision not to notify them when we had you guys. Damn. I guess what is, is. Also, the next step. This is so far out of my world. Guys like those two amaze me. Their contacts and experiences range so far. They really are one big Band of Brothers. Hell, I was just an airplane driver. My military world was the hull of a ship. Nothing compared to all the things career Army guys do. Jack, what is the name of that cool hotel in Antigua you booked the group into at the end last year?"

"It's the Meson Panza Verde. I always take my groups

there. Great place, great food and they take care of us as you know."

"Jack, here's my AMEX card. You're me. Could you set us up, two to a room for the guys, a large suite for Bo and me so we can gather there. Oh yah, that upstairs dining room where we had dinner – can we tie that up for tonight and tomorrow night? You know who to talk to. Watching those two guys, I think we'll need those spaces for a couple of days. Bet we're going in."

Blaylock said "Didn't you hear what Frank said?"

Mitchell said "Didn't you see the look on Stratton's face when he said it?"

Mitchell turned to Frank and said "Those inflatable boats – hope you can put them to use 'cause they're yours. Can't return them. They're private, not military, so keep 'em."

Frank said "Does the word 'wow' mean anything to anybody? These will be great for the Clinic to have. Thanks."

"Thought there could be a use. I remember some of those kids traveling by panga or launch for five or six hours each way to get to the Clinic. These may shorten that. Also, guess we need transportation to Antigua and the dentists to La Aurora. Got a bus for hire around?"

"Yes. Folks need some sleep. We need to arrange flights home for the dentists. My front desk will get a bus moving from the City – at least for you guys. Take about six or seven hours, depending. Take you eight back in. If there are flights, dentists can ride along. I'll handle the logistics."

Mitchell took a chair in the dining area where he could be alone and rang up Grazing. "Kenner. What came down? How'd it happen? From what Jack told me on timing we had them in hand over a half an hour."

"I had no call from you. Out of the blue for some unknown reason the demand changed. The FBI guy told the bank to transfer. I was there and concurred given the situation. There were several family members present and they were clamoring for payment. There was no denying them. Wouldn't have anyway. About forty-five minutes earlier Abernathy blew up at accusations he was delaying deliberately and blurted out that he couldn't transfer, that a rescue was underway. To answer your next question – nobody that heard that left, nobody made a phone call. Watson took a call from his partner, talked in front of us on business – nothing about rescuers. About an hour before Abernathy went to the restroom and the FBI guy went outside to make some calls. That's it."

"Damn me forever, I made the decision to let the captives inform their families themselves. Thought we had the full fourteen hours to comply so no rush. Any idea what was behind the change? Anything happen on your end that would warn someone?"

"Nothing that I'm aware of anywhere near that time."

"What do you mean 'near that time'? And how did Abernathy know?"

"In the afternoon, about three or so, people were pushing to transfer the ransom. To stop that I took Abernathy and Mrs. Villareal, along with attorney Williams, aside and informed them of the mission. I swore them to zip lip. I had no choice. They would have transferred before you hit the water. Later on, about four thirty, I had to sort of brief the FBI guy and an Interpol agent he had along. I left a lot out but they know we had a mission going. Not stupid guys. They are on the trace – both agencies."

"You think that sometime after the three o'clock thing and, say, eleven thirty one of those three people leaked to someone else?"

"That's exactly what I'm thinking. That change was a response to some stimulus. That's where my nose is pointing. By the way, the first two e-mails originated at an internet coffee shop in Ciudad Guatemala. Someplace called the

Global Internet Café. Don't know yet on the third. FBI let me know."

"Ken. Some years back you introduced me to a guy – Tom something – in Pamplona. I and Joanne took his seventies-something year old mother up to Roncevalles with us. You told me the guy was a Treasury agent – a super money tracker. What do you think about getting him on the trail? If I remember right he owes you when he got gored – and me. I took his mother off his hands."

"You're slow – and late, amigo. Already done. First thing I thought of. He was up and running with the transfer. He's parallel with the FBI – they don't know about him but he knows about them. Would probably piss off the Feebies if they knew. Those guys are pretty territorial. He'll be busy while transfers are going on. He expects multiple movements. We'll be informed as there is something we need to know."

"Kenner, you haven't lost a step. We'll be here a little longer. We've got a mission into Guatemala City. Mitchell proceeded to update Grazing on everything they had and what they were going to do.

"You're not going in yourself are you?"

"Nah. Stratton won't let me. Arrogant bastard and a racist – holds it against me for being Navy! Bo and I are waiting outside the perimeter. I do want to talk with this scumbag, though. He's the connection. He'll talk to me, one way or another. If he's difficult he'll probably curse his mother for giving him life. Taking those boys was a real bad mistake."

"Mitch, I'm playing with a bunch of things here. Don't have them put together yet but they are starting to gel. No need to bother you now about them – will later. My ruminations are all on tape in your office. Got more digging to do. You take care of business there. I'm on top of tracking and stuff here. Talk soon." He rang off.

Mitchell rose and went to each, Stratton and Hanson, saying "We'll be at Meson Panza Verde in Antigua tonight." As he wandered back, the ex-captives began to appear, showered, shaved and freshly clothed. Karen, Imelda and the boys had skipped the shave.

"Mr. Mitchell, excuse me. My name is Peter Rust. As I understand it, you generated this rescue. I would like to extend my heartfelt thanks. Quite a feat to have organized so quickly."

"You're welcome, Sir. Actually it was the other guys who pulled it off. I may have received the first call but it was Stratton and Hanson there who put it together. A lot of folks contributed in many ways. We're all delighted that you people are back safe and unharmed."

"Mr. Mitchell, I understand. Mr. Hanson had some interesting things to say about you. Something about 'ramrodded it', I believe. I've had a few days of forced relaxation, time to think about these events. Mr. Hanson – I mean, Bo – said you had some thoughts also. I think that when we return it might be constructive for us to have a meeting."

"By the way, it's either Doug or Mitch, your choice. Mr. Mitchell has been gone a long time. On the meeting, I think that would be a good idea. The sooner the better. I would be interested in your observations and thoughts on this thing. We've never met but I've heard you're a good man to listen to. I'll be back in a couple of days – got a small matter to attend to here first."

"So I gather. I inadvertently overheard the tape and arrangements with Frank."

Mitchell regarded the man with some reserve then coldly said "Somehow I think very little happens with you 'inadvertently'. Some things are best not overheard. I suggest that what you *think* you overheard might never have happened, a figment of your imagination after such a trying experience. Best to put such fantasies in the dump bin never to be spoken of. Ever. Are we in accord?"

"I understand. Call me when you wish to meet. And – good luck, Douglas." Peter went to the bar for a club soda and squeeze of lemon, smiling to himself. Now, given some time, he had penetrated the defense palisades of the operational cadre. He would eventually be allowed in and privy – even if only partially. They possessed knowledge critical to his analysis – knowledge the significance of which was probably unrecognized by them. Men of action, he thought, were not given to attention to detail and analytical thought. When he had the matrix complete he would present it in full bloom for appropriate action.

All the others had spoken to their ecstatic families. A great weight had been lifted. The reality of their rescue had sunk in and the obscenity of their taking washed away by the cleansing of the shower. Now, they were overwhelmed by hunger, a pure animal craving for good food, nourishing food, comforting food, familiar food. They ate, they drank, they laughed. Then the bottom dropped out. The yawns started. Their rooms silently beckoned. The adrenalin was gone. They didn't sleep – they crashed. Totally. Completely.

Soon, occupying couches or corners on folded rugs, all the team but Stratton and Hanson were asleep. Eventually phones clicked close. They lay down on the floor, throw pillows under their heads. They were asleep before their heads settled in.

CHAPTER 24

Outrigger Hotel
Rio Dulce, Guatemala
0930 hours local: Day 5

Frank strode into the bar lounge saying "Rise and shine, cowboys. Time to move. Got breakfast cookin'. Right through the arch and go left to the head. Everything you need is there, blades, towels, toothbrushes, whatever."

He turned to Mitchell and said "Mitch, we've got time for breakfast and such but we've got to be aboard the launch by eleven fifteen. The bus will be at Nana Juana's at eleven thirty or so. I let you guys sleep as long as I could."

"Great. Thanks. We needed that sleep."

The smell of cooking bacon and perking coffee wafted through the air beckoning them to move. It was stronger incentive than any order could possibly be. Move they did, all ablutions completed in short order.

When gathered together at the family-style tables in the dining area, plates full, Stratton said "Guys, we've got another little job to do. I and Bo have made some connections. We've got support coming from DEA and CIA guys in Ciudad Guatemala. We'll be briefed on the situation in Antigua. Mitch has us booked into a hotel there. Transport's arranged. When we finish breakfast we'll board Frank's launch. He'll run us upriver to the landing where a bus will be waiting. Time aboard the bus for more sleep if you wish. No need to talk on the bus. The driver, you know. We'll have time at the hotel. Somebody will find us there. We should be there before six tonight. Then, we'll see. Plans will depend upon the intel. Our goal is to extricate this son-of-a-bitch and have a little chat with him. Can't go in there, my ass!"

There were chuckles and some nods. "Got it, Boss." Gray said. They ate. Finishing, the men efficiently assembled their equipment, all weapons secured out of sight, all placed on the launch.

Frank said "We'll wait a little while. I want to arrive when the bus is already in the dock area. The less time you guys with your bags are visible, the better. Know what I mean? You aren't exactly the average tourists in appearance, if you get my drift. We'll leave in about fifteen minutes."

Mitchell said "What cabin is Blaylock in? Troia?"

He went to Blaylock's and woke him. A bleary-eyed Blaylock opened the door. Mitchell said "Sorry to wake you but wanted to say goodbye. We're leaving. Got a little more work to do. You will be leaving soon for CONUS. We'll be along sometime. Mark – I'm so glad everything worked out. It would have broken my heart if we'd failed. You be cool, old friend, and hug those boys for me."

Blaylock, with tears in his rheumy eyes, said "Somewhere, somehow I'll thank you for this proper. How the hell did Christina know to call you?"

"Good question but I suspect my wife talked to your wife along the way about some things she shouldn't have – another adventure. It appears that in her desperation I was the only life raft around. Appears she was right."

"Thank God she did! You know there are no words for how I feel."

"For nothing, hombre. For nothing. That's what friends are for. Gots to go now." Blaylock watched him go. There were more tears in his eyes.

Mitchell pounded on Troia's door. A clear-eyed Troia opened the door, saw Mitchell and said "You off?"

"Yeah. Thought I'd say goodbye. Take care of your chicks, Jack. Frank's working on your flights. We've got a little more work to do. We're going to track this damn thing down. I think it was organized in Monterey. Got a man in the City we need to chat with. You take care." Mitchell turned and walked away. Troia said to his back "Thanks, Mitch. Vaya con Dios."

Mitchell just waved his hand in the air as he walked away.

The launch ride was a short fifteen minutes up and across the river. They motored under the gigantic bridge, veering left into the marina nestled beneath its south end. The bus was waiting.

Mitchell gave Frank a hug, saying nothing. Then walked away. No words were adequate – or necessary.

CHAPTER 25

Meson Panza Verde Hotel
Antigua, Guatemala
1930 hours local: Day 5

Hanson rose to the light tap on the door. The muted conversation stopped, maps flipped over, files were closed. Gray silently moved to the back side of the door while the others scattered about the room, arms ready. Hanson said "Yeah?"

A soft voice said "Luke."

Hanson opened the door a crack. Before him stood a somewhat scruffy gent, feet slightly spread and hands held down and out displaying no weapons. One hand held a file folder. Hanson opened the door fully and nodded to come in as he took the folder. 'Luke' no sooner entered than Frank James was on him doing a full pat-down search. The 9 millimeter was taken from his back belt and the stiletto from his boot.

"Nice. Well done." said 'Luke'. "I've been sent to brief you on El Gallito. What's going down?"

"Nothing's going down." Hanson replied. "You're here

to do a brief. This is classified above your pay grade. We're not here, there is no 'here'. So, what does DEA have to assist us?"

"Hope you guys are better than you think you are. Knowing nothing about your business, I think this is going to be a bitch. No skin off my ass so let's get to it."

"Guatemala City is divided into 'Zonas' – with smaller numbers closer to downtown. 6th Avenue is the main drag in town. Avenues run north/south and streets east/west. Barrio El Gallito is in Zona 2. The barrio is very close to downtown. It begins exactly 7 blocks from 6th Avenue."

"I've googled and copied these maps I've got for you – no trace. Go west from 6th avenue towards the Puente del Incienso. This is a bridge that spans a large gorge that runs south by west then curving to the north. The Barrio El Gallito is located from Avenida Elena – which is really 1st Avenue – all the way to the bottom of that gorge. The housing area is *very* steep – running 30 to 40 degrees, more in places. It is a maze of extremely low income housing with narrow walkways and steps."

"The area that does not lie parallel to Avenida Elena and is closest to the gorge is where the drug boys hang out. That is *their* territory and no one – and I mean no one – goes in there without their knowledge and approval! The Army and Police have elements stationed on all the corners of the streets and avenues that define the perimeter of the drug Lords' territory but they do not enter. All the streets and avenues have been blocked off with huge concrete highway dividers so there is only one way in and out for all kinds of vehicles – including motor bikes."

"The drug guys have little kids – boys and girls – with cell phones on the *outside* of the perimeter calling in any traffic entering – wheels or feet. Their eyes are everywhere. Nobody knows an area like kids."

"Most of the players are young – fourteen to twenty. All

are armed – pistols to AKs, both 47s and 74s. Lots of other stuff, too. Many, if not most, are users. They are going through their induction into the underworld – hell, they're already there but the better ones are being selected for future heavier lifting. There are elements about it of a training ground and selection. All of these kids come from broken homes – or no homes at all – steeped in drugs. They are definitely abused kids whose future is yesterday! The only cure for them is to be dead. For them there is money to be made and they have nothing, absolutely nothing, to lose. Hope, for them, has never existed."

"The eyes are there twenty-four seven. I can't believe Al Quaida or the Taliban had anything like this but you all would know better about that. Probably did and its old hat to you. Just repeating this scares the hell out of me thinking you guys are going in there."

"Talking to myself, I'd say I'd look at entering and leaving through the gorge itself if I were going to do such an insane thing. And if I did I'd also look for trip wires and triggers for IEDs (Improvised Explosive Devices). Fewer eyes so more warning devices. The nearly vertical gorge walls provide the defense."

"Know any good restaurants in there? Guy might get hungry." Hanson murmured seriously.

"You gotta be shittin' me. Restaurant? No way. Wait. There is a restaurant club – owned by a complete piece of shit. We've got a four inch thick file on him. Name's Manny Bonano. Love to chat with him – in *our* house of course. It's a hang out for middle jefes – bosses – and a few of the really senior guys."

"Know where it is? On the map?" Hanson asked.

"Sure. Here, give me a map from the file and I'll mark it. You guys must really be hungry!" 'Luke' carefully twisted the map around some, thought for a few moments then placed an X midblock on the west side of a 'street'.

Hanson asked "If no one goes in there how does DEA know this stuff?"

"The air is ours. Our cameras have a long reach. Also, we've 'observed' some interrogations by the Guatemalan Army narco guys. They're pretty thorough about things we want to know. Seems the subjects never go back to inform of our interests. Whatever you're up to – you go in, don't be gentle because they're kids – they're deadly. Take 'em out – it'll improve planet earth *and* help your chances of getting out. Don't hesitate! Anything else?"

"Nope. Thanks for the information. You've been a big help. Take care of yourself."

"Adios – and good luck. You'll need it. Here's a number. If you need anything, ask for me. I'm your assigned contact." 'Luke' picked up his weapons and disappeared out the door. Hanson did a quick check of the hallway, both ways, and said "Do a bug scan on the file folder. Don't really trust the DEA guys – they live in a different world and might want to ride our coattails. I'll bet they seriously want to know what we're up to and our area of interest will give them some thoughts. Might try to steal our guy. Never know. Best to dispose of the folder just for drill. Deke, you want to take it from here?"

"Okay, guys. Looks like we need to reconnoiter that gorge and this Rio Chinautla, it's called. Garcia and Munoz dress down – time to go native. Shop today, go tomorrow. We need everything about that gorge. Think 'Luke' is right. Had already come to that idea. Reliance on barriers over time usually causes sloppy surveillance. Approaches first. Van location. The usual stuff. When that's all laid out – go in part way in daylight. Just a couple of derelicts. The rest of the way will be at night. Thought it kind of funny – him warning *us* about IEDs! Note any and mark but don't neutralize – we'll do that on our way in. We've got lots of study to do on the maps. We need to know that rat's nest like the back of our hands. Let's go to work, gents."

"Fellas, I've got a dinner arranged for twenty one hundred. Go up the stairs off the lobby. You'll see the private dining room. If you come to the beautiful little two - person dining room – that's for lovebirds – turn around. Our room is behind you. You won't believe the food here. Fantastic! I've taken the liberty of ordering our appetizers. One is prawns done in a butter, banana and brandy sauce that is to die for. The wine list is superb. They've got a Guatemalan rum that is eighty years old – not to miss after dinner." Mitchell said.

Stratton said "Remember when I said you couldn't go in with us? That you'd endanger us? This is what I was talking about. You've had too many of this kind of thing. You'll ruin my guys!"

"No, no. This is energy food. This isn't a luxury. Trust me. This sort of food is absolutely necessary. Otherwise, why would they have it? Guys, don't let the Colonel mislead you. You'll love it. In fact, I'm offering up the good Colonel's share to anyone who wants it. I'll call down for some MREs for him. Where's the phone?" Mitchell said with a smile.

Stratton said "Put your hands down, guys. I've had enough MREs to know I never want to see one again. I'll just suffer with the same chow as my men. It's a leadership thing. Duty and all that. Eighty year old rum, you say? Ahh, well, let's get to work."

"Skipping ahead, where you thinking we will talk with this clown? Bring him out or talk there? If we're bringing him out – which I think you should do – we've got to talk with a Company guy. Need a place."

Stratton looked at him then said "Let's make a call. For now, I think we have no time there. Let's see how our thinking goes. Can always cancel the safe house."

"Right."

"Bo, talk to your guy. Where can we get two seven or eight foot poles and some black canvass? About twelve or fifteen feet by six or eight. Some black plastic would be nice. Need a sail needle and line, also. Want to make a sling if we're bringing him out."

"Right." Hanson said as he whipped open his cell phone and drifted away. The pick up was immediate. After listing Stratton's request, he paused, listening, then said "Great. You've got another key to the van? Put the stuff in the van. Safe place location and key on the seat. GPS device? To-night? Good. Thanks. Be talkin' with ya." He turned and gave Stratton a thumbs up.

The team studied the maps. With pencil points they traveled every convoluted way. They discussed the merits and demerits of each possible route. The aerial photos gave them some feel of the vertical heights of buildings along the routes but only a feel. The narrowness of many of the routes was actually of some benefit. Any shooter from above would have to lean out exposed and shoot down – a diffi-cult shot to do with any accuracy. They mapped out several routes. The final decision would be made once the nature of the ravine was more known. The relief maps gave them several possible entry points. Garcia and Munoz would ex-plore each tomorrow.

They identified the building that 'Luke' had marked on the map. Each of the potential routes led there, splitting six buildings away one direction and five the other, to the front and rear. The building appeared to be three story, the adja-cent ones two story. In the photos there were two men in the back passageway and two more at the front in the tiny 'street'. One, in the street, clearly carried what appeared to be an MP5 or Uzi – short-barrel on a sling. It was assumed that this was a twenty-four seven practice of security for jefes. With those guards there it looked like 'Luke's'intel was on the money. Hanson sat with the team, observing. Mitchell sat apart, a horizon gaze focused out the window.

The team finished their work about a quarter to nine. They stood and stretched. Hanson went over to Mitchell who was still locked on the Horizon.

"Hey, Mitch! Come. Time for a drink. Hey, Mitch!"

Mitchell jerked, startled as he returned mentally to the room. He shook his head a couple of times to clear it. "Sorry about that. I was lost in thought."

"What are you chewin' on, fast mover?" Hanson asked.

"The strangeness of this whole thing. Of course, we need to get some answers from this guy but I don't think this is ground zero for the snatch. I think it's closer to home."

"What's new that's leading you there? I know you've thought that for some time but you seem more convinced." Stratton asked.

"The pictures are not from here. They weren't taken in Guatemala. Look at the clothes near the faces. Then, money. Besides the obvious stuff, they took Karen Smith and not the other assistants."

"So what?" Stratton asked. "She's one of the dentists, or dental assistant in her case."

"Yes, that's true. But her husband is Myron Smith – and he is the CEO of Berchel Construction, the third largest construction company in the U.S. Now, who in the hell in Guatemala would know that?"

Hanson and Stratton looked at him for a long while. Then Hanson said "I'll be damned! Let's go to dinner. My beauty belly needs reinforcement while I think about that!"

Stratton just nodded pensively.

CHAPTER 26

Meson Panza Verde Hotel
Antigua, Guatemala
0800 hours local: Day 6

"We're moving to the Hilton in Guatemala City. The day is open. Garcia and Munoz left at oh six hundred. They've got the van and they know about the Hilton. When they return to the Hilton we'll finalize our plans. Take it easy, relax. We'll be busy later. We won't be returning here so pack up. At fourteen hundred hours we'll meet for a refresh on routes. That's all I have. Let's go."

Mitchell beckoned with his head. Stratton, Hanson and Mitchell strolled out of the suite where room service had set up their breakfast. Once in the street, Mitchell said "Good to stretch our legs. Bo, I think we might want to have the Gulfstream positioned here in CG. If your guy says okay he should come in tonight. Otherwise we need to give Jake a heads up to be here to haul us to Belize. That might be better. He can get in and out of here easy. He'd be working with his own people. Let's have Jake come in tonight if he can. My guess is we'd want to leave sometime before dawn. Deke?"

Stratton said "No, I think we return to the Hilton after the mission. We don't know how long any of this will take. It's possible some medical care may get involved. I say we rendezvous at the Hilton, clean up, rest and schedule out, say, at ten or eleven. I like going out with Jake and meeting Ford in Belize."

"Works for me. Your call." Mitchell said. "Bo, can you make that happen?"

"On it."

"Our bus is here."

CHAPTER 27

Hilton Hotel
Guatemala City, Guatemala
1100 hours local: Day 6

"Why'd we go to Antigua, Mitch?" James asked.

"Knew we'd need time to organize so it might as well be in a superb place. Thought you all would like the experience. I love the place – and the food. The Hilton is – well, the Hilton. Now that we're operational this is better. Besides, Antigua is a better meet place for Luke and others. Fewer eyes, farther from the battle ground. And *we* have no contact with anyone here who may be followed."

"Makes sense." James said. "Thanks for sharing that place with us. I liked it."

"Fourteen hundred, my room." Stratton said.

* * * * *

Hilton Hotel
Guatemala City
1700 hours local: Day 6

A light tap on Stratton's door brought everyone to alert and positions were assumed. Opening the door, they saw Garcia and Munoz standing there, cuts and scratches all over their hands and faces. Stratton said "In, quick. Let's take a look at those. James, the med kit. In the bathroom, you guys."

"It's nothing ,Boss. They'll clean up easy. Just scratches from the damn brush. Ran into a bunch of Chollo cactus. We found a better way in than the ones we laid out – don't worry, you won't look like this. Talk with you in a minute, after we clean up."

Stratton said "You guys been drinking? Smell like hell."

Garcia said "Thought a derelict should smell like one. Wasted some Tequila on our clothes in case we ran into anyone. Didn't."

Each showered. James did his best on the deeper cuts and used a styptic stick on the shallow ones. A few bandaids were necessary. Cleaned up, they reentered the room.

Garcia said "Damned good idea to do reconnaissance in the daytime. As usual, up close is a lot different than the aerials. The escarpment in there is a real bitch. A real bitch. So bad they take it for granted no one will approach that way. There are two easier ways up and those are blocked. Saw a couple of kids near each one at the top. Even then one kid was asleep in the middle of the day. Great lookout but I understand. Even making it up the gully is a deterrent."

Munoz continued "We found three possibles. Each comes out near at least one of our sketched out routes. The best one didn't look so good at the start. We cut some hand and foot holes in the wall up about fifteen feet or so then it was relatively easy the rest of the way. The buildings are right up to the edge. They have no windows toward the ravine. The wind blows right up the face carrying stuff. The other two are fairly easy at the beginning but get tough at the top. On those the last twenty feet or so we had to go up like in a chimney. Doable. One comes out right on one of our routes. The other we'd have to slide along a building a ways. I'm thinking the first one I mentioned."

Garcia had the maps spread and was making arrows on it. "Here's number one, here's two and here's the one with the building at the end. Because we had to dig holes in the face of that first one, I think the folks up there think it's impassable. Actually, I'll bet they think all three are impassable. Bottom line? We can get in."

Stratton asked "Find a place for the van in the gorge?"

"No, but about a half mile down there's an area we can put it. The climb up to it is gradual and there's a trail. Found a hole in the brush to put it. Already cut brush to cover it. It'll wash. Up a ways there's an area you guys can wait. We'll join up and lead the way. GPS works. Checked it out." Munoz said.

"What's our enroute time? Want to hit this guy about 0300." Stratton asked.

Garcia said "We're about thirty minutes to the north end of town from here. Traffic should be light. From park place to the rim is about one hour. Figure fifteen minutes in – it's only three streets up. So, about an hour forty five if all goes well. Figure two."

Stratton said "Okay, let's do the tight planning but for now it looks like 0100 departure." Looking at Garcia and Munoz, he said "Anything else? Needs?"

Munoz said "We'll want rope to lower the guy down the face. Everything else we've planned is good to go."

"Okay. Jimmy, Scotty, Bob – you've got the back. Frank and Javier will be with me in the front. We're going in hot, no quarter with these assholes. Think ol' 'Luke' knows what he's talking about. Afghan rules. Jimmy, coming in the back there should be a crapper back there. Clear it. Any other door, clear it. There must be stairs up. Scotty, you've got those. Bob – cover the room. We'll clear the kitchen after we secure the room. We'll spread as we come in, same old, same old. There'll be folks there, I'm sure. When we come in, Javier you yell 'Manny'. Everyone look for a head jerk. Otherwise we look for short and fat. We'll put him down and hit him with a syringe. Cuff and tape him. Into the sling and out the front. Scotty, James, - you're carrying. Get the canvass sewn for the poles."

"Already done, Deke. Did it today." Garcia said.

"Okay. Any questions?"

There were none.

"Let's rest up. Going to be a long night. Put the do not disturb signs on your doors. Leave all unnecessary gear in rooms packed up. Wear the clothes you're going to wear to the airport. Change in the van."

"I've got us a small dining room for six o'clock. Anyone hungry? It's not like last night but it'll do. It's about that time. Sorry – they are all out of drinks." Mitchell said.

Garcia said "Man, I'm starved. A little food and a nap sounds good."

Munoz said "Me too."

CHAPTER 28

Rio Chinautla
Guatemala City, Guatemala
0030 hours local: Day 7

Separately each man made his way out of the hotel and to the van. Mitchell and Hanson together went to their rental full-sized car. Jimmy Munoz changed first. He would be driving. Javier Garcia changed next. He would be in the passenger seat. The others boarded and changed enroute. As the van pulled out, Mitchell dropped into a trail position. The caravan moved north across the city.

All men who have faced combat understand that time is elastic. It expands or contracts according to situation and need. An hour can seem a minute. A minute can seem an hour. At critical moments everything can shift to slow motion, creating a surreal perspective upon reality within which one has time to think and act. Maybe adrenalin's affect upon the brain has something to do with time perception – when shifts occur adrenalin seems to be present. As the van proceeded, the team's bodies began manufacturing small amounts of the stuff – not enough to become hyper but enough to heighten all the senses. Rookies get the jitters. Old hands get calm and focused.

The equipment had been arranged in order of need, everything in its assigned place on their bodies or in bags. No hunting or fumbling was wise in time of need. As the end of the pavement appeared two light taps on the brakes signaled Mitchell to break off. He spun a U turn then backed into a wide spot to the side of the dirt road just after the pavement ended. The van continued down the dirt road incline. Its lights were off. The night goggles gave Munoz all the vision he needed. At the assigned spot the men exited. Garcia pointed at the brush pile. It was swiftly pulled aside. Munoz backed the van in, nose pointed out and up in case a rapid departure was needed. Almost as swiftly the van was hidden with the brush. The men arranged themselves with Munoz and Garcia in the lead. Single file, they were off.

Mitchell and Hanson waited in their car. Fondling a Sig Sauer 229, Mitchell said "Now the hard part starts. Waiting."

Hanson opined "Guess it's not unlike slipping into a Taliban camp and stealing the commander. Wouldn't know, though. Never done such a thing. Don't think I'd want to do such a thing. Probably be scared out of my mind."

"You know, these guys are truly remarkable. I think I'd be like you but these guys, these guys seem on the outside like they're going to the market to get groceries!" Mitchell said.

"You know Mitch, it's what you're trained for and experienced in. Our stuff, back in the day, had everyone oooing and aaaing about the danger but we didn't think it was so much. Usually just another day at the office. I sure as hell wasn't scared or even nervous when it was time to mount up. Actually I was kind of exhilarated."

"Know what you mean. Same here. Time to play ball. Surf's up. Which bull did I draw? It was, and is, something else. The non-players don't understand. Even today most folks think carrier landings are fearsome. If you try to tell them that in an emergency, given the choice between a carrier or a field, experienced Navy pilots would choose the boat – they think you're kidding or lying. They don't understand that that is what you're trained for and that is within your comfort zone. These guys are us thirty years ago. And, god damn it, we *were* something. He laughed. "Bo, you remember the 23rd Psalm?"

"I know the answer to this question. No, I don't. Is this a trick question? Okay, tell me."

"Yea though I walk through the valley of the shadow of death I will fear no evil because I'm the meanest son-of-a-bitch in the valley. That's what these guys think."

Laughing, Bo said "And they're probably right. Thought I heard it a little different from you one time. Something like 'Yea though I fly through the valley of the shadow of death I will fear no evil because I'm passing thirty thousand feet and climbing'. Think I'll get in the back. Already removed the light bulb. Together up here too easy a target on both. Besides, folks could start talking if we're seen parked together in the bush at night."

"Wouldn't want that."

They both went silent, lost in their own thoughts.

* * * * *

The team moved silently up the gorge.

Broderick whispered "Feelin' nothing, Boss."

Stratton quietly said "Same." He knew what Broderick meant. Often, in the past, in the early stage of a mission he had sixth-sensed an intimation, or a warning premonition, of danger. Usually he had been right. Tonight he felt nothing. He sensed no threat. Felt no warning. If you get the 'feeling' and go against it you're probably making a big mistake. Probably – but sometimes you've got to go any-way. 'Not liking it' doesn't mean you can abort the mission. There are situations where one can abort but not for a 'not liking it' feeling. Had to be stronger than that. Guess that's what judgment is all about.

Munoz and Garcia had cut away some brush in dense areas earlier to open a slight path – not much but enough. Their cuts and scrapes had not been in vain. The passage to the base of the escarpment was swift. Using the cut out hand and boot holes previously made, they passed their gear up hand to hand. Once all were up, they laid out one rope to lower their prisoner later. No need to carry it in and out.

They paused and carefully scanned the unlit narrow pas-sageway called a street and the faces and tops of buildings along the way. Nothing. It appeared that the 'fortress men-tality' was at work. Inside the fortress one was safe. No need for vigilance. No one had ever come in so no one ever would or could. They could barely hear music some distance away. Up ahead they saw flickering light in several upper floor windows – televisions. No other signs of life. A light rain began to fall. It was welcomed.

Again single file but alternating on the sides of the pas-sageway, they moved to their split point. They had seen no one. With a swirl of his finger over his head, Stratton led his two men to the right, Munoz and his two went left. Strat-ton paused a short count to give Munoz a little time. His distance was a little further. Then he moved.

The two guards were leaning up against the wall, side by side two feet apart, half asleep from boredom. Stratton walked past the first guard to the second. The first guard, giving Stratton a startled look, started to say something as Frank slit his throat below his now turned head. Stratton, from in front, put the point of his knife up under the chin of the second guard deep at an angle into the brain stem. They were grabbed and slid to the ground soundlessly. Looking up they saw the sign over the door – 'Restaurante El Diablo'. Then they were in. In a blink they saw Munoz entering the back down a long hall.

The room was quite large, perhaps fifty by sixty feet. There were various tables and chairs arranged haphazardly around. There was a bar to the left that looked as if it had been installed into a cutout into the next building. And there was one large table occupied by six men playing cards. There was a seventh chair, empty.

Garcia yelled "Manny." All the heads turned but one turned harder. He was fat. The dark eyes flared anger at the interruption.

Stratton said "Him."

Irritation at interruption changed to defensive aggression in a nano second. Unfortunately for them their hands were all on the table. The man at the far end pulled his right hand off the table and reached down. A silent round through his head stopped that idea. At the same moment another made the same move with the same result.

Garcia said "Tranquillo, amigos, tranquillo."

Another started to make a move. Broderick changed his mind with one shot to the heart and another to the head.

Munoz said "He *said* tranquillo!" He then moved to Bonano saying "Esta Manny Bonano?"

A shocked and confused voice said "Si."

Munoz immediately hit him with a syringe, then a second because of his weight. Duct tape was slapped on his mouth. Hands grabbed each of his arms and he was stood up. He was patted down, relieved of his weapon and laid face down on the floor. His wrists and ankles were flex-tied. Munoz picked up the laptop off the table. The other two men sat with hands raised, one glancing down the hallway.

Deep fear and confusion registered on their faces. They were dead and they knew it.

Bob Gray had checked both toilets. Coming out of the second one he held up one finger then slashed it across his throat. There were stairs climbing beyond a door on his left. He was quickly up the stairs. Moments later he was back. Into the com mike he said "Door locked. TV on. I'll watch."

Stratton nodded. All seven chairs accounted for.

When they finished with Bonano, each of the other two men were handled in turn - taped, flex-tied and syringed. The three shot men were checked for life. Even thirty-eights have been known to ricochet around a skull. Subsonic twenty-twos didn't pack anywhere near that force. All were gone. Bonano's eyes had started to glaze from the strong dosage. Munoz and Broderick raced to the back and pulled the bodies inside. James and Gray did the same for the front. Gray returned to the stairs, watching.

When Munoz and Broderick returned they spread the canvass on the floor. They laid out the black plastic, set Bonano on it, taped the edge to him and rolled him up like a burrito. They centered him on the canvass.

Stratton looked at the eyes of the remaining two men. He then nodded toward the front door. Broderick and James lifted the poles holding the canvass and Bonano, placing one pole end on each shoulder. They connected each Velcro strap between the poles. The poles would stay on their shoulders while their hands were free.

Garcia was out the door. The way was clear. The others followed. Gray brought up the rear. The elapsed time inside was less than six minutes.

They moved single file down the passageway, Garcia some distance ahead. Stratton looked back then ahead. Standing directly in front of him was a boy with a pistol pointed at him. The boy appeared to be not more than eight or nine years old. With a gun, for Christ's sake! The boy began to speak when Garcia, who had come back up behind him, hit him on the side of the head with the butt end of his knife. The kid went down, out cold, or so they hoped. He was definitely down. Garcia had not been gentle – as 'Luke' had advised. They moved on at a rapid pace. The rest of the extraction was uneventful. All went according to plan.

At the edge of the cliff a rope yoke tie was formed around the ends of the poles. The package was lowered to the base, rope tie removed and the single file formation resumed for the trek out, Broderick and James in the middle.

Mitchell and Hanson were each squirming in their seats. Twice they had each exited to pee. Hanson had walked around and around the car until Mitchell had growled at him. The waiting was driving them nuts! Finally both were out of the car. Mitchell said "To hell with it. I've got to have a cigarette. I'm going to have a heart attack if I don't. I can't stand this waiting shit. No wonder the Captain was a grouch, waiting for his boys to return." He lit up.

He took one deep, satisfying drag when a hand grabbed his shoulder from behind and a voice said "That shit will kill you and on a mission will kill you even faster."

Mitchell spun around saying "Deke, you son-of a-bitch. 'Bout crapped my pants. You guys okay?"

"We got 'im. Let's go. Guys 'll be up here in a second."

Hanson put a bear hug on Stratton then said "Thank God," as they entered the car. Mitchell cranked up and pulled out as the van passed.

CHAPTER 29

Zona 9
Guatemala City, Guatemala
0345 hours local: Day 7

Jimmy Munoz drove the crunched, rusted, bedraggled old van through the streets of the city, not too fast nor too slow, guided by Garcia, his face lit by the glowing GPS unit. Threading their way through the convoluted, circuitous streets, Garcia thanked God for GPS technology. Without a 'local' they'd have been long lost. The CIA-provided empty warehouse lay in a light industrial area in Zona 9 not too far from La Aurora Airport. Convenient for transport purposes but not so close to be more upscale and more modern. It was just one of a thousand ramshackle, worn, innocuous buildings jammed together with no apparent plan in mind. It was perfect for its purpose.

In the back, Bonano lay supine, cuffed and shackled with black flex-ties, a strip of black duct tape covering his mouth. Gray sat watching James monitoring Bonano for any signs of awakening or breathing discomfort. He showed neither.

At enough distance to not appear together, Stratton, Broderick, Hanson and Mitchell followed along. Their rental car had air conditioning but they had turned it off. Its noise was thought-disturbing. They simply had all four windows down. The light breeze coming in was a comfort. Eventually from the back seat, Mitchell broke the quiet saying "A change. Think I'll take this one from the top. Plenty of time for other persuasions. I'll get to him. My name will be El Senor – just that. I'll take a coffee break – take that thermos along. Slip and call me 'General" about then. One of you will be 'corporal'. Sorry about the demotion, guys. Guess life's not fair – and after such a good job! Time to put psyche-ops to work. Hope to get more detail than one usually gets with fear or pain."

The van slowed, gave two taps on the brake and turned left onto an even smaller street lined on both sides with warehouses. The double-tap brake lights caused Stratton to close up. They were there. Both vehicles pulled into an indented truck entry. Broderick immediately exited and went to the padlocked personnel door alongside. The key did not release the lock.

"Garcia. This the right place? The key doesn't work." called Broderick.

"Says it is. The CIA guy plugged it into the GPS, said it would take us here. Shit."

Stratton said "Try the other locks around this building. Might be off a slot or two." Broderick took off, using his mini-light.

Gray slipped out of the van and went to the padlock. He inspected it briefly and returned to the van. He said to James "Give me your pliers." Reaching into his kit, Gray extracted a large paper clip. James handed him his pliers. Gray quickly straightened the clip. Using the pliers, a short distance from one end he bent the clip up at a forty-five degree angle. He bent that piece down at a ninety degree angle. That piece he then bent at another forty-five degree angle. The paper clip now looked as if had an upside down V on its end. Out of his belt Gray slid out a narrow, flexible metal strip. Returning to the padlock, Gray slipped the metal strip into the keyway. Measuring with his thumb, he withdrew the strip and, using the pliers, bent it to about one hundred degrees or a little more.

Holding the padlock in his right hand, he inserted the metal strip into the lock with the longer part below the beef of his hand. By pressing down with his hand he put a modest amount of torque pressure on the barrel of the lock. With his left hand he inserted the paper clip with the V up. He rapidly raked the clip back and forth inside the lock. Pop! The lock opened. "We're in." stated Gray semi-quietly.

Nobody made a comment. Actually, any of them could have done it. Probably best not to go through airports with the metal strip in the belt, though.

Gray said "Let's go. I'll get the bay door."

Munoz said "We don't know if it's the right place."

Gray responded "Who cares? It'll do. We'll be gone soon. Let's get it over with."

Stratton said "Man's got a point. Make it happen." A sharp whistle brought Broderick back fast. "We'll work here."

Amazingly, the bay door rolled up quietly! It was well lubricated and well used. Probably the only one in Guatemala that worked like that. Inside was a vacant storage area, a table and some chairs off to the side showing in the headlights. Both vehicles entered. Gray closed the door. When fully closed he hit the light switch. The area was well lit. "Looks like what the CIA guy described." Gray said.

James yelled that he had movement and eye flexing.

Stratton ordered "Cover." And all donned their balaclavas. A chair was brought to the center area. Several men extracted Bonano from the van, sat him in the chair, cut the flex-ties around his ankles and re-tied each ankle to a leg of the chair. The wrist cuffs were then cut and each wrist was re-cuffed to its side of the chair.

Enroute, approaching the warehouse, James had given Bonano an injection to neutralize the sedative and help him come back. Shortly after being placed in the chair Bonano opened his eyes. They were glazed and uncomprehending. Slowly his head turned, taking in the black clad, balaclava-covered men surrounding him. Lateral awareness came back slowly, his legs tried to flex, his arms pulled, all registering upon his mind that they were secured. He looked down and side to side then back up. Anger was beginning to rise. He could say nothing – the duct tape was still over his mouth. He began making various animal noises, the veins and tendons on his neck standing out. However, a change was taking place. Fear was starting to show its presence, supplanting the anger as his mind began to register its predicament.

Still not a word was said. Slowly, Mitchell brought another chair over and set it eight feet in front of Bonano. Mitchell looked at Frank James and pointed at the floor beside the chair. James quickly moved to stand there at parade rest. Mitchell did not sit. He slowly paced back and forth in front of Bonano, looking at him the whole time. He allowed the fear and confusion elements to grow.

Finally, he stopped in front. In a soft, calm, authoritative voice he spoke, in Spanish, "Buenas dias, Senor Bonano. Est muy temprano. Pueda llamarme El Senor. Ahora, yo sé que usted habla anglais. Tan, I will continue in English. I know about you. In fact, I know quite a bit about you. Escuchame! I'm sorry, listen to me. You should really calm down. For awhile I want you to listen. It would be best for you if you do and think about what I am saying."

"You should be happy that we have covered our faces. It

should occur to you that we don't want you to see our faces because we don't intend to kill you. That doesn't mean that we won't. Accidents do happen. But, we don't intend to. Senor Bonano, I think you are a very intelligent man. One doesn't survive in your business long if one is stupid. One doesn't become a jefe or cacique or boss if one is stupid. One doesn't own a restaurant in the middle of the most dangerous neighborhood in the most dangerous city in Central America if one is stupid. Yes, I think you are a most intelligent man."

"Now, those people you had kidnapped are friends of ours. You hurt them. You hurt their families. You hurt me."

At that moment Munoz, who had been studying through Bonano's laptop, raised a hand. Mitchell went behind Bonano to where Munoz stood and read the e-mail on the screen. Munoz held up a finger to wait. He pulled up another e-mail time-dated 0211 local. It read "Make them disappear. Rescue team coming now. Money paid."

Mitchell nodded and sauntered back to Bonano. "Where was I? Oh, yes, you know what? I think that you weren't going to release them at all. I think that you never covered their eyes or hid from them where they were being taken. Your cousin, Felipe, was unconcerned. Yes, we've had a chat with Felipe. He was most cooperative as you can see by our presence. They were never going to be able to lead anyone there or identify anyone were they? Why? Because they would be dead."

"Senor Bonano, I think you are a very bad man, a man who deserves to die very, very slowly. I think you have killed many people even if I don't count the many your drugs have killed. Well, Senor Bonano, you are not alone. Every man in this room has killed many people. That's true, everyone in this room. But – we are not brothers. You see, you kill anyone, good or bad. It doesn't matter to you and it doesn't bother you. We kill bad people like you, people who have earned the privilege of dying by our hands. Ugly people in their morals, evil people God should have aborted, people like you who are animals, not humans. But, when necessary, we have killed innocents."

"Senor Bonano, now you should start becoming very afraid. You see, I said we didn't intend to kill you. I said nothing about your wife and your two small children. I said nothing about your son in private school in Phoenix, did I? Your wife would be a shame. Your children? We could justify it by wiping out your genetic line for the betterment of the planet."

"But you are a lucky man. A very lucky man – yes, very lucky. You have something I want. You have information that I think will let you off the hook, save the lives of your family. Senor Bonano, I'm sure in your career you've had occasion to seriously question people who didn't want to answer you? Nod your head. Okay. Did any one of them ever not answer eventually? Good. That's the same for me. I've never had even one not answer my questions in the end. Not one! Think on that."

"I have questions that I want to have answered fully and detailed. That's all. You give me those and, as a man of honor – which you may not understand – I will not kill you or your family. In fact, I'll add more. You give me that and you will leave here in the same condition you entered. Don't be enticed by the false pleasure of evasion. It won't last. I want you to tell me pleasant news, pleasant so I won't have to hurt anyone. I have experienced an ocean of untruth so I know it well. You don't want to test that."

"I've talked enough for the moment. It is time for you to talk. You take a little time to think while I take a cup of coffee." Mitchell turned and said "Corporal, a cup of Guatemala's finest, please. Did you all know that Guatemala coffee is considered among the finest in the world?"

"Certainly, General."

"El Senor." Mitchell corrected.

"Yes, Sir."

Mitchell wandered over to the table where the cup sat steaming. He picked it up with his right hand and a hammer with his left, looking at it with contemplation as he stood in profile to Bonano. He took a sip of coffee and replaced the hammer. He picked up the pliers and looked carefully at those too, turning them side to side. He replaced those also. Another sip of coffee was followed by a look of curiosity. He reached forward and picked up a syringe, rolling it between his fingers at eye level. He laid it down, took another drink of coffee and laid down the cup. Bonano had watched every move as was intended he do.

Mitchell returned to Bonano and said "You know what those tools are for. The syringe is another problem – the tool of last resort. Most of the so-called truth serums aren't all that good. People say all kinds of nonsense when on them – a lot of it no good, fantasy, make believe, goofy stuff. Certainly not good detail. I want detail. Accurate, usable detail. This serum, however, is high-tech military 'liquado de verdad' that works marvelously and the subject is lucid, answers clearly and in detail. Unfortunately, the side effects are terrible, eventually irreversibly damaging the brain. A shame. Well, so much for that. I trust you've had enough time to think."

With that he gestured towards Bonano with a sideways flick of his hand. James ripped the duct tape off Bonano's mouth. His head twisted down and away, a grimace of pain flashing across his face. Then he raised his head, looked at Mitchell and said "General, do you really think you could get to my family? El Gallito is now warned and waiting."

"It is El Senor. There is no General here, wherever here is. I make the point that we got to you when the wisdom was we couldn't. You believed no one could get to you. Trust me, we can get to anyone we choose. We certainly can get to Phoenix."

"You can't find bin Laden."

"*WE* are not looking for bin Laden. That is the U.S. military and they are not us. But now that you mention it – they did find bin Laden and couldn't get clearance from the politicians in time to take him. We have different methods and rules. We don't ask. We make our own rules. Here you sit and I offer that as proof. There are dead men that I offer as proof. The U.S. military would not have done what we did. And they never do what I am prepared to do to get my answers. Does that ring true to you?"

"It does, Senor. I will take your deal. It seems I have no choices here."

"Good. That is an excellent and intelligent decision. First – who set up this kidnapping? It wasn't you. That we know. You had no way to get those pictures or any reason to pick and choose as you did. So – who?"

"His name is Ricardo. I do not know his last name. He lives somewhere in the United States. He came to me more than a year ago with the proposal. I could earn half a million dollars. Then, about ten weeks ago he said it was on."

"No last name and he came to you – a man of importance – and offered a deal? Senor Bonano, you don't want to hand me this as an answer."

"No, I'm serious. We were friends as little boys. My mother was Maya. She came with my father to La Ciudad, to the university. My father wanted education, to become ladino – not Maya. He became political. My mother got a job at the U.S. Embassy as a housekeeper. She was pregnant with me when the Army death squad decided that my father had too loud a voice. After I was born another housekeeper, a special live-in housekeeper, got the Embassy to make my mother a live-in housekeeper. The special housekeeper also had a small son like me. My mother and his mother were very close. Her name was Tia Sophia. We were the only live-ins. His name is Ricardo, mine is Pablo but I changed mine later."

"Why did you choose Bonano which means banana in English?"

"A girl once told me my thing was like a banana. I thought it was funny. I took that name. Others have said the same thing. Besides, it sounds like that American Mafia guy so I liked it."

"Too much information. Back to Ricardo."

"We grew up together. We attended the American school for Embassy kids and some others. The other kids lived not at the embassy but the school was nearby. We had to take English and Spanish classes – right from the beginning. Most of the others came and left. Some of the older ones went to schools in the States. I was the only Maya kid. Ricardo was mestizo."

"Wait. Digame – mestizo?"

"Peninsulares are people from Spain. Creoles are Spanish people born here. Mestizo is a mix of Indigenas and Spanish. Ricardo's mother was mestizo. Ambassadors come and go but the one who was there when we moved in, I heard someone whisper he was Ricardo's father. Ricardo looked more anglo than mestizo. Anyway, we were always together until we had about ten years or so. Then one day his mother tells mine that they were going to the States. The old ambassador was going to sponsor her and Ricardo. They were so happy. My mother didn't want to be at the Embassy without her, she'd be so lonely, she wanted family. So she took me back to the puebla. I couldn't stand it there. Family is okay but my mother died. I was a city boy, I had school. I spoke three languages plus some Poqomom. I left for the City at sixteen and got into the drug side early on. The doors there were open to a Maya boy, nothing else was. My hungry belly and hands were attracted to the treasure."

"After the first ten years, Ricardo gets a hold of me, here in CG. I don't know how he found me but he did. After that, four or five times, maybe six, he'd show up here and we'd connect. I'd given him some numbers to reach me anytime. He'd call, we'd meet. Not in El Gallito. He never gave me a way to reach him in the U.S. I asked a couple of times. The last time he gave me an e-mail address to use for this project. He gave me the laptop. That is how we connected."

"Did you pick the Global Internet Café as your contact point? It is fairly close to El Gallito."

"How the hell do you know that? Never mind. Yes I did."

"Where did he live when he went to the United States? Where did he go to school?"

"At first I think San Diego, then Los Angeles. He's mentioned both. He never said but I know some university in California."

"What does he look like? Describe him."

"He is about five feet eleven, much taller than me. Remember what I said about only a quarter Maya? His skin is light brown like a tan on an anglo. His hair is blackish brown and his eyes are black. He is a very confident looking man. He stands tall and dresses like money is no problem. He speaks without accent, English with no Spanish accent and Spanish with no English."

"Any tattoos?"

"No. None I could see."

"Hair – long or short?"

"Sort of short."

"The ransom has been paid as you know. Fortunately for you we arrived before you finished it – as you were instructed. Who made the decision to kill the hostages and when and why?"

"Dios, is there anything you don't know? Fortunate for you as well. I was busy on my stuff and didn't expect anything coming down then. Didn't get the message until three yesterday morning. Couldn't get Felipe to come up. Killing the hostages was part of Ricardo's plan from the start. Too risky to turn them loose. Take the money and take no chances that one of them could have seen or heard something."

"So you didn't send the change in the ransom demand message?" Mitchell said.

"What change?"

"As I was saying, lucky for you. Your half million. Give me your account numbers." Mitchell said as he nodded Munoz forward. "Tell him what he needs."

Bonano did so. After a few moments of rapid key punching, Munoz looked up, nodded at Mitchell and said "Got it. There's a lot more here than the half mil. Four point three total."

"Move it all. Senor Bonano, you played for half a mil and lost. View it as a cost of doing business. As they say, 'Sometimes the bull wins'."

Bonano said "You do realize there are going to be some unhappy hombres when payments aren't made. That's an operating account."

"Senor Bonano, that would be your problem, I'm thinking."

"It's moved. There are other things in here that will take me time to work out."

"Where was it?" Mitchell asked.

"Lichtenstein." Munoz answered.

"Senor Bonano, There are more accounts than that. Please give my associate the information he needs to access those accounts. It will save him some time and you some discomfort. He will find them eventually but your help will be noted."

Bonano recited a list of places, account numbers and passwords.

When he finished Mitchell continued "Lichtenstein? Senor Bonano, that is a pretty sophisticated place for a Maya boy to be putting money. Did Ricardo set that up for you?"

"God damn Gringo! You Anglos always assume as easy as breathing that we 'Indians' – as you call us – are stupid and can't do anything without a white man telling us how. Goddamn you arrogant assholes! Hell no, he didn't set me up with it. *I* explained to *him* how to move large amounts of money around. In my business we have to move big monies around. I showed him how to use cutout servers in Uzbekistan and Tajikistan. I'm a university graduate in finance, for Christ's sake, although I didn't learn how to do anything until long after university. They don't really know how to do anything but talk. God, I hate you people for thinking the way you do. It's all of you. You know, while I'm on it, Senor or general or whoever the fuck you are, you could have just asked your questions to start with – you'd have gotten your answers. I knew the situation immediately. Anybody who could come into El Gallito and take me is not to be fucked with in any way. But no, you had to play your little psych game with the simple Indian boy. Jesus, you people make me sick. Now, you got any more questions? I've given you all I know. Kill me or let me go."

Mitchell stood frozen. He was shocked at the outburst and stunned by its accuracy. Those had been his automatic assumptions and had been the underpinnings, truthfully, of his whole approach. He couldn't believe he'd been dressed down so succinctly and so to the point. He gathered his thoughts.

"Senor Bonano, do not bare your fangs at me. I cannot forgive your actions against my friends. I do think it a shame that your intelligence could not have been focused better. The drug trade is evil but it is the users, the demanders, who are truly at fault. If it was up to me, I'd say let them have it. Laws of economics would price it so low that it wouldn't be worthwhile to produce and transport. The associated violence and social disruption would sure disappear. Look at liquor after prohibition. But it is not up to me."

"I will keep my word. You gave me what I asked. You will leave here in the same condition you arrived. Goodbye." He turned to Garcia saying "Sedate him."

Garcia came forward with another syringe, injected him and said "I wish this were the other one!" Bonano said nothing.

The chairs and table were returned to their original locations. As Bonano's eyes closed the cuffs were cut and replaced with new cuffs as before. Mitchell side-nodded towards the van. Bonano was carried to the van, his chair joining the others.

Mitchell looked at Stratton. "What do you think? A little gift to 'Luke'? A thank you? Think the guys take the van to the hotel parking lot and call Luke? Get some sleep. Jake planned for ten. Leave the hotel at eight thirty."

"Sounds like a plan." Stratton concurred.

On the way to the hotel a call was placed to 'Luke' who answered on the first ring in spite of the time. The information on the van's soon- to-be location was passed and the present inside. It was also mentioned that it would be nice if he called the CIA when the van was empty – it was their van. Luke was given a number to call.

Luke was astonished at the success of the penetration, at the capture and no friendly casualties. When he expressed the idea that perhaps it wasn't the fortress that everyone thought, he was informed that it was precisely because it was a fortress for so long that it was vulnerable. The fortress mentality was its Achilles heel. To them any risk was frontal. They simply couldn't conceive that anyone would mount that escarpment and enter their domain. No different from the French and their Maginot Line of long ago.

Another call was made to Jake the Snake. The ten hundred pickup was confirmed.

Jake commented that this was the best phone call he'd received in a long time. He'd be happily and thankfully airborne in thirty minutes on his way to La Aurora Airport.

CHAPTER 30

Hilton Hotel
Zona 10
Ciudad Guatemala
0400 hours local: Day 7

The team had changed clothes in the van. This time they had to enter together through the one night door opened by security. The night watchman eyed them nervously. After depositing their gear in their rooms they gathered in Stratton's quarters.

"Gents," Stratton said "Quite a night. We've got four hours till we leave for the airport. A little sleep might be nice but we've got a lot of air time to catch up on that. By coincidence I have here a bottle of Cardinal Mendoza brandy from Spain and eight glasses. Anyone care to join me?"

Bob Gray said "Colonel, I'd like to say what a pleasure to work with you again. Two operations that go according to plan! Unbelievable! Except for that cluster-fuck in 'ganistan, you seem to walk on water. Everybody loves working with you."

There were mumblings of "Roger that!", "Here, here." and "Damn straight."

The brandy was poured. Mitchell spoke up "I have a series of profound toasts I'd like to make. First – here's to the Deke."

Everyone clinked to that saying "Here, here."

"Second, here's to Jimmy Munoz." Clink.

"Third, here's to Scott Broderick." Clink

"Fourth, here's to Javier Garcia." Clink

"Fifth, here's to Frank James." Clink

"And sixth, here's to Bob Gray." Clink.

"Gentlemen from the bottom of my heart – thank you. There are nine other people and their families who also thank you from the bottom of their hearts. To quote an Admiral of long ago who said as he launched young pilots on a mission from which many would not return – where do we get such men? You are 'such men'. One warrior to another – you have my deepest respect. It has been an honor to be associated with you. And again, thank you."

Hanson said "It has truly been such an honor to have served with you in a tiny way on this mission. It is an even greater honor to know you. I, too, thank you."

The six tipped their heads and raised their glasses to the two old warriors in acknowledgement of the sentiments. Nothing needed to be said. A silent wind-down period, a shift to non-combat, a burn of adrenalin, a sip of fine brandy – all familiar to these brothers of Mars.

Frank James broke the spell and said "This is great and it's been fun but has anyone thought about *how*, exactly, we're getting back into the States? That's a lot different than leaving it. And we didn't exactly check out."

Garcia added "Homeland might not like these weapons and stuff."

Hanson responded "Don't worry. We're covered. We go

into Hobby. Customs and Immigration, one each, with a dog to sniff the airplane for drugs and explosives, will come aboard. It'll be a walk through. JSOC is handling it. Then we're off to equipment return. Then to Monterey. Your passports won't be recorded in because you never left."

"Cool." someone said. "Any more of that Cardinal whatever? That's damned good!"

* * * * *

La Aurora Airport
Ciudad Guatemala, Guatemala
1000 hours local: Day 7

Full power was brought up on the C119. The old Flying Boxcar shimmied and shook as the propellers bit hard into the air. She struggled trying to reach her rightful domain, wriggling like a hooker down the runway. Eventually she found her element, her wings finding lift and straightening her roll. She was airborne; her nose rose, sniffing the sky and liking it. She changed from a hooker to a courtesan once in her domain.

Jake looked back and yelled "Deke, won't be too long. Gerry Ford has the Gulfstream out of our hangar and will be ready to roll when we arrive. My guys will help with the gear. Why no boats? We could have hauled them."

"No way to get them to CG. Left 'em for the Clinic to use hauling kids. No need on the gear. We'll handle it all. Would like to move directly to the Gulfstream when we land."

"Understand. I'll taxi close. That was sure some trick you guys pulled off. The guys in CG filled me in. They still can't believe it even though they've got the guy to prove it! That asshole is giving them a lot of info. He's asking protection and giving up everything he knows. The debrief will take some time. Apparently he's somewhat worried about an American General and his outlaw guys coming back. Something also about stealing his money – lots of it. Can you believe it? A General? Where do these folks get these ideas? You say anything to him about his family? Perhaps his boy in Phoenix?"

"Might have been mentioned but only as an inquiry about his grades and his health – you know, neighborly concern. The dispatch of his buddies might be influencing him. Bet he's not sure who the hell has him. Probably thinks the rules of the game have changed and for him they have." Stratton replied.

"Well, none of the guys in CG can get over it. So quick, so efficient, so impossible. Word is that El Gallito is in a major uproar. Guatemalan Army guys have asked our guys if they have any idea what it's about. Nobody knows what's going on in there. Some bodies have been sent out. Higher ranking guys, they think. Police have them. Seems twenty-twos were used. Not common around there. Narcos like big calibers, lots of noise, and lots of impact. Speculation that some sort of a coup within the narcos is happening. Of course, our guys were surprised and know nothing."

Deke nodded. Then he laid his head back and was asleep. Like the others.

* * * * *

The Boxcar slamming into the runway woke everyone. Once again it was raining and gusting. Jake finished his rollout and taxied to the waiting Gulfstream. The 550's engines were idling. The stairs were down, waiting. Jake's associates were standing in the warm rain and began clapping as the team disembarked. Deke, Hanson and Mitchell each thanked Jake before they left the aircraft. Seeing the clapping men, they broke into grins. Each stopped and saluted the rain-drenched men. Then they continued to the Gulfstream.

Once aboard, Clara closed and secured the hatch. The taxi began immediately.

Garcia said "Man, the accommodations here are a lot nicer than that Boxcar."

Clara announced that "Mr. Ross personally instructed that champagne was to be poured, once airborne, for everyone. He has ordered that his personal supply be used – the Blanc de Blanc from Gruet Winery in Albuquerque, New Mexico - which is almost Texas. He loves this wine. He says it is the finest made in America – better than most French Champagnes."

"I have also prepared, at his direction, a lunch which I will serve after I pour. Hope you like filet mignon from prime Texas beef, garlic mashed potatoes – grown in Texas, sautéed mushrooms and onions – grown in Texas and asparagus spears – grown, you guessed it, in Texas. Mr. Ross says "Well done! Welcome home."

The takeoff roll began and almost immediately the nose rose up. They were on their way home. Mission complete.

They were expected at Hobby Field in Houston. The inspection was cursory. The dog was happy with the airplane. They never shut down the engines.

The jump to the remote field was routine. The JSOC Air Force plane waited. The transfer of all the 'borrowed' equipment went fast. Again, the engines of the Gulfstream never shut down.

During the flight, Mitchell and Hanson thanked each of the team then sat with Stratton.

Mitchell said "Deke, this part is over. You and your men

were awesome but it ain't over 'till it's over – as Yogi liked to say. There's a big part still to do. We may be calling for some of your back-channel contacts - with your permission. As this unfolds we'll keep you posted for curiosity if for no other reason. This fellow, Jimmy Munoz, seems to be handy with the computer. He's very smart. It would be nice to have a techy that's truly one of us. What's he got going at home? Any chance of him hanging around a few days, maybe longer?"

"I don't know. I'll ask him. He's an independent contractor, consultant on computer stuff. You read him right. He's single so he might want to ride it on out." He left to speak with Munoz. The two returned.

"I'm aboard. We tracking the money? Finding out who's behind this? This is going to be lots of fun! Hell, yes I'm aboard. I want to bring down the sick son-of-a-bitch behind it. Besides, work on Bonano's laptop will take me some time. There's lots there about a lot of things. From time to time I'll have to service some clients though."

"Great. Not a problem." Hanson said. "You'll bunk at my place. Go with me when we get to Monterey. You drive there?"

"Yes."

"Okay. Follow me when we get there."

Mitchell said "Good. I've got to see Grazing as fast as I can. You guys join up at my place after you touch base at home."

Hanson went forward to speak with Ford. "Tell Ross Jr. 'thank you' and that his support made possible the success of the mission. It couldn't have been done if you guys hadn't stepped up to the plate. Gerry, thank you. You're one hell of a pilot. I'm glad you had the stick at Punta Gorda. Tell Jr. that I'll try to keep this down to every twenty years or so. We'll de-plane as soon as you're at the terminal. So – goodbye and thanks again."

Ford said "Bo, this was something else. I'm so proud to have been part of it. Never dreamed that as a corporate pilot I'd be involved in something like this. This has been one of the most gratifying things I've ever done. Thank God you got them out. They probably won't make a movie about this one though! Suspect this won't see the light of day. Anyway, I'd like to thank you for letting me be part of it. I really enjoyed meeting you guys. Not often in life one gets to meet legends. I see why you guys are. It was a thrill for me. You've got my numbers. If I can do anything for you or if you just want to have a beer in Texas – don't be a stranger."

"Same for Monterey. You take care, Gerry. Adios."

CHAPTER 31

Monterey Airport
Monterey, California
1800 hours local: Day 7

The landing was a thing of beauty, the wheels gently kissing the runway then the nose gracefully easing down until that wheel found the earth. Shortly they were at the Millionaire Terminal. Grazing was waiting on the tarmac when the Gulfstream pulled up. With a warm feeling of pride in his chest he watched as the team descended the ramp. As they approached he pulled himself to ramrod attention and snapped the crispest salute he'd done since he was a Second Lieutenant. He held the position until all had passed. As they passed, each stopped, returned the salute with big grins and moved on. Inside the terminal, Grazing said "I'm so damned glad just to know you guys! Proud doesn't even begin to describe how I feel! These people here – well, I don't have words to tell you how they feel. They can't tell you but I can. *Thank You!*"

Deke said "Aww – just another day at the office, Colonel."

"Colonel, my ass. I'm Ken Grazing, Deke."

"Right, Ken. Bo and Mitch told me quite a lot about you. You couldn't handle the ground stuff so well, eh? Went to flying? Gut shot can do that to a guy."

"Deke, those guys have been known to lie. Got to be careful what you believe if their lips are moving. In fact, that's how I tell if they're lying – their lips are moving. Dead give away."

"Ya – sort of noticed that myself. Nice meeting you, Ken. Need to take care of my guys. Be seeing you. Later."

Mitchell walked up and said "Kenner, we've got work to do. Sorry about that fucked-up decision to let the captives break the news to their families. Should have kept you informed. Stupid. Can't do anything about it now. See you at home."

THE DEVIL'S RANSOM

PART TWO

THE INQUISITORS*

*a person making an inquiry, esp. one seen to be excessively harsh or searching

—The New Oxford American Dictionary

CHAPTER 32

Mitchell home
Carmel, California

Hanson and Munoz arrived early. Hanson made the introductions when Grazing answered the door. Grazing had long been up and about, already finishing the half pot he had made. Mitchell, struggling awake and moving slow, began to prepare a fresh pot. Munoz watched the ritual and asked "Wouldn't happen to have some tea, would you? Preferably green." To the raised eyebrows he said "Hey, acquired a taste for tea in Afghanistan." The eyebrows dropped back down.

Mitchell nodded and looked in a cabinet, saying "Earl Gray, English Breakfast, Black, Chamomile and – ah hah – Green." He put on a pot of water.

"I don't know about anyone else but I'm damned tired. It's hard work getting old. Was a time a few hours sleep fully recharged. Going to take some extra stretching to loosen up these travel kinks."

Hanson looked at Munoz and Grazing saying "So that's

what's ahead of us when we get old! Wonder what it's like
– think we're not going to like it. It hurts watching an old
man hurt so!"

"Afraid it's not that far away for ya, Bo. Let me know
what it's like when it hits." Grazing chuckled.

"Warms my heart to be among warm and loving friends.
Ah, well, beggars can't be choosy. As soon as this caffeine
kicks in we can put these old brains together and see where
we are. Jimmy, your young brain is a welcomed addition.
Kenner, I asked Munoz to join up with us. He's a magician
with the computer. I think he'll be a big help. Liked what I
saw in Guatemala."

"Welcome aboard, Jimmy." Grazing said. "You really said
yes when this squid asked?" Munoz nodded. "Sensibility of
the troops has gone downhill if that's true." Grazing continued.

"Enough abuse, Kenner. The kid's smart enough to side-
step bullets. That's smarter than someone else I know."

"That's true. I surrender." Grazing laughed.

The caffeine infusions poured, Mitchell headed for the
patio without a word. Grazing fell in alongside. Hanson
moved to follow while Munoz gave him a questioning look.
Hanson said "The addict needs a cigarette. We work outside. Bring your laptop. By the way, up here in Monterey we
always have sweaters and a light jacket available. This ain't
L.A. Gets a little chilly here if you're not used to it. Even in
August."

Mitchell set the pot in the middle of the table and nodded at the chairs. "Guess I'll start. Jimmy, you any good
at taking notes on that laptop? I know you're not a secretary but I saw those fingers fly. Would you mind taking on
that role? We'll also tape to make sure we don't lose any
thoughts but it would be nice to print out the sessions. We
old guys, we're better at reading from a piece of paper than

we are from a screen. Easier to make margin notes too. Life-time habit."

"No problem, Mitch." Munoz answered.

"Okay. I'll try to summarize the southern stuff. Bo – jump in anytime. We have the Maya jefe, Felipe, fingering his cousin, Manny Bonano, as the man who recruited him and his group to highjack the dentists. He offered two hundred thousand dollars for the job. There was clearly no intent to release the hostages alive. Bonano stated that and that it was part of Ricardo's initial plan. The tribal members were all apparently aware of that because there was no effort to conceal their identities or the location of the puebla. The hostages said that the captors were nervous or unsure but I think that's because they'd never done this before – take captives and kill them."

"The jefe had a notebook of pictures, this one, telling him exactly who to kidnap. It had been planned out in advance exactly who would be taken. The notebook had been given to him by Bonano who received it from Ricardo. The pictures in the book had been taken somewhere other than on that trip to Guatemala. Kenner, later today could you make copies of the pictures and visit each hostage? See if they can recognize where and when their photo was taken and, if so, who took it. Their spouses are used to seeing you."

"Good idea." Grazing responded.

"All the people taken were people of wealth. This Ricardo was a childhood friend of Bonano's. Ricardo brought the plan to Bonano. He offered 500,000 dollars for the proj-ect. Bonano drafted his cousin to do the grab. Bonano and Ricardo, last name unknown, communicated by internet using Global Internet Café in Guatemala City – it's near Bonano's barrio called El Gallito. Bonano knew Ricardo from childhood. Both lived with their mothers in the U.S. Embassy. Ricardo's mother, Tia Sophia, might have been mistress to the Ambassador and Ricardo might be the Ambassador's child. Later, that Ambassador sponsored Sophia and Ricardo's entry into the United States. Ricardo was educated at some university in southern California. Ricardo is one fourth Maya, one quarter Spanish and one-half anglo. He is perhaps five feet eleven, is slender, has blackish-brown short hair and black eyes. He is about thirty-five years old and dresses expensively according to Bonano. We are told he speaks English with no Spanish accent – pure American neutral."

"We need to find this guy. Jimmy, you need to search the records. Who was Ambassador then, who was Tia Sophia, what was her last name, did the Ambassador sponsor her and her son and, if so, when did this occur? Anything you can find on them. If government records, INS, etc. are a problem, talk with Kenner and Bo. They may be able to guide you. Don't do anything illegal that can be tracked to you. If you run into any such situations, talk with us. There are ways – don't charge in. View old guys as assets to be used. We know things and people. I mean it. Sadly, we have had people, friends, killed doing searches for us that were tracked to them. It still pains us deeply."

"I understand, Mitch. Broderick and I talked. I realize exactly how dangerous this is. Jeez, these guys were in the process of killing seven adults and two kids. And that Bonano bunch – who knows who else he knows down there. If the guy gets wind of who was involved in the Bonano grab – we've all got problems. They would hunt us down one at a time. For sure they want that money back."

Grazing said "What money?"

Mitchell said "We sort of liberated four point three million from Bonano."

Munoz said "Mitch, the other accounts he gave us? I worked through them. Transferred out an additional three point eight. The total is a bit over eight point one. I put the three point eight in a small Lichtenstein bank. Friend of mine helped me set it up fast. The four point three is still in the Swiss bank. That bank isn't on Treasury's monitor list, I wouldn't imagine. It's tiny and flys below the radar. Treasury can get in there if their interest is attracted. What are we going to do with the money anyway?"

"Oh, we'll find a use for it. It's nearly half the ransom. If we don't recover the twenty this will help those folks. Then there are expenses. We've got lots of time to figure that out. We need it to be in safe places. Caicos and those other islands are out. Treasury watches them like a hawk. What do you think?"

"I'd probably suggest Singapore but I'm certainly no expert in legal stuff on big money or how to hide it. I've heard that Singapore is particularly non-responsive to Treasury's overtures about co-operation on financial matters. That little city-state seems to think that being a safe-haven for money is critical to its wellbeing, or so I'm told. Working with the U.S. Treasury would be counter-productive and the U.S. has no real leverage in other areas to force their compliance with Washington's wishes. Their only products are business and financial center plus transshipment crossroads. From the air their harbor looks like one humongous ship parking lot." Munoz replied.

Grazing said "Think I'll make a call. Time for me to check in anyway. When we're done I'll look into it. I'll get back to you, Jimmy."

Mitchell continued "Okay. This Ricardo guy is our main string to follow. Ken, you want to pick up here? What have you got from the northern front?"

"Not a hell of a lot. I looked at what went down prior to that last demand e-mail. Who could have passed the word that we had the money ready and that a rescue force was on the way. We know that at the bank Abernathy exploded about the rescue team but nobody left between then and the demand. Abernathy went to the restroom at one point and could have made a call. He's the obvious one but it's too obvious."

"Watson took a call, not made one, and talked business in front of us. There was no mention of a rescue team or money ready. He was talking percentages and points on a property loan package. Something about twelve point seven two percent and five basis points, waive the brokerage fee and close right away – within fifteen days. Would lose the asset if they didn't foreclose. Couldn't hold the rate offer open longer than that. Nothing else – he did a lot of listening. So did I."

"The demand e-mail came through Uzbekistan – not Guatemala City. Harrison, the FBI guy, called me early today. They blanked out there and so did Interpol. What I don't know is if anyone text-messaged surreptitiously without me seeing but don't think so. As it is, those are the only two people with any possible outside contact except the FBI and Interpol guys. They were on their phones a lot. But they suspected in the afternoon. Have to ask them if they commented on their suspicions to anyone. The problem with Abernathy is that he knew since the afternoon also – so why go to the head and make a call when I'm there to see? Doesn't work."

"It was strange to me that all the parties fell in the same general area for collateralization percentages to make their ransom share – a share determined by the kidnappers. All the accountants used sixty-five percent, the common margin, and each could just make it. When Abernathy dropped the bank's loan percentage level none but Villareal could – and he was covered by the bank's executive insurance whatever it was. What do you think the odds are that six families, selected in Guatemala, would have roughly the same usual percentage of collateral needed to make a specified ransom demand? So --- it would seem someone knows the assets of the selectees. Others of lesser net worth were not taken."

"Initially had a feeling about the Watson guy. Martha Wilson, wife of Charles – the auto guy – quietly called Watson a liar when he carried on about his wife wanting to go help in Guatemala. Seems she didn't want to go, hates flying, scared. Watson forced her to go – for the business, he said. Pretty ugly according to her. Mrs. Wilson heard the whole thing. She doesn't care for him personally – at all! But – he could have been schmoozing things. All these people are investors in his PineTree Financial business."

"This is a mortgage investment business. It's been returning over ten percent for a long time. Monthly payments. Local real estate. Extremely well thought of locally. Bank loves 'em. So do most of the investors, or so it seems. Now, he probably would have knowledge of his investors' net worth in some fashion. But, his wife was taken and his collateralable assets fell into the same range as the others. He also had to borrow to fund his portion of the ransom."

"Earning ten percent in real estate in the demolished market was somewhat intriguing to me so I visited his office – as a potential investor. He had really talked up how well PineTree was doing at the hostage families financial meetings. Talked business the whole time – no real drift into concern about his wife after the first inquiries. He is definitely business oriented to the exclusion of everything else. Possibly he is burying himself in it to avoid thinking about her situation. I think his secretary, MaryLou, has the serious hots for her boss. She lights up when he walks into the room. I mean seriously lights up. He doesn't seem to react. I picked up a bunch of his brochures and a prospectus he uses. Haven't looked it over thoroughly yet."

"The FBI and Interpol are trying to track the money. No word from them yet. I'm guessing because the last demand came through an Uzbekistan cutout we'll find the money goes through one of the 'stans on its way to wherever home is. If that's so then I bet the Feebies run into a block. Interpol, I don't know. They've got different rules."

"Mitch, should I go on?"

Mitchell said "Yes, he's in all the way."

"Okay. My man Tom is on it. He has all their Federal assets at hand plus some special ones of his own. He'll brief me as to progress. I'll talk with him shortly. That's about it from here. Got no vibes or suspicions on the other participants. Feebies are running BIs on all the principles – hostages and spouses. Said they'll share when they have anything. By the way, they did BIs on Bo and I right off. Me because I was here. That led to Bo and a few months back. That pulled in you, Mitch. They wanted to know if we'd terminated those two – didn't buy the suicides. Told him we had absolutely nothing to do with it. Warned me that if it turned domestic we had to share everything and not interfere. Told him we did last time – with the authorities *and* the media, that we're equal opportunity sharers."

"Right – when we have it all, if we can. Might have to skip a few minor points." Mitchell said. "Those BIs on the principles would be interesting reading. But I think we should dig ourselves. Feebies might skip a few minor points as well. They have their own agenda and absolute truth isn't always on their list. I've been told that sometimes things like politics and closure rate affects their actions. Can you imagine such a thing? Too much work piling up for Jimmy alone. I think we're going to need some more help on all this."

Munoz said "I know a couple of people – a guy and a lady – who are excellent on Background Investigation work. Set up some systems for them. They'll cost though."

Mitchell said "Hire them. You're on the payroll as well at your regular rate. Stratton told me that you're an independent consultant – so you're consulting. You're on the job."

"Thanks. That'll help. I'll call them. Need full names of the principles and any other information. Everything helps them."

"We'll get that to you when we wrap up here. You're the contact point. Ken, you have all that?" Mitchell asked.

"Yah, I can fill him in. It's in my daily summaries."

"Okay. Honoring that great philosopher, Deep Throat, when he said 'Follow the money', the only nexus we have of all the parties is the PineTree Financial thing. I'd like to explore it deeper. You have the prospectus, right?"

Grazing nodded.

"While you're filling in Jimmy, I'd like to read it."

Hanson said "I've got one at home also. Watson pitched me on it but I passed. Some things didn't make good sense to me. Other things I flat out didn't like. Serious conflicts of interest involved with no oversight, controls or recourse. I'll discuss it with you after you read Ken's copy."

"Really? First negative word about PineTree I've heard here." Grazing said.

"Gents, think it's time to go to work. We're a wrap unless anyone has something more. No? Okay, we're done for the moment. Bo, went light on you for now. Know you've got a full plate at your office. I'm sure this'll get heavier. We'll put this stuff together. Brief you later."

"Good. I've got to herd some cats back into their cages. They're good cats but still cats. Some days I wish I didn't have employees."

CHAPTER 33

Mitchell home
Carmel, California

"Paula? This is Jimmy Munoz. What's your work load now? I've got a paying project for you if you've got the space."

"Great. Here's what I need. I'm going to send you four names. I'd like full background on them and their spouses. Every little detail you can find. Expense is not a factor. Time *is* – I'd like it a week ago. Confidentiality is also. You report to me – and you bill me. If for any reason you cannot reach me I'll give you a backup name and number where you can report. Do not attract attention from authorities. You could be parallel with the FBI. They are not to know about you. Cover yourself."

"No, this isn't interfering with police work. Yes, it's possible that one of them could be a criminal – a murderer at heart. So keep yourself untraceable – you hear me? You know how to do that even though it takes longer to get the data. Use your cutouts."

"Yah, I know. I'm a real sweetheart but it's a job. It's what you do. I'll e-mail the info. Bye – and you're welcome."

He sent the e-mail:

> James Villareal, wife Jane
> > Chairman and CEO, Central Bank Holding
> > Monterey, California
> Imelda Watson, Husband Winfred
> > Husband President of PineTree Financial
> > Monterey, California
> Peter Rust, wife Marianne
> > Private Investor
> > Pacific Grove, California
> Archibald Abernathy, wife unknown
> > CFO Central Bank Holding
> > Monterey, California
> Your alternate contact is;
> > Doug Mitchell
> > Phone: (831) 629 4177
> > E-mail: jdmitchell44@aol.com

Punching in another number from memory, he waited then left a message to call him. He sent another e-mail:

> Karen Smith, husband Myron
> > Husband Chairman and CEO,
> > Berchel Construction
> > Monterey, California
> Charles Wilson, wife Martha
> > CEO Peninsula Motor Group
> > Monterey, California

    Mark Blaylock, wife Christina
      Pediatric Dentist
      Carmel, California
    Jack Troia, wife Kelly
      Pediatric Dentist
      Monterey, California

Soon 'Randy' returned his call. Jimmy outlined the work as he had done with Paula, not mentioning Paula's employ. No need to ruffle competitive feathers. He also briefed Randy on the self-protective needs and the reasons. He verbally gave Randy the alternate contact information.

When he finished with Randy, working from his rough notes, he put the essence of the meeting into usable order and printed six copies. He found five three-ring notebooks in Mitchell's office. He printed and taped each name – plus one called MASTER – to a different notebook. He loaded each with a set of the minutes of the meeting and spread them out on the desk.

He moved a small coffee table next to the couch, found a yellow legal pad and pen and with his laptop he sprawled out on the couch. He started hunting Ambassadors to Guatemala - and their mistresses. He intended to bag just one – a trophy size.

* * * * *

Mitchell took the prospectus and brochures from Grazing, refreshed his coffee in the microwave and went to his smoking den of solitude on the patio. Sufficiently supplied with his main comfort food diet – caffeine and nicotine – he leaned back and proceeded to scan the brochures. They were typical hype glossies and of no merit for his purpose. He turned to the prospectus – the lure for investors.

He slowly and carefully read the entire document – even the usual boilerplate legalese. He went inside, made several copies, saw Munoz fast asleep on the couch and returned to the patio. Then he read it again even slower making various markings on the margins of a copy with his pen. When finished he leaned further back and drifted into his contemplative trance.

Grazing, carrying an opened bottle of wine and two glasses, found him in that state. Making some noise, Grazing set down the glasses, poured and returned to the house. He reappeared with crackers, sliced apples and cheese. Again, he sat them down noisily.

When Mitchell looked his way, Grazing said "I like this hotel. They know how to stock a cellar and mini-bar. The wine selection is fantastic. Found this one. Hope you like it. It's one of my favorites."

Mitchell glanced at the bottle and said "Yeah, mine too. Think I have some of this at home. Wait a minute, I am at home. Christ, don't drink it! This is a special wine I was saving for my mother-in-law. It has cyanide in it! Fortunately I'm immune so I'll drink it. I've some Hearty Burgundy in the furnace room. You'll love it – stored just like in Reno."

Grazing said "Fortunately for me the VA Hospital found that I, too, am immune to cyanide so we can share. We'll bring out the gallon jug for the boy. He won't know the difference. Too young!"

Mitchell sniffed the glass and exclaimed "Man, you're expensive to have around. That's the 93 Syrah, isn't it? What a beauty!"

Grazing, sipping his wine, said "You've got that right. Reminds me of a girl in my sophomore year. Looked good, smelled good, went down easy! Full bodied, well rounded and great legs. Ahhh yes, definitely a lot like this wine. Loved that girl."

"Believe I knew her. Used her as the role model for the wine. Appreciated her virtues. She mentioned a guy with a big nose that wasn't much good in the sack. I'm sure it was the same girl, the more I think on it."

"You wish. You'da met her you'da had ten grandkids by now."

"How'd you miss her, then?"

"I was poor but that was okay with her, sorta. Couldn't afford baggage then. But – she flunked out and went home. Heard she cried herself to death missing me. Shame! What a waste!"

"You sure you didn't play around with those funny white powders in 'Nam? Sometimes wonder about your engine missing a few pistons." Mitchell inquired.

"Nah, nothing to do with white powders. It's just that sometimes the fumes from your wines make it sputter. Strange when it happens. I surprise myself with what comes out. Have to be real careful in mixed company. Bo says he has the same reaction. He suspects you put formaldehyde in them. Rots the brain, he says. Do you?"

"Only in the special bottlings for my dearest friends – and my mother-in-law." Mitchell said. "Keeps the cyanide potent."

"Sure makes them taste good, whatever it is." Grazing said. "You know, when I came out you were out there in space somewhere. Find anything?"

"Nothing earth shattering. That prospectus, if it works – and you say it does – is incredible. I see why Bo took a pass. I made copies and we can go over it later when Bo is here. Joanne said she'd barbecue up some dinner here when she gets home. The Hansons are coming. What did you hear from Tom?"

"He's been busy. As he expected, the funds were split up and vectored on. At the second stage the funds rested. Whoever he is, let's call him Mr. X, he knows about algorithms and patterns. Even though he's going into countries resistant to U.S. exploration of their lucrative financial dealings, he's aware of traffic pattern monitoring. Treasury can get to specific accounts officially but there are hoops they have to jump through. Takes time and those countries drag their feet deliberately. Funds would be moved but it is a trail."

"One shortcut is to use algorithms to do traffic analysis to follow destinations *assuming* it's the subject funds. The Echelon system at NSA has been alerted to the FBI's interest. Tom receives all generated hits, same as the FBI. Most of their encryption has been compromised, de-crypted automatically and read directly – but not all. The point here is that there is so much electronic money movement that it is overwhelming. If the exact same amount is moved it can be easily spotted. But broken down and moved at different times – days apart – without knowledge of the bank's internal actions it is nearly impossible to track in useful time."

"However, Treasury, over time, has established 'worm holes' through the shields of most of the commonly used banks in popular areas. It seems our government, from time to time, does not appreciate legal niceties adequately. They seriously do not approve of others breaking laws but view themselves above and beyond it – particularly if money or ego is involved. As much as I abhor the practice it is to our benefit in this instance that they have such moral lapses. The gist of this is that Tom is, in fact, inside the bank's system and had the account immediately identified and tagged to tell him of activity."

"It was shortly broken into five holding accounts one of which held 500,000 dollars and was transferred to an account in Lichtenstein. That account – which already held substantial funds – was depleted not long after. The transfer instructions originated in Guatemala City. The funds – some four point three million – went to a tiny bank in

Switzerland, one very secretive and not on Treasury's commonly used bank list. Seems Tom has no entry to that bank. If, in the ordinary course of chasing wrongdoers, it appears that Treasury may be making progress in that direction he will let me know. Get my drift? One of Tom's outside hackers may have toddled around in there would be my guess."

"The four other accounts were still dwelling and fully loaded. He expects a flurry of activity any time – probably further broken down and spread over later today and tomorrow. He says that the guy is good but not that good – so far. We'll see what he does next. Probably do something through the 'stans. A couple of other guys at Treasury are tracking for the Feebies. They're making no efforts to cover their explorations. He's got a visual on them all the way. Interpol has been making inquiries. That's about it for now. He's on it tight."

Mitchell had listened carefully. When Grazing finished, Mitchell said "Excellent. Deep Throat was truly one of our greatest philosophers. But, when the money comes to a final rest, it still might not give us the person. That will take more work. Twenty million – or nineteen five minus transaction fees, which will be stiff, is a lot of money. You don't take it out of a bank in a suitcase. Probably stays in one or a series of interest earning accounts. And that interest money *can* be carried out in a briefcase! After management fees, five percent return is a million bucks a year, tax-free. Lots of places on this earth one can be comfortable on that."

"Those small private banks have the account numbers on the system but the associated human name is kept elsewhere in a card file or book. There's the rub. The fund is managed, earnings converted to actual cash and transferred in the privacy of someone's office. Of course, if the *fund* can be *absolutely proven* to be the proceeds of criminal conduct – according to the laws of its country of residence, treaty with the U.S. or international law – then the *fund* could be seized. But that doesn't give us the name of the person behind it. Even there the name used isn't necessarily the real name. In that case I'm sure for a substantial fee the bank manager will have misplaced the identification card for awhile. It seems to me that aiding the government in such an endeavor might not get us to the evil bastard but it would eventually recover some or all of the ransom money. It would be earning interest while the legal battle raged, though I'm sure lots of folks would find reason to dip into the fund before the remainder was returned. Funny how that works. Let's evaluate carefully before any serious sharing. Good job, Kenner. Keep on the trail. Reminds me, I've got a couple of calls to make. Jimmy, you got anything yet?"

"Yeah, I do. I'm thinking that the Ambassador in question was named Jon Anderson, a long time Foreign Service light-weight. I'm also looking at the guys on either side of him but I'm pretty sure he's the one. Those housekeepers must have been paid by the Embassy so I'm hunting the employee pay records. Tedious but I'll find them. Can't go direct to the Embassy without answering inconvenient questions. As a second route, I've contacted Luke in Guatemala. They've got a legitimate reason checking out Bonano and all with the Embassy. Told him I was after the name of the other live-in housekeeper with a boy. Asked him to press Bonano for a last name. Told him the first name was Sophia. He will get back to me one way or the other. My people are on the BIs. It'll take time. I told them to be super thorough, no detail too small. By the way, Ken asked me to add Abernathy to the list – just for the hell of it while were at it. Said the guy bothered him for some reason."

"Great idea, calling Luke! Knew I liked you, kid. How come you weren't an officer?"

"I was a poor kid. Went in right out of high school. The Army gave me my chances, paid for my college education, trained me on computers and electronic stuff and made available everything I have. The Army gave me the confidence that I can do anything I set my mind to. They let me find out that I'm pretty damned good. I gave them eight years. Now I want the challenge of the civilian world. See if I can master that. You know, it's tougher in a lot of ways."

"I know what you mean. I gave the Navy seven. It was scary leaving the womb of the University for the Navy. Seven years older it was scarier leaving the womb of the Navy. In the Service all your physical needs are taken care of and the where, when and whats are scheduled. Yeah, I know exactly what you're talking about. You'll handle it just fine. Takes a little time to get used to deciding things for yourself, that's all. Guys, relax and hang loose. I'm making those calls. Dinner's at seven thirty. Sami and Bo will be here around six."

CHAPTER 34

Mitchell home
Carmel, California

Mitchell called Jack Troia. After the social rituals and chit-chat, Mitchell asked Troia when the list of people for that Guatemala trip was firm, specifically when had each future hostage committed to the trip. Troia would call him back.

He called Peter Rust to set up a meeting the next day. They arranged a ten o'clock at the Carmel Roasting Company coffee bar in the Barnyard center. They could sit inside or, if too many ears were about, could stroll the adjacent courtyard.

He checked in with Joanne. All was well in the office. He called the winery. Miguel had everything under control. There were no issues needing his attention. It was one of those slow periods in the winegrowing world. The grapevines were slowly doing their thing. The wines in tank and barrel theirs. Attentive nurturing at this stage was the norm, husbandry in its true meaning, allowing each to become what the wine gods willed they be.

Troia called back. "Mitch, I've got it in my trip book. Of course, intentions are subject to change but first commitments are noted in my trip book for planning. Often there are cancellations or on again, off again changes. Mark and I are a standard go. His boys always go. Villareal has been a big supporter and wanted to go for years. He was on board about a year ago. Same with Wilson. Same with Watson. They committed together at our fund raising party. Actually Watson said Imelda would go. She's a tech. She didn't confirm until three months ago. Rust about three months ago also. Karen Smith almost always goes. She's on unless she cancels. Is this a help?"

"Don't know. Working on every angle trying to figure this out, Jack. Thanks. I'll let you know if we have any successes. Ciao."

He checked the time. He had a good hour before he had to set up the dinner service on the patio. Joanne had prepared the beef tenderloin from Costco, now marinating in ziplocks in the reefer. He made some guacamole and aioli, covered them and put them in the reefer to diffuse the flavors. He picked four Japanese cucumbers, peeled then sliced them into a mix of Greek yogurt, mint and garlic. That, too, went into the reefer. Bottles of Chardonnay and Sauvignon Blanc joined. That done he returned to his chair on the patio.

* * * * *

Sami and Bo arrived shortly after Joanne. Grazing made the introduction of Munoz to each of the ladies. Sami joined Joanne in the kitchen for last minute touch-ups. Mitchell had prepared everything as far as could be done early: Broccoli was in a pot ready to steam, the rice cooker was chugging away, sliced vine-ripened tomatoes covered with diced bell peppers and sweet onions dosed with herbs de province vinaigrette was covered and in the reefer, a Madras curry for the rice was on simmer, crackers and thin-sliced baguette were out with dips, cheese was on the olivewood board, the barbecue was heating up.

Sami said "Mitch really does his thing in the kitchen. Must be nice to have a husband that loves the kitchen."

Joanne laughed saying "Yes it is! He does love it. It relaxes him. Me? I cooked in a previous life. Can do without it. Once in a while I get the urge but only once in a looong while. Only trouble is his recipe book was captured from the French Army and he cooks enough for a Division! Happily, he washes and cleans as he cooks. Makes it easy for me after."

Mitchell was handing out copies of the PineTree prospectus when the ladies joined them. Sámi had her glass of Chardonnay. Bo was finishing preparing Joanne's and his Cosmopolitans. Mitchell handed each a copy saying "This is the prospectus for PineTree Financial. Each of the hostage families is an investor in PineTree. The only connection of all financially is PineTree. That's probably not too startling because it's local and apparently well-thought of according to Ken's take. We don't know if it has anything to do with the taking but we're following every possibility no matter how minimal the connection. Bo was pitched but turned it down, wisely. Didn't like it. He'll tell us why. Today I read the prospectus. Found it amazing."

"Frankly, I can't believe that smart people and their advisors bought into the thing. You'd have to believe that the principle, Watson, is a saint. It is so full of conflicts of interest and opportunities for the principle to reap monies that it blows the mind. The whole thing is probably, at some point, a lawsuit or fifty waiting to happen. During good times everyone would be happy and shenanigans wouldn't become apparent. During lesser times there is a lot of room to hide for awhile but eventually investors will come out on the short end – not the principle. He'll still make money. The legalese and disclaimers give the principal the ability to maintain that the investor was warned and that the principle was knowingly authorized to act in any way he saw fit at his sole discretion."

"Let me mention a few of the things. There is a corporation that employs Mr. Watson. He is the president and owns the stock. That corporation 'manages' the mortgages for a fee of one point two percent per year. The investor is not part of the corporation. The investors are members of individual LLCs organized for a specific mortgage or pool of mortgages. The corporation takes a portion of each but only as a member like the others – so he can say he's investing right along with the investor. But it doesn't actually put in money. Its share is from promotional work – in essence, another fee. There is no liability beyond that as a member which is loss of invested capital which is zero for Watson. Watson is the licensed broker. When the LLC has its pool of funds available for investment it employs the corporation – read Watson – to find a mortgage vehicle, a borrower. It charges a 'finder's fee' for 'finding' the borrower. The mortgage broker – read Watson – 'finds' the willing lender – his LLC – and he receives the broker finder's fee. He dips both sides of the deal. Nothing illegal about that – just inappropriate because it's not disclosed. He siphons off three to five percent of the investors' funds but if the return is enough to please the investors – everyone is happy. Except maybe someone who thinks that there is a fiduciary responsibility in there somewhere.

"The hooker lies elsewhere. The prospectus specifically states that *none* of the mortgages made will conform to requirements for Federal mortgage protection. That is an alarm. These are going to be very risky loans – to people who can't qualify under Federal rules. Thus the high interest rates that generate the returns that everyone is giddy about.

But, it's worse. The prospectus clearly states that qualified appraisers 'may' NOT be used or required to determine loan to value ratios. In fact, it goes on to say that the corporation 'manager' – read Watson – may personally determine the value of the asset at its sole discretion! What you have is a pool of investor money that one person, with no oversight, can evalue, approve a loan using other people's money and service it making a fee at four points in the process – two commissions, service fee and participation."

"The accumulation of monies phase generates no interest for the investor while the pool builds in preparation for a lending. Wonder where the earned interest goes? Bet I know. The investors cannot have access to the corporation's books. They have no standing because they're not stockholders. For the LLCs, 'sole discretion' means he can't be challenged. The sole recourse if one is unhappy is return of principal when and if it is available – at the discretion of the manager. Wow!"

"What did Santayana say – 'Those who do not know history are condemned to repeat it' or something like that? Well, in the late 1980s, early 90s, there was a massive wipeout of mortgage company lenders and credit unions. They had made many marginal, or below, loans during the go-go days. They retained and serviced their mortgage loans to generate those cash flows. The economy declined. Mortgage default rates shot up. Wiped out those companies – industry wide. In fact, most of the industry."

"The next cycle starts. What did the industry learn from the previous debacle? Don't make marginal loans? No. Absolutely not. They thought the message was 'Don't hold on to the mortgages'. Generate the loans, package them and pass them along somewhere else. That, along with some pandering political moves, led us into the economic disaster we are well into presently. But the Watson guy didn't even learn that lesson! He's making unsound high interest loans and keeping them – or the investors are keeping them. The very program that killed in the eighties. The investors are in the 'Tulip' mode – they think house values will never go down, only up, and that they are perfectly safe with a mortgage as collateral. If there is a default they could actually make more money by foreclosing then re-selling. The prospectus covers that asserting that the corporation may engage in that though not as its primary business. Guess what – more fees will be involved in any such activity. The corporation may even act as attorney in fact when thus engaged."

"Apparently local folks believe that this area is immune. What nonsense! The values of homes here are already starting to collapse. A portion of the market pressure was speculative – buying with the intent to sell as values soared. The whole house of cards is tumbling down. Look at Bear Stearns. Five months ago they were one of the biggest, most profitable of the big boys on Wall Street. Four months ago they don't exist at all. Lehman Brothers disappeared in a blink. Why? Home mortgage sub-prime market."

"Historically, U.S. house value to annual income has been about three to one. Last year, 2007, it was four to one. But in California and Florida it was *ten to one*! Why? Speculation. Prices were only going up. People bought second and third homes. Signed up for easy loans at low teaser rates that adjusted in two or three years – up to very high rates. No problem. They figured they'd sell, grab the appreciation and be out before the high rates hit. The next guy was thinking the same – in at teaser, out with money. Tulips all over again. – but with some wicked twists."

"We're immune here? Look at how many of our already overpriced homes here are seconds, in some cases thirds. Clinton's easy house money, easy house credit, made it possible for anyone to get a home loan – almost no matter their situation. I know one truck driver down in the valley earning around 60,000 per year who bought an $800,000 home up here! True! So who the hell has PineTree been lending to at twelve to fourteen percent? How are they paying out ten? What happens when the defaults soar?"

"Ken, you indicated that PineTree was still pitching, bringing in investor money to loan on mortgages. What are they doing – going into buying foreclosures with the money or what? If Watson was making super-good loans – and no one knows but him – then maybe his default rate is super-low. Hard to believe but could be the case. So what's the new money for? Many of the old investors had, and chose I'm sure, the option to roll their monthly earnings back, re-investing in new pools. Where is that money going – no one knows but him."

"Other than that I have no opinion on the subject. Bo, you were wise to pass."

"Mitch, you covered my thinking although I didn't know those ratios. My God, this collapse is going to be worse than I thought." Hanson said.

"I wouldn't be surprised if our local property values declined to half for a long while. A long while – then stabilize around seventy percent of boom value, maybe a bit higher. There are some unique features of the area. But that means many of the homes are going upside down..."

"Wait. What does that mean, 'upside down'?" Sami interjected.

"It means the mortgage is bigger than the value of the home. When that happens and someone loses their job – they walk. Enough of those and you've got a tsunami hitting the financial community. And that will freeze everything. Banks will fail. Business will shut down. A disaster. The government will have to step in to prevent a global collapse – if they can. The next couple of years are going to be brutal."

"There is a funny quirk. These coming bailout programs

will be so massive that one effect down the road will be hyper-inflation. They can't politically run up taxes to pay for it so they'll tax it secretly by using the money supply system – print lots of it. That will devalue it and pay the nut with low value dollars – that is, inflation. So - in the long run owning property will be one protection. Property tends to adjust to the value of money."

"Reno is getting hit pretty hard already. We're seeing high-end houses for sale reduced by a couple hundred thou and not moving." Grazing commented.

Joanne interjected "I, for one, am really glad we have no money in PineTree. I know some people who have half a million and up invested there. I've heard some people put their life savings into it and some even borrowed to invest. How sad if the home market does what you say."

Hanson said "As a businessman, if I read the situation as you describe and if I were in the real estate game, I'd see an upcoming – if not already here – need for a magical source of big bucks to float me over this tsunami. Looks to me like Watson might be candidate for very close scrutiny."

Mitchell said "Exactly the point that hit me this afternoon when I read that prospectus! Along the way I asked myself who here has the motive for an operation such as we saw? I mean, one doesn't wake up one morning and, over coffee, say 'I think it would be fun to kidnap and kill a bunch of folks'! There has to be some driving force behind such an elaborate operation. It was planned out – well, as a matter of fact. How could anyone anticipate that a group of ex-Special Forces guys could, or would, be put together, much less that fast, or that a rescue could be mounted? The only rescue effort possibly attempted might be from the Guatemalan Army and that would be too late if even tried. No, the planning was excellent, well conceived and meticulous in application. A slam-dunk on paper. No one could possibly imagine or consider the speed and abilities of a

Stratton or a Hanson to bring the assets to bear required to foil the project. Like so many plans, criminal or otherwise, conception may be brilliant but as one moves down the operational path, intelligence and commitment of the people required to carry it out can slide way down the scale. Felipe and Bonano gave up their info readily – well, yah, with a little persuasion but still pretty easily. Once pressured they were not committed to protection of the guy up the chain. Anyway, all the thinking kept bringing me back to the big 'WHY?'. And who the hell thinks in terms like twenty million? An individual thinks small. What is driving the size of the demand? I think we may have found a plausible answer to those questions. At least it needs exploring deeper."

Grazing said "I concur. Another thing. It really bothered me that the ransom demand was broken down as it was. It was almost as if an accountant, or someone used to thinking with lists, had prepared it as a guideline to what each could raise then simply sent it without realizing the implications. The FBI guy was surprised about it also. There's a lot of accountancy mentality involved in real estate work. That connection had already struck me. But, it also struck me that Abernathy fit that mentality. That's why I had Jimmy add him to the BI list. Keep in mind that bankers think in big numbers and have an accountancy mentality. Also, Mitch, in your scenario of doom, you mentioned bank failures. There might be motive to save one's bank"

Hanson said "But the president of the bank was taken and meant to be killed."

Grazing responded "So was the wife of Watson. Watson is out his ransom money – money he came up with willingly, even anxious that it be sent quickly to save his wife. The bank is *not out* Wilson's ransom money – the insurance company is. The bank itself has no loss exposure nor does Mrs. Wilson. And bank people know how to move money around. Real estate people usually don't move big money around. Banks do it for them. They move paper around, not money."

Hanson nodded appreciatively and said "Good points. Looks like we have more than one suspicious area. But, Abernathy is an employee, not an owner of the bank. Why would he, or someone like him, conceive of such a radical effort? To protect a job? Seems bizarre, if true."

Grazing said "At one point, in the financial meetings, Mrs. Villareal, while publicly chastising him for lowering the banks collateralization rate, called him 'Dear'. Now wouldn't that raise some interesting possibilities as to motive?"

"You've got to be kidding me!" Mitchell said. "I love my brilliance at having you be there, Ken. Jesus, you don't miss a thing do you? I thought I had this thing narrowed down and you open up a whole new possibility that makes a lot of sense and fits what few indicators we have. Further along that line, I'll bet the bank and Mrs. Villareal both have substantial life insurance policies on Charles – with Mrs. Villareal as beneficiary. What a sweetener!"

Grazing said "Mrs. Villareal is very proud of her grandfather and father's building of the bank and its development of this region. Pride of place is a strong force in and of itself. A twenty million infusion to preserve that could go to motive. Add in personal gain from life insurance, elimination of a burdensome spouse, a new love and you've got some powerful forces at work. Mrs. Villareal comes across as a sweet lady but behind it is one smart, tough person. However, she doesn't strike me as a killer. Then again, if she's a closet psychopath she probably wouldn't. Who knows?"

Mitchell said "We've got to pursue both possibilities. Anyone got anymore curveballs for us to swing at?'

Sami said "Mitch, you kept referring to 'tulips'. What in the world were you talking about?"

"I'm sorry. I should have mentioned that about two hundred years ago in Holland the market for tulip bulbs went crazy just like housing has here. People believed prices would only go up – just like housing here. The crash was devastating – just like now. It is the classical textbook case of the mob mentality that causes these sorts of things. Some of the same thing was at work in the nineteen twenties leading to the twenty-nine crash and the Great Depression."

Jimmy Munoz spoke up "I'd like to thank the Mitchells for this wonderful dinner. I really enjoyed the 2001 Ventana Grenache Noir. Went great with the tenderloin."

Grazing looked over and said "Jimmy, how'd you know it was the 2001?"

Munoz said "Looked at the label, Sir."

Grazing said "Mitch, my faith in age and experience was just restored. Knew he couldn't know that."

Munoz said with a smile "Actually, I prefer the '99. It has a little more depth to it but you'd expect that – a warmer year up here. The '97 Syrah is my favorite of Mitch's reds but Mitch is famous for Syrah so no surprise. Have you had that one, Ken?"

Grazing looked at him for a moment then growled "Go-damn kids."

Munoz said "Ken, I made all that up just to jerk your chain."

Mitchell said "Don't think so, Jimmy. Ken, '99 was a warmer year and it does have more depth. Very good, Jimmy. Ken, do I know how to pick 'em or what?"

"Jimmy, I'm impressed." Joanne said.

"Aw, shucks, M'am. It was nothin'." Jimmy answered in his best southern drawl. Everyone laughed, even Grazing.

"For dessert we've got cheese and fruit. Joanne will bring it out once I take our dishes in. We've an eighty-six Malvados Port, Duca d'Alba brandy and I smuggled back some of

that Guatemalan rum. There's de-caf coffee or tea. To accompany your choice, if you wish, I happen to have some
Monte Cristo Especiales, fresh from Guantanamo Bay. The
Navy takes care of its own. Tomorrow should be interesting
and busy. Let's just enjoy the evening." They did.

CHAPTER 35

Mitchell home
Carmel, California

Though all were civilians, old habits die hard. The three men were up at the crack of dawn, Grazing first. He had the pot perking and water heating when the other two strolled into the kitchen. Munoz was now housed at Mitchell's, the easier to work and brief each other.

"Good morning, gents." Grazing greeted. "Are we ready for a busy day? I have a feeling things are going to get exciting soon."

Mitchell said "I will be as soon as that coffee is ready. I've got a ten o'clock with Peter Rust. I don't know him – met him when we recovered them. I've heard he's quite the thinker. Wanted to meet when we returned. I know he listened outside the lattice work wall when we played Felipe's tape. Pretty sure deliberately. He overheard the entire thing including our intent to go after Bonano. I didn't like it but what could I do? Not sure about him but I want to hear what he's got to say. Have a few questions for him too. Think you guys have a lot to check on."

Munoz said "Yeah, I do, anyway. Saw that I've got a lot of reading to do. BIs are starting to come through – partials. I'll print out what there is and put it in your binders in the office."

"Good. I'll check in with Tom and summarize yesterday as well as today, print and put it in the notebooks too." Grazing added. "Mitch, I think I'll hire a local private investigator to sniff around on Archibald and Jane. It's amazing what locals can find out fast. I'll call a PI I know in Reno. He'll be able to give me the name of a local guy who's good."

"Nice. I like it." Mitchell said. "Jimmy, print what you have before you read. I've got a few hours and I'll read what you've got."

"Sure."

"Ah – the coffee's ready. Think I'll pour, go out to the patio and run a few laps. Nothing like a vigorous run to loosen up."

Munoz said "Run?"

Grazing said to him "It's bullshit, Jimmy. He can't even spell run. What he means is he's going out for a cigarette. He does virtual running. Stands, smokes and pretends he's running. It's his commitment to his doctor. One time the Doc told him he had to lose weight and get some exercise so he got a haircut then went to a casino to walk between slot machines. He's lucky his mother gave him good genes."

"If God had meant for me to walk or run He wouldn't have given me an airplane or a car, now would He? For His own reasons, He picks some people to slog through rice paddies or poppy fields. Others – a very few, select others – He chooses to put in air conditioned cockpits far, far above the mosquitoes, the dirt and, oh yeah, the bullets. Go figure. It's truly a mystery."

Munoz cracked up laughing. "You guys always go on like

this? Jesus, first stuff out of your mouths at daybreak is this nonsensical patter."

"Should have heard us when we were young and our brains worked correctly." Mitchell then said seriously "Jimmy, it breaks the tension, it's a cover up for the seriousness of what were working on. A lot of pilots are motor-mouths. What it is is a stress release. Behind it they are coldly efficient, calculating technicians. Like you SF guys. But with you guys it's not every single day. For us, every day, every time we mount up we know that in military flying there are no round trip guarantees. Even training flights. Particularly training flights. If you don't laugh at this world, you'd have to cry. And crying hurts your reputation. Jeez – grown men crying – embarrassing! So – we laugh." Mitchell moved off towards the door.

"Pretty good philosophy, Boss." Munoz said as he headed for the office.

Grazing just nodded, looking away, remembering.

* * * * *

"They've got a lot of info in. Here's some to read while I'm printing more." Munoz said as he handed Mitchell a stack of papers.

"Thanks." He said as he arranged himself for a long read, legal pad and pen at hand, glasses sliding on his nose. "Damn things." He thought.

* * * * *

At nine o'clock he sat those papers, and the others Munoz had delivered, aside, performed his morning ablutions and departed for his meeting with Peter Rust.

Peter Rust rose, all six feet four of him, as Mitchell entered, extended his hand and said "Good morning, Douglas. So very good to see you. At the expense of seeming repetitive, thank you again. It was quite a time. I took the liberty of buying you coffee. Hope you like their Jamaican Me Crazy blend. I do."

"Good morning, Peter and thanks, I do like it. No problem on the rescue. We had nothing else going on that morning. It broke the boredom."

"Right." Peter said, chuckling. "I've thought about it quite a lot since. That was incredibly amazing to organize and pull off so fast. So fast hell – to pull it off at all."

"Peter, it really wasn't that big a deal. Among us we know a lot of people. Old guys accumulate a lot of friends if you've lived your life anywhere near right. Good military officers look after their men. The men look after the good officers and they have long memories. After all – it is a Brotherhood – at least among the ones that count. It never dies."

"I suppose it is so. Still, those of us who have never experienced that find it amazing. Incomprehensible to us, really."

"I know. Civilians sincerely don't get it and never will. It can't be explained, only experienced. Even then it doesn't always connect with everyone. Just among the club. Anyway, talk to me. Tell me about your take on the event then I have a few questions I'd like to ask."

"Gladly." For the next half hour or so, Rust gave Mitchell a concise sequential rendering of the event, his observations and his thoughts thereon at the time and subsequent. He finished saying "Now ask away. When you're finished I have a few of my own."

"Here is a picture of you. Any idea where and when this was taken?"

"Ah – so that's the one the jefe had." Rust studied it carefully. "No, I have no idea. I am looking almost directly into the camera but not quite. My eyes are slightly up as if I'm looking someone in the face or eyes and the camera lens is a ways below. See that? But I can't relate it to any specific place. Just don't know."

"Okay. Think about it. Call me if you come up with anything. How do you suppose anybody acquired knowledge of your assets?"

"Not really that hard, I would imagine, in this day and age of electronic access. The bank certainly has enough information to get a solid picture. I have an open line of credit for my activities – it's with Monterey Central Bank. Nine months ago I had to do a thorough listing for them. Had a large deal I wanted to go into. Some stocks had a few months to go before long-term capital gains tax reduction kicked in. Others weren't ripe. Borrowed short-term. Paid off now. My computers are not encrypted – too complicated for me and what for? Guess a hacker could get in easily if they wished."

"Who did you work with at Central Bank?"

"Archibald Abernathy himself. It was a large sized loan. He approved it. As I said, it's been paid back."

"How'd you come to go on this trip?"

"Jack Troia was our children's' dentist forever. We've been regular supporters of his projects for the indigenous children. He's been pushing me to go for years. A few months ago I saw I had some slack time – you know how crazy the market has been. Thought it wise to not be active – just watch it. My wife thought it'd be a good time to go. When Winfred suggested I go I thought why not?"

"When did Watson suggest this and why?"

"About four months ago or so, at one of his soirees. Said his wife was going, why didn't I go."

"Did he bring up the subject?"

"Hmmm. No, I think my wife did. No, he did – about his

wife going, talking with my wife. You know him, always pitching what he does for the community."

"What brought you to invest in PineTree Financial? A professional investor such as you should have seen through that thing part way into the first reading – long before one finished."

Rust paused for a second, gathering his thoughts, then said "I put in ten thousand only. Many people put in hundreds of thousands. It became the 'in thing' to be an investor in PineTree in some quarters. My wife socializes with a group of ladies who are heavily invested there. Tell me, have you ever done anything you're against simply viewing it as a price for marital peace? Simply to stop the noise? To me, the ten thousand wasn't that big a deal, possibly wouldn't lose all of it and, if I did, it was cheap for my wife's happiness. Thus, meaning mine. Make any sense?"

"I understand completely. Been there. Got that T-shirt. You said you've thought a lot about this. Any conclusions or suspicions about who's behind it?"

"It's apparent that with these questions you're on a mission to find the guy or guys. No, I've reached no conclusions other than I'm positive it's someone from here. Who – I don't know. I can't put it together. I'm missing too much information, too many disconnects and gaps. Could be somebody at the bank. PineTree has some financials on me but so do several other investment entities."

"Douglas, I really want this bastard. It's not every day someone sets out to kill one. I want him bad. Now, I have questions to which I'd like answers. I want in on the search. I want to be part of it, to contribute in some way, to bring my abilities to bear. Most important to me is any information on this guy so I can work with it."

"Peter, I'm sorry but the answer is no. I understand your feelings but any such search, if there was one, would be far out of your league. If you searched and it became known to this fellow, remember he was about to kill nine people. What do you suppose would happen if you became to be known to be hunting him? I myself am remaining far away from that. He could already be pissed off enough about the rescue now that word on that is beginning to spread."

"Douglas, I understand about the risk. However, frankly, I don't believe you about the search. That Bonano fellow had to give you something."

"Who? I have no idea who you're talking about."

"Douglas, don't give me that crap. I have a right to know everything about who tried to murder me."

"Peter, I can't give you what I don't have. You are making an intuitive leap to a wrong conclusion – and a dangerous one at that. You're not hearing me."

"God damn it. I want in. As a victim I have rights in this matter, a vested interest if you will. If I have to use leverage, I will."

Mitchell, very quietly, asked "What do you mean 'leverage'?"

"I know about the Bonano fellow and the Guatemala City expedition. I think many laws were broken – U.S. and Guatemalan – that you don't want to see the light of day. Am I making myself clear? I want in. Period."

Coldly, Mitchell said "Mr. Rust, I have no idea what you are talking about. Nor would anyone else. You should refrain from conjecture. Once again, I seriously suggest that you have suffered severe psychic trauma from your capture. Such assertions would only damage your reputation and credibility as they have now with me. You are quite correct – you do have rights, as you have put it twice. You have the right to your life and your right to freedom which, by the way, *we* gave you. Sir, it was not you. If it had been you alone we would not have come. You, Sir, were collateral baggage. You should be thankful that you were saved. You should be grateful for your life and to those others who were with you. You should thank your god for brave men such as those who risked their lives to save yours. This time, save your own life – don't search for the guy. Drop it. Throwing threats and wild accusations around would not be wise. If you feel the need to continue in that vein, I would advise professional help. If ever asked I would state that I so recommended to you. Good day to you, Sir, and goodbye." He rose and departed, shaking his head slightly.

Rust murmured to himself *"I think I profoundly blew that. Never thought about the hunted hunting the hunter. I do hope they find the bastard. I might have been wrong about action people. Some of them anyway. But I will look - carefully!"*

"Well, well, well." thought Mitchell as he drove away. "That was interesting. Hope I just saved his life again."

* * * * *

Munoz looked up from the screen when Mitchell came in. "Hi, Mitch. Got a bunch more paper for you to read. Might want to get Ken reading too when he comes in. Lots of stuff happening. We've got a name! Luke confirmed. Ambassador Jon Anderson sponsored one Sophia Ortiz and son Ricardo for entry to the United States old INS records show. Later naturalized. Anderson is serving in a higher venue, departed this earth fifteen years ago. Mother Sophia died about the same time. They all lived together in La Jolla. The bad news is son Ricardo cashed out his inheritance from Anderson and disappeared. So far, no record of his movements or activity, at least under that name. I'm still looking. How'd it go with Rust? Anything?"

"Some. I'll cover it when Kenner gets back. Basically, though, there's a connect to both Abernathy and Watson. Guess two leads are better than none at all. Would have liked to have had only one connection. Nobody said it was going to be easy. I'll be on the patio. It'll take awhile to read this stuff."

Several hours later Grazing returned. After grabbing a glass of lemonade he joined Mitchell and Munoz on the patio saying "We've got ourselves a PI. Her name is Gloria Ashly. Salinas office. Besides Abernathy and Mrs. Villareal, I added Watson. She already had a file on Watson. We're not the first to inquire on him. Some investors – actual and potential – have taken an interest in him. Two lawyers also. She opened up after I explained some things to her. I cautioned her about being extra discrete and told her why. She accepted the hire – with pleasure, she said. She'll report when she has anything."

"Talked with Tom. Money is moving. All over the place. The move orders are coming through a cutout server in Uzbekistan. He thinks a re-assembly is beginning in The Southeast Asia Bank in Singapore. That might or might not be an end point, at least for some of it. It's not yet clear but after trotting around Europe the switch to Asia fits a pattern used by some drug cartels in the past."

Mitchell said "Ken, the BIs from Jimmy are giving us some info. It seems Jane Villareal, nee Alderete, and one Archibald Abernathy are both graduates of the University of Washington, both attended 1970 through 1974, he was a Delt, she a Tri Delt. Back then, the sleeping porch of the Delt house looked directly at the Tri Delt house. In all probability they knew each other. Those two houses often socialized together."

"I read the report." exclaimed Munoz. "Where'd you get that about the porch and socializing?"

"I was a Delt at the U.W." said Mitchell.

"Small world." said Munoz.

"Yes, it is that. I think Kenner picked up on something.

Ken, why don't you ask the Feebie to look into life insurance policies on James Villareal? If this is the right path, an insurance payment could be nice frosting on the cake for those two – and no messy divorce. Wait a minute. That would tip our hand that we're seriously looking domestic, not foreign. He'll demand what we have. If he does and we're not forthcoming, that's obstruction of justice. They get touchy about that. When was the last time you saw a Feebie smile?"

"You mean the first time? Never! I'll call Tom. He can get it. Even though I brought it up, the more I think on it I'm having trouble seeing these two as the engineers. Usually I can feel evil vibes. Don't get it with either one. She seems so real, so what you see is what you get. He seems the methodical, anal-retentive, contrary banker. This project was way outside the box. He's inside the box genetically. If it is them, they're the greatest actors on earth – consistently. But they do need to be looked at."

Mitchell said "Don't like coincidences. The U of W connection is bothersome."

"For me, too." Grazing mused.

"The rest of the BI stuff hasn't rung any bells with me. Don't have anything on Watson yet. Lots of other things that would be exciting for the gossip circuit but nothing for us. Think I'll forget I ever knew those other things. Fortunately, at my age, forgetting is easy to accomplish. Hope I don't forget to forget." Mitchell said. "Too bad there's more to read. That's more to forget."

"The meeting with Rust didn't narrow things down. He made a big borrowing from the bank. Worked with Abernathy directly because of the size. Approved. Had to list out assets so Abernathy had knowledge. Invested in PineTree to keep wife happy, only ten thou, same opinions as us. PineTree had some knowledge of finances but not much. No encryption on his computer. He decided to go on this trip only four months before. Watson encouraged him at a social gathering. Apparently Watson was talking with Rust's wife about his wife going and suggested Peter go as well."

"Then it took an ugly twist. The guy wants to be part of the search for Mister X, demanded it when I said no. Told him there was no search. Told him how dangerous it was if Mister X heard about any such thing. Hope I scared him off. Anyway, he threatened me with exposure of the Bonano thing if we didn't let him in. I got pretty tough with him. I think he's not going there but one never knows when amateurs get the bit in their teeth. He could become a problem if I wasn't successful."

"He actually threatened you?" Grazing said.

"Directly. Straight out. No sugar coating." Mitchell responded. "Surprised me, actually. Silly bastard is pissed off that someone tried to kill him, which is understandable. Didn't understand that by letting the guy become aware that he was looking he could become a target again. He did make one informative observation. When I showed him his picture he pointed out that in the picture his eyes were not focused directly on the camera lens but slightly above it. He thought that he was looking at someone's face or eyes and the camera was slightly below. I had missed that. When I came home I looked at the other pictures and in all of them there is that offset of eye focus."

Munoz exclaimed "Button lens. You can buy them at any spy shop. Those folks would never know that their picture had been taken."

"Right. Again, careful planning." Mitchell said.

CHAPTER 36

Mitchell home
Carmel, California

"Mitch, you're not going to believe this." Grazing said as he strode rapidly into the patio waving a handful of papers. "New stuff on the BIs. Abernathy worked for four years at The New World Bank of Central America in – guess where? Guatemala City! Ten years ago to six years ago. Can you believe it? The background papers say he left under some cloudy circumstances – unclear, looking deeper but definitely terminated – fired. Unemployed the next two years until hired by Central Bank of Monterey four years ago. Sure looking worse for Archibald. Damn, I simply don't feel it!"

"Starting to look like your radar's out of whack. Old equipment malfunctions from time to time. Still not definite, though. We need a lot more. Looking forward to what she finds."

At that point Munoz approached with more papers offering them to Mitchell. "Info on Watson is coming through."

Grazing said "You took care of Rust. No one else could place where or when their picture was taken. None had seen it before. The background had been closely cropped. Karen Smith recognized the edge of her blouse but she wears it often. Didn't have it with her in Guatemala. Imelda Watson wouldn't see me. The housekeeper said she was seeing no one. Doesn't surprise me from what I've been told about her condition."

"Didn't take Tom too long. There are two life insurance policies on James Villareal. One is by the bank – key man policy – for five million, bank is the beneficiary. The other is for two million, wife Jane the beneficiary. Par for the course – normal for a man in his position. Proper for her age for lifetime care, maybe a shade light. Nice but not dramatic."

"Spoke with Loddington – the Interpol guy – in London. He says that they are making some progress on penetrating that Uzbekistan server system. They hope to be able to browse around inside soon. They've got reasons of their own to want to go in there, not just us. They've breached several walls without triggering alarms. He says it's slow going. Says they – the server – charge a heavy fee for the cutout service. Uzbeki government gets a cut – taxes – so no interest in stopping it. Same in all the 'stans. Lucrative cottage industry."

"Harrison sounded frustrated when he spoke with me. Echelon has triggered on nothing. No alerts. Nada. The Uzbeki thing has them stymied. NSA has all the electronic transmissions stored, of course, but without exact times of instructions to the Uzbeki cutout they have no idea of which message to backtrack to its source. The Uzbeki service regularly delays re-transmission to defeat that very thing."

Munoz said over his shoulder as he headed back inside, "I don't buy the thing about penetration of the server system. I'll bet the Uzbek's are playing with them, giving them something to occupy them. Basic protection would call for installing new barriers every day particularly when you know that every major power is trying to penetrate 24/7. I would."

"Makes sense to me but I don't know squat about that world. You'd think that Interpol would know that." Grazing said. "I'm going to be gone for awhile. Got a meeting with Mrs. Ashly over in Salinas then going to get a haircut. I'll take these papers with me. It's so gorgeous out I might go sit on Carmel beach and read if time works out. I'll see you later." He waved backhanded as he left.

"One problem with dredging up mud is that some of the mud sticks to the dredger!" Mitchell grumbled to himself as he read. Watson was born in 1959 in Pasadena, California, had attended a community college off and on four years and received an AA degree in Business Administration. He'd taken employment with a credit union in Glendale, California as a clerk rapidly advancing to loan officer. He'd found his niche. Newspaper publicity releases showed him receiving various awards for his community and real estate activities. He was mentioned in two articles as a graduate of UCLA.

He had left the credit union for the larger playing field of Bear Stearns in Los Angeles pitching in a new league – real estate mortgage packages. With investors – individuals more so than institutions – he was exceptionally successful, a born salesman. Bear Stearns, culturally, was a believer in publicity press releases exalting their employees' superlative successes. Several covered Watson's awards for superior performance. After four years he left the pressure cooker of the brokerage house for Monterey, California to open his own independent real estate mortgage company – PineTree Financial. While at the credit union he had acquired his California real estate license. While at Bear Stearns he'd acquired his Broker's License.

Along with his move in 1990 he married Imelda Agana

of Salinas, California, no children. Imelda Agana, first generation Filipina-American, AA degree from Hartnell community college, Salinas, worked as a dental technician in Monterey, California for eight years. Subsequently not employed.

The file was full of county recordings of real estate transactions. Paula had extracted the ones of personal nature, consolidating those in a separate folder. In 1992 acquired home in Pebble Beach for $684,000, 10% cash, financed balance. 1994 purchased Pebble Beach home for $1.2 million, 10% cash, financed balance. In 1994 sold original home $801,000. 1999 acquired home at foreclosure sale, Pebble Beach, $2.0 million appraisal, paid cash $1.4 million. No recorded loan. 1999 sold second home $1.7 million. 2000, purchased home Santiago, Costa Rica; $212,000; no loan recorded. 2002; acquired at foreclosure sale home, waterfront, Tahoe City, California; $489,000. No loan recorded.

"Wow." Mitchell thought. "Even riding the boom of home price escalation this guy must have been printing money! County property taxes on those homes was a big annual chunk of money. In addition to that he comes up with nearly three quarters of a million after tax cash within two years unless there are loans we haven't found. Still, I'm definitely in the wrong business!"

He leafed through the huge stack of recordings that involved PineTree. He surmised that there were many recordings by LLCs that didn't reference PineTree. He realized that any rational organization of the data was beyond his competence. Analysis of the data after organization was probably also beyond his competence. The team did not possess the ability among them. They'd have to go outside, to professionals.

Mitchell put the papers aside and called his business attorney of long standing. A meeting was arranged for thirty minutes hence. Mitchell checked out with Munoz and was off.

Mitchell requested guidance employing people to organize and analyze the documents, find other documents as indicated along the way, preferably from a forensic point of view. He said "You hire them. Makes everything work product. Possible at some point the FBI may try to force information out of me."

His attorney stared at him then said "Mitch, what the hell are you into now? In our thirty years together you never cease to surprise me with the bizarre crap you walk in with! Did you ever think about just being a winegrower?"

"Sure. A couple of times. Something always seems to get in the way. Nolan, this is important. Whoever you bring on board has to understand that absolute confidentiality is critical. And – super important – they must protect themselves in searching for information. Their cover could be inquiring for an investor or a lawyer for an investor."

"Mitch, where are you really going? How bad is whoever you're after?"

"Nolan, no doubt you have heard some talk about a kidnapping and rescue in Guatemala. That might have been Bo, Ken, myself and some other guys. The ransom demand was twenty million. That's not Maya indegenas. Someone here is behind it – we don't think it, we know it. And whoever he is, he gave an order to kill all nine captives – including Mark's two boys. We're hunting that son-of-a-bitch. Right now, the indicators we've developed are pointing at either PineTree Financial or inside Central Bank. This part is all on PineTree."

"You're thinking PineTree, Watson? Jesus Christ, Mitch. You're after a murderer? You do realize that he may shift his focus to you guys if he smells you coming? And any of your scouts?"

"That's why I raised the self-protection aspect for anyone you hire." Mitchell answered.

"Mitch – you're making me a scout."

"Well, yeah, but you got used to that in 'Nam. You loved getting shot at so much you became a lawyer. Normal for you to go in harm's way. Can – or will – you put this piece in place? I can meet with whomever, whenever."

"Damn. Okay. Wait a minute." he said as he picked up his phone. He spun his chair to face the window, his back to Mitchell. After a long, whispery talk he hung up and turned his attention to Mitchell. He said "A gift from me to you. You're on. Peterson, Peterson and Jones. San Jose. You're meeting with Ralph Peterson as soon as you can get there. 'Nam vet. He's the head of the firm. They are forensic accountants, both accountants and lawyers. Go – and you're welcome. The bill will be in the mail. Hope you don't get a heart attack when you open it. Better have Joanne open it."

"Thanks, old friend. I'm on my way."

"Hey Mitch – I was kidding about the bill."

"I know."

* * * * *

An hour and a half later he arrived at Peterson's office off Stevens Creek Boulevard. He was shown in to Ralph Peterson instantly. They introduced themselves. At Peterson's hand gesture to talk, Mitchell gave him a briefing on the points he thought were germane – both to the work and to the self-protection. When Mitchell finished Peterson swiveled his chair to look out the window. He sat like that for some time. Mitchell waited. He spun back and said "He ordered all nine killed, the kids too?"

Mitchell said "Yes."

"And you think it might be someone at PineTree? You know, there's only two guys there."

Mitchell said "How do you know that?"

Peterson shrugged and punched a button and said "Howard, could you come to my office, please?"

"Sure, Dad."

"My son." Peterson said unnecessarily.

Mitchell waited for an answer to his question. He didn't get one.

Howard entered. Peterson introduced the two.

"Howard, we have a priority project. You will lead it. Use assets as you need. Hire our usual temps if you need them for non-sensitive work. Report to me. I will explain the project to you. It concerns PineTree Financial.Mr. Mitchell, does that suffice? If so, you will please leave those documents with us. We apparently have a lot of work to accomplish." He stood up. So did Mitchell. They shook hands at the office door and Mitchell departed.

Driving away, Mitchell thought "That was certainly strange. Short and to the point. How'd the guy know about only two principles at PineTree? And why the hell did Nolan put me with this specific outfit? There were local folks who could do this job. Something else is at work here. A 'gift', huh, Nolan? Seems to me that you've just told me something – someone else is already seriously looking at PineTree. Howard didn't ask his father who PineTree was. They are already there – working on it. Nolan, you rascal! This is getting more curious all the time. These guys can't be working on the ransom thing – they didn't know anything about it. Whatever it is, it's been ongoing longer than our interest."

"I'll be damned! Civil business lawyer, forensic accountants and lawyers, all high powered – there's a lawsuit in the wind! A big one! Somebody is unhappy with PineTree.

That is very, very interesting. *There* is another reason to need money besides the economy downturn. Mr. Watson, you are getting my attention."

CHAPTER 37

Over dinner that evening Mitchell enlightened the others about the events of the day. Hanson had joined them.

"A big time civil lawsuit, if one had exposure, would certainly create a need for big money. Not just for settlement. Such a lawsuit in and of itself could destroy a business such as PineTree that depends on local acceptance. Even if ill-founded it could trigger a run on the company, a bailing out of old investors and no new ones coming in. Instead of being 'cool' to be in it would become 'cool' to be out. A hidden twenty mil would be a nice personal safety net." Hanson said.

"I'd like one of those nets." Munoz mused.

"Wouldn't we all!" Grazing said. "Don't think I'd kill for one, though."

Mitchell said "Keep in mind that this is conjecture on my part. Neither attorney said one thing to me about knowledge of PineTree separate from my inquiry. But the whole sequence tantalizes one's mind. Nolan would never breach a confidentiality but he is capable of nudging one in the right direction. I think I was nudged."

"Worth watching. Spoke with Gloria Ashly today. She, so far, is turning up nothing on Abernathy and Villareal, no rumors, no innuendos. But – it's been only a day." Grazing reported.

"Also spoke with Tom. The Singapore account is growing. The account is held in the name of a Singapore corporation that lists a Singapore attorney as the attorney in fact and uses his address. Singapore doesn't require the corporate officers and major stockholders to be filed. Another account is growing in Gibraltar, same form. A local attorney acting as principle for what Tom calls a 'mailbox' corporation. He also said a new one on the Isle of Guernsey is showing up. This one will be a temporary accumulation point. The EU has been trying to close down the Guernsey laundering route but no progress yet. It's a lucrative money-maker for the island and a tax haven from the British Revenue guys. The typical pattern here for the drug guys is Guernsey to Aruba to Singapore or Kuala Lumpur in Malaysia."

"I've got to go back to Reno for a few days. Some things need taking care of. I'll be back. I'm leaving after dinner. Want to miss the Sacramento traffic." Grazing concluded.

"Figured that. Saw you having club soda and lime. Knew you were driving. Get back as quick as you can. Things will be breaking before long." Mitchell said. "We'll hold the fort as long as we can."

Grazing excused himself and left.

Munoz said "I think I've got a trail on Ricardo Ortiz. The La Jolla high school forwarded a transcript to USC. I found a *Richard* Ortiz enrolling that fall. Tomorrow I'll have the USC records and should have his Social Security number. I put Paula on it. She'd essentially finished her BIs. Told her Ricardo was higher priority. I'm going to be getting some bills before long."

Mitchell said "Transfer some funds from the Bonano account to your business account. Pay as you need to. Pay yourself as well. Be sure to report that as income to your business. Should ultimately wash out – income and expense. For me, I'll pay the Guatemala charges, keep a tally then cover later from the Bonano account."

"Works for me, Boss."

Hanson said "The other night you mentioned Guatemala rum. It just occurred to me that eighty years is probably sufficient aging time. Do you suppose it is possible that it would be ready? Don't want to rush things if it needs more time. But that and a Cohiba seem appropriate about now."

"Bo, I believe you might be right. However, I mentioned Monte Cristos, not Cohibas. Can you suffer through an Especiale?"

"Believe I could but it would be a step down. Always a problem when one dines at these low-end greasy spoons. Fortunately, I've learned to adjust to hardships in life."

Joanne came flying in the door. "Thank God it's Friday night! What a zoo the office has been. Bo, make me a Cosmo, please. I'm going to dump this stuff and join you guys in a minute. Mitch, I'm starving!"

Mitchell assembled a plate for her while Hanson prepared her cocktail. Glasses and the rum, very similar to an aged Armagnac, were taken to the table by Munoz. Mitchell turned on the gas overhead heaters then set Joanne's dinner service. When she arrived Hanson presented her the Cosmo. Mitchell hit the microwave button. She had her cold drink and hot dinner in front of her within minutes of arriving home. She sat, exhaled deeply, looked at everyone and said "Hi."

Mitchell said "Hi, Precious. Seems you're thankful to be home. Been a busy one? Here, guys, I've got the Especiales but let's wait until Joanne is finished with dinner."

She said "Thanks. So bring me up to date on the great manhunt. Anything developing?"

"Some things are falling into place but no definite track yet." Hanson said. "We've been going over the points but all we've come up with is that we've got to focus on this eighty year old rum from Guatemala. Sometimes, as they say, en vino veritas or in rum, if present. We're hoping the rum will clarify our perception."

Mitchell summarized for her their new information and observations. When he raised Archibald and Jane's attending school together and Jane's use of 'Dear' when speaking to Abernathy, she leaned back, thought for a moment then said "No."

Mitchell said "what do you mean – 'no'."

"They are not a couple. No way. That's what I mean."

"Oh." said Mitchell. He knew better than to ask why she had that opinion. He also knew it was not opinion. It was fact – in her mind. But take it as true, he thought. These things she knew. Still needed to be verified.

CHAPTER 38

Sunday morning early Mitchell received a call from Ralph Peterson who asked him if he was able to come to Peterson's office in San Jose straight away. He was. Peterson had asked if his full day was open. It was – he would make it so. Peterson had given him no reason. Mitchell had not asked. A Sunday morning call for a meeting meant only one thing to Mitchell – whatever it was it was important. He would find out soon enough.

When he arrived the security guard unlocked and showed him in. A phone call caused the presence of Ralph Peterson three minutes later, fully dressed for business in blue suit and tie. Mitchell, in his Levi's, felt a little under-dressed for whatever was in store.

"Good morning, Mr. Mitchell. You made good time." Peterson said. "Shall we?" gesturing toward the elevator.

Peterson led the way to his office. He went to his chair while pointing at the one in front. Mitchell sat.

Peterson tented his fingers, index fingers to his chin. He paused then he began "I spoke with Nolan more in depth after you left. He speaks highly of you. He tells me that you have possessed some of the highest security clearances our country bestows. He tells me that you are a man that has experience keeping secrets secret, that your brain rules your mouth. He also mentioned that you have been known to bend the rules when they are in the way of what is right."

"It seems that earlier this year those two murderous, drug-dealing politicians that were all over the media were brought down by you and your friends. I was in 'Nam. A cousin of mine was there also. He became involved in the drug transport – and used. Later he was discharged, cleaned himself up, married, and had two children. We were friends as well as family. Years ago he and his family were murdered – executed, as it were. I attended the funeral. Then I went hunting. Would you like to guess where the trail was leading? It dead-ended for me, walls I couldn't penetrate."

"In my career I have adhered to the highest standards of ethics and have always striven to do what is right. Those two things are not always the same. Choices are made. I am committed to the interests of my clients – all my clients."

"Today I have a report prepared for you. Over there is coffee and, there, is a comfortable chair. You may smoke here but open the window. Close and lock it when you leave. That door there is my restroom. I am leaving and will not return today. You have several hours of reading to do. When you finish, leave the file on my desk, close the office door – it self locks – and the guard will let you out. Here is your report. Good day, Mr. Mitchell."

With that, Peterson rose and departed. Mitchell looked at the closed door in amazement. Eventually he looked down at the thin folder he was holding. He opened it. There was a single sheet of paper. On it was a summary of yesterday's meeting. Nothing else.

"What the hell?" thought Mitchell. *"What did he mean by hours of reading then handing me this?"* He went to the soft chair expecting papers there. Nothing. Hands on his hips, he looked around, confused. Then he saw, on one side of

Peterson's desk, a stack of files perhaps eight inches thick in total. Mitchell smiled. He understood!

He opened the top file and saw PineTree Financial in the first paragraph. *Yes!* He took the entire stack to the chair setting them on the small end table adjacent, fetched a cup of coffee and settled back for a day of reading.

He saw that in the top thin file was a lawsuit, not yet filed, against PineTree Financial and Winfred Watson, jointly and severally. The complaints were a long list of frauds, larcenies, wrongful enrichments, missing trust funds, breaches of this and that. The short version was that Watson had been a bad boy, stealing from his investors. The rest of the files were the research and work product, analysis, argument and law.

He had no legal pad and pen with him. He could find none in Peterson's office. He got the message – read, don't write. So he read. For hours he read. And his photographic memory took a picture of every page.

CHAPTER 39

It was gathering dusk when Mitchell headed home. Dropping onto the 101 heading south, he was glad he wasn't going into San Jose on a Sunday evening. He wondered where all those people went every weekend. It was always like that on Sunday evenings – heavy traffic going north, heading home.

Looking at the traffic, he thought of looking at ant nests when he was a boy. He had observed them scurrying to and fro diligently accomplishing some purpose. But what was it that their pin-point brain was directing them to do? Whatever it was they were serious about it. He thought that if an ET spaceship hovered over the earth looking down studying the strange earth creatures how similar it would be. Why were these creatures moving three thousand pound pieces of metal around? They appeared to have a compulsive need to move more of them twice a day, five days of every seven, to different locations. Other pieces were moved continually. Sometimes only a few were moved about. The aliens would wonder what the pin-point brains of those little creatures were directing them to do, what they were about. His cell phone rang, breaking his ridiculous reverie.

"Mitch, Jimmy. Turned on the evening news. Channel

eight reported that Peter Rust was found dead on Asilomar Beach this morning, shot in the head. Thought you should know."

"Oh my God." Mitchell exclaimed. "Damn it all to hell! Jimmy, it's escalating. I think we need help. Bo, Ken and I are known to have run the rescue – and Stratton. The rest of you were never introduced to the hostages by name. Looks like Mister X is getting nervous. That was a terrible mistake on his part. Call Scotty. Let's employ Blackstone Security. We need protection on each of the four. Don't think you're exposed yet but you are staying openly in my home. Nah, he'd go after me first. Let's get Blackstone moving. Is Joanne there?"

"No. She's over at the Hanson's. She and Sami went to Nordstrom's up in San Jose – Stevens Creek, I think she said."

"Okay. Thanks Jimmy. I'm on 101 on my way home. See you in about an hour. Bye."

He called Joanne's cell. When she answered he said "How much did you deplete Nordstrom's?"

She laughed as she said "You've talked with Jimmy. You'll love your new tie. It has whales on a blue and pink background. Not."

He told her of Peter Rust. He told her of his concerns about escalation, that he had expected it at some point. That point was now. Then he said "Joanne, I think I know how much you and Sami love San Francisco. I think you and she should go to the St. Francis Hotel for a few days. Shop, dine, see a play – all that stuff you two love. I think you two should leave now. Do not come home to pack stuff. Borrow from Sami or buy what you need. Leave now. And tell Bo to call me right away."

"Oh, Mitch. This is getting seriously dangerous isn't it?

What are you going to do? You don't even know who it is. Damn it, Mitch."

"Sweetheart, it is what it is. We'll handle it. I've got some protection moving into place for us. We'll be fine. You and Sami get out of there – now. That's the important thing right now. Be cool. We'll talk. Bye."

Mitchell took Hanson's call and explained the new chessboard arrangement. He then called Grazing and discussed the events and his moves with Blackstone. Grazing was at that moment coming through Sacramento picking up Interstate 5 for Monterey. He would arrive in three and a half hours. They signed off.

Mitchell called Stratton and informed him of Rust. He told him of the warning he'd given. "Deke, you're known to all the hostages just like the three of us. Who knows what this fellow is thinking or will do. He may think you are part of the hunt. I've instructed Blackstone to put cover on you as well as us. Thought it would be wise. Munoz is setting it up with Scotty as we speak."

Stratton said "Thanks for the heads up and the cover. I thought it would come to this when he smelled the hunt. When Bonano went missing he had to get nervous. I've been carrying since we got back. No surprise. No way were nine people going to keep their mouths shut. Mitch – get the bastard – soon."

"I hear ya, Deke. We're making progress. Sun Tzu said something about needing to shake the grass to startle the snake into exposing itself. Looks like Rust shook the grass for us."

Afraid so – too bad he shook the grass so close to the snake. The guy should'a listened to you."

"I know but it still saddens me. I've got to look into what he did after I spoke with him and Saturday night. If I can find that out it might tell us what made the snake strike. I'll be talkin' with ya. Stay alert. Adios, amigo."

When Mitchell arrived home Munoz and Broderick had Blackstone men moving, all licensed to carry. It would be some hours before operatives were in place. Munoz informed Blackstone of the change in Grazing's location from Reno to Monterey.

Hanson had arrived at Mitchell's home before Mitchell. He was seated at the kitchen table with various pistols spread out on a towel. He was methodically re-cleaning and oiling each one by one and checking their operation. Several loaded clips for each were to the side.

Mitchell said "Looks like you're going to war, Bo."

"Think we're in a war. We should be prepared for this guy. He's shown his hand. Can't have too much firepower just like you can't have too much fuel!"

"That's true – unless you're on fire. You have that nice Beretta 9mm you had me carry last time? Liked that thing. Comfortable grip for my hand."

"It's there. Loaded. Safety's on."

Munoz came in from the outside. He was dressed in black.

"Where have you been, Ninja?" Mitchell asked.

"Outside. Cleared the area before you got home. I wanted to make sure no one was waiting for you. Also strung some fishing line and cans around the yard. If this guy comes I'd like an announcement of his presence."

"Jimmy, it seems like you almost know what you're doing! Not bad for a youngster."

"I also brought in your wheelchair and walker, old man."

"Careful kid. If you hurt my feelings that's elder abuse and you could go to jail for that. This is California, you know."

"Boss, it'll be some time before Blackstone can have everyone in place. I suggest that tonight we rotate, one of us awake at all times. This guy hit last night. He's on the move. By hitting Rust he's nervous, maybe panicky. That means unpredictable."

"Good idea. Bo, Jimmy – you guys decide who's first. Ken will be tired when he gets here and I am mentally exhausted. Wake me when it's my watch. Tell Ken that tomorrow morning he and I will make a couple of visits. Tomorrow, after the visits, I'll fill you all in on what I learned today. The end game is near. Jimmy, here's a tape for holding in a safe place. It's a summary of today I dictated on the way home. I'm crashing. 'Night all."

CHAPTER 40

It had been a tranquil night with no unwanted interruptions beyond the mind- numbing boredom of night watch. Over their morning coffee, Grazing commented "Quite a reception last night! As I was coming in I felt a presence then caught motion off to my right. Thought our Mr. X might be visiting. Made a move for the house when Jimmy called out to me. What a relief. Once inside Jimmy told me about the visits today. Who are we seeing? The ladies?"

"You got it right. I'd like you to make the calls. They know you. I'd like us first to visit Mrs. Villareal – alone. Then we should see Mrs. Rust. I know it's a bad time but there are questions I have to ask. You may have to push her some for an appointment. I think today we will have our target identified. By that I don't mean we'll have hard proof, hard enough for a court, but *we* will know for absolute sure."

"You already know who it is, don't you?" Grazing said.

"I think so but we've got to let evidence lead us to a 'for sure' position." Call Mrs. Villareal when you think she's up. I'm going to grab a shower. Think I'll dress nicer, sport coat and tie today. You too, amigo." Mitchell headed for his bedroom, coffee cup in hand.

He had finished his shower when he heard Grazing yell

from the hall that Mrs. Villareal would see them when they arrived. He stepped it up a notch. He decided that today called for classic attire, formal in a sense and in its affect. Light gray slacks, dark blue blazer, white shirt and tie with regimental stripes accomplished his goal. Couldn't get any more classical than that. Eye comfort food for two ladies of some age. He hoped it would soften the effects of some of his questions.

When he entered the kitchen Munoz said "Gee, Boss. You got a hot date or something?"

"Or something." Mitchell answered. "Here's the addresses of the two places we'll be. If Scotty's people show you can vector ours that way. Each interview should not take long. We'll check in before we move. No calls to us except emergency. Don't want interruptions during the interviews. Have I forgotten anything, Jimmy?"

"Nothin, Boss. This may sound like nonsense but until the Blackstone guys are here and on you, I suggest that a default word in communication be used if you are compromised in any way. I suggest the word 'son' used either way – your son or that big yellow ball. That word would alert me."

"Strange. What're you thinking, Jimmy?"

"You're focused here but what if this guy has contacted the narco guys in Guatemala City? We're interested in getting the twenty mil back. They might be interested in getting their eight mil back. A hostage would be one way to do it, a bargaining chip if you will."

"That is certainly a possibility. I think that's a good thought. I'll pass it on to Ken on the way. If any of us use it – even you here – the alert is on. I like it. Kenner, you about ready?"

"No need to yell. I'm standing right behind you. How the hell did you ever survive as a fighter pilot? Jeez!"

"Sometimes it beats the hell out'a me! Did you hear Jimmy?"

"Got it. Like it. Let's roll."

* * * * *

They pulled into the long drive of the Villareal home – or castle, however one wills. It was on the Seventeen Mile Drive of Pebble Beach, hidden far back from the road out of sight behind tall stone walls. The old oak gate had been open for them. Mrs. Villareal waited at the entrance door.

Her warm smile greeted them as they approached. She said cheerily "Good morning, Ken, Mr. Mitchell. It is so nice to see you. Come, let's have a cup of tea – or coffee, if you wish." She led them in.

"Mrs. Villareal ...." Mitchell began.

"Please, call me Jane. I am far more comfortable with it and respond better." she said with a chuckle.

"And I go by Doug or, more commonly, just Mitch."

"Well, hello then ... Mitch. I haven't had the opportunity to thank you personally – so, thank you, deeply and sincerely. And tell those wonderful young men the same for me."

"You're welcome, M'am and I will do that. Believe me, they were happy to be of service."

"According to my husband, those young men are about ten feet tall and leap over tall buildings in a single bound. I suspect he may be exaggerating a tiny bit but with what they did it could be true."

Grazing and Mitchell laughed with her.

"Mitch, did you enjoy your mini-vacation there after the rescue? Peter Rust came to visit us – actually to ask a bunch of questions. He said you were off to Guatemala City to 'explore', as he called it. He put it in a strange way."

"It was quite beneficial. I learned quite a lot. It was fascinating. Jane, we asked for this meeting to ask some questions of you, not your husband. Yes, black." as she tendered a cup of coffee.

Grazing said "The same, thank you."

She said "Let's sit here. You were saying, Mitch?"

"I have some questions but first could you tell me what Peter was asking? I was unaware that he was asking questions of people."

"Oh, yes, of course. He made it very clear that he believed that someone here on the Peninsula was behind the kidnapping, not some natives in Guatemala. The things he said made a lot of sense. Most of his questions concerned access by others to his financial information he had supplied to the bank. James could give him no satisfactory answers – satisfactory to him, anyway. He left visibly not pleased but it was all James could give him. He was particularly interested in Archibald but, of course, James can't accommodate questions on personnel. I surmise that you, also, are of that opinion. Asking for a meeting and asking questions indicates to me that you are looking."

"Jane, are you aware that Peter Rust was found Sunday morning on Asilomar Beach, dead by gunshot?"

Her hands flew to her face as she said "Oh my God, no, please tell me it isn't so. Oh my God." She held the sides of her head. Slowly she recovered her composure. She said "Do they know who did it? Did they catch the person?"

"No, Jane, they don't know. Yet." Mitchell said.

"Why, for God's sake. Nobody gets hurt on Asilomar Beach. Oh my God – do you think it was the person he was searching for?"

"It very well could be, Jane, but we truly don't know." Grazing offered.

Jane went dead still. She dropped her hands to her lap and slowly looked from one to the other. Her eyes grew larger. Then she said "You two are looking for that same person. I know it. Your words avoid it. Your body language screams it out loud. Please, do not lie to me. You are."

Mitchell quietly said "Jane, I must ask you some questions. Normally, I would not at this time but I do need to know. Will you assist me?"

"Oh, I wish you wouldn't do this. This is dangerous for you."

"Jane, we are known to this person because of the rescue. We are in no more danger than before. Now, let me tell you something. A lot of information has come into our awareness. We need to clarify some things so that we can eliminate them from consideration. On others we need to see if they are relevant. I'd like to ask you about Archibald Abernathy. Ken says you indicated he has worked for the bank about four years. Is that correct?"

"Yes, that's about right but Archibald could not be involved in this. I know he couldn't do such a thing, any of it. He simply couldn't."

"And how do you know that, Jane?"

"I know him and I feel that his heart wouldn't let him. He is not a devious or violent person."

"You know him that well, Jane? He is, after all, just an employee of the bank."

She gave Mitchell a withering look and said "Our employees are family of the bank. No one is *just* an employee."

"Okay. I apologize for my choice of words. Where did Mr. Abernathy employ before coming to Central Bank?"

"Dear, you are going into an area I cannot – personnel

information. I will not answer that or questions of similar nature."

"I understand. Let me come at this differently. We know that Archibald Abernathy was unemployed for two years prior to joining Central Bank. We know that he had an exemplary banking career prior to seeking and taking employment with the New World Bank of Central America in Guatemala City. We know he was fired after four years there. You can see, I'm sure, why the Guatemala City employment connection has captured our attention."

"Oh my goodness, Mitch, Ken. In Guatemala City Archibald was suspected of some serious embezzlement. He had been set up by a co-worker. The bank acted without full investigation. He was terminated and his reputation destroyed. Afterwards, the bank's investigator, with the police, found that the co-worker was in fact the guilty party and Archibald was exonerated. But, the damage to his reputation had been done. Reputation goes a long way in the banking world. After two years of unemployment he called me. We hired him. He is brilliant, you know."

"Why would he call you, Jane?"

"We were acquainted."

"From school days?"

She looked at Mitchell coolly, the beatific smile absent. She said "I think you know entirely too much, Mr. Mitchell. Yes, from university. We both attended the University of Washington. We were friends."

"Friends, Mrs. Villareal, or more?"

Grazing looked at Mitchell in shock and disbelief at the question.

Her look was pure ice. Anger flared in her eyes then subsided. Intelligence took back control. Her head tilted to one side. Then tipped to the other, slightly. She was thinking.

Then she burst out laughing, deep bursts of laughter that

took her breath away and caught in her throat. She slowly recovered herself saying "Please...excuse...me, I'm... sorry... it is...just so...funny. Give... me...a moment."

Mitchell and Grazing stared at her not understanding what she found so hilarious.

Finally gathering herself, she said "I'm sorry for that. You have generated some information on all the people involved, I see. You have surmised that Archibald and I knew each other in school. You found the Guatemala thing of his. My husband was taken and was to be killed. I think you have put Archibald and I together, eliminate my husband and we live happily ever after – is that it?"

Mitchell said "From our perspective it is one possibility."

She chuckled again and said "Mitch, stay with winegrowing. Don't go into the private investigator business. You see, the flaw in your research and analysis theory is – Archibald is not attracted to women! Never has been."

"Abernathy is gay?" Grazing asked surprised.

"That I don't know, Ken. I think he's more a-sexual. I don't think he's attracted to either side physically."

Mitchell said "Jane, I intend to remain a winegrower but on this we must be investigators. There is a killer on the loose among us. Please, tell us – what *is* your relationship with Abernathy?"

"Oh, Mitch, it is difficult to describe but I will try. Archibald has a brilliant mind. At university I was fascinated by how it worked. I was gifted intellectually. My father encouraged me to explore everything. Yes, I was in a sorority and participated in the brain-dead giggly stuff but I had to have my intellectual time. Archibald was one – just one – of my outlets."

"Archibald is a unique character. It is possible that someday he will write a book that may change part of history as you know it. He has had two pets since university. To this day he does his bank work and then disappears into his world of research. He has neither time nor desire for attachments of lovers or family. In all probability he is on the autistic scale, probably Asperger to some degree, as are many fixated intellects. I understand his work, challenge him, argue with him, and play that devil's advocate role so necessary for his type to thrive. And me."

"James and I have a good marriage and have had for a long time. The truth? Yes, at times he's a pompous ass but so are most men. He makes me laugh – with him and at him. And when I put my foot down he minds. He is a very good bank president and that is important to me. He is a wonderful father to our children. He has sat through some of the times with Archibald and was bored to tears each time. He has no comprehension of our conversation. It is not his world. I was laughing so hard because I saw how it must look to those with the partial information you possessed."

Mitchell said "Jane, why was a brilliant banker working in Guatemala City? That is not exactly a world center of finance."

"Archibald has two lines of interest. He is totally focused to the exception of almost everything else – except his bank work. When the bank opens he is able to shift to banker. At closing time he shifts to researcher. Ken, you saw how he has extreme difficulty telling a falsity or bending rules to fit an emotional situation. To him, it was okay to tell the families the facts about risks because it was factual. Classic Asperger. That's when I stepped in. I put on a bit of a show for the others. He knew he wouldn't be put on food stamps. I thought it was a great bon mot – for the peace of mind of the others."

"One of his lines – not the one he may explode history with – is that the Shakespeare of history is not the Shakespeare of reality. There have been a plethora of gifted students working on that for hundreds of years. Sufficient data simply isn't there in my opinion. Archibald is a gifted linguist as well. He contends that in those days, a poor boy from the hinterland could not possibly have acquired past-youth the language used in the writings. The language screams formal education in the style of the day for the noble class alone. He has amassed reams of cogent examples and learned argument. He has a further belief that Shakespeare of history never left England, a belief supported by many other students of note. Yet, plays accurately depict knowledge of Continental locations such as Denmark – Hamlet's castle – or Verona, Italy of Romeo and Juliet, among others. He believes the real Shakespeare, the writing Shakespeare, was Edmund deVere, an Earl, a close friend and family of the Queen and widely traveled on the Continent."

"However, his mark may be made with Columbus. He is of the opinion, again, that the Columbus of history is not the Columbus of reality. In pursuit of his goal, one must remember that Antigua was not the capital of 'Guatemala' – that came later. It was the capital of the entire Spanish empire of Central America. As such it was the repository of documents and writings from throughout the Spanish New World. When the earthquakes severely damaged Antigua the government *and archives* moved to Guatemala City. Those archives are why he went there."

"He is of the opinion that Columbus was not the son of a Genoese rag merchant, that that was a cover story. Again language, bearing and schooling of the time. As a rag merchant's son he would never have been given the opportunity to learn navigation as he did – particularly a boy from Genoa. The Portuguese guarded their charts brutally. It was a death penalty for misplacing one. Columbus sailed with Portuguese charts. He also had the Portuguese tables correcting Astrolab readings – a must have. A rag merchant's son from Genoa would never have been granted an audience with Isabella and Ferdinand, especially while they were busy laying siege to Granada and driving the last of the Moors from Spain. He contends that Columbus was a Portuguese noble incognito. Many nobles had fled to Spain for sanctuary in1484 after a foiled attempt to cast out King John, many just peripheral. John later pardoned many of them including family members of the subsequent King Manuel. He thinks Columbus was one of them.

No educated person of the time believed the earth was flat – that had been dispelled long before. Portugal had the school of navigation – Prince Henry and all that. The Portuguese and King John already knew of the landmass between Europe and Asia and that it was empty, occupied only by natives. They'd been there. They'd traded there. Columbus carried Portuguese coin, not Spanish. They knew fairly accurately the size of the earth and that it was a waste of time and money to go that way. They were intent on going east to India directly for spices and the incredible riches that offered – and preclude the stronger Spain from competing. They needed the diversion while they worked out treaties that involved the Pope's power to control their stronger neighbor in the future. That resulted in the Treaty of Tordesillas giving Portugal essential control of the spice routes easterly! It was a scam to get Spain to focus on going west for India. In fact, when Columbus returned from his first voyage – the discovery voyage – he sailed first to Lisbon and King John before continuing on to Spain! *He conferred with King John for two days*! Archibald's facts and extensions thereon go on and on. They are cogent and erudite – and exceptionally persuasive."

"You must understand, Mitch, Ken. Your possible scenario depends upon hunger for money and sexual gratification of sufficient magnitude that rational thought becomes irrational. There is neither present in this reality. I'm sorry, gentlemen, but I and Archibald are not your culprits. At my age, though, it is rather touching that I would be thought of as the femme fatale. My goodness, when I think of it I'm rather pleased that you thought that I was a possible. Wow, I do like it! I'm going to take that as a wonderful compliment!"

"Jane, I'd like to thank you for seeing us. We have some other calls to make." Mitchell said, rising from his chair and moving towards the door. "When this is over I'd like to go deeper into the Columbus thing. It's intriguing."

Grazing said "Jane, thank you for trusting me that day. It was tense trying to buy time for the guys. I appreciate your help. I couldn't have stopped them without full disclosure. It was critical that the funds not go then. Had they gone all the hostages would have been dead when the team arrived. We know that for fact. You were a huge part of saving their lives."

"Thank you, Ken. I can't tell you how good that makes me feel. I will cherish that thought." She said as she held the door for them.

They left her standing on the porch waving and flashing her beatific smile.

"Kenner, I think you were right. It is not her. She was telling the truth. As you said, if it was her she's the greatest actress in the world. Nope – it's not her."

"I agree. Funny how one set of facts can have two so radically opposite stories that fit."

Grazing took out his cell phone and placed a call to Gloria Ashly. "Gloria, Ken Grazing. We need to shut down on Abernathy and Villareal. It's not them."

"Ken, I was about to call you. I have come up with nothing. It is my opinion that they are as they appear. My report is finished. It will come with the bill. Thank you for the business. If I can do anything else – call. And good luck on the rest. Bye."

"Bye, Gloria." He said and clicked his phone closed.

"Ken, time to work your magic on Marianne Rust."

"Yeah, I know. Sure don't want to do this. It is a tough time for her. She's a quiet, nice lady. Well, here goes."

He received her permission to come to her home. She would meet with them. The home was a charming, functional structure in Pacific Grove within comfortable walking distance from Asilomar Beach. They approached with some trepidation – this was not going to be fun. Asking questions of a grieving woman deep in her sorrow would have to be done with care. It had to be done though. They needed the answers only she could give. If she had them.

Marianne had seen them arrive. She and her sister, Sally, both were at the door as they climbed the steps. Marianne said with a wan smile "Good morning, Colonel, Mr. Mitchell. Please come in."

Grazing said "Thank you for seeing us, Marianne. I am so sorry for your loss."

"Thank you, Ken. Let me introduce my sister Sally. Sally, this is Ken Grazing and Mr. Mitchell. Mr. Mitchell, I'm sorry but I don't recall your first name. Things were so confused that day."

"I go by Mitch, Mrs. Rust. I, too, am sorry for your loss. I feel the loss. I knew your husband."

"Yes, I know. He told me of you. He was sorry about your last meeting, about his conduct. He wanted to find a way to apologize, that he was in the wrong. Will you accept an apology from me on his behalf? It is what he wanted to do."

"Accepted, and thank you. I knew he was stressed. I had already put it aside. Mrs. Rust, we are sorry to intrude during this sad time but we have some questions. Are you able to talk with us?"

Marianne nodded yes and gestured toward chairs in the

living room. Her sister, with a frozen glare, said "Gentlemen, is this really necessary now?"

Marianne said "Sally, shush. I know why they are here. This must be done. It is what Peter would want. It is what I want. If they are to find the killer they need answers. I expected them from what Peter had said."

"Find the killer? Sis, they are not the police. What are you talking about?" Sally loudly inquired.

"Sally, these are the men who rescued Peter and the others in Guatemala. This is bigger than our police. Find something to do. Leave us. Let us talk. Please. I am alright." The sister frowned then departed.

"Before you start I'd like to thank you for saving the hostages. That was incredible. I'm so thankful for those boys. What a terrible experience for them so young. Now, how can I be of help?"

"Mrs. Rust, I met with Peter on Friday morning. We need to know everything he did after that meeting – if you know. Anything would be of help."

"Yes, okay. Let me see. After that meeting he came home. He was agitated. He paced the floor in the kitchen where I was working. Since he came home from Guatemala he had been focused on who had tried to kill him. No, obsessed is a better word. He was upset that you would not allow him to help you hunt the madman. He told me that you warned him about the danger, told him to drop it. He said he understood and told you so but he was going ahead on his own. He said 'By God, no one tries to kill me and walks'. As I understood his ramblings I asked him to let it go, to let you take care of it. He wouldn't. It was normal for him to ignore others, ignore me, when he has an idea. Nothing new."

"Later, he said out loud 'Abernathy' – just that and left. Later, one of the assistants at the bank called me. She is a good friend. She asked if Peter was alright. She said Peter stormed into the bank and marched into Mr. Abernathy's office unannounced. He had closed the door but the yelling could be heard all the way to her desk. Peter was waving his arms and yelling. After a while Peter stomped out."

"When he came home I asked him about the bizarre conduct at the bank and what did he think he was doing. That was around three thirty. He wasn't home long when he said 'That god damn Watson' and he left again. He returned home near six o'clock. He was dejected and seemed exhausted. He fell asleep in that big chair over there. Later, about ten o'clock, he received a call on his cell which woke him. He listened, got up and said that he had to go out for awhile, that he'd be back later."

"Peter often walked at night thinking and relaxing. It was normal for him. I was not alarmed by his going out. Sometimes I walked the beach with him. I was tired and went to bed. In the morning when I awoke he was not there. Then I became alarmed and called the police. Two hours later walkers on the beach found him. That is everything I can remember. Like I said, I've been expecting you. I've thought through everything I can recall. I've also said the same things to the police detective."

"Mrs. Rust, thank you. I know this is difficult for you. I think you've covered everything we wanted to know. Ken, do you have any questions? No? Mrs. Rust, again my condolences. We'll let ourselves out."

"Good bye, Marianne. We will do our best to solve this. I'm so very sorry." Grazing said.

In the car Mitchell said "Wish the guy had listened to me."

Mitchell's cell phone rang as he drove past Pacific Grove's high school. Jimmy Munoz' voice blared on the car speaker "Assets in place on both of you. Bo's covered. So's Stratton."

Grazing said "I thought that might be the case. Let them know that I picked up the black Chevy when we left the Rust house. Don't have the other. I presume there are two in case we split."

Munoz said "Aw, shit. They're supposed to be better than that. Scotty won't like to hear that. He's a supervisor, you know."

"That's why I told you. He should know. Shouldn't be that easy for me." Grazing responded.

"I'll let him know. Adios."

Mitchell said "Ken, you gotta be shittin' me. You picked up on a tail? That fast? Hell, we just left."

"I get kinda sensitive when someone might be trying to kill me. Been that way ever since I got shot. Funny how that works. The car pulled out too fast when we left, like a kid but then didn't accelerate like a kid would. Figured it was our cover. Not too amazing – I did know it was in process remember. Mitch, I seriously do wonder how you ever survived. Again there's a guy on your six and you don't even know he's there."

"You know – it must have been a miracle. In fact, I'm sure of it. God's always liked me. She thinks I'm cute. Anyway, that's what wingmen are for, to clear your six. Seriously, I'm impressed ol' buddy. Gives me comfort to know you're on my side. Kinda scary for the other guy, you bein' after him."

"Too bad *he* doesn't know that. Be better for us if he did. Would probably sneak far away in the night if he knew *I* was after him. As long as he thinks it's *you* after him he'll think everything's alright. No problem."

"Maybe it'd be best if we somehow let him know that it's you, not me, that's hunting him. The more I think about that idea the better I like it. Yeah, definitely that's what we should do, alright."

"Not likin' that approach, fast mover. Probably looks good to you but not to me. I don't mind you covering me but your eyesight bein' what it is you might shoot me, not him. Bein' shot hurts no matter who pulled the trigger. Nah, we'll let him keep thinking that you're the threat. I like it better that way."

"Okay. But I am impressed you picked up on that tail. Let's go home. Round up Bo, see if he can join us. Make sure Munoz warned him of the cover. You Army guys scare me. Bo might draw down on his protection. Not good. They'd probably double the bill for that. Mr. Bonano might object to the surcharge."

Grazing laughed and punched in the number. Finished, he clicked it closed. "Mitch, I'm feeling good. Kinda exciting to be in the trenches again. Sure hope the guy sticks his head up so we can get a clean shot."

"Know what you mean. We'll get the bastard."

THE DEVIL'S RANSOM

PART THREE

THE AVENGERS*

* inflict harm in return for an injury or wrong
done to oneself or another

—The New Oxford American Dictionary

CHAPTER 41

They gathered on the patio. Their light jackets, needed in Pacific Grove, were off. They were not needed in Carmel Valley beyond the fog line. The afternoon was a comfortable eighty two degrees, the usual breeze calm. Munoz had placed a coffee pot and tea pot on the table, cups, water and glasses and a plate piled high with sandwiches.

Mitchell said "Jimmy, you've been busy. So you're a chef also. This is great. Thanks."

"Thought everyone might be hungry. Made a special California treat for you guys – jalapeno sandwiches."

Grazing said "Hey, Mitch. You have any tuna fish in there?"

Munoz, laughing, said "Ken, don't worry. I can't eat the damned things either. There's tuna, egg salad and cheese sannies there."

"Better." Hanson said.

As they sat down to eat Munoz' cell phone rang. He listened then clicked it closed. "Stratton's on his way in."

He no sooner said that when Stratton came through the patio gate. After the greetings and the invitation to join and eat, Stratton said "Thanks for including me in the protection. Guess things are heating up or the cover wouldn't be needed. I appreciate the call, Jimmy. Scotty had called me already – the minute you hung up, even before he had assets moving. Some nonsense about warning his old boss. Anyway, I thought I'd wander over to see if I could be useful. I saw that the shooting had started with that Rust fellow going down. Shame!"

"Deke, I met with him and warned him off. Tried to, anyway. The guy wouldn't listen. Obsessed." Mitchell said. "Glad to have you here. The more the merrier. What I really mean is the more targets the less the odds the guy will shoot me. I like that. I'm a little worried about you, though, volunteering to step forward into the line of fire and all. I'd come to the idea that you were a pretty smart fellow. Guess I should re-visit that conclusion." Everyone laughed. "After we eat we'll bring all of us current. We've had a lot of separate activity going on. We need to bring it together today."

Stratton nodded and reached for a sandwich. Hanson went into the house returning with a bucket of beer bottles on ice and an opener. He said "The Sergeant did a nice job of setting up but he doesn't understand high level, command staff strategy meetings. Here's the beer."

"About time." Stratton said.

* * * * *

When they had finished eating and cleaned up, Mitchell said "Gents, we're getting close. I had an interesting day yesterday up in San Jose. I'll fill you in but first we should hear what everyone else has to report. My information will take time and be more relevant when you have the other information. Ken, what's happening with the money?"

Grazing said "Talked again with Tom. Money is flowing in bits and pieces into the Singapore account. We have the account number but not the password. He has a track on the actual money movement but not the transfer instructions. Those contain the password in order to effect the transfer. And those could be different for each account. We do have the name of the attorney of record who filed the corporate papers and legally represents it. It is probable that he does not possess the password for the account. No password is required for deposit, only withdrawal. I'm afraid our Mister X is the only one who has it."

Mitchell said "Good. We'll get it. Do something for me. Call Tom and see if there are life insurance policies on Imelda Watson and, if so, how big and when subscribed – and, of course, the beneficiary."

"What about Winfred?"

"Not important. Jimmy, bring us up on your work."

"Okay. As you all know, Bonano gave us a 'Ricardo' guy and the Embassy connection. I tracked Ricardo and Tia Sophia into the United States, sponsored by Ambassador Anderson, living with Anderson in La Jolla, both naturalized. Found one Richard Ortiz at USC – and his Social Security number........"

"What?" yelled Grazing. "Ortiz? How long have you known that? Jesus Christ!"

"Ken, what's got you fired up?" Mitchell asked.

"God damn it. PineTree Financial. Watson's junior partner is named Richard Ortiz, an MBA from USC!"

"You've got to be kidding me." Mitchell said.

"No. That first meeting I had with Watson when I checked them out for curiosity. The receptionist, MaryLou, got the papers from Richard's office. Watson mentioned his name, called him his junior partner."

"Damn. We've known that last name for several days. You weren't here when Jimmy reported to me."

"It's in the summary books." Jimmy said.

"Haven't had time to read mine." Grazing said. "That's the guy though. I didn't meet him but I'll bet he matches the description that Bonano gave you. We are definitely on the final stretch."

"Tomorrow let's get pictures of those three folks at PineTree. From a distance. Don't want to tip our hand at this stage. Truth is, we have no proof of anything at all. But at least we know where to look." Mitchell said. "Today Ken and I spoke with Jane Villareal. She and Abernathy, in our opinion, are not behind this. Ken and I both believe what she said. The suspicious connections between the two are totally benign and of non-interest." Mitchell said.

"Before you get into your San Jose stuff I need to cover something. Yesterday, while you were in San Jose, Bo sent over a young man that does some work for him. Seems this fellow, Paul Garvin by name, has had first hand involvement with Watson and PineTree. We sat out on the patio and Paul shared his story. This may answer some of our questions. Jimmy, I taped it if you wish it for the files. About two and a half years ago, plus or minus, Paul and his wife acquired a nice piece of property in Marina. They intended to divide it up and build three houses on it. They would live in the first and sell or rent the next two. They hired architects, worked with the city – which was an unmitigated bitch, constantly changing this and that. He wondered why they don't know what they want in advance. Anyway, they complied with all the picayunish bullshit and received word that their permits were approved about a year and a half ago."

"Getting loans then was no problem. They were even giving 'no-doc' loans – loans with no documentation required. Banks were not only mortgage brokers. They wrapped everything into a five hundred thousand first mortgage for him – no problem."

"Then they ran into minor delays getting the physical permits in hand. It was time to begin land preparation and construction. They started. They had seen right along that they would need a bridge loan, a construction loan. That was common, no problem they thought. Then there was a sea change – the banks had started acting squirrelly, as he put it. Somebody told him about Watson and PineTree. He went to them."

"They reached a deal. PineTree would advance seven hundred fifty thousand. That is, an LLC would provide the funds through PineTree and be given a first mortgage on the properties. Of the proceeds of the loan five hundred thousand would payoff the existing first mortgage and the remaining funds would be advanced as progress payments to pay contractors. Watson himself had determined the finished value and approved the loan as justified by that value."

"Everything went fine for awhile. Monies were advanced for construction payments. Then Paul ran into delays from Watson with excuses. Then he couldn't get through to Watson. The first two houses were essentially finished. The Garvins had moved into the first. The second needed a little fluffing and it would be ready for sale or rent. The third was about half done. The contractor, not being paid, walked off the job, filed a mechanics lien and filed suit."

"Their life became hell. They didn't know it would become worse. They started getting notices that they were in default on their first mortgage – the five hundred one. PineTree had not paid it off! It appears that Watson sold a first mortgage to an LLC of investors for one point five million, didn't pay off the five hundred existing first – just pocketing the seven fifty and five hundred – and also the remainder of the two fifty! Paul's attorney can't believe the brazenness of it. Suit will be filed but the Garvins have a damaged credit rating, reputation and all that. What they will recover remains to be seen. He can't be planning to survive when these things start unfolding"

"I asked him if Watson walked in and gave him the money to finish construction, paid off the old first and covered all his expenses to date would he be willing to drop all charges and claims against Watson and PineTree. He said sure. The property would be complete, the value there. He could get a regular loan at far less interest and if even one of the two units sold he would need far less money as principal. The phony seven fifty is between Watson and his investors. The documents he signed are for seven fifty only."

"It looks to me that that is what Watson is trying to do. He's scrambling to keep up appearances with high interest returns to established investors to buy time using other monies he's not supposed to. He's hoping to cure before the crap really hits the fan. He'll probably cure the Garvins shortly."

Mitchell said "It looks like that's one of the ways that he's kept the balloons in the air – paying the monthlies with false money. That dog won't bark for long! It certainly fits with what I learned in San Jose. Watson had sixty-eight LLCs he had formed and taken monies against first and second mortgages. No problem there except he recorded the mortgages in his name, Ortiz's and MaryLou Novak's, not the name of the respective LLC! During the deposition time they frantically re-recorded all sixty-eight in the proper names. There are others that were upside down to begin with – supposed mortgages laid off to LLCs that are greater than the actual borrowings, even value, and the difference used to pay returns to investors giving the appearance of profitability."

"Even worse are the valuations he made that were so high that he and friends could purchase homes with zero money out of pocket, resell, pay off the mortgage out of the transaction and pocket the appreciation – all unbeknownst to the investors. At the same time he generated new fees for the new transaction. That is a breach of implied fiduciary responsibility – and that is a tort, or so attorneys are maintaining. Along that line, as defaults occurred with this collapse he failed to notify members of the LLCs of those defaults such that the investors, if they so chose, could step in and cure the default or bid in at the foreclosure sale to protect their position. There are instances where positions were lost, payments to investors continued and no one knew of the lost positions until the deposition disclosed them. They may be missing around twelve million dollars of funds held in trust accounts or so one investigation asserts. If so that would cover a lot of those high interest returns or he's got a big chunk rat-holed somewhere. Probably both."

"There are many people who borrowed their entire home equity from banks to invest in PineTree, people with no source of current income to pay back the loans if the investment failed. Of course, people believe that mortgage security is fail proof – or, at least, they did before this collapse. Many of those folks hear the word mortgage but don't dwell upon the words second or third and what that means. The effect upon this community in human terms will be devastating. There are many whose belief in this sure thing will lead them to a life of poverty with no way to recoup, the elderly, the frail, the sick."

"Let me backtrack for a minute. I gleaned background information on the three PineTree individuals from the depo and investigative reports. It seems our principal, Mr. Watson, never finished university, certainly not UCLA as mentioned in those credit union press releases long ago. He did attend a community college on and off and eventually received an AA degree."

Grazing broke in saying "On the wall of fame in his office he has diplomas from Harvard and Wharton displayed. There's nothing there about an AA degree from where-the-hell community college. Most strange."

"That appears to be the least of his crimes but it fits in. He did acquire legitimately his real estate sales license and Broker's license from the State of California and has maintained them throughout the years. He lied on his application both to the credit union and to Bear Stearns years ago, which is no surprise, asserting that he had a Bachelor degree in Business Administration from UCLA as repeated in the press releases. He has claimed that so often for so many years that he probably has come to believe it himself. The Harvard and Wharton representation probably came later. He has been continually active in all phases of real estate since he left Bear Stearns in the mid-eighties. He received huge fees from Keating's Lincoln Savings and Loan debacle down south. You may remember that mess cost the government more than three billion bailout and more than twenty thousand people lost everything. He was not actively associated with, nor employed by, the scam – he was an independent operator and was paid fees accordingly. He left the area before the meltdown in 1989, coming here to Monterey. So far, he is the only one named in the forthcoming suits. He is the one deposed and that was earlier on one suit based on a state reporting error."

Richard Ortiz, age thirty-six, is for real – he is a graduate of USC – a Bachelor Degree in finance. Also an MBA. He was naturalized as a teenager – from Guatemala. He also worked at Bear Stearns. He was well thought of there, an ambitious young man on the make. The word was that he had bought into the 'greed is good' creed but no indications there of any illegal conduct. He had strong entrepreneurial urges, felt confined by corporate limits. He left with high praise and recommendations. He joined PineTree five and a half years ago and has conducted many of the pitch meetings with potential investors. He skillfully handles the professionals – lawyers and accountants, speaks the right language, and projects an impressive aura of professionalism, competence and honesty. Watson allowed him to work one on one with clients – potential or actual. He had signing power the last four years. Beginning four years ago some mortgages were held and recorded in his name. Four days before Watson's deposition all were re-recorded under the proper LLC names. No other potential malfeasance was noted in the investigative reports."

"MaryLou Novak, age twenty-nine, joined PineTree five years ago. She also has a degree in finance – from Phoenix University. Small town girl from Gustine, father a dairy farmer. Ambitious. Money-hungry hometown commentary. She, too, has participated in potential investor pitch sessions and her degree has been touted – but not her school. She has been introduced as operating in a professional capacity – not as a receptionist secretary. Commencing before but near the same time as Ortiz, some mortgages were recorded in her name and re-recorded the same day as those of Ortiz and Watson. She is single, no history of marriage and lives alone although it is reported that Watson visits often. She has had no law enforcement contact. She handles the lion's share of paperwork, contracts, banking, filings, recordings and such. She handles cash distributions and has check signing authority. She signed all the interest checks forwarded in the last four years including those on lost foreclosed properties. So far, no to-be-filed suits have listed her as a defendant. In her capacity she had to be participating in the deception. The intent is to turn her as a witness during depo or, failing that, adding her name as one of the John Does."

It appears that Watson ran a clean business up until about four years ago. Even then, the recording in their own names is not, per se, illegal. They can be construed as agents of the LLCs. It is not clear what they – or he - had in mind with that. It is possible – or probable – that Watson directed that with the others just obeying the boss' orders but not understanding the reasons. He may – and this is pure conjecture

– have intended to package the mortgages and sell them to the securities market then abscond with the cash. It would appear to be legit to the buyer if they bothered to vet the paper. Often no one bothered. The money involved was not trivial. The total on those mortgages was thirty-three million. With the one suit and upcoming deposition he apparently changed his mind and re-recorded them."

Hanson said "He had this kidnapping plan formulated by then. It was in process. It looks to me that he needed time for it to come to fruition. Best to re-record – no harm, no foul. The mortgage sale scam would mean abandoning everything and an international run for cover before long. The kidnapping and insurance plan couldn't be traced to him – or so he thought."

"You've got a point. Sounds right to me. That's probably his thinking. Starting the mortgage filings when he did, he must have been planning a long-term run out back then. He wasn't in any trouble four years ago. In fact, his business was booming. He was riding the bubble and making out like a bandit! That would have been 2004. The guy certainly had the experience of the eighties. No doubt he saw that the bubble would burst someday. There *were* guys who had it figured out then – they were betting against the bubble. With the collapse they are making billions – yeah, with a B – with the credit default swaps they had bought for next to nothing from big banks, insurance folks and investment houses. Watson may have been reading the same tea leaves as those folks."

Grazing interjected "What the hell is a credit default swap? When you use market jargon I get lost."

"A credit default swap is essentially an insurance policy on a position. When a bunch of mortgages were gathered together into a 'bundle', into one unit, that unit was called a Collateralized Debt Obligation or CDO for short. Each CDO had a value. There was the principal portion to amortize monthly and the interest portion to be paid monthly, creating a fixed monthly cash flow. These fixed flows were of value to investors like insurance companies, pension funds, trust funds and the like. Anyone could buy an insurance policy against any given CDO failing – if they could find someone to sell them one – and that someone also had to have the financial where-with-all to cover the guarantee. Everyone so believed in the safety of the CDOs that some big players sold insurance policies – called credit default swaps – very cheap, almost gave them away, and viewed the premiums as free money. By big players I mean like AIG, Deutsche Bank, etc. When the mortgage default rate began to be big enough to cause the collapse of a CDO, the insurer had to pay off the face value to the insured – that is, the purchaser of the insurance, not the CDO itself or the investor. By the way, that stuff is a big part of the bailout need."

"Actually, home prices peaked in California in early 2005 and commenced a steady decline. In 2004 home prices were over ten times average annual income while the American average was about four to one ratio. Watson could have seen that warning flag. Hell, it was his profession. He must have seen it. 2004 was when he began the recording game and his bail out. By that time he'd had more than a year to become involved with little Miss Novak. Perhaps he started thinking with his other head."

Hanson commented "He seems to have been a pretty straight guy until he hired Ortiz and MaryLou."

"I think that may be a coincidence. The market shifts hadn't occurred yet thus no need to get kinky. When he saw the indicators of the eventual collapse he began planning for an escape, a grab the money and run. The MaryLou element was probably a factor. Sweet young things tend not to be enamored with fat old men who have no money. Ken commented on her lighting up when he's around. He probably wanted to keep that light burning." Munoz opined.

Mitchell continued "Then, about two and a half years ago, the first default hit him. He had a second and bought out the first which ate a lot of cash. He used a new LLC for that mortgage with himself as the debtor. Eventually he sold the property at a loss but made up the capital shortfall himself. No investor was aware of the manipulations. He maintained the image of success and fail-safe."

"Throughout '06 and '07 home prices continued their steady decline in California. The adjustment from speculation to reality was beginning its run. The effects were slow to hit the Monterey Peninsula but they did hit it subtly. Demand for mortgages on those spec homes declined. That impeded cash flow but didn't eliminate it. In early 2007 a couple more defaults occurred. Not a big thing in itself but he was in a cash pinch and didn't cure. That is when the phony payments to investors began. It was at that time that deals like the Garvin scam began – doubling the asserted mortgage, not paying off liens and using funds to maintain image while his kidnap and insurance plan came into play."

"We know the time frame on this. The folks on the mortgage shenanigans didn't know anything about the kidnap thing until our digging led me to my business attorney who recognized the implications immediately and, as I said, nudged me in the right direction for this confidential background information on our guy."

"This guy is a real sweetheart. It is a shame about the nice folks who are going to get severely damaged when this comes down. On the other hand, their greed was a factor, but we all have that to some degree or another."

CHAPTER 42

"And that, gentlemen, is that. While we think about all that I have related to you, I suggest that contemplation is best done on a full belly. I asked Jimmy to order us in a Limo. It awaits us. I thought it also best that we each not wander around alone. There is a wonderful restaurant in Pacific Grove called Favarolo's – on Lighthouse. Everything is made on premise. Mom, Pop, and son operation. The food is to die for. Shall we?"

Stratton begged off. There was a previously committed engagement with his wife.

They returned home well into the night. Mitchell found two bottles of a twenty four year old vintage Port from Quinta da Noval and some Monte Cristos. They turned on the gas overhead heaters and settled back to enjoy and talk.

Munoz' phone vibrated. He took the call. He looked up and said quietly "Guys, we have visitors. Have your weapons ready. Careful, our guys are out there. They've got six spotted moving closer. They'll take them down. If any get through be ready."

Mitchell said "I believe we should continue talking. Sound normal." Maintaining their talk, they smoothly glided to defensive positions in the shadows along the walls, weapons at the ready.

Munoz, monitoring his phone, said "Two are down and secured. These guys, whoever they are, are not very good. They're working in pairs and not staying near each other. They're moving toward the house. One more down. Another........What? What? Oh, Jesus Christ! Identify yourselves. Yell stand down. Bring 'em in." He snapped his phone closed sharply. All eyes were upon him.

He said "They're god damn FBI!"

Mitchell said "You're not serious. Really?"

"That last one? They didn't get the tape on quick enough. He said FBI. Our guy didn't put him down."

The patio gate opened. Three black-clothed men, their arms behind them, were marched in followed by three different black-clothed men. They were followed by the rest.

Mitchell said "Who's in charge here?"

One man stepped forward and said "I am. We are FBI. Get these damn ties off of us. You are interfering with a Federal officer. You have assaulted Federal officers. You are under arrest."

Mitchell said to Grazing "Get that god damn Harrison on the phone. What does that silly son-of-a-bitch think he's doing?"

Grazing was already punching in numbers. When Harrison came on the line Grazing said "What the fuck do you think you're doing? You god damn near got your incompetent idiots out here killed! What the hell is the FBI doing at Mitchell's house?"

Harrison said "What? What do you mean 'killed'?"

"We've got your people here in the yard. One of your guys is trying to put us under arrest. It's a little ridiculous because his hands are flex-tied behind his back. I'm taking pictures. Come out here and collect your children. Now. Out."

Grazing looked at the young FBI agent who had tried to arrest them and said "Son – you heard that. Would you like to re-think about putting us under arrest? Mitch, are you getting their pictures?"

Mitchell said "Yeah, I've got them. Nice poses."

Grazing said "Are these guys dis-armed?"

One of the Blackstone men said "Yes, Sir. We have their weapons."

"Take pictures of those too, Mitch. Then give the camera to Jimmy. Jimmy, download the stick. Send them to me and to another safe place. Your call. Now, for you clowns. Please indicate to these men in which pocket you have the warrant authorizing your entry onto this Citizen's property and home. Where is it? Answer me! Now!"

"What, no answer? Surely you agents of the law would not come here without one. There is no public safety issue involved. Why in the world would you violate the Constitution of The United States like this? I can't wait to hear your answer."

"Sir, I will wait for ASAC Harrison to arrive and answer. Could you please remove these flex-ties? They are very uncomfortable." The agent said. The others nodded, concurring.

"Think we'll wait for Harrison. I'm not sure you all are who you claim to be. Probably should wait for Harrison, whom I know, to identify you. You could be Muslim terrorists with false IDs. You could be narco killers. Even worse, you could be wine geeks after his cellar. God only knows what you are. Besides, handing you over trussed up might make a point."

Mitchell said "Colonel, the pictures make the point." He

was not sure where Grazing was going with this. No point in pissing off the FBI too much.

Grazing said "You've got a point. Cut 'em free."

They stood there rubbing their wrists when Harrison came through the gate, took in the situation and said "I assigned them for your protection. After Rust was killed I knew you were next on the list. They've been on each of you since about noon."

A Blackstone man said "Since eleven forty eight. That's when mine showed. Been monitoring his curiosity."

Another Blackstone man said "The guy watching the house got in position at one thirty seven."

Harrison said "One thirty seven?" as he looked at the subject agent.

"Took me time to get here, Sir. Traffic out of San Jose."

Grazing said "Harrison, what the hell were you thinking, not informing us?"

"You wouldn't act normal if I did that. Besides, I thought you cowboys would refuse if I offered and I didn't want to chance losing any of you." Harrison responded.

"Why do I feel less than protected and more like bait? Anyway, what are they doing closing on the house at night? That's a no-no. They're on private property."

"That's something I'd like to know as well. Agent Johnson, would you like to explain this? To all of us."

"Sir, we moved in to be closer to the wall so we could be looking out to any potential threat from all sides."

Munoz said to a Blackstone man "Carpenter, please tell us what came down out there."

"Sir, each time we had their man spotted when they came on duty or soon thereafter. They were monitored. They were viewed as threats. When they made their move to penetrate the house we made our moves to negate the threat. The first three, from behind, had tape slapped over their mouths and a pistol placed against their skull and ordered to their knees. They were pushed down and flex-tied, wrists and ankles. They were dis-armed. That operative then went to defensive search for potential re-enforcement assaulters. You were informed at all times of our actions – after the fact."

Harrison said "You put guns to their heads? To FBI agents?"

"Yes, Sir. That was unknown to us. We are all licensed to carry. We knew they were armed by bulges in their clothing. Their actions indicated they had deadly intent. They appeared to be the deadly threat that caused you to put them there to begin with. We broke no law. We used no more than reasonable force. Sir. Colonel?" the Blackstone supervisor nervously said looking to Grazing.

Hanson said "Special Agent Harrison, we have not met. I am Bo Hanson. I am of the opinion that what our agent says has merit. There have been some errors made, forgivable ones at this level. I believe that procedure calls for a tender of protection which the Citizen may accept or reject. A certain question of competency has arisen – not to the benefit of the FBI. May I suggest you gather your children and depart? Oh yes, and send them somewhere for proper training. Say – to the Army?"

Harrison had turned to face Hanson. "Ah, the other Colonel. At least this time there are no dead bodies for us to clean up. Johnson, take the men and go. Stand down. Your assignment is finished." He turned back and said "I guess we screwed that up royally. I was trying to protect you gents."

Mitchell said "Special Agent Harrison, I'm Doug Mitchell. Please don't dismiss your men. Let me talk with you for awhile. I've got some thoughts to run by you."

"Of course, the other Musketeer. Sure, I'll hold them. When would you like to talk?"

"I may change this but I'm thinking about three tomorrow afternoon. You'll probably only have to hold two agents in the area. The two and you are sufficient to handle anything that may come up. Early on, Colonel Grazing told you that we would cooperate if it turned domestic. We think – not know, think – that it has and we intend to cooperate if we have definitive evidence that it has. I think we will tomorrow afternoon. If so, I want to turn further action over to you immediately. I would need to have you close by, not further than one or two minutes away. At that point I would turn everything over to you for full credit if any is due. We would disappear. Would that be workable for you?"

"Under the circumstances I guess I can work with you fellows. I know that you won't tell me exactly what you've got going but as long as you're not breaking any laws I have no legal right to know. You old guys are something else but somehow you get to the heart of the matter. I'm positive you guys are breaking laws all over the place but what I don't know I can't act on. So keep me ignorant. By the way, if your plans have anything to do with Winfred Watson, he's in L.A. He flew there yesterday, ticketed to return noon tomorrow."

Mitchell tipped his head slightly, giving the Special Agent a curious look then said "We'll keep you in the loop if anything changes. Otherwise, three tomorrow at the Starbuck's on Sixty-eight. And Special Agent, you say we're breaking laws all over the place. I assure you that that is incorrect – only the ones that are in our way. But I'm sure the FBI can understand that, no?"

Harrison laughed and said "You know, I'm a little uncomfortable about those pictures. Embarrassing. Could hurt some good young men's careers. FBI's not too fond of embarrassment. Not really fair – rookies against Special Forces, you know."

Mitchell said "I'm sure those will never see the light of day. I'll see to it. Good night Harrison."

Soon after Harrison departed Hanson left for home. Munoz called it a day begging exhaustion, which was understandable, leaving Mitchell and Grazing to enjoy their Cuban cigars and vintage Port.

Taking time to thoroughly inspect the glow on the end of his cigar and sipping some of his Port, Grazing lazily asked "Mitch, what was that all about?"

"Tomorrow late afternoon is the end play if I'm thinking right. Here's what I have in mind." After he explained they argued into the night.

CHAPTER 43

Tuesday morning came with a roar, wind and nearly horizontal hard rain. Its pounding against the house woke everyone early. As usual, Grazing was the first up. He had both the pot and water going when Mitchell, followed by Munoz, strolled in.

"Damn, not ready yet? Jeez, you're turning into a banker, Kenner. Guess old guys need more sleep."

"Nah, not more sleep. Heard your snoring clear out here. So loud I couldn't think through the steps for the coffee maker for awhile. Got the water going okay though. Jimmy, yours is ready. Fast mover, yours'll be in about half an hour."

Munoz said "God, you guys never stop, do you?"

"If you don't keep him in line he'll start doing strange things like his plan for today. I should'a smacked him up alongside the head yesterday. Only thing that keeps him between the lines." Grazing said.

"What lines?" Mitchell queried innocently.

"That rain is really pouring down. I thought it doesn't rain around here this time of year." Munoz said.

"Doesn't. This isn't rain. This is a god damn hurricane

from Hawaii. Pineapple Express they call it. Grapes aren't going to like this. It's not so much the rain itself but the warm airmass with it. I knew this was coming. My guys are all set to blow-dry the vines when it breaks. That'll be day and night till they are dry then we'll cover it again with fungicide spray. Never ends." Mitchell said.

"Blow-dry the vines? Are you serious?" Munoz asked.

"Yeah. We use fans and blow the water out of the vines. Takes a couple of passes through the vineyard then the fungicide to fight the rots. Feel sorry for the guys on heavy dirt. They can't get into their fields for days. Real rot problem for them."

The patter continued until a break for showers, shaves and dressing. They decided to go to the Wagon Wheel restaurant close by in the Valley for breakfast. Mitchell called Bo.

"Don't know if I can make it, Boss. It usually takes two people to get my boat out of storage but I'll do my best."

"Right. See you soon. We're heading out."

He then called Stratton who jumped at it also.

The Wagon Wheel is one of the great breakfast restaurants of the world, perhaps the best. No one knows when it first opened. The word is that it was operating when the first white explorers came over the hill. Normally there is a waiting line outside. Not so today. They had no delay and took the big table back in the corner. Stratton arrived. Hanson rolled in shortly after.

Hanson came inside shaking water off his head. "This can't be too good for the grapes, Mitch." He said as he came to the table.

"It's not but it will save on the electric bill. How're you doing this fine day, old buddy?"

"I'm good. Funny how rain makes the knee joints stiff but they loosen. How about you?"

"Knee joints are fine – no problem. In fact, I went water skiing earlier. Knees felt great. Don't have any idea what you're talking about but I am feeling sorry for you." Mitchell jibed.

"It starts already, huh? Jeez, my brain's still at idle." Hanson said.

Grazing said "Bo, it's almost always at idle. What's new about that?"

They ordered. Breakfast came. They ate. Grazing's cell phone rang about half past nine. Grazing took the call saying "Uh huh" several times then "Thanks for the call."

He leaned back in his chair, looked at his companions and said "That was Harrison wishing me a good morning. Oh, yes, by the way, Richard Ortiz was found shot to death in his apartment this morning. Found about six thirty by the manager of the complex. The wind gusts were slamming his front door back and forth against a wall. A neighbor had called about the noise. Now isn't that a curve ball? I know that guy was our Ricardo. Double damn!"

Stratton put the fingers of one hand to his forehead, rubbing the area gently. Then he spoke saying "Ken, check with Harrison. I suspect that you will find that both Rust and Ortiz were shot with a thirty eight. Also, later, forensics will find the bullets are from the same gun."

"How do you get there, Colonel?" Munoz inquired.

"Jimmy, remember at the Restaurante del Diablo? When Bonano was disarmed he had a thirty eight snub nose. I think Ricardo was enchanted with his real-life bad guy playmate. He would copy him. Ricardo would have the same kind of pistol. He shot Rust. Watson probably offered to dispose of the weapon. Probably told him it was dangerous to keep. Once Ricardo handed him the weapon Watson shot him."

"Why?" Munoz asked.

"The money has been accumulated. One less to share. And, most important, it cuts the connection to Watson. Watson can claim that any wrongdoing was done by Ortiz without any knowledge by Watson."

"Deke, Watson flew to Las Angeles Sunday. Ortiz went down Monday night sometime. Watson 'll be back today noon." Mitchell said.

"Somehow he got back. He did it. He's clearing the deck, eliminating shares and connections. When the bankruptcies hit he'll be cleaned out, have zero. Then he'll disappear only to cash in his retirement policy in Singapore. He did it."

Mitchell said "Deke, I think you're right about the same gun but I'll bet Watson has an airtight alibi in L.A. or somewhere south. The planning through this whole thing has been too good for him to leave himself open there. He'll be covered. The flight was for that very purpose. Another flight up and back would give him away. A rental car would also give him up unless he had good false ID.

Their phones rang almost simultaneously. Grazing flicked his open, listened, grabbed a pad and pen and said "I'm ready to copy. Say all that again."

Mitchell said "Mitchell." then "Morning, Nolan."

Nolan said "Did you enjoy your Sunday?"

"Did I ever! Absolutely fascinating day. Thank you."

"Thought you might find it so. You realize we are monitoring everything there. I have another little tidbit for you. Last Friday morning Imelda Watson filed for divorce citing irreconcilable differences."

Mitchell yelled "That's it. God damn it, THAT ... IS ... IT! Nolan, I love ya. If you were built different I'd marry you! That is it!"

Nolan said "She doesn't know it but she is jumping an empty ship."

"She knows something else! Far more important. I'll tell you later. You just gave me the keystone. Bye and thank you, thank you and thank you."

His table mates were staring at him.

"Guys, I was just informed that last Friday Imelda Watson filed for divorce!"

"So?" Hanson said.

Stratton said "Poor woman was pretty zonked out. Badly traumatized, catatonic even."

"By god, no she wasn't! She wasn't catatonic. Her eyes were clear and she had no catatonia twitches. Confused me at the time. She was *understanding* and it first shocked her then deeply saddened her. She began contemplating her possibilities. At the hotel, sitting on the couch, Peter and I nearby, she said in a moan 'I was supposed to die'. I thought it a strange expression at the time. Rust figured it out his last afternoon. That's why he said 'That god damn Watson'. She *knew* he had forced her to go to Guatemala to be killed! She *knew* it. How? Ken, we need that insurance info fast. Ring up Tom. See if you can build a fire."

Grazing had been waving his pad in the air. "Mitch, stop for a minute. I have it here. That was Tom. Here it is: Four years ago, one million on each, each the other's beneficiary. Three years ago, an additional mil, same beneficiaries. Sixteen months ago additional policies, four million each, same beneficiaries including a double indemnity terrorist rider but two year delay. That's all."

"And there you have it. She knew about the one, one and four. She knew she was worth six million to him – dead. She knew he had forced her to go. She also knew he was in severe financial trouble from the market collapse. That's why she said what she said! Now we know. It is Watson for sure!" Mitchell finished.

Munoz was pointing his index finger toward the room. Mitchell turned his head. The people at the other tables and counter – all the way to the door – were looking his way. He smiled and said "Sorry for the disruption, folks. I'll be quieter."

Those close by who had clearly heard the words were filled with curiosity and continued to look at him. Mitchell stood and, while nodding smilingly at each, departed. The others followed. Hanson paid the check.

In the car, Grazing said "We don't have one damn thing that constitutes usable proof of anything at all to do with the kidnapping. Ricardo was our possible connect. The PineTree financial stuff will sort itself out over the next few years and, besides, that's not our thing. He could answer to criminal charges as well as civil but all that will be relatively minor in the end. Ortiz will be the fall guy. He'll try to lay everything on him, even the kidnapping stuff if it should come up for any reason – which it won't. To seriously bring him down we need hard evidence on the Ortiz murder or Rust. I don't think there's any way to tie him to the kidnapping itself."

"No – except to the Singapore fund." Munoz offered.

"Yeah, but we can't give up Tom's work or even participation. It would finish him. Beyond a Treasury agent going around the FBI, some of his methods were beyond legal. We give the FBI that Singapore account info – they're going to seriously want to know *how* we know about it. That's not good." Grazing answered.

"We've got lots of time to work out the legal niceties. Right now we need that password to transfer those funds back. We'll get it later today if the plan works, which it will. Hell, it might even generate some of that proof we're after. It is in the hands of the gods now." Mitchell mused.

CHAPTER 44

It was precisely three in the afternoon. The outside tables at Starbuck's in the Stone Creek mini-mall were usually vacant at that time of day. Harrison was seated with two Grandes, waiting. Mitchell sat down as Harrison was looking down at his watch, jumping as Mitchell's chair scratched the concrete.

Mitchell took his cup and thanked Harrison saying "I assume this is for me. Glad you consented to this meeting, Mark. We are at an impasse, all of us. In summary, we have nine people kidnapped and nearly killed. We have two dead people here. There is no usable evidence to convict whoever is responsible and it doesn't look to me to be any in the future. All I see is no progress. Do you concur with that assessment?"

"That would be a fair assessment, yes. That would be my take on it." said Harrison.

"I think I know exactly who the doer is but I can't prove it in a fashion that would sustain in Court. I won't go into how I know this but I do. And please don't ask. What you need, Special Agent Harrison, is for the bad guys to expose themselves to you in a fashion that will let you bring them to justice. It is up to them to give you the evidence you need, perhaps in their own words."

"That would certainly be nice. And interest me. Profoundly. I want whoever it is!" Harrison commented.

"Mark, I know this is domestic now and is on your turf. We are supposed to back out. But you cannot go where we can and you cannot do what we can do. It is not a turf war between us. Together we can end this I believe. Today. These people are truly amateurs in spite of the brilliance of their planning. Outside their rigid plan they come apart, they panic, they make unplanned moves. To one of my compadres I made a comment about Sun Tzu and the art of war. At one point he said 'One must shake the grass to startle the snake'. I am afraid Peter Rust shook the grass too close to the snake and it bit him – a mistake I damn well won't make but I do intend to shake the grass. I believe *they* will make the mistake."

"I need you and your men standing close-by so when we yell you can arrive within two minutes – sooner the better. We would call on your cell. I believe you will find the weapon that was used on both Rust and Ortiz. I believe you will be able to arrest the perpetrator and have the proof you require."

"What the hell are you going to do?" Harrison asked.

"I'm going into the lion's den. I'm going to face the tiger one more time, nose to nose. I am going to say things and lay bare facts that they believe only they possess, that only they could possibly know. It will startle them beyond control, I believe. There may even be an attempted strike against me but I will be gone before it can occur. There may be deadly discord between them after I leave. You must enter quickly to prevent that."

"This is nuts! This is so far from acceptable protocol! I'll draw lifetime duty in Mossy Hollow, West Virginia! Why the hell am I even listening to you?" Harrison exploded.

"Because you want these bastards. And I'm the only way you can get them." Mitchell said softly. "I will be just fine. There will be armed protection around me. Mark, listen, we are big boys, and we know exactly what we are doing. There is no personal risk. There's a song that goes 'you don't pee with the puppies and crap in the big dog's yard'. Mark, when they kidnapped and murdered, they crapped in our yard. And for damned sure – we're very big dogs!"

"Mitchell, that, I've got to agree, is true! I'm damn glad you guys are on the side of the angels. Against my better judgment – or maybe going along with it – where do you want me and when?"

"At four forty-five I'd like you to be in the parking lot at PineTree's offices in Ryan Ranch Business Park. We will be arriving at PineTree's offices at a couple of minutes before five. The call to you should come at ten or fifteen minutes after five or thereabout. Ken will have your cell number on speed dial. Give Bo the cell number of one of your associates. Both will call. Timing is so tight that I don't want a failed connection to delay your arrival. There are stairs by the elevators. Come in that way. We will be using the stairs at the far end. We should be out of there, out of sight, when you and your men arrive. You and your men will see none of us so you have nothing in that area to testify about if ever necessary. We will depart out the back and be gone."

"What will be my probable cause for entry? I've got to have one." Harrison asked.

"It is an office open to the public so you have a right to enter. However, you will have one. It will be on the phone call. If necessary we will stand behind it. Testify if we have to. Even your presence outside the office will be supported by me, if necessary. I would testify that I thought my life was potentially at risk and I asked your presence for protection. Okay? But make it not necessary. Try the old anonymous tip thing. We'd prefer to stay below the radar."

"Mitchell, when this is over I've got a bunch of questions I'm going to ask." Harrison said.

"I'm sure you do and will. And I certainly will cooperate with the FBI to the best of my ability. I do point out, though, that at my age anything before nine o'clock this morning and thirty years ago is rather blurry. It comes and goes. Frustrates the hell out of me. I'm sure it will you as well. Damned memory."

"Mitchell, you guys are so full of shit!"

"Funny. Bo said the same thing about the FBI. Just this morning, I think. But then, it was before nine o'clock so I could be wrong." Mitchell said, laughing.

Harrison laughed as well, shaking his head.

Mitchell stood, looked at his coffee and said "Thanks for the coffee. Finally got some of my tax dollars back – I'll be damned. This is a great day! Four forty-five. Adios." He left.

Harrison nodded thoughtfully. To himself he said "This will either be a coup or a career-breaker. Hope that crazy bastard really does know what he's doing."

* * * * *

There were seven of them, The Magnificent Seven, three in Levi's and four in black. All were openly armed, pistols on hips, loosely holstered. They marched into the offices of PineTree Financial at four fifty-nine. They went through the empty reception area into Winfred Watson's office. Winfred and MaryLou looked up, startled, from documents spread on the desk, a paper shredder grinding merrily alongside.

Watson said "What the hell? What is going on?" Apprehension trying to grow into fear developed in his eyes.

The men spread to the sides of the room as they came through the door and assumed parade rest stances facing

Watson and MaryLou. One moved behind Watson. They were intimidating. Extremely intimidating. Intentionally so.

Mitchell said quietly "Winfred, sit down and be quiet." He nodded to the Blackstone man behind Watson who placed a beefy hand on the muscle running from Watson's neck to his right shoulder, squeezed with iron fingers and pressed Watson down into his chair. Watson grimaced with pain.

"Take the young lady to the reception room and hold her there. I will speak with her later. If this gets ugly she should not be here." Mitchell directed.

Two men took her arms to guide her to the door. She looked at the hands on her elbows then at Mitchell and said "Please let me go. I don't know anything. I'm just the receptionist."

Mitchell said "MaryLou, we both know that's not true, don't we? I'll speak with you when I've finished with Winfred." He gave a quick sideways snap of his head toward the door. They brusquely escorted her out and closed the door behind them.

Mitchell turned back, facing Watson, "Watson, it is over. It's done. Accept it. I want one piece of information from you and we will leave. No harm. Tell me the password for the Singapore account."

"What Singapore account? I don't know any Singapore account. What are you talking about?"

"What I'm talking about is an account in Singapore, specifically one in the Southeast Asia Bank, account number Z493601- 521Q containing eighteen point nine million dollars. Those ransom dollars that went from Central Bank to Grand Cayman to Lichtenstein to Guernsey and to a bunch of other places whose names and numbers I can give you if you wish. The dollars that traveled Europe reducing in size until they ended up together in Singapore. In the account that you set up through attorney Lee. The account that holds the monies belonging to the hostages. *That* is what I am talking about. Are we clear on that? I will not accept any more silly questions. The password, please."

Watson's left eyelid began to twitch, his lips quiver. He said nothing.

Mitchell nodded at Broderick who carrying a bag. The Broderick unzipped the bag and extracted two rolls of duct tape and a pair of water-pump pliers, sometimes called adjustable pliers. He stepped forward and laid them on Watson's desk, Watson watching every move, his eyes growing larger.

Broderick began tearing off arm-lengths of tape and sticking the ends to the edge of the desk.

Mitchell said "How'd you come up with the routing of the ransom? That's not something you'd do in your business."

Watson's quivering voice said "Richard got it from his Guatemala friend. What is he doing? What are those for?"

Mitchell put his cold, steely fighter pilot's eyes on him and said "You have not answered me. Answering me is the smart thing to do. Those things are persuaders. The tape will cover your mouth and bind you to your chair. The pliers are for loosening things, perhaps breaking them. Watson, you surprise me. I thought you were an intelligent man. Think on it. A tribal chieftain in the jungle chose to speak to me. A seriously bad-ass narcotics chieftain in the heart of Guatemala City chose to talk with me. Is it possible that you are not as smart as that tribal chief? Is it possible that you are tougher than or not as smart as that narcotics boss? It is fair that I tell you that every person that I've ever questioned seriously has given me what I sought. Every one – one way or another. I strongly advise your cooperation. I do not enjoy inflicting pain although your case would be an exception. Ordering the deaths of those boys and my friends profoundly disturbed me. Pissed me off, actually. Enough talk. Give me the password, now!"

Watson began to cry. Tears flowed down his cheeks as his plans and future disappeared in front of him. His mind realized that the magnificent life ahead he had envisaged, had planned for, had anticipated, had hungered for was dissipating as fog before the morning sun, had become nothing. He visibly diminished, collapsing in on himself.

As the Blackstone man approached him holding a strip of tape, Watson, in a barely audible voice, said "No. Eyewin."

Mitchell said "What? You win? What do you win?"

Watson said "The password is EYEWIN, spelled E,Y,E,W,I,N."

Mitchell looked to Munoz saying "Do you have that?"

Munoz nodded, his fingers flying over his laptop's keyboard.

The Blackstone man gathered the pieces and rolls of duct tape and the pliers returning all to his pouch.

"I do have one more question. The missing trust account funds. Where are they?"

"A lot has been paid out to investors as returns. There's only around two and a half million remaining. That is for distribution to investors. Keeping the ten percent return rate up on one hundred and fifty million or so ate up cash pretty fast the last year and a half." Watson mumbled.

"Where is it kept – which bank? Under what name and number?" Mitchell inquired. He looked at Munoz and said "We'll leave this alone and pass it along."

Watson, demolished in his defeat, whispered out the information.

Mitchell said softly "Thank you, Winfred. Now we wait for the transfer to be completed. That plan was brilliant. That was an amazing project you put together."

Watson, recovering somewhat, raised his head and speaking in a flat voice said "Yes, it was brilliant. No, it was genius. No one in their wildest imagination could have anticipated anyone trying a rescue in the time we gave much less succeeding. Such a thing was never considered. You bastards had to do the impossible."

Mitchell nodded his head agreeably. "What were you going to do with the money – cure the funny financial stuff and clean up your mess at PineTree?"

Watson said "Hell no. We were going to send everything into bankruptcy. I'd cure a couple of things to get rid of potential criminal charges. I'd let the receiver and the Court handle the mess and the people. There are still lots of assets of value. The investors would get some of their money back eventually, whatever was left after the receiver and lawyers took their cut. I was just going to disappear to some sunny place."

"You and Miss Sugar-pants in there were going to marry and ride off into the sunset hand in hand?"

"God, no! As soon as we divided up the money I was going to disappear again. Cold day in hell before I would marry her."

Grazing said "Bet that's not what she thinks. She's really got the hots for you."

"That's her thing. I go along with it but it was never going to happen. God, at times she's got body odor that would gag a maggot! And she is evil to the core. I would be afraid to turn my back on her. I want away from her as fast as I can."

Mitchell said "What do you mean by 'evil'?"

"What do I mean by evil? This was her plan – all of it! She shot Rust and Ortiz. That's what I mean by evil!"

The enormity of the blasphemy struck him. "Come on, Winfred. You're laying this whole thing on that young lady out there? That's not very gentlemanly or believable – although I do know she shot Ortiz." Mitchell said.

"Mr. Mitchell, she is not what she seems. You simply don't understand. When Rust showed up I wasn't here. She was. His ranting told her that he had put it together, had tied us to the Guatemala thing. He had to go. She called him to meet her on the beach. I didn't know about it until afterwards when she told me. She sent me out of town so she could eliminate Ortiz – the only connection to Guatemala. If Rust thought it then someone else must also. She said we had to cut that connection. Besides, financial stuff could also be laid to him. She also said it would now be a two-way split, not three. See what I mean about not turning my back?"

"Winfred, I would guess that you didn't let her and Ortiz know about Imelda's life insurance, you know, the six million dollars, did you?" Mitchell mildly inquired.

Momentarily surprised, Watson dejectedly said "No, that was a nice bonus for me. I paid the premiums, not them. MaryLou would get what she wanted – money and Imelda gone. Me, too. But the six million was mine. Could buy a lot of Coronas with an extra six million and a nice place to drink them. And nice brown girls to drink them with. Girls that smelled good. God, it would have been nice!"

Mitchell nodded at Grazing who left, going to the reception room and leaving the door open.

"Winfred, how did it all come down? I mean, nobody wakes up one morning and plans something like this, do they?"

"No. It sort of evolved. I saw early on the housing price collapse coming. Everything was too wacky. Prices climbing out of control driven by speculation. The multiples growing too big. We were really exposed but we couldn't stop bringing in money to shore it up. There was a time when I was going to sell off a bunch of mortgages in a package deal, grab the money and scram, probably to Brazil first. No extradition from there for financial misunderstandings, you know. There are other places as well. Somewhere along the way, over a lot of drinks, Richard started talking about his narcotics big-whig childhood friend in Guatemala. Mary-Lou said maybe we should have those dentists I helped support kidnapped for a big ransom and use the money to clean up the problem. I came up with the insurance play when I saw that the kidnapping plan was so good. The real estate problem grew to the disaster it is today. There wasn't a cure. I changed my plans. Let someone else clean up whatever there was to clean up. I could leave eventually with no one chasing me."

Munoz raised a hand and nodded yes.

"How did you pass the message that a rescue was in process? You had to do it from the bank. Did you have Ortiz call you?"

"Yeah, that was easy. I know enough about money mechanics to know the transfer was being delayed for some reason. I knew it would take time but it was getting ridiculous. The FBI doesn't put holds on private money. They don't have that power and they don't want that responsibility. If somebody dies they are responsible. The funds were easily available to a bank like Central. No- something was going on. There was some reason to delay. I told Richard to call me after half an hour. By then I knew of the rescue attempt and that it was in process. Frankly, I was shocked that such a thing was being done."

Mitchell said "Winfred, the warning on the rescue was cleverly done. My take on it was you suspected something was up because of the delay, as you said. You arranged for Ortiz to call you at the bank. Once you pushed for the answer you just waited for the call. Gutsy. In front of everyone you passed the message. The fifteen year deal meant fifteen minutes. Waiving the points meant no negotiation – right?"

"How the hell did you figure that?"

"In your BI report, you gave a talk to a Chamber of Commerce gathering. You were quoted at one point on profits to the effect that you never waive a fee for any reason whatsoever, never chase deals. Waiving points was something you never did, by your own words. It was non-negotiable. Your comment about losing the asset if they didn't foreclose is pretty apparent, given this context."

"It wasn't Ortiz that called. It was MaryLou. It took her some time to figure out what I was trying to say. I had to be pretty blunt with that one. She finally did get it. She directed Ortiz to send that message."

Winfred, I am curious about the collateralization percentages being so close. How did you come up with that if you don't mind telling me? I mean, it's not important but I would like to know. The pictures were easy but the percentage business befuddles me."

"I was somewhat surprised myself when the accountants spoke. Actually I was patting myself on the back when it came out. I made educated guesses at the net worth of each based on what I knew combined with surmises from comments over time. I used that number at sixty-five percent to determine the amount each could raise quickly. The actual number I came up with was higher but we wanted speed. I thought if we were too far off on some they could get community help. It wasn't all that complicated. We did it that way so there would be no arguments about who had to come up with what. Like I said, we were interested in speed." Watson said with a smile.

"*Jesus Christ.*" Mitchell thought. "*The son-of-a-bitch is pleased with himself.*"

* * * * *

Grazing had set his recorder on MaryLou's desk behind which she was standing. He turned it on. She listened, her head down. She said nothing. At the body odor comment her entire body sagged. She twitched slightly at the insurance comments. She appeared to be a young girl stood up for the Prom. She radiated dejection and hopelessness. Profound sadness enveloped her.

Grazing said loudly "Finished."

* * * * *

Mitchell said "Watson, the transfer is complete. Thank you for the correct password. You sit there for awhile. I will speak with MaryLou for a minute or two and then we will be gone. If you don't already have one, find a good attorney. You're going to need one. We are not the law but I know they are not far behind us. From the deposition you've given you know a lot more of the civil stuff is coming. Probably some criminal stuff as well. Good bye."

Mitchell thought *"Well Winfred Watson, if the rest doesn't go as I think it will this tape will certainly hang your miserable ass. By God, we got you, you worthless bastard. Time to find out if I've read MaryLou correctly. And time for the goddess Justice to use her sword – not her scales."*

Mitchell gestured out to his companions.

CHAPTER 45

They entered the reception area and gathered between Mitchell and the door. Mitchell was facing toward Mary-Lou. Her backpack was upright in the chair in front of her. She was ever so slowly, glacially, methodically unzipping the top compartment.

Mitchell said "MaryLou, it is over. All of it. Killing Rust and Ortiz was a mistake. Rust more so. The FBI will be here shortly. They will find …."

Someone yelled "GUN". Her hand was ever so slowly retreating from the backpack pocket. The butt of the pistol could be seen. Immediately five weapons were drawn and aimed at her.

Holding his arm out, palm down, Mitchell said "Guns down. Leave. Now."

They looked at him in shock – except Grazing.

Grazing said "You heard him. We're leaving now!" as he held the door open.

Mitchell said "Now, Ken."

Grazing exited and immediately hit the auto call button on his cell. So did Hanson on his. As the last man came out Grazing was saying into the cell "Move now. Gun in play."

The door closed.

Mitchell slowly moved toward the door as MaryLou, gun in hand dangling at her side, turned toward Watson's door, head still down, shoulders slumped.

Mitchell said "MaryLou, give it up. It is over. It's done."

She stopped and partially turned his way, eyes still down, gun still dangling loosely at her side.

Mitchell said "No, MaryLou. You don't want me. You want him. Let it go."

Her shoulders straightened. Her head rose. Still looking away, she said quietly "You are *so right* – it *is* over. But you are also *so wrong*. My plan was perfect, absolutely perfect. You assholes destroyed it, destroyed me. I *do want you* because you are the head asshole." With that she turned fully toward Mitchell.

The look in her eyes froze Mitchell in place, stopping his progress to the door. He was a deer in the headlights, immobile.

She smoothly raised the gun and pointed it directly at him.

She said "See you in Hell, asshole!" and she squeezed the trigger. At that instant Mitchell unfroze and leaned toward the door.

The 150 grains of 38 Special copper jacketed, hollow-point lead slammed into his body. Drops of blood and pieces of flesh painted a Jackson Pollock-style mural on the wall behind him. A nano-second later his body slammed into the artwork. He stood there dumbfounded. His eyes glazed. His knees gradually gave way. His body slid gently down the wall leaving a bright red smear through the fresh mural. He came to a stop sitting on the floor, his head sideways toward a shoulder. The large blood droplets and larger pieces of flesh formed tears for Mitchell and cried their way down the wall.

Marylou stood looking down at Mitchell's body. Watson appeared in his doorway, saw the carnage, saw MaryLou standing over the body. He promptly went into shock at the scene. MaryLou turned to him and again smoothly raised her pistol and fired. Watson disappeared backwards from the doorway.

* * * * *

Harrison and his two men were coming at a run down the long hall when they heard the first shot. Grazing and Stratton, Munoz, Broderick and Hanson close behind, were coming from the stairs, from the other direction in the hall. Guns were drawn. Grazing had yelled "No Mitchell" seconds before the first shot and they were already on the way back when they heard it.

Grazing was saying "Shit.Shit.Shit." as they approached. The FBI agents were holding palms up ordering the civilians to stop, to hold. They did. Harrison turned the doorknob as the second shot came. His two agents charged into the room, guns at the ready as the third shot was fired. Mary-Lou had fired into the roof of her mouth, painting another mural on the ceiling with human debris. Within seconds one, then the other, of the FBI agents yelled "Clear".

Stratton and Munoz raced to Mitchell's body. Grazing was calling 911. Harrison was on his cell doing the same. So was Hanson.

Stratton was on the wound, pressing hard, trying to stop the blood flow. Munoz had torn off his shirt and was wadding it up to create a makeshift pressure compress. Blood gushed as Stratton released pressure to insert the compress. He immediately reapplied pressure.

Munoz said "Pulse is weak."

Stratton said "Christ, there's blood everywhere. He's lost

a lot. Get those EMTs here fast, Ken. We're gonna lose him. Jimmy, stay on me when the EMTs get here. They won't be able to handle this. The pressure must stay on. We're in the wagon with him. I might not be able to maintain this much pressure. You may have to relieve me at some point."

Grazing said "EMTs on the way."

Stratton said "Call Joanne, find out his blood type then call emergency at CHOMP. Tell them to be ready for immediate whole blood transfusion upon arrival, several pints, before anything else. Have thoracic surgeons on standby. Use your rank, national emergency, whatever. Tell EMTs to bring the gurney up with them."

Grazing punched in Joanne's number. She answered. Grazing bluntly asked "What's Mitch's blood type?"

She answered automatically "O positive. Universal donor. Why?'

Grazing said "He's been shot. We're going to CHOMP." He hung up as she began screaming.

Stratton held pressure. The pool of blood was beginning to congeal. "Where are those fucking EMTs?" he cursed over and over.

The EMTs arrived. The lead EMT said "Okay, Sir, we'll take over now."

"The hell you will. Everyone, get under him and place him on the gurney. Jimmy, help me maintain pressure. Put up pressure on his back directly below my hands. Now, everyone."

Stratton walked alongside the gurney pressing down.

The lead EMT said "Sir, I really must insist. You are not qualified and you cannot be in our vehicle."

"Son, I'm a Colonel in the United States Army, Special Forces. I know exactly what I'm doing. If you try to interfere with any directive I give you will be taken into custody.

Sergeant, if he opens his fucking mouth again, shoot him or something. I don't have time for his bullshit."

The lead EMT then saw that all the men were armed, weapons in some hands. He saw one with FBI on his jacket. He said "Yes, Sir."

Thanking God for the elevator, they got Mitchell to the EMT truck and loaded. Lights flashing and siren screaming they headed for The Community Hospital of the Monterey Peninsula –CHOMP. "How long?" Stratton asked. Twelve minutes was his answer.

"Jimmy, I've got maybe five minutes left in me. Let's start the exchange. You'll have to carry the ball the rest of the way. It's got to be from this side to hold it right."

Munoz moved closer to Stratton's side. He slowly started to insinuate one hand under Stratton's. Once that was accomplished they began with the other hand. At the same time Stratton eased to the side, Munoz replacing his body position progressively. It took four minutes to complete the transfer. No new blood appeared.

The lead EMT had changed from boss to blood pressure monitor. He said "Colonel, we're losing him. There's almost no blood pressure."

Stratton yelled "Don't say that! We are not losing him, God damn it! We're not. Mitch, you stay with us, god damn it! Fucking Navy pussy! Don't you give it up. The going's getting tough so you get going. Let's see what you're really made of. Navy pilots – all show, no go! Come on, stay with me!"

* * * * *

Hanson, Broderick and Grazing followed, Grazing at the wheel. "Oh, Christ" Hanson whispered as he pulled out his cell phone and placed a call, saying "Come on, come on".

"BioBanc USA. Robert Hayner speaking. How can I help you?"*

"Robert, Bo Hanson. We've got a situation. Mitchell's been shot bad and is enroute to CHOMP. Stop your techs or get them back. I'm just guessing on blood loss but figure six pints throughout so pull fifteen percent and start augmentation to the full forty times. Start now!"

Hayner said "They've gone but, Bo, There's no real rush. At any time they can pull up the cells and have them at proper temperature in a few hours. First we need to have a company in New Jersey overnight the recipe, the ingredients and a copy of the FDA IND – the authorized protocol – to CHOMP's lab. They work closely with FED-EX and they can probably get the shipment out quickly. They're staffed twenty-four seven and there's a FED-EX terminal nearby. We are not authorized to manipulate – only store. CHOMP's lab will do the augmentation. We're on it – don't worry, there's time."

"Didn't know all that. Let's make it happen as quick as you can. Keep me posted. Thanks" Hanson answered as he hung up.

Broderick asked "What's that all about?"

"He has his White Blood Cells in storage at BioBanc. That was the president of the company. His technicians will pull fifteen percent of his cells from cold storage, warm them up and send them to the lab. They will multiply them forty times. It will take them about seventy-two hours, or so. Then they can be injected into his blood stream."

Broderick said "I don't understand. Wouldn't they be transfusing whole blood into him?"

---

* The technology of White Blood Cell storage as presented in the story exists. BioBanc USA exists. For more information see the Appendix.

Grazing said "Whole blood, as it's called, isn't really whole blood."

"Wait a minute. What is it?" Broderick asked.

Hanson said "Long ago when folks first started playing with transfusions the results were disastrous. Eventually they figured out things like A, B and O types, then the Rh thing. But they also figured out that the White Blood Cells (WBCs) were unique to each individual person. Introduction of those into another would trigger an immune system response to those foreigners. Thus, all donor blood has the WBCs spun out before use. They absolutely cannot be introduced into a patient. Whole blood is everything else."

Hanson continued "In essence, the blood he has lost contains his WBCs. The transfusion blood does not. With massive blood transfusion there would be a radical reduction in WBCs and, thus, loss of his immune system. He'd have no defense against all the bad stuff floating around. I just guessed at maybe six pints. We've each got around eight pints. At normal two billion per pint I figured twelve billion are needed. Divide by forty – their multiplier capability – you get three hundred million which is fifteen percent of his two billion in storage. Once the doctors fix him we'll know how much blood was actually used and can start another batch if necessary."

"That's just the dilution aspect. Another aspect is that even in less massive trauma than Mitchell's, after about seventy-two hours the immune system deteriorates – going into a shock thing. Not only does reproduction of WBCs cease but the efficacy of the existing cells declines or halts. No immunity! The replacement WBCs did not suffer the trauma, are viable and fully functional while the immune system recovers itself. Often enough, eight to ten days after successful surgical procedure the patient nosedives. You know – the surgery was successful but the patient died. Sorry, folks. There are many who believe this is because of the immune system failure. This process is intended to provide protection during that critical period."

Broderick looked at him in amazement saying "That's incredible! Why haven't I heard of this?"

Grazing said "The technology is very new. It's also outside the box of conventional medicine and in this litigious society 'new' isn't necessarily accepted by fearful doctors. In fact, I've heard doctors first call it 'voodoo medicine' and then, after a few hours of thought commenting that there may be something to it."

"Mitch is really lucky that he's right here in Monterey where his cells are stored."

Hanson said "Most areas of the country are within twenty-four hours. Actually, BioBanc can get the cells to much of the world within the time frame – even to battlefield hospitals."

"Why the hell isn't the military putting these down for soldiers?"

"I don't know. You'd think they would. They're looking at it. They've been informed." Hanson answered. He looked at Grazing then said "Suppose I should call the General and give him a heads up. He'll probably be needed later on."

Grazing quietly said "I hope so. Bet you're right about that. Good thought."

Hanson pulled up another number.

* * * * *

The ambulance swung off Highway One onto Highway Sixty-Eight. Within seconds they were at the emergency door of CHOMP. Mitchell was offloaded, Munoz at his side.

They wheeled Mitchell directly to an operating room. An effort was made to deny Munoz entry to the sterile area.

In his command voice Stratton said "He's been unsterile for half an hour. You get transfusions going first. Once you have two pints in him we'll release pressure and you guys can take over. He has no blood. We release – he dies!"

The doctor heard the tone, saw the blood covered armed man in front of him and nodded at the wisdom of the order. A transfusion commenced immediately. While blood was being pumped into Mitchell, two doctors were exploring the area around Munoz' hands.

Eventually one doctor said "Alright, Sir, you can release. We'll take it from here."

Munoz released. Fresh blood spurted. The second doctor rapidly applied pressure. Munoz was shown the exit by a nurse. He left looking back over his shoulder at Mitchell.

The ante room looked like a war zone. Armed men, blood-covered men, men in black, a jacket yelling FBI, local police, a sheriff, many with tears streaking their faces, paced the area. Then screaming pierced the somber air as Joanne arrived.

Hanson and Grazing took her in hand. Slowly her hysteria declined. Her rationality returned to some degree and she was able to register, somewhat, the answers to her questions about what happened. She vacillated between periods of calm and outbursts of trembling and sobbing. Hanson and Grazing did their best to console her while struggling themselves with their own despair.

At one calm moment Hanson quietly told her that he had initiated the recovery and augmentation of Mitch's white blood cells and that she would be required to authorize the re-introduction.

With a startled look of remembrance she said "Oh, yes. Thank you for thinking of it. I guess this is why we laid them down." She then drifted back into an introspective trembling state.

Hours later a doctor appeared asking for the next of kin. Joanne leaped up, extricating herself from the comforting arms of Grazing and Hanson. She raced to the doctor followed by Grazing, Hanson and Stratton.

Joanne said "I'm his wife. How is he?"

He introduced himself as Dr. Larson, looked at the three men, and said "This is for her alone."

She said "They stay. Tell me."

The doctor gave a slight shrug saying "He's alive. He's out of surgery and in intensive care, post op. It is touch and go but he has a chance. He has a good constitution. Most people probably wouldn't have made it this far. The blood loss was tremendous. We don't know about brain damage from the blood loss. Had it not been for the pressure treatment he wouldn't have even gotten here. He's in a very critical state and will be for some time. Now we wait. That is all I have, Mrs. Mitchell, for now."

"Thank you, doctor, thank you."

The doctor turned to Stratton and said "Sir, judging from your appearance and that man over there I would guess that you two are the ones who got him here. A job well done. Not many folks know to do that."

"Thanks. It wasn't our first rodeo, Doctor." Stratton said.

"Yes, I gather that. The EMT told a nurse something about Special Forces and an order to shoot him if he opened his mouth again. I see he didn't open his mouth. Probably a good thing."

"You've got that right, Doctor, but I don't think my men would do that. We should be going, clear your waiting room."

"Yes. It would make the other people much more comfortable I'm sure."

They passed the word to the others and all departed.

CHAPTER 46

Three days later Dr. Ralph Emerson (Brig. General, U.S. Army Medical Corps, Ret.) called Dr. Marlin Larson requesting a meeting concerning their patient – one Douglas Mitchell. The two doctors were acquainted and both were credentialed to the hospital. A time to meet was easily arranged.

Emerson and Joanne arrived promptly at one o'clock. When they entered the conference room Larson awaited.

"Hello, Mrs. Mitchell, General." Larson greeted.

"Hi, Marlin." the General said while Joanne nodded in return. "Thanks for all you've done. Quite a mess I understand."

"Mrs. Mitchell has informed me of your care of him. Thought I'd see you about now." Larson responded.

"How's our boy doing today? What's his CBC and Diff? Sepsis showing up?" Emerson asked.

Larson paused, thinking, and slowly looked at Joanne then back to Emerson. "Ralph, maybe we should consult alone."

"No. I want to hear." Joanne stated firmly.

Emerson nodded at Larson.

Larson cleared his throat then spoke slowly in language that Joanne could understand "His White Blood Cell count is next to nothing. Ralph, we've got a cytokine storm that is ravaging what few he has left. Sepsis – an infection – has set in and is growing. We've been hitting with antibiotics and we're not gaining. His condition is extremely critical and worsening. We're doing everything we can, Mrs. Mitchell, but it might not be enough. I'm very sorry."

"Marlin, I need you to listen to me carefully. Doug Mitchell put his White Blood Cells into storage at a company called BioBanc for just such a problem."

"I've heard of that. Thought it was nonsense." Larson commented.

"For the last couple of days his WBCs have been undergoing a multiplication manipulation here in CHOMP's laboratory under an FDA approved protocol. By about six o'clock this evening there should be about twelve *billion* of his *own* WBCs available to be returned to him. We should plan on doing so."

"Ralph, that is not an approved procedure. I don't know about this. I'm very uncomfortable with it."

"Marlin, the man is extremely critical – as you've said. You've reached the limits and we're losing. Mrs. Mitchell has with her notarized releases of liability for both CHOMP and you personally."

"Okay. I can see the logic. My God, twelve billion? Really? Of his own? So – no rejection. Are they viable?"

"Yes. They haven't been subjected to trauma so no shutdown. They've got a hell of a fight on their hands, though. Marlin, the procedure is really no different than the oncologists have been doing. We'll feed them in over about six hours. We can go directly into the saline drip. I will take charge, if you wish, of the procedure."

At seven o'clock that evening the re-introduction began.

CHAPTER 47

Mitchell opened his eyes. He looked about, not twisting his head. It didn't seem to move. He saw Hanson in one chair, chin on his chest, asleep. He saw Grazing in another chair on the other side in the same condition.

It hurt to breathe but he took in enough air to squeak out "I know I'm not in Heaven so where am I?"

At the first squeak both Hanson and Grazing jerked awake, fully alert.

Grazing said "Hi, Mitch. You're back! Thank God! You're in CHOMP. But how do you know you're not in Heaven?"

"'Cause you and Bo are here and you guys don't stand a chance of making it to Heaven."

Hanson said "Jesus Christ! He's really back, the crazy bastard!"

Mitchell croaked out "Where's Joanne?"

Grazing said "She's been here right along. She went to the cafeteria to get food. I'll call her." His trusty cell phone was put in use.

"How long have I been out?"

"Six days." Grazing answered.

Mitchell's eyes closed lazily then re-opened.

Minutes later Joanne flew into the room followed by Mitchell's son Chase. Chase just looked at his father with tears in his eyes. Joanne took his left hand in hers and held it to her cheek. Tears flowed down her face. "Oh, Mitch. I thought I'd lost you. Oh, Mitch."

He said, groggily and seriously, "I said goodbye."

She said "What?"

"When she started to raise the gun everything went to slow motion. As it came up I said inside 'I love you JoJo, Chase. Goodbye.'" He said, serious like a little boy looking for approval.

She cried even harder. So did Chase. So did Hanson and Grazing.

Mitchell slid back into sleep.

* * * * *

A day later Mitchell awoke again. Grazing and Joanne were bedside. Joanne was reading, Grazing slumbering. Mitchell said "JoJo, don't you have anything better to do than watch two old men sleep? Hi, Sweetheart. Hi, Kenner."

"Hi, Baby." She said. "Glad your back. How're you feeling?"

"Don't know. Hurts a little to breathe. More to talk. Other than that I don't know yet. What does the doctor have to say? How bad am I?"

"Mitch, the doc will tell you what damage there is but you're out of the woods. For awhile it was iffy. Stratton and Munoz saved you with heavy duty pressure. Later I'll tell you the story. Now you have to heal and gain strength." Grazing said.

"Where'd she hit me?"

"Upper right chest near your right shoulder. Tore up muscle and some bones. The surgeons think they got everything back in its proper place. They think that with time you'll be able to use that arm, that you'll be okay, Darling."

"Sounds like I'll be able to predict the weather with it, though. How long have I been here?"

"Seven days." Grazing said.

"I've been asleep for seven days? Jeez. That's a first. Never did that even as a teenager. Wow. Kenner, do me a favor, get Stratton and Munoz here. You, too. Got some business to take care of."

Joanne erupted "No you're not! Business? Are you crazy? Never mind, I know the answer to that. Mitch, the doctor won't allow it. I won't allow it. You need rest, not work."

"JoJo, did she shoot me in the brain? No! So my brain doesn't need rest, just my body. So – I won't move my body. Really, JoJo, I need to take care of stuff."

"Absolutely not – isn't going to happen!" she declared.

"Okay. Ken – notes. Munoz determine exact amount of return transfer. Make up difference to twenty million. Transfer from Bonano account. Today. Second, contact your Tom. Ask if his Treasury contract is exclusive or can he receive fees for outside work. Ask him about any expenses incurred. If any – reimburse from Bonano account. Third. Joanne, you should be getting bills for stuff. Talk with Jimmy. He will provide money for payment. Kenner, I'll need a phone in here. Hey, how long they going to keep me? Is this a smoking room?"

"Mitch, you know CHOMP is no smoking anywhere. You should stop anyway. You know I hate it."

"It's a cult, that's what it is." He said

"What is, Dear?" Joanne asked.

"Nicotine Nazis. I'll bet they won't give me coffee either. They run together, you know. Nicotine Nazis and Caffeine

Crazies. Tell the doctor I'm going home tomorrow. I'd go now but I'm rather liking this self-administer morphine button. It's helping stave off the desire for a cigarette. Man, you'd think after seven days that wouldn't show up."

"Joanne, are we absolutely sure she didn't shoot him in the head?" Grazing asked.

"Yes, we're sure. This was caused by a severe bicycle accident when he was seven. Never been right upstairs ever since. His mother warned me. I should have listened."

Laughing, Grazing said "By the way, Harrison wants to talk with you – when you're able of course."

"Hold him off for a few more days. We've got some things to clean up and besides, with time, pressure decreases. I'm sure he collected my tape from my stuff. Did you give him yours?"

"No and no. I grabbed yours from your pants when we lifted you to the gurney. He never asked about tapes. Never came up."

"Good. Take mine, rewind and erase everything up to where you yelled 'finished'. If he asks about the missing portion comment that it just happened like the seventeen missing minutes on Nixon's tape. Mysterious, actually. He does need that for his report and it will help him and the FBI let go. They do not need to know anything about that account or how we knew about it. We really don't want to lie to the FBI – at least any lie that can be proved. Think I'll pump the morphine now. I'll probably go spacey soon. Come to think of it, I am a touch sleepy. Ken, I need to talk with Frank about …. the ….."

"He never wants to stop. His recovery time is going to be hard. What do you suppose that last thing about Frank was about?" Joanne asked.

"I think he wants to talk with Frank about setting up an education trust fund for the two boys – Enrique and Emilio.

That would be my guess." Grazing answered. "We do owe those two boys. They were heroes, leading the men as they did."

* * * * *

When he awoke he heard Stratton, Hanson and Grazing talking. He listened, quietly enjoying their banter, glad to be alive.

"Hey, guys." he finally said. "Where's Joanne?"

Grazing said "She's at home freshening. Bo and I have the watch. Deke came by to see how you are. He's been here quite a bit but you've been asleep. He had trouble the first time back. They wouldn't let him in until he promised not to shoot anyone."

"Mitch, that's a bunch of crap and you know it. Welcome back, my friend. I can't tell you how great that feels – to welcome you back!"

Hanson said "Mitch, that might not be true. He called you a Navy pussy. Said fighter pilots are all show, no go. Said lots of nasty things to you. I'm not sure he means welcome."

Grazing said "Bo, he did order Munoz to shoot that EMT guy if he didn't obey. He might not have meant those nasty things he said. Maybe."

"I admit I was a little excited at the moment. Maybe they were a little strong. But, hey! They got him mad enough to hang on. I mean, he's here. Isn't that proof?" Stratton said.

"Okay, okay, guys. I'll show you mine if you'll show me yours. I'll tell you what happened after you left up to being shot. You tell me the rest. I seem to have forgotten it."

Stratton said "You *were* sort of sitting down on the job."

"Anyway, when you guys left I was coming out but I needed to say a few things to her. As I told you before I was positive that she was the shooter of Ortiz. I was surprised when Watson said she shot Rust also. But, it made sense. Rust would never have gone out at night to the beach to meet a man but he would a young woman offering information. It made perfect sense to me at that point but didn't affect my plan. Hearing him denounce her I thought would trigger action by her. I was more right than I thought there! I thought she was a young woman who would do anything her amor would ask – and react murderously against him if rejected and denounced. We had no way to bring him to the justice he deserved through legal action. I thought I could trigger that woman scorned thing in a known murderess and boy, did I."

"You should be able to hear it all on the tape. But the tape doesn't tell it all. Not by a long shot! I will tell you what's not on the tape. Many times in combat, and a few times in civilian life, when a dangerous event occurs the happening goes to slow motion but my thinking is functioning normally. An example is once at the aircraft carrier I didn't come up with power on the landing. I'd never had a bolter – missing the wires. When I realized I missed the last wire I knew I was going over. It takes time for a jet engine to wind up. As I went over the edge of the deck I checked my airspeed and tickled the stick up. The nose responded. I knew I could fly in 'ground effect' – basically you can fly slower than you can really fly, if you're close to the ground. I didn't eject. I knew all that absolutely! I still recall flying alongside the carrier looking at it like a tourist. Eventually, I gained enough speed to climb."

"The same thing happened here. The event shifted to slow motion. Except this time I froze instead of continuing to the door. When she straightened her shoulders and raised her head I knew she was going through some sort of change, a resolve, a metamorphosis, if you will. A terrible smell filled my nostrils. When she turned and looked into my eyes I froze. Those non-human eyes were on fire, fanatical, insane. I've never seen anything like it. Kenner – ten thousand times more fearsome than the bulls in Spain."

"She confirmed Watson – it *was her plan*. Her perfect plan. And I destroyed it. And her. I thought she would go after Watson. Never dreamed she wanted me as, what she called, the head asshole. She had the gun in her hand dangling full arm length at her side. The extended arm rose smoothly upward with no hesitation, leveled and fired. I swear I saw the bullet coming out of the barrel. I overcame the freeze and lunged left toward the door. Too late. There was no pause on her part. A simple raise, stop and fire. It felt like a truck had hit me slamming me back into the wall. I couldn't stand up. I slid down the wall. I knew I was in deep tapioca. Really deep."

Grazing interjected "Now you know what it's like, old friend. Too bad, wish you'd never found out."

"Yeah, me too. Anyway, she stood looking at me for a moment, the weapon back down at her side. Watson came to his door. She turned and without any pause raised her arm and shot him. Then I remember nothing. No shining light, no luminous tunnel, no hand reaching for me – just out! Nothing! Guys, she was not human! There wasn't the faintest hint of humanness in her eyes. At that point she was as close to Satan as anything I can imagine. It actually is giving me chills to recall it. Our language provides me no words to give you the image. Totally heart-stopping fearsome. With time and thought I may be able to describe her better. If I haven't struck fear in your heart, I haven't described her properly. That is everything I have."

The others stood looking at him trying to digest what he had said.

"Wow." said Stratton. "And I thought I had seen all the evil the world had to offer."

"Me, too." said Grazing. "At least I never saw the rifle or

even where the shot came from that got me. You watched the gun come up, point at you and fire! Jesus, God Almighty!"

"Hope I never find out what it's like." Hanson said. "I'll tell you what happened next. These guys and Munoz were all busy. I was an observer because it was my coffee break time. I never work when I'm on break time so I watched." He then continued filling in Mitchell on all the subsequent events of the evening.

When he finished, Mitchell looked at Stratton and, with tears in his eyes, said "Deke, how the hell do I thank you for saving my life?"

"Easy, my friend. You bring the wines to dinner for, say, two years. That should be enough. Don't need anything else. See, now I can brag about rescuing a Navy pilot who froze when he shoulda jinked. Isn't that what ya'll called it – jinking? Besides, isn't that the price *you* charged when somebody else tried to thank *you* for *their* life?"

"You're right, that was the price. Deke, did you really order Munoz to shoot that EMT if he said another word?" Mitchell asked.

"That would be a yes but I may have overstepped my authority then. Then again, they would have killed you if I'd have let them. They simply hadn't seen this kind of wound before. Jimmy and I have. Couldn't let that happen."

Mitchell lay quiet, deep in some sort of contemplation. Eventually he spoke "Guess I really came close. I've always thrived out on the edge. To tell you the truth, I thought the bullet, shell or SAM hadn't been invented that could kill me. I was golden, invincible, and nearly immortal. Lately, my body has been betraying me on the immortal thing but I still thought I could walk in harm's way and emerge alive. I've learned some lessons from this."

"What?" said Hanson.

"I've learned that I was god damned right! No bullet has yet been invented that can kill me. Here I am as proof! But I've also learned that it's important to have fantastic friends. And keep them close! I was once told to pick your friends carefully. Boy, did I pick great ones!"

They all laughed. Grazing said "No one but you would come to that conclusion on the bullet. You are so fucking unbelievable at times. Guess that's why we love ya. That lunge to the left was the difference. You are one lucky son-of-a-bitch."

"Yeah, I know. I never leave home without it."

Hanson said quizzically "Your American Express card?"

"No. Luck." Mitchell said as he drifted off to sleep.

Stratton said "He's going to be alright. I have to admit, his analysis is logical. A little bizarre, but logical! I'll see you guys. Adios."

* * * * *

When Mitchell again awoke Joanne and Jimmy Munoz were his attendants. Mitchell said "Good morning or whatever it is. Hi JoJo. Hi, Jimmy. God, I would love some coffee. I smell some somewhere."

After some husband and wife chatter Joanne left to find him some coffee.

Mitchell immediately said "Jimmy, did you take care of the transfer to total twenty mil full restitution?"

"Yes, Boss. Done."

"Good. How much?"

"One point one and change."

"Okay. Give me your cell phone. Ahh – wait. Dial this number for me then give me the phone. And listen."

"Nolan, Mitchell. Yeah, everyone is saying that. In a week

it'll stop. Look, I've got two boys in Guatemala that I want to set up an educational and support trust fund for. The trust and funding can be set up anywhere outside the United States. The funds have never been in the States. There is an ex-pat American, Frank Lombard at the Outrigger Hotel in Guatemala. Work with him on their names and needs. Jimmy Munoz works with me, staying at my place. He will give you phone numbers or anything else you need. When you determine the needed amount he will transfer funds into the trust."

"Nolan, don't go there. I can't answer those questions. No, the money is not mine. No, I'm not messing with the IRS. Yes, I'm just a facilitator for the foreign owner of those foreign funds. No, the United States has no interest in the money but no need to excite their interest. You know how those parasites are when there's money around."

"Thanks Nolan. Here's Jimmy." And he handed the phone to Munoz. He smiled as Jimmy went to work.

Joanne returned with coffee and saw Munoz on the phone, his laptop open. She said "I'm glad that is Jimmy working and not you. I've told you - no work. I would have been less than pleased if I'd have found you on the phone."

"I know, Dear. I've got to rest and repair. I hear you."

Munoz wandered out still on the phone.

Joanne and Mitchell talked together for another half hour before he drifted off to sleep. He never touched his coffee.

* * * * *

When he next awoke only Grazing was present. Mitchell looked around not seeing Joanne or a nurse. He said "Kenner, I've got a mission for you if you're up to it. I've got to handle this while Joanne's not here."

"Go."

"You, Bo and Deke need to put your heads together. You guys decide. I've asked Nolan and Frank to create a trust fund for the boys. Jimmy is coordinating. You need to decide a proper finder's fee for Tom, if he can accept it. Then, you guys decide a bonus check to each of the rescue guys. Are you okay with money? I know Bo is. What about Deke? It is up to you three to get rid of the Bonano money. Keep what you wish. I don't need any. Make the payments for services rendered or consulting. Jimmy will transfer the funds. Make sure he is well paid, sweeter than the others. He will know the transfers and he's contributed more. That should clean everything up. I'd like all this done ASAP. A fait accompli is harder for anyone to unravel. I suppose I'm going to have to talk with Harrison before long."

"Yeah, he is pushing pretty hard – particularly with everyone coming in and out. On the other matter, we've been discussing it. We figured the right thing was to spread the fund out to the participants. The hard part was figuring out the split after I took my five million."

"Yeah, I bet that was tough. With that and my four million I didn't tell you about, we can have fun at the Atlantis Casino. I do love that place. Seriously, we need to get it done fast. And Ken, don't give the guys a choice, don't ask. They'd refuse. Let the checks arrive. Use checks, not electronic. We want a paper trail from a foreign bank if ever needed. Tell them they must report it to the IRS at normal time as ordinary income. We don't fuck with the tax man!"

"Gotcha. Good plan."

"Get on it. I'm fine. Think I'll wait here for Joanne. I'll let her inform Harrison that I'll see him tomorrow. I may have to take the truth and bend it a little. I think Harrison is on our side – he seems a good man. But he *is* FBI. Would like you and Bo here - in case I start screwing something up you can intercede. Can't trust the effects of these drugs."

* * * * *

The next day Special Agent Mark Harrison was given permission to visit. Hanson and Grazing were present, by arrangement. Joanne was not, by arrangement.

After the cordialities Harrison said "Mr. Mitchell, I, personally, am curious about several things. These two Musketeers have been amazingly forgetful – claiming it's a common old age affliction. Perhaps your memory would be better, if you have the strength of course. I know you briefed me to be on site and ready to arrest. You told me it was Watson for the kidnapping and Rust and the woman for Ortiz. How did you know?"

"The planning was so good. Watson was going to have an airtight alibi. She was the only possibility. Turns out she did Rust also." Mitchell said.

"Okay but what did you need to talk to Watson about? Why not just give them to us?"

"There was nothing to give until they gave it. You had no proof, as we discussed. I had no proof, as we discussed. I had to convince them that we had proof, had undeniable facts, that it was over. I did a lot of bluffing and guessing but presented it as fact. The exact content was something important. I'm sure it was. It will probably come to me. God, I hate these lapses."

"Could it have had anything to do with an eighteen point nine million dollar transfer from Singapore to Central Bank minutes before the shooting began? That is, while you were in PineTree's offices? And we don't quite understand why yesterday's transfer of the balance of the ransom came. Loddington tells us it was from a small private bank in Switzerland. When we get around to it we'll look into it."

"I'd be happy to guess that our encouragement caused him to return the remnants of the ransom money to the rightful owners. I would guess the balance was perhaps a delayed transfer, an electronic glitch, so to speak. Think kindly of him for that. I do."

"How did you 'encourage' him to do such a thing? It doesn't fit and that vixen surely wouldn't have allowed it – voluntarily, that is."

"We basically pointed out that it was over, as I've said. He'd lost the money. Jail was coming. The FBI was right outside. It would work better for him if it was given back willfully before the FBI came up. That's about it."

"What do you mean by 'lost the money'?"

"Well, I knew he had it. The FBI knew he had it. The FBI would find it eventually. Or so I told him."

"It took seven of you, armed, to pass that friendly message?"

"I sorta thought that armed men might be a little intimidating and thus encourage him to see the wisdom of my advice. The main thing was those armed men were there as my hired protectors while I was in the presence of a known killer or killers, or so I had reason to believe. That was their primary purpose. The intimidating factor was beyond my control and would be moot with an innocent man."

"Why did you send the others out and not accompany them immediately?"

"To defuse a situation a man must, occasionally, stand alone. Or to point the way."

"Mitchell, you came close to siccing her on him, to shoot him, according to the tape. It could be taken that way."

"Special Agent, nothing could be further from my mind. I'm sure I counseled her that it was all over."

"Yes, that you did. What I don't understand – and it's not apparent on your tape – is what did you do to trigger her, to fire her off?"

"I'm sure I don't have a clue. I've never understood women. At times they seem to be controlled purely by emotion, not reason. It befuddles me when it occurs. Have you ever run into such a thing?"

"Christ, I'm not going there. I'm still a young man, relatively. I need my job. We've had some inquiries, off the record, if we know anything about an American General running around Guatemala robbing narcotics people. You wouldn't have heard anything about that, would you? Perhaps during your recent visit to Guatemala?"

"Special Agent, I can't imagine anything more preposterous than an American General doing such a thing. Unless he were a closet Democrat, of course. Then there's no accounting for behavior."

Grazing and Hanson fought to hold back a snicker.

"Would you be able to tell me what happened in that room with her?"

"As well as I can. When she took the pistol out she was moving as if in a trance. I started to leave. You had been called to disarm her. Boy, did I misjudge the whole thing! I knew she was the shooter on Ortiz but I thought Watson was behind the whole thing, thought he had conned her into it. He was behind it but she was the planner and driving force."

"I've never experienced such as her and never want to again. Her body language was a dejected little girl. Then she changed. When she turned and looked at me her eyes were afire – literally. The look on her face was pure evil. Her eyes had no hint of humanness, no trace or vestige of morality. They were pure predator's eyes. They were Satan, the Devil incarnate. I was moving toward the door but those eyes froze me. Everything shifted to slow motion. As the gun came up and fired I leaped left. I was slammed against the wall and slid to the floor. She looked at me on the floor as if I were a chunk of meat or road kill, with no emotion. Without a word or any hesitation she simply turned and blew Watson away. After that I remember nothing. My tape recorder was running. Did you find it?"

"After she shot you it is as you said. She shot Watson. And yes, we've listened. Mr. Grazing was kind enough to bring it to us. We found it disconcerting that the discussion with Watson was missing for some reason. Mr. Grazing could give us no explanation saying only that it was your tape and that technology befuddled him. Can you explain it for us?"

"I would have to put myself in the same category as Mr. Grazing. I can barely turn on my computer. My son has to work it for me. And when I learn something about it I forget by the next day. Again, it's very frustrating. Someday you, too, will experience this phenomenon, I'm sorry to say."

"You say she looked like the Devil to you?"

"Yes – although I've never met the Devil. At least until her."

"Mr. Mitchell, we have listened to your tape. You may be the most incredibly lucky man on earth. At the end, just before she shot herself - she said something very strange."

"What was it?" Mitchell asked.

Harrison, on his way out, said "She said 'I wonder who I should be next'."

APPENDIX

The technology concerning White Blood Cells as described in the story does exist, is available and is a tool that should be considered by all. The entire technology is only a few years in existence. As new it is outside conventional medical thought at this time. However, it is supported by many world-class immunologists. To name one – Professor Dominique Charon, head of immunology at the University of Paris and president of the World Immunological Society. There are too many more to name. Additional information can be acquired from:

> BioBanc USA
> Biobancusa.com
> (888) 246 2262
> Robert Hayner, President

Our immunity to foreign invaders resides in the family of our WBCs. They are of different forms and functions working together as a system. For example, some have 'tentacles' and wander about touching other bodies in the blood stream 'testing' them as friend or foe. If foe, they grapple the offending entity and haul it off to killer T cells, another form, for termination. The WBC system constantly 'polices' our blood looking for invaders. They are police, judge, jury and executioner all in one. It is a constant war ongoing within our bodies. Absent the WBC system we are defenseless against viral and bacterial forces.

WHY STORE WHITE BLOOD CELLS?

As stated, our immunity and defense resides there. Those cells are unique to each one of us. At the level of present knowledge, those cells cannot be used interchangeably among us as can Red Blood Cells (within known limits). Introducing another person's WBCs into your system will cause a disastrous response of your immune system to those foreign invaders.

As a result of that feature, among others, early experiments with blood transfusions were less than happy – often fatal, in fact. It took time to identify the A, B, and O aspects and the Rh factor. Early on the necessity to separate out the White Cells was exposed.

Thus, when medical personnel refer to 'Whole Blood' transfusion from donors it is not a technically accurate phrase. The white cells have been spun out and the recipient receives everything else.

The efficacy of the normal immune system is function of density – in my layman opinion. With a lot of variability, humans have around seven to eight pints of blood. There are around two billion WBCs within each pint. That density is there for reasons known to the gods of evolution. It is apparently what we need to do the job. The body corrects its needs in response to smaller events or invasions.

It is far different for highly traumatic events and large transfusion requirements. In those cases, studies indicate that the immune system goes into a slow decline for about seventy-two hours post-event then goes into a 'shock' characteristic, strongly receding and shutting down. WBCs are not produced nor are existing WBCs active in their work. Often enough, eight to ten days after otherwise successful surgical procedure the patient goes into decline and failure. Hospitals can be ripe with infectious disease. Well-meaning visitors carry agents into the area.

Replacement of the patient's WBCs provides the needed immunities. The returned WBCs have not been affected by the trauma event, are viable and active.

HOW ARE WBCs TAKEN AND STORED?

The WBC taking procedure is simple. BioBanc USA identifies locations throughout the United States where one's blood can be taken. They take one pint – the same amount taken when donating blood – in the same manner as when donating blood. Special packaging and shipping instructions are supplied by BioBanc USA to the facility where the blood is taken. The blood then goes to BioBanc.

When received, the blood is processed through a centrifuge procedure separating and capturing the WBCs. BioBanc harvests and stores about two billion WBCs from your one pint of blood. The cells are stored in special super-cold tanks charged with liquid nitrogen. The storage technology has been around for decades. We are all familiar with viable egg, sperm and umbilical cord-blood storage and viability upon retrieval. WBCs respond in the same fashion. The WBCs retain all the immunity memory they possessed at the time of their taking. Portions can be retrieved with the balance remaining stored. The portion retrieved can be multiplied up to forty times in a lab.

OTHER APPLICATIONS

There is still much to be learned about white blood cells, their forms, functions and procedural applications of that knowledge.

There appear to be cancer applications. Chemotherapy and radiation therapy can be damaging to WBCs. Post such treatment the immune system can be substantially compromised for a period of time – often prolonged. Re-introduction of one's own healthy WBCs provide immune protection during that period. There are a variety of other applications being appraised.

NOW – THE BIG ONE

Immunization operates by a new foreign agent entering the body and the WBCs don't recognize it as foreign immediately. Then they do and manufacture WBCs with the ability to recognize, fight and kill. While that is going on and the battle rages you may be 'sick'. When the good guys win – you get well. If the bad guys win – you don't. In the future, after your survival, The WBCs recognize that agent immediately and kill it when it arrives. That's a layman's over-simplification but, in essence, that's how it works.

Vaccination works by taking dead or weakened virus nurtured in egg, horse blood or some other base, making a serum and introducing it into the body providing the WBCs the recognition ability from a weakened form of the infection. The manufacture of the vaccine takes time – lots of time. We've all heard of health officials speak of eight or nine months until sufficient vaccine will be available.

Further, many viruses mutate rapidly – particularly the flu virus. The flu vaccine one gets in the fall is for the virus form that scientists *think* that it will mutate into by the time you get the vaccine. At best, it is an educated guess – year after year.

We all know that flu can be deadly. Just how deadly many have forgotten or never knew. In 1918 the Spanish Flu killed over forty million people accounted worldwide. It was probably far more. The survivors acquired immunity.

They no longer exist. There is no acquired immunity to that virus in the living population.

That virus still exists on earth. It is not gone. It exists sealed up in government laboratories – both Russian and American – as part of the old biological warfare work. The question is – where else? Long frozen bodies in the arctic now thawing have some people concerned. That virus jumped from pigs some believe. We've recently seen another virus jump from chickens. Some think Ebola jumped from monkeys.

So what's the point? The point is that if a deadly virus gets on the loose, during the augmentation stage of one's white blood cell expansion, the virus or its deactivated form can be introduced. The WBCs will pick up recognition as an enemy. Upon insertion into the body they not only have recognition capability but they immediately begin 'teaching' the other WBCs the recognition! All within seventy-two hours! Not nine months! Not after one is dead! Forty- eight to seventy-two hours to acquire immunity! And with no allergic reaction to egg or horse blood or whatever base!

The White Blood Cells of my family and myself are in storage in BioBanc – as well as the cord blood of my granddaughter.

—DM